If there are three hundred Ramayanas...
There might be three thousand
or thirty thousand Mahabharatas.

~ A.K. Ramanujan

Abbreviated Reviews

A New Scribe for the Mahabharata: It is so difficult to achieve a combination of the ancient and the modern, the historical and the imaginary, the authentic and the innovative. But [with] Kamesh Ramakrishna, we have it. The Mahabharata comes alive with a twenty-first century zest... This allows an entirely new approach to the tale (to my knowledge, never attempted before). The usual Mahabharata is inclusive of fantastic elements, magical weapons, gods and goddesses, rebirths and reincarnations. This novel steers clear of all that... So read this book with respect for new views. The Mahabharata is always evolving... Dipavali Sen, Associate Professor, Sri Guru Gobind Singh College of Commerce, D.U. & Freelance Writer

***

Considerable control is called for while re-imagining myth so that it does not degenerate into fantasy... This is where Ramakrishna's novel, the first in a series of five, comes as a welcome surprise. He re-imagines the events as occurring in 2000 BC. This is India north of the Vindhyas, with a non-literate oral culture, bereft of iron, horses and chariots; of cattle-drawn carts, mud-wattle cottages, bows, arrows and bronze weapons. There are no missiles, no aircraft, no huge gem-encrusted palaces and gleaming silken attire... We certainly look forward to the sequels. Pradip Bhattacharya Ex-Additional Chief Secretary, West Bengal & Comparative Mythology Specialist

***

This is a book of historical fiction that transports readers on a journey of imagining what might have been, of how things might have happened and how history may have been created by the rich, varied and sustained traditions of oral story-telling in ancient India. In doing so, the author reveals the thoroughness of his research, the historical analyses and the attention to period-specific details that make the reading of this novel not just an exercise in fantasy but also a master class in history and literature. Girija Sankar, Global Health & Development professional, Atlanta, Georgia

***

A must-read for anyone enchanted with the Mahabharata. To truly appreciate this book one needs to know and love the textured epic…the protagonists are tinged with darkness...the antagonists show glimmers of righteousness…the gods are Machiavellian… I love the little details of how the story is told [here]. It takes us back in time and [we view the] Mahabharata not as spectators from afar, but up close. It transports us to the tent in the dusty Indian plain where the mighty general lies on his deathbed. It provides a textured look into the old soul's last helpless days and sheds light on the formative events of his youth and adulthood. It also puts forth a brave alternate hypothesis on the root cause for the war. In that sense it is also a novel that makes us think deeply about contemporary issues like climate change and the impact of immigration on society. I commend Mr. Kamesh Ramakrishna for a brave attempt at the thirty thousand and first Mahabharata! [Amazon Review] Mukul Sheopory, Mountain View, California, USA

***

This is an extraordinary book. Anyone remotely familiar with the Mahabharata will be hypnotized. Together, the theme, the structure, and the style all make the perfect novel. In fiction, it is rather rare to find rich character studies together with a fascinating plot and a lively style, yet, this novel has all three. But the most interesting is this: the book is convincing and it sometimes reads like historical fiction rather than epic fiction. Dr. Jean-Philippe Belleau, Associate Professor of Anthropology, College of Liberal Arts, University of Massachusetts/Boston, USA

***

A creative, compelling and accessible version of Bhishma's origins. I enjoyed reading it for its format, complexity, and captivating writing style… It allows a creative perspective that connects an ancient story to relevant political issues of environment and population, and thus sticks in the minds of readers [today]. [Amazon Review] Vidya Viswanathan, Philadelphia, USA.

***

The author's re-imagining of the Mahabharata in a time of radical ecological change is a very interesting perspective. In general we do not fully appreciate the impact of climate change on the waning and waxing of civilizations and empires. The author stays with the traditional protagonists but the ecological backdrop changes everything that transpires…The lack of written historical accounts from ancient India has frustrated many a researcher. But it is also a blank canvas for storytellers, and the author [has] made a good start by casting the Mahabharata in the context of ecological disaster. [Amazon Review] Jawa Tembulkar. Lexington, Massachusetts, USA

***

A contemporary view of the Mahabharata: Kamesh Ramakrishna provides a very different perspective on the grand old story of the Mahabharata…a contemporary look at the characters of Satyavati and Devavrata (Bhishma) and others. Strangely enough…they sound quite real in the current context of the 21st century. Overall, a very interesting book. [Amazon Review] RKM

***

Well written with a completely different view point! The author has dared conventional wisdom and written what he strongly feels. [Amazon Review] Medysurya

***

In Ramakrishna's retelling of the Indian epic, the Mahabharata warrior Devavrata Bhishma recounts [the] long road of intrigue and misunderstandings that led to his renunciation of a crown and the eventual eruption of war... It is a joy to see how the characters and their understanding of each other shift. The Author uses Devavrata's descriptions to capture the Hastinapuran civilization, drawing from historical record... A unique and entertaining attempt to reconcile the ambiguities of ancient myth with archaeological record. Kirkus Review

FALL OF THE KURUS

BOOK I

THE MAKING OF BHISHMA

A NOVEL

KAMESH RAMAKRISHNA

ISBN 978-93-52010-17-2

Cover Design: Tina Patankar
Layouts: Hitanshi Shah
Printed in India by Nutech Print Services, India

Published in 2018

PLATINUM PRESS

An imprint of LEADSTART PUBLISHING PVT LTD
Unit 25, Building A/1, Near Wadala RTO,
Wadala (E), Mumbai 400 037, INDIA
T + 91 96 9993 3000 **E** info@leadstartcorp.com
W www.leadstartcorp.com

Marketed & Distributed by:
A Division of Bennett Coleman & Co. Ltd.
The Times of India, 10 Daryaganj, New Delhi 110 002
Phone: 011-39843333 Email: tgb@timesgroup.in
www.toibooks.com

AUTHOR DISCLAIMER: I take full responsibility for this work of fiction. Its contents and the opinions in it are products of my imagination. All my life I have read widely in the fields of history, archaeology, mythology, philosophy, science and technology, and I have drawn on these to create this story. I do not claim historical authenticity or scriptural validity. This novel does not represent what may 'really' have happened. Nor does it represent the views of the Publisher. It is not endorsed as authentic or historical by the Publisher or anybody else.

For my Parents

About the Author

KAMESH RAMAKRISHNA grew up in Bombay (Mumbai). On graduating from IIT-Kanpur, he went on to obtain a Ph.D. in Computer Science from Carnegie-Mellon University, Pittsburgh, specializing in Artificial Intelligence. He was on the faculty of The Ohio State University; he was a software engineer & architect for some computer companies; he received some patents for his work in artificial intelligence; was the CTO for a startup, and in recent years, a consultant software architect.

For over twenty years Kamesh has been an avid student of history, archaeology, science and philosophy, drawn to the latent interconnections between these disciplines. His interests have had a tremendous influence on this book, the core ideas underlying which have been previously published in two peer-reviewed journals – *The Trumpeter* (Canada), and *The Indian Journal of Eco-criticism.*

Kamesh lives with his family in Massachusetts, USA, and can be reached through the web-site www.themakingofbhishma.com

Contents

Appendices

Author's Note
FALL OF THE KURUS
THE SERIES

FALL OF THE KURUS is a series of five novels that tell the story of how an empire grew out of a crisis that overwhelmed a Bronze Age culture in South Asia of 2000 BCE. Panchnad (we know it as the Sarasvati-Sindhu Culture or the Indus Valley Civilisation), a great matriarchal urban culture mostly on the banks of the Sarasvati, collapsed when the river dried up. Its inhabitants migrated to the Gangetic plain through the small border town of Hastinapura. Hastinapura was hardly a settlement – it was more or less a trading centre established by the Kuru family to manage trade with the forest-dwellers of the Gangetic plain – the Nagas immediately to the east and the Rakshasas further downstream the Ganga, who occupied the Eastern Plateau that bordered on the Eastern Sea. The Nagas were slash-and-burn agriculturists – at the request of the ruling family of Hastinapura, they initially helped the refugees. The refugees had intended to return to Panchnad but as time went on and the crisis worsened, they became immigrants who created permanent settlements on land left fallow by the Nagas. The Vyaasa, head of the Kavi Sangha (Society of Poets), of Panchnad, which had helped Hastinapura deal with past crises, helped the Kurus formulate and implement policies for managing the crisis.

Arable land was scarce as the Nagas did not clear vast tracts of forest for farming. The Naga way of life could not support the large number of Panchnad refugees. The Panchnad refugees wanted to recreate their way of life in Panchnad, which would demand much more from the land. Meanwhile a long drought threatened to create famine. Mutual knowledge was lacking; respect and tolerance did not exist. Conflict was unavoidable.

Conflict came in the form of a Great War. The leaders of the clans/settlements involved – the Panchalans, the Kauravas, the Pandavas, the Yadavas, and other, less prominent clans – manoeuvring between different strategic goals. Coincidentally, the Matriarchs of the various clans failed to produce heirs and war justified the privileges claimed by men. The victorious alliance compromised on Hastinapura's patrilineal model of inheritance for the short-term. The last act of the Great War was the expulsion of the Nagas – that cemented the primacy of the male King and the relegation of Matriarch as consort to the King.

BOOK 1: *The Making of Bhishma,* portrays the world of Hastinapura as its rulers try to manage the crisis. This novel explores the impact of this conflict on the life of Devavrata (also called Bhishma), the eldest son of Shantanu the ruler of Hastinapura. Major events in Devavrata's life are collateral damage – his mother's suicide, his father disinheriting him, the death of his half-brothers, etc. – even as he struggles to create an empire that would address the immigration problem. At the end of his life, Devavrata muses over all that he gave up in his personal life to create the empire, all that he had left unmade in his own life while he made the empire, an empire over which the Great War was fought.

BOOK II: *The Last Matriarchs.* The Great War ended with the collapse of all the matriarchies of Jambudvipa, leaving the Pandava-led Hastinapura patriarchy in control of an empire. The Vyaasa Lomaharshana (the young Kavi Sangha Archivist of Book 1) collects the life-stories of Kunti Bhojamata and Agnijyotsna Panchali Draupadi for the Annals of the Hastinapura Empire. The two matriarchs lament that they do not have daughters to succeed them. They describe their struggle to keep their sons and husbands relevant in the power struggle with the Kaurava patriarchy ruling Hastinapura.

Kunti succeeds in obtaining their patrimony for her sons, the Pandavas, only to see it crash in a murder conspiracy of their Kaurava cousins. The Pandavas then ally with Draupadi, the Panchalan Matriarch to demand and receive a share in the Hastinapura Patriarchy. The Kauravas are jealous of the success of the Pandavas and Panchala confederation and their Yadava ally. They provoke a war, the Great War, ends in the death of all the children of the Pandavas, the Yadavas, and the Panchalans.

Draupadi closes her narration by observing that there were no Matriarchs left among all the clans that survived the war. Draupadi functioned as Matriarch for Parikshit, the son of Abhimanyu and Uttaraa, but Parikshit did not have daughters either. Hastinapura's form of patrilineal inheritance had become the norm in the new empire. The era of Matriarchs was over.

BOOK III: *The Great War.* Devavrata's nemesis and love, Amba, met Lomaharshana (the young Kavi Sangha Archivist of Book 1). They exchanged stories – she told him of her time with

Devavrata, and he told her the story of the Great War that he was composing.

SUMMARY: The Kauravas exposed; Assault on a Queen; Krishna saves Krishnaa; The siege of Indraprastha; The Pandava Escape; The siege of Kampilya; Draupadi defeats Drona; The capture of Bhishma; The murder of Abhimanyu; Disarming Drona; The killing of Drona; Violating a Truce; Trapped in Mud; Death of Karna; Capture of Duhshasana; Draupadi and Duhshasana; Draupadi rejects a rebuke; A mace-duel ends in cheating; Massacre at Midnight; The split with Draupadi

BOOK IV: *The Last Naga.* The Naga warrior Takshaka had surrendered in the hope of stopping King Janamejaya's massacre of the Nagas. The Vyaasa Suta, (the son of Krishna Dvaipaayana, Satyavati's son by Parashara) narrated the history of the conflict between Takshaka's family and the Pandavas. It had begun with the murder of Kindama, Takshaka's great-grandfather.

SUMMARY: Pandu kills Kindama; Pandu's punishment; Takshaka kills Pandu and Madri; The Burning of Khandavaprastha; Takshaka's vendetta; A Great War; Naga neutrality; Yudhishthira offers Arjuna; Takshaka suspends his vendetta; Parikshit is crowned; A Collective Punishment; A King is Killed; Janamejaya is crowned; Genocide; Takshaka surrenders; Takshaka's trial; The Vyaasa Suta tells the story; Janamejaya's decision; Takshaka accepts.

BOOK V: *The Last Yadava.* The wound had turned septic and Krishna was suffering from fever. The hunter's young son asked Krishna many questions about his life. Krishna realized that he would probably die and narrated the story of his own life.

SUMMARY: Kamsa takes over; Krishna is hidden; Krishna comes of age; Krishna kill Kamsa; Meeting the Pandavas; The Pandavas disappear; The Pandavas reappear; Alliance with Panchala; Krishna recommends acceptance; Jarasandha; Govardhana Village runs away; The Burning of Khandavaprastha; The Building of Indraprastha; The killing of Jarasandha; Krishna saves Draupadi; The Great War; Massacre at Midnight; Yudhishthira the Emperor; The Abdication; A Civil War?; The Depopulation of Dwaraka; Krishna the Wanderer; Injured by Jara; Death by Jara.

Introduction

As a child the *Mahabharata* fascinated me. Not only did it have heroes, heroines, villains, and fast-paced action, but it also raised profound human questions about fairness, the thirst for revenge, the horror of war. When I became interested in history and pre-history, I struggled to fit the stories into what the archaeological record showed. The histories of other vanished cultures of the ancient world – Greece, Egypt, and Sumer – seemed to be grounded in verifiable fact, while the Mahabharata, a self-proclaimed *historical* epic of a still-alive-and-breathing culture in South Asia and Southeast Asia, seemed to lack any foundation in reality we could unearth.

This book is a revised version of *The Last Kaurava* a novel published by Leadstart Publishing in 2015 in India, where readers have easy access to the story of the Mahabharata through books, in school, or by way of stories told by parents, grandparents, or the many uncles and aunts who populate the family environment. To many readers of the epic, the world of the Mahabharata appears exotic, though metaphors and allegory from it often appear in ordinary conversation, even today. My hope is that this revision will make sense to readers outside India as well; who know the basic story of the Mahabharata but who have only experienced it as exotica. Mostly these readers are from the South Asian diaspora, but others may find the book interesting as well. An extended summary of the original Mahabharata is included in the boxes, as an introduction to the reader completely unfamiliar with the original, as well as a reminder for readers who know some of it.

The Mahabharata: Summary of the Original Epic

Shantanu, the king of Hastinapura falls in love with Satyavati but is unable to marry her because her father asks that Shantanu should disinherit his son Devavrata and pass on the crown to her sons. When Devavrata finds out, he voluntarily relinquishes his inheritance, but that does not satisfy Satyavati's father who is concerned that Devavrata's own children would not accept this. In response, the young Devavrata vows celibacy, which earns him the title (usually translated as 'The Terrible').

Satyavati's sons, Chitrangada and Vichitravirya, die childless but she arranges for Vichitravirya's two wives to bear two sons fathered by her pre-marital son Vyaasa (also author of the epic). These two sons are the blind Dhritarashtra, the elder, and the pale Pandu. Dhritarashtra, being blind, cannot be king, so Pandu inherits the throne. But he exiles himself as punishment for a murder he commits. Bhishma is Regent during the various periods when there is no functioning king on the throne of Hastinapura.

Dhritarashtra has a hundred sons, called the Kauravas, headed by Duryodhana and Dushasana; Pandu in exile has five sons, the Pandavas, named Yudhishthira, Bhima, Arjuna, Nakula and Sahadeva. When Pandu dies, the Pandavas go to Hastinapura with their mother Kunti, to be raised with the Kauravas. Duryodhana, who had expected to inherit the kingdom by default, resents the return of the Pandavas as Yudhishthira becomes Crown Prince. The result is enmity between the Kauravas and the Pandavas.

Duryodhana plots against the Pandavas, who escape a burning palace and disappear. They come out of hiding at the wedding of the princess Panchali Draupadi, the daughter of Drupada, king of Panchala. Panchali chooses Arjuna as husband, but in order to fulfil their mother's mistaken injunction to share his 'winnings', all five Pandavas marry Draupadi. The reappearance of the Pandavas with a powerful new ally leads to a compromise. Hastinapura is divided and the Pandavas are given the barren south-eastern half where they establish the city of Indraprastha.

Duryodhana's plots continue. Yudhishthira is invited to play a game of dice and finds himself facing an expert opponent, Shakuni. Yudhishthira loses everything, including his brothers, himself, and then Draupadi. In a confrontation, Draupadi is assaulted and Bhishma refuses to intervene. In order to settle the conflict and prevent war, the Pandavas agree to go into exile for at least thirteen years, with an additional twelve years of exile if discovered during the thirteenth year.

After thirteen years, Duryodhana refuses to return Indraprastha to the Pandavas. War is unavoidable. This becomes a Great War in which many, many kings from all over the world (i.e. India) participate – almost two million warriors converge on the field of Kurukshetra. The war lasts eighteen days, with almost all the warriors dead.

Bhishma fights for the Kauravas and is fatally injured on the ninth day, but stays alive on a bed of arrows for another fifty-six days, well past the end of the war. Yudhishthira comes to him for advice and receives it – almost fifteen thousand verses of the canonical total of one hundred thousand verses of the epic are Bhishma's advice to the newly crowned King of Hastinapura.

Many scholars have viewed the vow of celibacy to be the root cause of the chaos described in the epic. In that case, one would expect Bhishma to be a central character of the narrative. But he is not. After the vow, there are only three occasions on which Bhishma appears and makes a fateful decision. These three episodes span three generations. For a central character, he receives little time on the stage leading to the war. But after the war is over, Bhishma's instructions to Yudhishthira are a sixth of the verses in the epic.

The reader of the Mahabharata may be confounded by the setting of the story. Technologies from a variety of stages of development (Iron Age or Bronze Age or even Stone Age) are indiscriminately mixed together. Social organizations from different social systems are placed in the same time period. Tribes or peoples from different eras take part in the Great War. The war takes place within a few weeks of the end of the period of exile, but armies and warriors come from thousands of miles away to take part in it.

So what is the truth? Archaeology provides some hints.

We know from satellite images and excavations that around 2000 B.C.E., in South Asia, a great river with over a thousand urban settlements on its banks, dried up and disappeared. This river, the Sarasvati, is mentioned in the *Puranas* and the *Vedas*. The vanished settlements were the Sarasvati-Sindhu Culture (SSC), called the Indus Valley Civilization after the settlements first discovered on the banks of the Indus and spread over modern-day Pakistan and western India. When the river dried up, the SSC towns collapsed, sending refugees in all directions. Refugees moving east into the Gangetic plain would have encountered a native, forest-dwelling, non-urban population, leading to conflict over land and its uses. These were unresolvable conflicts with no compromise – one side had to lose and the other side had to win. War would be the solution, both awful and unavoidable; with peace would come a new way of life.

Fall Of The Kurus is a series of novels that tell the story of this crisis. *The Making of Bhishma* is Book 1 of the series. Changing the context has resulted in many differences between this book and the story in the original Mahabharata. This novel is set in 2000 B.C.E., against the backdrop of the crisis caused by the drying up of the Sarasvati. Hastinapura, on the Ganga, is a frontier town that is overwhelmed by immigrants. Social policies set up to manage the crisis fail and this set the stage for the Great War that ended one civilization and established the first empire in the region.

The story told in this book was memorized by the *Kavi Sangha*, an organization of bards and poets, whose annals comprise the historical archives of the cities in the Panchnad culture. The archives of Hastinapura contained the memoirs of Devavrata, also called *Bhishma* (The Terrible), who was a central figure of the time leading up to the Great War. The Head of the *Kavi Sangha*, called the *Vyaas*a, was a respected figure, who also played a part.

I followed some ground rules for establishing the context. Fantasy has been eliminated – there are no gods, goddesses, or demons; there is no magic or magical weapons; there are no miraculous conceptions or divine reincarnations; the *Law of Karma* (that depends on the concept of rebirth), is not used to explain behavior. Situating the Great War in 2000 B.C.E. has limited the technologies available. For instance, there are no nuclear weapons. But more to the point, no horses or iron or million-man armies. Iron was scarce or unknown; armies were small; horse-drawn war chariots would not exist for another two hundred years; transportation was by carts drawn by oxen or onagers (Asian wild ass). The people were not all that different from us – they loved, they hated, they were kind, they got angry, they acted without thinking, they plotted, they lied, they demanded the truth, and so on. In short, they were not better than us, nor worse than us, but just like us. The one big difference was that the culture did not use writing but was an oral one – history was memorized and recited, not written and read.

What is the difference between *The Making of Bhishma* and *The Last Kaurava?* The first tells the story of Bhishma's life as narrated by Bhishma, lying mortally wounded and a prisoner of his grand-nephew. The latter embeds the same narration within the context of a second crisis, over twelve hundred years later, and results in a project to write down the history of Hastinapura. The advanced and sophisticated culture of South Asia in 850 B.C.E. was non-literate (to the best of our knowledge), and a script had to be invented. Hence the frame is the story of the invention of a syllabic script (called *abugida* by linguists), that is the presumed root of all later South Asian and Southeast Asian abugidas. But readers of *The Last Kaurava* felt the frame story interrupted and slowed the main narrative and was a significant barrier to continuous reading. I too, felt the frame story distracted readers from mapping the reimagined life of Bhishma to that described in the original Mahabharata. I decided that readers, especially those unfamiliar with Hindu mythology, would be better served by a more condensed version.

There is one other major modification with respect to the original epic – I have changed many of the conventional names. The Mahabharata often uses descriptive names or titles. Some characters are never called by their names while other names are descriptive or honorific. Devavrata is called *Bhishma* (The Terrible), *Pandu* means 'The Pale'; the wife of the Pandavas is *Draupadi* (Daughter of Drupada) or *Panchali* (Princess of Panchala), and so on. Some names are clearly invented to label the villains. Thus the eldest Kaurava is *Duryodhana* (Bad Warrior) and his brother is *Dushasana* (Badly Seated). Some 'put-down' names have lost their sting. For instance, the martial arts teacher who fights for the Kauravas, is *Drona* (a wooden jar that holds intoxicating drink/*soma* during rituals). Conversely, some names, for the heroes, are intended as praise. *Yudhishthira* means 'Firm in War'. Others may have been humorous – Bhima is *Vrikodara* or 'Eats like a Wolf'. I have attempted to identify the given names of the major characters in the original Mahabharata. For example, Duryodhana is *Suyodhana* (Good Warrior), and his brother *Sushasana* (Well-seated). Drona is *Kutaja* (Mountain Peak). It is possible that Kutaja was transformed to Drona by his detractors. A list of names transformed in this way appears in the Appendix.

Cast of Characters

[Those not in the original Mahabharata are marked with an asterisk.]

Major Characters

SHANTANU: Devavrata's father, who unexpectedly becomes King of Hastinapura. He imposes the one-child-per-person policy proposed by the Kavi Sangha. His first wife Ganga commits suicide over the loss of her children, traumatizing Devavrata, his firstborn. Driven by lust for Satyavati, he disinherits Devavrata, and later dies of depression, caused by guilt.

SATYAVATI: The beautiful Naga woman of the Meena clan who asks her brother Shukla for help to discourage Shantanu from wooing her. Shukla's plot backfires spectacularly and results in Devavrata's disinheritance and vow of celibacy. The mutual distrust between Satyavati and Devavrata casts a shadow of deeply conflicted enmity over the following years.

DEVAVRATA/BHISHMA: The Kuru scion who takes a vow of celibacy after being disinherited by his father. It is his vision that creates an empire over which he refuses to reign as King, but acts as Regent, initially for his step-brothers, and then their sons and grandsons. His personal life suffers as he feels betrayed by his first love, unable to save his step-brother, and finds and loses a second love. He is ignorant of the existence of his son, Shikhandin, who leads him to his death. At the end of his life he is unable to stop his father's descendants from fighting over the empire.

AMBA: The second woman loved by Devavrata watches him earn the title 'Bhishma', suspects him of plotting to kill her, escapes, and raises their son Shikhandin to be unaware of his father, but to hate him.

SHIKHANDIN: Son of Amba and Devavrata is raised to hate his (unknown to him) father. He leads Devavrata into an ambush. Devavrata kills him but is mortally wounded in doing so.

YUDHISHTHIRA: Eldest son of Mahendra/Pandu, grandson of Vichitravirya (Devavrata's step-brother). Yudhishthira and his brothers are the *Pandavas*. Yudhishthira follows in his father's footsteps and opposes Devavrata's vision of empire because of its fundamental flaws (that his father was unable to correct as King).

SUYODHANA/DURYODHANA: Eldest son of Dhritarashtra, grandson of Vichitravirya (Devavrata's step-brother). Leader of Dhritarashtra's hundred sons, collectively called the *Kauravas* (opposing the *Pandavas*, the sons of Suyodhana's uncle, Mahendra Pandu). Suyodhana has a chip on his shoulder as he is considered younger than Yudhishthira and hence not the heir apparent. He is angry with his father for being weak and not fighting when he was ousted from the kingship by his younger brother, on account of his blindness. Suyodhana feels cheated of his rights.

LOMAHARSHANA: The Archivist in Indraprastha when the war begins, he stays with the Pandava army and is encouraged by the Vyaasa Shukla, to record the history of the war for the Annals of Hastinapura. Lomaharshana's task is to identify key events and compose memorizable entries for the Annals.

* SHUKLA: The Vyaasa (leader of the Kavi Sangha) just before and during the period of the Great War. Brother to Satyavati, he advises her to make impossible demands in response to Shantanu's wooing. But this strategy backfires when Shantanu's

Chief Minister Sashidhara counter-plots. Shukla, as Vyaasa of the Kavi Sangha, supports the project to add the story of the Great War to the Annals of Hastinapura and also contributes to it.

* SASHIDHARA: Shantanu's friend and an actor by profession, he becomes his Chief Minister despite his lack of qualifications. A quick study, he is diplomatic and becomes indispensable. His memory of events during Shantanu's reign helps to fill out Devavrata's and Shukla's version of events.

SECONDARY CHARACTERS

* GANGA: The Queen, Shantanu's wife and Devavrata's mother. She commits suicide by drowning, while Devavrata watches helplessly.

DVAIPAAYANA KRISHNA: Son of Satyavati by the Vyaasa Parashara. He grows up to become Vyaasa after Lomaharshana, and edits the Annals of Hastinapura.

CHITRANGADA: First son of Satyavati by Shantanu. Impulsive, like his mother's family, he is killed in a conflict with the Shakas, who try to enter Hastinapura from the north.

VICHITRAVIRYA: Second son of Satyavati by Shantanu. Becomes King after his brother's untimely death and leaves the administration of Hastinapura to Devavrata, while he enjoys life with his two wives. He dies childless, thus leaving a mess that Satyavati tries to fix.

AMBIKA & AMBALIKA: Vichitravirya's wives and Amba's younger sisters. They try to help Amba escape Hastinapura and side with Satyavati in her dispute with Devavrata.

MAHENDRA/PANDU: Son of Vichitravirya by Ambika and Krishna Dvaipaayana (son of Satyavati by Parashara). Albinism makes him hideous to gaze on. He sides with the Nagas in their dispute with the immigrants. He abdicates as King when he realizes the limitations of what he can do to change policy. Founder of Indraprastha.

DHRITARASHTRA: Son of Vichitravirya by Ambika and Krishna Dvaipaayana (son of Satyavati by Parashara). Blind from birth, selfish, and susceptible to emotional outbursts like his grandmother Satyavati and grandfather Parashara, he sides with the immigrants and Devavrata in the debate with Mahendra/Pandu over the treatment of the Nagas. His sons, the Kauravas, are like him.

KARNA: Advisor and friend to Suyodhana, his origins are unknown in *The Making of Bhishma* but his story is revealed in Book II of the series: *The Last Matriarch*.

The Prisoner

1
Amba's Visit

"Remember me? AMBA?"

The voice rang in Devavrata's ears, cutting through pain to a melody of long-forgotten joy shadowed by a fading anger. He felt a warm light grow and envelope him like dawn breaking out over the river Ganga. Images lost in time veered in and out of focus. Questions came flooding into his mind: *How could it be Amba? What was she doing here?* But the words stuck in his throat, refusing expression. The voice in his ear, silenced by a grey miasma – a grey he associated with pain and anger. The glow faded and the grey fog grew until it shadowed every color. *Amba. She is here. I must see her.* He tried to turn his head. Agonizing pain shot through him from the arrow head in his left armpit, compelling him to pause.

"You killed my son! You killed Shikhandin."

The greyness grew deeper. *Yes, he had killed Shikhandin.* His mind raced. Shikhandin had lured him into an ambush. He had dealt the man a fatal blow. The ambushers had attacked and a well-aimed arrow had penetrated under his arm to his lungs, rendering his arms useless. He had fallen, by Shikhandin's side. A prisoner, he had been transported in the same cart as Shikhandin, to the Pandava camp. He had listened to Shikhandin moan as he died.

Shikhandin was Amba's son? He should have known. It explained so much. He understood now why trusting Shikhandin had been so easy. Amba's profile as she looked out at the sunrise over the garden town of Varanavata, his model town for resettling the Panchnad refugees, melded into the profile of Shikhandin looking out over the Ganga at the remains of a war ravaged settlement, making him drop his guard and follow Shikhandin into the ambush. He recalled the surge of anger when he discovered Shikhandin's betrayal; fury that had made him slash Shikhandin. *Shikhandin 'the arrowhead', well-named and well-aimed; truly an arrow aimed at him.* He was the only one he had killed in this war. At his age he was more an asset in conducting the war than fighting battles. *But…there were so many buts.*

"You killed your son. Now die!"

The greyness turned darker. Devavrata tried to face Amba and deny the astounding charge. But he felt her hand push down on his left shoulder, against the broken shaft of the arrow. Pain exploded through his body; a burning flame that would not go out. He was a warrior. *I will not scream,* he thought, struggling against the roar he had once used in battle. He was *Devavrata Bhishma,* The Terrible, four times Regent of Hastinapura, bulwark of an empire built to last for eternity; an empire that must now save the refugees fleeing from their ancient home of Panchnad in the west, into the embrace of the Ganga and Yamuna. He was the savior of a civilization.

He would not scream! But his mind's defiance did not prevent the arrowhead (*Shikhandin!)* from pushing in deeper, past his lungs to his heart, already torn by Amba's presence. His last memory was of a glimmering haze in which guards rushed in and pulled Amba away…and regret that he had not looked upon her face.

2
A Father's Boon

"I give you this boon, my son: You may choose the time of your death." On his deathbed Shantanu had laboured to whisper the words to Devavrata, his son.

If they had sounded like the mutterings of delirium to Devavrata then, they seemed yet more irrational now. He must be dead, for he was floating. All about him was white nothingness, unrelieved by color or shadow. This must be death. But that was not possible, for he had not yet chosen to die. Then he heard a voice behind him.

"Will he die?"

Devavrata could see nothing but his hearing was good enough. He recognized the speaker as his grandnephew, Yudhishthira. His mind formed questions: *Was this a dream? Why am I floating? Who is Yudhishthira talking about?*

An unfamiliar voice came from his left. "Not right away, Sir. When he wakes he will be in pain. I will do my best to ease it."

The whiteness began to fade into grey. *Where am I? How can I hear a discussion between my grandnephew and a stranger? Someone was to awaken soon. Who were they talking about?* Devavrata felt a touch on his chest. He looked down. There was nothing to see. He could feel four fingers, close together on his invisible chest. The greyness turned into blackness. The fingers on his chest moved. There was a spot just below his left nipple that was sensitive. If they touched it, he would feel it. A moment later he felt the fingers touch the sensitive spot. He felt his muscles twitch.

The voice said: "His heart is in good shape. I don't hear any worrying sounds but the tip of the arrow is almost touching his heart. Do not move the arrow. Any movement can puncture his heart. Blood will then pour out into his lungs, and he will die."

Devavrata suddenly remembered the voice. It was the who had worked on Shikhandin when they were first brought in. The conversation he was listening to was taking place in the medical tent. He was floating again, in blackness. He could not see but he could hear. Yudhishthira and the *bisaj* were discussing someone with a lung injury from an arrow. *Just like me.*

"Will it heal at all?"

That was like Yudhishthira. *His voice reminds me of his father; caring about everyone, even a wounded prisoner.*

"No," said the *bisaj*, "the Regent will die sooner or later."

The Regent was going to die. The Regent...I am the Regent. They are talking about me. He must be in the medical tent, not floating around. He was not dead, he was dying. *What happened to my father's boon?* It had been a strange utterance, possibly the strangest from his father, on his deathbed. Even in delirium Shantanu had been serious and convincing. In his idle moments Devavrata had wondered what his father had meant. Apparently nothing, for here he was, fatally wounded and soon to die.

Why can't I see? He was prepared to die but he had always imagined himself entering death with eyes wide open, seeing everything. Moments passed, feeling like an eternity; feeding a growing sense of panic. He found himself back in his body. Now he could feel the pain in his shoulder, pulsing and alternating with his heartbeat, impossible to ignore. He opened his eyes. The *bisaj* was sitting by his side, along with Yudhishthira. The *bisaj* bent low and placed his right ear on the Regent's chest. Devavrata closed his eyes.

Devavrata heard Yudhishthira ask, "How long?"

"Two days…a week perhaps…no more. I will return in the morning to check."

Silence.

The first thing that struck Devavrata when he opened his eyes was the sunlight streaming in through the open flap. His bed had been turned around to face the entrance of the tent. He could no longer see the mat on which Shikhandin's body had been laid. His left leg was tied, as before, to one of the tent poles. He could turn a little more freely to the right, but a roll of felted cotton placed behind him prevented him from rolling onto his left side. It felt rough on the skin of his back. His shoulder was sore; he could not move his arm.

"He has opened his eyes."

It was Yudhishthira, his grandnephew. Devavrata now realized they had been talking about him. *I am going to die, and fairly soon at that.* Amba was nowhere to be seen. Yudhishthira smiled down at him; his grave eyes giving his smile the lie. Calmness radiated from Yudhishthira and seemed to calm the people around him. That alone made him different from his cousin, Suyodhana.

A sensuous pout characterized the descendants of the old Queen Mother. *My stepmother*, he thought. She had it, as did her father and her brother, Shukla the Vyaasa. It marked her descendants, making them seem attractive, encouraging people to defer to their wishes. Her grandson Dhritarashtra too, had the pout, and despite his near-complete blindness, women were drawn to him and he did not turn them away. Dhritarashtra's son Suyodhana too, had the pout. But it made him seem dissatisfied, which indeed he was much of the time.

But Yudhishthira, also her great-grandson, had not inherited the pouted lips. That had settled the matter for the Queen Mother – she demanded proof that Yudhishthira was truly Pandu's son and thus the legitimate heir, *her* heir. There was no proof and no known way of establishing the truth. "Yudhishthira is not my descendant," she had declared. "You must support Suyodhana's claim, for he is my only true heir." His stepmother was another reason the cousins could not compromise.

That curve of the lips, with its hint of subtle pleasures, also drew people to Suyodhana and his brothers. Devavrata knew the look, for despite all that had happened it still had the power to make him want to please his stepmother. After his father's death, he and his stepmother had clashed frequently, but he had often compromised, even when a compromise was not warranted. And when his anger at his stepmother had been too great, and a compromise seemed impossible, her brother Shukla, with the same facial feature, the same look, would bring him round.

The unanswered questions about Yudhishthira's legitimacy was one of the reasons why Devavrata supported Suyodhana.

But it was not the only reason for this war. *The Pandavas will destroy what I have built,* Devavrata thought. His life's work, accomplished over four long, self-sacrificing terms as Regent for one or other of his father's descendants, was the Kuru Empire he had built around Hastinapura. The refugees fleeing the famine in the west, caused by the drying of their great river, the Sarasvati, could have been sent back to face certain starvation and probable death; they could have been forced to go further east into the land inhabited by the forest-dwelling Nagas[1] and Rakshasas[2], and left to fend for themselves, to die or to survive on whatever terms they could get. His father, King Shantanu, had tried and failed for the forests were not easy to clear, the land hard to till, and, bar some, the refugees were urban dwellers, not farmers. They all wished to immigrate to Hastinapura.

Despite their poverty they did not consider themselves refugees but immigrants. Before the present crisis, immigrants had been welcome in Hastinapura. The Kauravas[3] themselves had been immigrants, as were all the non-Naga residents of Hastinapura. But circumstances were far from normal. The river Sarasvati[4], which hosted most of the Panchnad cities and received snow-melt from the Yamuna, which flowed about ten

---

[1]The Hastinapuris gave the name *Naga* to the forest-dwelling, matriarchal bands living along the Ganga. The Nagas had many names for themselves, derived in different ways such as from a totem animal (Matsya, Naga, Meena, etc.) or from the name of the founding matriarch and sometimes her spouse.

[2]The Nagas gave the name *Defender* (in their own language) to the hunter-gatherer tribes that dwelt in the forest to the east of modern-day Patna. The Hastinapuris translated that name into the Panchnadi language as *Rakshasa*.

[3]*Kaurava* means "descendent of Kuru," but the term is usually applied specifically to Suyodhana and his brothers.

[4]*Sarasvati* is the hidden river of Hindu legend, flowing invisibly to merge with the Ganga and the Yamuna near Allahabad.

yojanas[5] to the west of Hastinapura, and from the Sutudri[6], which flowed farther west. But earthquakes in the Himalayas had changed this. The Yamuna had shifted east, and the Sutudri had turned west, depriving the Sarasvati of water. This had forced migration.

The Yamuna's eastward shift was not an immediate gain for the eastern lands as the waters had no channel to flow into and simply flooded the land. The Khandava forest to the west of Hastinapura, and areas further south, were flooded and could not house the immigrants. Any settlements they built had to be in the lands to the east and south of Hastinapura, lands already occupied by the hitherto friendly Nagas.

These immigrants did not seek to be pioneers, creating new settlements that would take a generation or more to become as livable as the towns they had left behind. They sought urban rather than frontier lives. Devavrata's accomplishment had been to marshal the unhappy refugees into work crews that built dams, created lakes, constructed waterworks – thus forming the infrastructure to support the new settlements.

But all this had come at a cost. The Nagas, traditionally friendly to Hastinapura, were being squeezed out of their traditional land.

---

[5]*Yojana* is a measure of distance, estimated variously to be between seven and ten miles.
[6]*Sutudri* is the river Sutlej.

Permanent immigrant settlements took over the lands the Nagas had left fallow to recover from the stress of slash-and-burn agriculture. As each new settlement grew, all the arable land near water bodies would be taken. The Nagas could no longer live in the way they were used to. Either they had to give up their way of life or leave. They were pressurized to leave.

The Pandavas would undo all that he had accomplished. They would justify their rebellion, just like their father had justified his, in the name of fairness and justice for the Nagas, Devavrata thought sadly. But Suyodhana would not do that. Like his father Dhritarashtra, he did not care about the Nagas and had many ties to the immigrants – a few friends, many lovers and numerous allies. *He will soon outdo his father in the number of wives and concubines he takes from among the immigrants.* Hastin's descendants had come a long way, transitioning from the trading family that founded Hastinapura to the warrior-rulers they now were. No, Suyodhana would not interfere with the administration of the empire Devavrata had established.

"Pitamaha, do you feel any pain?" It was the *bisaj.*

Devavrata's heart no longer raced as it had done when Amba had pressed on his shoulder. *Where was she?* His breathing was ragged and he could feel the stubby edge of the broken arrow against his upper arm. *It had not been removed; it was still there.* "A little," he said, trying to smile.

The *bisaj's* serious face did not change as he continued to gaze down at the Commander of the Kurus.

Yudhishthira said quietly, "Pitamaha, your injuries are grave, aggravated by what Amba did. She was upset by her son's death.

I approved her request to collect his body, not anticipating her actions when she saw you."

Did they know what Amba had told him? Did anyone? Had Amba told the truth? I must talk to her. I must reassure Yudhishthira that I am not afraid of her. Devavrata tried to smile but the pain turned it into a grimace. "She has reason to be angry. He was her son. I wish to talk to her when her anger cools – perhaps in a month."

Yudhishthira's eyes dropped away from Devavrata, his shoulders slumping a little. Slowly, he raised his head and looked straight at his granduncle. "That is not likely."

What did he mean? Devavrata frowned.

"You are dying, Pitamaha." For a brief moment a ripple of worry crossed Yudhishthira's face and calm eyes. "The *bisaj* advises against removing the arrow. Amba pushed the arrowhead past your lung. It missed the vital spots but now lies near your heart. You are alive because the arrowhead is plugging its own hole. If it had not, you would have bled to death. The *bisaj* does not expect you to last more than a week. If the arrow was removed, you would last only a few *ghatis*[7]."

Devavrata had listened with eyes closed. *So this was how it was to end after so many years, so many battles, so much pain… Was this how my father's boon is to be manifested?* "Do you mean I can choose when I will die?"

"Yes. That is one way to put it."

[7]A *ghaṭi* is defined as one-sixtieth of a day (from sunrise to sunrise) and is twenty-four minutes. A *vighati* is one-sixtieth of a ghati and is twenty-four seconds.

3
Yudhishthira's Request

Devavrata had not expected the pain. He was a warrior, an old one at that. He had survived much. He had been cut by the sword and lived. He had felt the sting of a sharp arrow before. He had felt the bone-numbing pain of falling down a hill but had recovered to keep fighting. That was just physical pain; he knew how to overcome physical pain.

But this was different. The thoughts that echoed in his mind could not be subdued like bodily pain. They grew with each reverberation, tearing open the old wound he believed had been cauterized by the passage of time – over five hundred moons[8]. But Amba's visit had re-opened it; angry because he had killed her son. He could understand that. *But why did she leave in the first place?* That was a puzzle he had never found the answer to. If he had known she was pregnant, he might have… He was surprised to find he no longer recalled the cause for his absence when she had disappeared. If he had known of her pregnancy he would not have been absent. *Shikhandin was my son!* He thought he had become inured to surprises and yet this revelation astounded him. The onset of war at Suyodhana's

---

[8]A solar year is about thirteen moons, or lunar months. So five hundred moons (or months) is about forty years. Bronze Age cultures appear to have used a calendar that used the month to measure the passage of time and the years for agricultural purposes. In the interest of readability, I will use "moons" when characters are conversing but "years" during description.

instigation, the Pandavas' escape, their alliance with Panchala, the Yadava alliance with Panchala, led by Krishna Gopala, the cowherd, the list of surprises was long. But this one left them all behind. The dead Shikhandin was his son. *I killed my own son!* Shikhandin was the son he had vowed would never exist. He had kept his promise; he had no son. *Truly I deserve to be called Devavrata Bhishma.*

Shikhandin's paternity appeared to be a secret from everyone else too. His great-nephew Yudhishthira had apologized for Amba's attack; he had not imagined she would use the opportunity to finish off her son's killer. Nothing in Yudhishthira's words had indicated that he knew Shikhandin was his granduncle's son and uncle of a king in his own right; nor that he knew of any past relationship between Amba and Devavrata.

Yudhishthira had taken care to see that Devavrata was safe and comfortable. The other Pandavas – Bhima, Arjuna and the twins – had come by, their voices subdued, their broad shoulders slumped in his presence. The attendant assigned to care for him was brusque and abrupt, his dislike of the enemy Commander clear in all his actions. *Only my grand-nephews, leaders of this camp, care whether I live or die. To the rest I am the enemy, better dead.* In the Kaurava camp, neither Suyodhana nor Suyodhana's hangers-on seemed to care whether he lived or died, and yet the army, nominally under his command, deferred to him.

The tent entrance was on the eastern side. A leather flap blocked the rays of the morning sun. Devavrata's bed had been placed along the southern side, his head towards the entrance. On the western side there had been the bed bearing Shikhandin's body, laid out on its back. Devavrata had puzzled over the profile, wondering why it tugged at a corner of his mind. With Amba's revelation, that mystery had been explained. She must have taken her son's body away the previous night. Realizing Devavrata was in the same tent, she had returned to kill him. Long years ago, those wide eyes and high cheekbones had touched his heart, giving it life; now they had returned to reclaim that life. *No matter, I am a fortunate man.* Before death finally claimed him, memories from so long ago that he almost doubted their reality, had come to lighten his heart. Those memories assuaged the sorrow that welled within him now as he recalled watching his son die – the son he had not known he had. *Just once, before Yama takes me, I am permitted a glimpse of pleasure from lost time. You are not to blame, Amba. You were the only light in my life. That was enough.*

His grandnephew posed a different problem. Yudhishthira looked subdued, depressed by the thought of Devavrata's imminent demise. If there was one thing he could change, it was to relieve Yudhishthira of his misery. He had always had an innate affection for the boy and the man. The slight youth with the distant gaze had changed into a dignified man who held himself like a warrior and behaved like a commander of men. However, the legitimacy of his claim to Hastinapura's throne remained in doubt. The compromise Devavrata had forged many years ago and made Yudhishthira Chief Magistrate of Indraprastha (City of Indra), the breakaway republic, had collapsed under the weight of Suyodhana's ambitions. Devavrata had not expected the compromise to stand forever, but it had not survived the first generation. His plans for the empire envisaged that Hastinapura would eventually rule all the surrounding lands, including Indraprastha, but the compromise had failed, lasting only a few years.

"Pitamaha, would that I could change what the *bisaj* has said!" Yudhishthira's manner reflected genuine concern.

"Yudhishthira my boy, I am an old man and have seen much. That my wound is fatal, I know. The *bisaj* is right. I do not have much time left. I accept it."

"I beg forgiveness for capturing and disabling you, but it was necessary. This war was unnecessary. But no matter now, we must win."

"You did what you had to, my son. I swore to protect the dynasty and ensure legitimate succession. As long as I live, I have to oppose you."

Yudhishthira did not respond. Devavrata's public oaths were well known, as was his acceptance of his own disinheritance. Nevertheless there were whispers hinting at treason. There were secret oaths as well, of celibacy and unquestioned support for the Queen Mother's children, made to his father and known only to a few. Sanjaya, the family bard would have sung publicly of Devavrata's vows were he not terrified of Devavrata *Bhishma*. Vyaasa Shukla, the golden-voiced Head of the Kavi Sangha, knew all that Devavrata knew and more. Lastly, the secret oaths were known to his nephew, Dharmateja *Vidura*[9], known for his wisdom, intelligence, closed mouth and open mind, born alongside his royal brothers Mahendra *Pandu*[10] and Dhritarashtra, the child of a royal wet-nurse; perfect in every way that the other two were not, yet ineligible to be king as his

[9]*Dharmateja* was called *Vidura*, meaning "the Wise." He was not a warrior, but due to his intelligence and wisdom, he was appointed Chief Minister to Devavrata Bhishma and later to Mahendra Pandu and Dhritarashtra.
[10]*Mahendra* was called *Pandu*, the Pale, possibly because of his albinism.

mother was neither royal nor a wife, merely a maid-servant of the Queen and occasional bedmate to their father, the dead King Vichitravirya, and wet-nurse to his sons.

Did Yudhishthira know of my vows? Is he about to question my decision to oppose him? Devavrata did not think so. *And why would he touch on the subject of succession? It would be resolved soon enough, through battle.* Yudhishthira had always refused to be drawn into the ancient debate over legitimacy. Pandu had acknowledged him as his son, making him eligible to become Master Trader of Hastinapura, and that was the final word.

"Our dynasty will live on," Yudhishthira said now. "The survival of the Kurus is not what worries me. What concerns me is the crisis that began with you and continues to confront us. My father rejected your chosen path for the empire, and now I reject it as well. We may not undo all you have done, but we *will* stop the continual grabbing of Naga land and their eviction. The Yadavas have promised not to go further north. We have more than our share of refugees. The next lot can go further west, beyond the mountains to Bahlika.[11] I want you to explain why you chose to create this empire. It will perhaps help us follow a wiser path, one the Matsyas, Yadavas and Panchalas will support. My Kaurava cousins felt threatened by our proposals. You too, saw them as a threat to the empire. War became inevitable. You may be too old to fight but your mind is revealed in the strategies they have adopted to fight this war. That is why we had to capture you. We intended to capture you, never to maim or kill you thus. We thought that with you as our prisoner, Suyodhana would be left with

[11]*Bahlika* is believed to be either Bactria or Baluchistan. It is said to have been founded by Shantanu's brother Bahlika who abdicated and left Hastinapura.

Kutaja *Drona*[12], Master of Weapons and martial arts teacher, as the only competent advisor on the conduct of the war. What grieves me is that your injuries are fatal and you will die my prisoner. I have no option in this. I cannot send you back. I must hold you prisoner. My men are afraid of you and your cunning. Even now they ask when we will execute you."

Cunning? Devavrata mused over the description. They were right of course. Only the cunning survive to old age. He had survived. "What do you want from me?" he asked, his voice a mockery of the thundering roar of old. "The crisis continues. Clearly we have not been wise, for we have added war to the flames."

"I wish to know the history of the crisis. How it came about, what was tried, and what did not work. You are the only one whose knowledge goes that far back."

"No, not the only one…"

"The only one I can talk to now," declared Yudhishthira. "The Queen Mother refuses to have anything to do with us. Uncle Dharmateja Vidura tells us he supports our claims, but being Vidura, chooses to remain in Hastinapura, at Suyodhana's side, refusing to explain his actions. He always helped us when we lived in Hastinapura. Mother Kunti says she will not move out of Hastinapura, that I should fight for my rights. Vyaasa Shukla can move freely within the city but takes care to speak in parables that nobody understands.

A sour taste rose in Devavrata's throat. He was being asked to remember. Remembering was all he had done since he had

[12]*Kutaja* means "mountain peak", but also "jar". Later, the martial arts teacher would be called *Drona*, which means "jar", specifically one used to hold the hallucinogenic drug *soma* used in Vedic ritual. Drona is possibly a pejorative name.

been captured. But those were not the memories anybody wanted. "I need time to think. I am tired and it is late. Ask me tomorrow." *With luck I shall be dead.*

"I will," Yudhishthira said. "I will come ten ghatis after sunrise and bring along Indraprastha's Archivist."

An archivist! So they were getting help from the Kavi Sangha, Devavrata mused as he carefully eased his aching shoulder against the cotton roll.

4
Archivist of Indraprastha

Lomaharshana[13], the Archivist, woke that morning to find one of his younger colleagues sitting by his bed.

"We have a message from the Vyaasa," his junior said. "He will visit us soon – a quiet visit without any ceremony. The Pandavas are rumored to have a senior prisoner in their camp. It is imperative that you archive his memoirs. Ask the eldest Pandava, Chief Yudhishthira, for permission, and take note of any questions he might want answered. There can be no delay."

As Lomaharshana was readying himself for the day, a verbal message arrived from Yudhishthira: *We have a prisoner whose memoirs must be archived immediately for he is on his death-bed. I have told him what I wish to know and he understands my requirements. Start as soon as you can.*

Lomaharshana completed his morning rituals and meal and then hurried over to the hospital tent. He recognized the prisoner immediately – *The Regent, Bhishma.* It was a shock to see the man whose name had terrified him as a child, bound and confined in a hospital tent. As he stood gazing down at the stern face, he realized that this capture could well mark the end of the war. The morning meal in his belly suddenly felt lighter.

[13]*Lomaharshana* means "one who makes hair bristle or stand on end."

Capturing Devavrata the Terrible was a great achievement. If this does not bring peace, what will?

The Regent was still asleep. An attendant was replacing the bloodied cotton roll behind his shoulder with a fresh one. "There is an arrow stuck in his armpit," the man said. "He acts as if it matters not, but from time to time he admits to discomfort. The *bisaj* says he will die if we extract the arrow, but then he will die in a few days anyway. Why they cannot let him die, I don't know. They are not even questioning him. I would have put him on the ground and jiggled the arrow till he told us everything. Instead, we are taking care of him, doing what we can to comfort him. I clean the wound with fresh turmeric water and keep it covered. While you are with him, just do whatever makes him comfortable. Not too much though." The nurse gave a crooked grin and left.

Lomaharshana sat down at the foot of the bed and waited for the Regent to awaken.

"Amba!" Devavrata mumbled in his sleep. Lomaharshana leaned forward to catch the word. *Who was Amba? Maybe he had said Amma? Was he calling for his mother?* Despite the coolness of the autumn morning, Devavrata's face and throat had beads of sweat; his cheeks glowed with a thin sheen of moisture. Lomaharshana cleared his throat loudly but the Regent did not respond.

The attendant returned and said, "Look, he is awake." Before Lomaharshana could protest, he had prodded the sleeping Regent's injured arm with one finger.

Devavrata flinched, trying to turn his head. The pain brought him completely awake, his eyes wide from the effort to control his response. He saw the Archivist sitting near his feet and his eyes narrowed. "Who are you?" he asked.

The Archivist replied, "Lomaharshana, Sir. I am the Archivist. I have been instructed to work with you. Please do not trouble yourself; there is no hurry. The Commander will explain it all to you. I am waiting for him."

"Commander?"

"Chief Yudhishthira. Consort and Head of the Queen's Council. He will be here soon, Sir. I am ready but we must wait for his arrival."

"So you are the Archivist. Does Shukla know you are here?"

"Shukla, Sir?"

"Vyaasa Shukla, your leader."

"Yes, Sir, he does."

"Where is he?"

"I do not know. These days his movements are secret."

Devavrata looked around – the tent was large and empty, as if erected just for him. The sun was bright outside though it was still early, the shadows shorter, their fuzzy edges sharper. It was a month since the monsoon had ended and the autumnal equinox had been celebrated. Usually the grain would have been harvested now and in a few days the farmers would have been busy again, preparing for the winter crop. 'I am a warrior, not a farmer!' Suyodhana, encouraged by his friend Karna, had proclaimed when Devavrata had counselled patience. They were both wrong. A warrior needed to know all that a farmer does in the cycle of seasons.

It would not be easy to satisfy Yudhishthira – what did he really want to know? Devavrata had had few choices in policy. First Yudhishthira's father, and now Yudhishthira himself, seemed to think there had been choices. But the supply of agricultural land had always been limited. The Nagas, with their slash-and-burn practices, had used the forested land inefficiently. They had not created permanent settlements, just ramshackle villages that were abandoned after ten or twenty years.[14] The spent fields were left fallow for at least two generations, until no one in the community recalled living in that spot. Any itinerant settler could have exploited the situation; all he had to do was occupy the fallow land and yell if a Naga threatened him. Yudhishthira's father had rejected a policy of patience. He, Devavrata, had tried his best, but there was no 'fair' solution. And now Yudhishthira seemed to be in a hurry. Devavrata looked around. The Archivist had closed his eyes and appeared to be meditating. He had assumed the *nishkamkarnarpana*[15] pose. *He has the right idea; use our training. There is no hurry. I too, can be patient.*

Yudhishthira came alone. Yet again Devavrata was struck by the difference between the cousins. A King was followed by an entourage. Suyodhana was a King. He called himself King. He moved around Hastinapura with a coterie of courtiers,

---

[14]For agricultural purposes, the solar year is defined from one winter solstice to the next winter solstice.

[15]*Nishkamkarnarpana* pronounced niche-calm-cur-narp-un-u(h) means "paying attention without attachment" were a set of skills to memorize. This is one of the techniques the Kavi Sangha teaches its bards to enable them to memorize, recall, and forget what they heard.

who waited on him. Yudhishthira did not call himself King, or for that matter, Emperor, as some of his troops did. He walked around the camp without an entourage. He had chosen to make his city a *janapada* – a State governed by a Council chosen by the people – a practice in the cities of Panchnad, the land between the Sarasvati and the Sindhu. A hereditary Matriarch, advised by the Council, headed the janapada. A Matriarch had never ruled Hastinapura in its unusual evolution from caravanserai to city. But Indraprastha, Mahendra Pandu's town, a new settlement born of Hastinapura, had chosen to return to Panchnad practice, with some changes.

Yudhishthira sat down by Devavrata's head. His voice soft, he asked, "Did you sleep well? Are you comfortable?"

Devavrata found himself smiling at the courtesy; he had become used to the forceful language of Suyodhana's court. "Your people carried out your instructions perfectly, my son. You have competent hospital staff. They propped me up so the arrow would not be dislodged. A boy attended to me every time I awoke. Why care so much for a dying man, an enemy at that?"

Yudhishthira smiled. "Should I torture you to get information about Suyodhana's war plans? I have been asked to do that. Fortunately I do not need that from you. I have other questions. Do you remember our conversation?"

"Yes. I thought about it all evening, and was concerned I would not be able to sleep. But when night fell, fortunately sleep took me. You want me to recall ancient memories?"

Yudhishthira nodded. "There is much I do not know. I was young, perhaps too young, when my father told me some of the history. He died just as I came of age. When we returned to Hastinapura, my mother was concerned that all the children were only being taught martial arts. She asked Uncle Dharmateja Vidura to take charge of our education, but he had to deal with all five of us. He taught me about your administration of the Hastinapura Empire, but there was no time for anything else."

"True, we did not have any time for you, or for your innumerable cousins."

"Pitamaha, that is not the history I wish to hear now. Tell me about your childhood. Tell me about your father, my great-grandfather Shantanu, and what he did."

It is so easy to like this man, Devavrata thought. *He is direct, just like all of Satyavati's descendants. Maybe we are wrong to doubt his parentage, lip or no lip. There are differences – he is polite, whereas Suyodhana and his brothers are arrogant. He wants history, not an artful story with the twists and turns that please storytellers. I cannot give him either version.* "My childhood? You cannot understand my childhood without knowing everything else that was going on at that time."

"I am here to listen. Begin with the founding of Hastinapura, if you will."

"I need some time to collect my thoughts."

"You can work with Lomaharshana here," Yudhishthira said.

"Yes, I have met him," Devavrata said, nodding to the Archivist standing silently at the foot of the bed.

5
Where Is Devavrata?

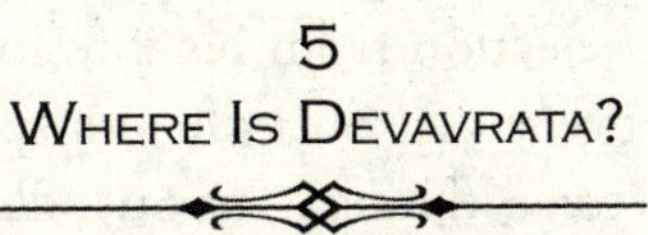

Suyodhana could not be still. Karna watched him pace back and forth across the vast chamber.

"Damn it! Damn, damn, damn it, Karna! I do not wish to make peace with those Naga-loving Pandavas. I want war!"

"Suyodhana, my friend, there is no need to be so agitated," Karna said from where he stood beside a casement opening onto the wide vistas below. He had come as soon as he had been summoned, having heard that Suyodhana had stormed out of the Council meeting.

"That meeting was a waste of time. Why did I even call it?"

"But you got what you needed – permission," Karna reminded him.

The morning had begun with bad news. Devavrata Bhishma was missing. He had left on a secret mission with Shikhandin. It had been a week but he had still not returned. It was frustrating to work with the stubborn old man. He had ruled as Regent for so long that he could not stop ordering people around and doing things without permission. Now he had gone off on a mission that Suyodhana and Karna had tried to ignore, a fool's errand to make peace.

I do not wish to make peace with those Naga-loving Pandavas. Only Karna understood how Suyodhana felt; only Karna had tasted the bitter fruit of rejection from his inferiors that Suyodhana now experienced every day. Suyodhana's spies relayed to him the word on the street, diluted, for Suyodhana's anger would scorch the messenger. Yudhishthira was wise, Suyodhana was not; Yudhishthira was a mature man, Suyodhana a spoilt boy; Yudhishthira tried to be fair to all, Suyodhana favored his immigrant friends.

The siege of Indraprastha the previous year had been an extraordinary success, bar one inexcusable failure. The Pandavas had been trapped and with their allies, the Panchalas and Yadavas, unable to come to their aid. Suyodhana's men had blocked the upstream dam and cut off water supply to the capital city. Then they had diverted the spring snowmelts into channels that went a long way away from the city. The Pandavas' *City of Indra,* Indraprastha, had become a cemetery with thirsty, starving people and dying children. In another day or two, the people – both the citizens of the republic, the *janapada* whose *janas* ruled, as well as the common people, the powerless and leaderless *ganas,* whom the Pandavas had so publicly championed – would have handed the Pandavas' heads to him on a platter. *It could even have been seven heads if his guards had not been tricked by the wily Yadava Chief, Krishna, and the arrogant Panchala Matriarch, Panchali Krishnaa Agnijyotsna.*

The inexcusable failure had allowed the Pandavas to escape from the city into the surrounding forests. *And those fool soldiers had let them go!* Suyodhana's troops had looted the city and he had ordered its destruction. The citizens were ordered to settle elsewhere. His granduncle, *Regent* Devavrata, had objected. *For somebody called Bhishma, The Terrible, he was soft as butter.* Their victory would have been complete for the Pandavas had left everything behind – wealth, clothing, slaves.... The victory should have made his life glorious, but for the singing of Yudhishthira's praises by the exiles of the destroyed city. His glorious victory had tasted like mud in his mouth. It was a botched victory.

Recalling that failure reminded him of the debacle that morning, which had left him angry and despairing. There was only one man who could pull Suyodhana out of the depression that gripped him whenever he thought of the Pandavas – Karna.

"Send for King Karna," he had commanded the guard at the door. The man had hastened to do his bidding.

It was then that the news of Devavrata's disappearance was brought to him. As Suyodhana awaited his friend's arrival, he heard a commotion outside and found a man lying sprawled on the ground near the door of his chamber, panting.

"He asked for King Suyodhana," said one of the gatekeepers.

"Bring him in." Suyodhana turned and walked back into his chamber. The guards picked the man up and brought him in. Looking at him more closely, Suyodhana recognized one of Devavrata's attendants. "What do you have to say?" he asked.

"Regent Devavrata has disappeared, Sir! He was last seen with a stranger, Shikhandin by name, who has also disappeared," replied the man.

Suyodhana shook his head in disgust. The old man was becoming a liability with his eccentric behaviour. "Karna!" he said in relief as his tall friend appeared at the door. "What are we to do? That slippery Shikhandin has disappeared, along with our Field Marshal! I knew we should never have trusted that Naga. Bhishma may even be dead."

"Does it matter?" asked Karna. He did not look upset by the news.

Suyodhana looked up and paused. "You are right; we do not need the old man. We captured Indraprastha without his help. If it had not been for the interference of my treacherous uncle Dharmateja (He does not merit the title Vidura), we would have the Queen of Panchala serving us. We do not need our commander Bhishma, but we cannot have him captured either, for he knows all our defences, our strategy. If he is not dead but a prisoner, they could torture him to extract that knowledge."

A meeting of the War Council was in order to deal with the crisis. The Council consisted of Devavrata, now absent, Kutaja Drona, Suyodhana, his brother Sushasana, and Karna. Sanjaya, the Court Poet, attended in place of blind King Dhritarashtra. *King by the grace and sufferance of Devavrata, the generous, abstemious, self-sacrificing, ever-critical Regent*, Suyodhana thought. All his life he had endured taunts about being the son of a blind king. Though his uncle, Dharmateja Vidura, was a member of the Council, Suyodhana did not inform him, thus ensuring his absence from the crucial session. Vidura had been one of Devavrata's appointments to the Council, but Devavrata was missing. *What was the point of having an avowed critic of the war on the War Council?*

Suyodhana summoned the others, asking the martial arts teacher, Kutaja Drona, to chair it. He had all but begged him to focus on the immediate crisis caused by Devavrata's death or capture. But Kutaja Drona, another of the old guard, was an obstinate, unyielding disaster as moderator; nothing Suyodhana or Karna proposed was to his liking.

Did he think he was the king? fumed Suyodhana in silent frustration. *His attitude has established negativity as the order of the day.*

Drona declared there was no point in organizing an expedition to find and rescue Devavrata, if he was still alive, for they did not even know where the Pandava camp was. And nothing was possible in Panchala or Yadava territory. Instead, they should collect intelligence from their spies in order to find the Pandavas, who could even be hiding with the Matsyas. Suyodhana could not imagine a drearier place.

Only he and Karna were for the proposal to sending out a full-scale war party. The Council wanted more information before they decided. Devavrata's man, who had brought the tidings, was suspect. He had revealed very little useful information, saying the other guards had run away. Suyodhana considered threatening him with torture to get at the truth. But Kutaja Drona recommended that a small troop investigate the site of the kidnapping. The Council agreed.

They will support anyone but me, Suyodhana thought as he left the session in a rage. It had been a waste of time. It made him furious. *Investigate first indeed!* Turning to his friend he asked plaintively, "What am I going to do, Karna?"

"Calm yourself, my friend. What you have is good. The Council has not appointed an investigator or specified the size of the troop. Until the Council meets again, you are in charge."

Suyodhana smiled. "Of course! I may not be King yet but the Regent is absent. My father will do what I say. You can be the lead investigator."

"I will need three hundred men."

"You will have them. I will mobilize the rest of our army so that we are prepared to act on whatever you discover."

The Past Through Shantanu

6
Devavrata's Education

"Tell me about your childhood; your father."

At Yudhishthira's request, Devavrata narrated the story of his early days. Much came to mind, the memories of a child. Like the memories of most children, there was no trace of crisis or turmoil, either then or to come. He knew his mother was sometimes pregnant, and as he grew older, he realized that his newborn brothers and sisters disappeared soon after their birth. His siblings were born, and then, suddenly, they were gone. But these events hardly affected him.

Devavrata skipped past his earliest memories with brief descriptions – the occasional regal visits from his father, King Shantanu, and his mother, Queen Ganga, interrupting an endless routine of playing with the attendants who took care of him, crying when they demanded obedience to some rule, ordering the servants, running along the river bank and building sandcastles... When he learned to talk, visits from his mother became more regular and patterned. She hugged him, calling him *laḍla* (sweet boy). He, in turn, called her *avva* (mommy). He would wait for her hugs even as he moved from one caretaker to the next and from one teacher to another.

In the beginning the King did not seem to know what to do with a toddler. Devavrata was his only son and Shantanu envied the boy's easily expressed affection for the Queen. As Devavrata learned to speak, becoming articulate, his father came by more often. He asked his son to call him *bābō* (papa), rather than *Rājan* or *Mahān,*[16] or the other titles Devavrata had been taught by his caretakers, who were always deferential to the King. The switch was awkward at first but Devavrata wanted to please his father and tried to be informal with his father.

Shantanu took Devavrata to public events, and Devavrata took pleasure in his father's pride in him. The king took Devavrata to Council sessions, where the boy sat quietly to the right and slightly behind, his father's high seat. It seemed reasonable to be proud of this indulgence. He observed how his father conducted himself as Head of Council, a role Devavrata was being groomed for. He observed the decisions involved in being the Chief – judging, rewarding, punishing – and facing the consequences of those decisions. His family seemed happy and secure, his days predictable.

Then his mother died. Devavrata's voice trailed away.

Yudhishthira watched him as he stopped speaking. "If it pertains to this war, you must tell me," he said, his voice quiet but holding the authority of a Ruler.

---

[16]*Rājan* is usually translated as "King," with the connotation of "Glorious One" or "Resplendent One;" *Mahān* means "Great One".

Is what happened to my mother relevant today? Devavrata wondered. It might bother him like the incessant flapping of a humming bird sipping from a jasmine flower, but that did not make it relevant to others. But what had happened to his mother that day was not inconsequential; it had cast a shadow on the rest of his life. Those events made him the Regent he had become. They influenced his key decisions, leading to certain actions that forced more decisions. It could be said that the events leading to his mother's death did indeed lead to this war and were relevant to Yudhishthira's questions about policy.

Devavrata said, "When my parents had a disagreement, the house would darken and the air become hot and humid, as if heralding a monsoon storm. Perhaps this was only in my mind, for the mansion itself was never dark or oppressive. The staff walked on tiptoe when my parents argued, trying to avoid attention. Even though I was only eight years old, my parents would be short-tempered with me as well. My mother tried to make up for her irritability with an impulsive excess of unexpected hugs. I made occasional attempts to ask her what the matter was, but she did not answer. I later concluded that she was preoccupied and had not heard my questions. I was unused to being taken seriously by my parents, so it was no surprise. This is a report of my observations. I understood the situation many years later, and my memory is undoubtedly colored by that knowledge.

I was eleven years old when my mother died so I understood everything that led to her death. You may be surprised by that. It was a result of my education, which had deviated from the traditional. I had learned to memorize conversations I heard, even if I did not understand them, so I could recall and understand them later."

"What was different about your education?" Yudhishthira asked.

"As was customary for the first son and heir of a great trading family, I began my schooling at the age of six. Yes, the Kauravas were becoming warriors, but they continued to be a trading family as well. My schooling followed the established pattern appropriate for a future caravan master. That pattern changed as the Kauravas became warriors first, as our ancestor Samvarana wished. Suyodhana's cohorts, warriors all, now look down on traders, forgetting their own origins. My father's descendants today would not recognize the education I received.

I had a trader's education. It began as soon as I could speak meaningful sentences, describing others' actions. Speech proved I was not mentally disabled. The test showed I could interpret simple actions and sequence of actions performed by others, and describe them in simple sentences. Once schooling began, I advanced rapidly in comparison to the other traders' children of my age. Bored, I joined the bards in their training sessions. By the age of twelve they were expected to accurately memorize complete conversations that lasted for at least half a ghati, recall shorter conversations with intonation, and the core content of longer conversations of up to three ghatis. I enjoyed these classes.

Trading families believed in training[17] their children in multiple skills. Trading was the only Guild to do that systematically. Memorizing the manifest of a caravan was a skill; being prepared to fight off bandits to protect the caravan was

[17]More details on the training of an apprentice trader may be found in Appendix A.1.

another. Both were necessary. Thus we also trained to fight, which consisted of exercise routines to develop the strength of various muscles in the body so that the hands and feet became fighting instruments, the centre of the body the source of power, the eyes became windows that not only allowed one to view the world, but exposed an enemy's innermost thoughts.

After memorization and martial arts, the third aspect of my education was unique to me as the son of the Kaurava ruler of Hastinapura. We Kauravas had to do more than defend ourselves; we had to inspire the warriors we led into battle. The Mercenaries Guild selected promising apprentices to undergo training in command, called officer training. Guru Vasishtha, the first Vyaasa, had persuaded the Mercenaries Guild Master of his time to train the officers in Samvarana's army. He also persuaded the senior-most Matriarch of Panchnad that some form of the training prospective Matriarchs received should also be provided to Samvarana, the Master Trader of Nagapura, and his chosen descendants, as long as they were the guardians of the Panchnad frontier.

There is still superstition and gossip attached to this training. No, we do not have a command voice that compels obedience. We do not enter a mystic trance in which we consult with past Matriarchs before we arrive at a decision. But we do learn what it feels like to be at the reins of a runaway cart; to steel our gut and take decisive action in the face of uncertainty.

This brings us to the greatest difference between our world and that of Panchnad. The Master of a caravan is a man who wields supreme power, while in a Panchnad city the Matriarch wields power, with the advice of her Council. This is as it should be, since a caravan may have to go through hostile bandit territory or confront criminals who pretend to be friends while acting as spies for the enemy. The Master must have a free hand to make crucial, life and death decisions under pressure. Guru Vasishtha and King Samvarana made this the model of governance for Hastinapura. The ruler of Hastinapura, like a Caravan Master, is thus ever ready for battle. Panchnad was a land in which cities settled conflicts without war; Hastinapura and its neighbors settle conflicts by war, nothing else."

"Pitamaha," Yudhishthira said, "you have spoken of this before. I recall you telling me many years ago that in Panchnad conflicts were not settled by wars. I was unable to understand you then, for all my life the prospect of war has never been distant. How did Panchnad settle conflicts without war? All the foreign cultures I have heard of from travellers and traders, engage in war. So how did Panchnad become a war-free culture?"

Devavrata took a long breath. "I'll tell you what I know. Traders who have travelled in caravans to the west attest to the unique features of Panchnad, and the unusual way society is organized. It was key to the absence of war. Most of the ordinary citizens, not being traders, did not know these were unique features of their culture. The people of Panchnad did not understand how special they were.

The practice of war, so common in the west, was considered strange in Panchnad. The scholars of Takshashila have an explanation. They call the period in which Panchnad developed, the Third Age. It is tempting to call the present times we live in the Fourth Age, the baleful Age of Kali, the Age of Strife. I say this with conviction because the world has been at war for most of my life. The coming of the Age of Kali was presaged by its shadow on the lands to the west. Parsaka[18], Sumer[19], Elam[20], and even powerful Lauhityapada[21] abandoned trade as the path to prosperity and succumbed to war, with external as well as internal enemies. The effluent of war clogged and then blocked the river of trade, eventually stopping it completely.

My son, you want to know how this one-of-a-kind society came about. I will tell you, but remember this, it is impossible to recreate. That was your father's confused goal."

Yudhishthira replied, "I want to know more about Panchnad and the world in the Third Age. Tell me what you know of that Age, of the world at large but Panchnad in particular."

---

[18]*Parsaka* is the ancient name for Persia in South Asian literature.
[19]*Sumer* is the name for the group of city-states that began the urbanization of Mesopotamia (around 3000 B.C.E.).
[20]*Elam* was an ancient non-Semitic culture in southern Iran that frequently came into conflict with the Semitic Sumer and Mesopotamia. In 2000 B.C.E., Elam was the hegemon, and the once-powerful Sumer was reduced to poverty.
[21]*Lauhityapada* means the "Land of the Children of Red (soil)," or maybe "People of the Red Way." One of the names used by Egyptians for their country was The Red People's Land.

7
Pandavas Will Lose The War

Devavrata paused in his narration, eyes closed. He spoke slowly, seeming to choose his words carefully.

"Yudhishthira, our own world is disintegrating around you. You are struggling to save yourself and your brothers. In my opinion, you are losing. Why do you wish to know about the Third Age?"

Yudhishthira replied somewhat urgently, "Pitamaha, you are one of the few people who know the greater world. Suyodhana and his cohort have no interest beyond the immediate. The immigrants and the Nagas struggle to maintain themselves. The Kavi Sangha keeps its secrets. When peace returns, we will need to know more about the rest of the world. This is not idle curiosity."

Devavrata nodded. Alone among his many grandnephews, Yudhishthira had a sensitivity to life unusual in this age of conflict and aggression. "I regret your father's decision to separate himself from Hastinapura, but that is in the past. What I say may fill the void in your education. I regret that it may be wasted in pursuit of a lost cause."

"I lay my gratitude at your feet, Pitamaha."

Devavrata said, "My education, as I have described, was very different from what is taught now. As a trader, I learned some bardic skills, some warrior skills, some linguistic skills, and some skills in observing cultures. Now the Kauravas are only warriors and this war, your war, is like no other event in Panchnad history. The Kurus are not traders anymore; they are warriors and empire builders.

This change had its origins in Samvarana's exile by the Panchalas, your ally. Hastinapura was just a border town, a glorified caravanserai. The Nagas of Panchala drove out the Kuru leader, Samvarana. But he returned and re-took Hastinapura with the first Panchnad army that was trained to kill, not capture. Samvarana's guru, Vasishtha, helped create and train this army. It became a permanent institution to protect Hastinapura from the Panchalas. Hastinapura was no longer a Panchnad town but a militarized State, perpetually ready for war. Meanwhile, Vasishtha's organization, the Kavi Sangha, became the foremost advisor to the Kuru family."

"I understand now what my father meant," Yudhishthira said reflectively, "when he denounced the patriarchal city. That it came through war and was sustained by an army. In turn, the army presented a fierce face to the world and ensured the continuance of hostility."

"Yes, the Kauravas were traders and warriors, but we also created the first patriarchal State in our world. My policies were built on this framework. As you point out, your father disagreed, strongly enough to exile himself rather than work in a State he could not change. He took you away and raised you and your brothers according to his values. In hindsight, that was a mistake; he should have stayed. You would have been educated in, not ignorant of, the necessary knowledge and skills of kingship.

As it was, when you and your brothers turned up in Hastinapura, we could still train your bodies. Bhima and Arjuna have become formidable warriors. But your minds had developed according to what your father taught you. You could not have become traders even if you had wanted to. There is much more to being a warrior than brute strength, and we left you to learn those skills on your own."

"For what I know, I have to thank Uncle Dharmateja Vidura," Yudhishthira said. "But you are right. My brothers were enamored of the warrior's path you showed them and did not choose to learn from our wise uncle."

"Yes, Vidura tried, but I do not believe he could have succeeded," Devavrata said. "I was surprised when Vidura took such an interest in your education. For most of his life he had seemed like a restrained version of his brother, Dhritarashtra. I knew that Mahendra Pandu's defiance of my policies and self-exile had somehow impressed Dharmateja Vidura. He paid many visits to Indraprastha, and brought back useful information; truly Vidura the wise."

His voice pensive, he added, "If only Dhritarashtra and Suyodhana had listened to Vidura."

But I don't care anymore, he thought.

"His visits were welcome," Yudhishthira replied. "When I was young I had no idea who he was. He played with us, brought news of events in Hastinapura to my father, and to my mothers, Kunti and Madri. He was kind and taught me a great deal."

"Dharmateja Vidura was the child of a servant, hence not a Kshatriya, so even though he was a son of the King, he was not educated as a warrior," Devavrata explained. "But as he was raised alongside Mahendra Pandu and Dhritarashtra, he learned things he would never have otherwise. Even so, he could not have made you into a greater warrior than Suyodhana. Do you understand why I say you will lose to Suyodhana? I have little use for tact now. Suyodhana received the education that you and your brothers did not, the education of a warrior."

For the first time Yudhishthira raised his voice. "Pitamaha! I do not take offence at your critical statements regarding my education or that of my brothers. Surely, it is irrelevant to the story you are telling. How does it relate to the immigrants, to this war? What in your opinion do I need to know, that you can you teach now? Can you tell me why the Nagas opposed the establishment of Hastinapura and the consequences of that opposition?"

"The deficiencies of your education, and that of your brothers, is very relevant," said Devavrata. "Suyodhana is a skilled warrior. He has skilled strategists working for him. His education, like mine, trained him in war. Unlike me, he was trained to be only a warrior. He is capable of recognizing a thousand distinct sounds in their context and reacting accordingly. His hands and fingers were trained to be flexible and strong, to be sensitive enough so that, blindfolded, he could identify objects by touch, and strong enough for his grip to be unshakeable. That is the origin of his battle-name *Duryodhana*[22]. I know it has been used to mock him, and he is

[22]*Duryodhana*, means "Bad Warrior". However, the connotations of the adjective "Bad" are controversial. It could be interpreted as "difficult" or "malevolent" rather than "unskilled," the last being pejorative while the first two might imply great skill.

easily irritated by insults. Nevertheless, he had the best teachers on strategy we could get from Parsaka, where war is a persistent way of life. This too, I do not expect you and your brothers to have learned to appreciate. You may have tactical successes, like my capture, but you will fail to win the war."

"That may be. If we fail our consolation will be that we tried to move our world down a kinder, gentler path – one my father wished to travel."

Devavrata sighed. Had Yudhishthira not understood him? Had his own bluntness clouded the message? But Yudhishthira had asked to be educated, and that was something he could do.

"I will answer your questions first and then continue with the history leading to my father's policies," he said.

Annals of the Kavi Sangha

One thousand and two hundred years after the start of what would be called the Kali Era, Hastinapura suffered a crisis – a flood destroyed the city, killing most of the kavis. The oral archives, memorized by the kavis, were in danger of being lost. The Vyaasa Vaishampaayana initiated a project to write down the oral archives.

In addition to stories with heroes and heroines and gods and goddesses, these archives contain information of interest to historians. The answers to many of Yudhishthira's questions fall in this category. These questions and answers are rarely recited in public, but they are an important piece of the archives. These are the Annals of the Kavi Sangha.

Appendix A.2: The Four Ages of the World

Yudhishthira said, "What did people believe about the state of the world, in particular, the concept that we were on the brink of a Fourth Age of extreme evil; that the transition from one Age to the next would be calamitous and traumatic; and, that all humanity would be destroyed at the end of the Fourth Age."

Appendix A.3: The Rarity of War in Panchnad

Yudhishthira said, "All my life the prospect of war has never been far away. How did Panchnad settle conflicts without war? All the foreign cultures that I have heard about, from travellers and traders, engage in war. How did Panchnad become a war-free culture?"

Appendix A.4: The End of the Third Age

Yudhishthira said to Devavrata, "I want to know more about Panchnad and the world in the Third Age. Tell me what you know of the Third Age: the world at large, and Panchnad in particular."

Appendix A.5: Naga Reaction: Panchala and Nagapura

Yudhishthira asked Devavrata how Hastinapura had been established despite the hostility of the Nagas. The Annals record Devavrata's opinion.

Mother

8
Devavrata Listens

Devavrata said, "Now that you have heard all there is to know about the history of Hastinapura, do you have any questions, my son?"

Yudhishthira nodded. "Pitamaha, permit me to ponder awhile on what you have said. I have many questions, but I will reserve them for now. I would rather know how your father's policies affected the people and the State. Please continue with your childhood memories."

Devavrata smiled, the lines of pain easing on his face. "I had joined the Bard Guild classes, being bored with my own. I began as a precocious student, in listening. Less than thirty moons[23] into my education, I could report conversations lasting as long as a ghati. I could memorize lists exceeding a hundred entries. I could identify over a hundred sounds. I had arrived at the level of expertise expected of an eleven-year-old

[23]About two-and-a-half years.

apprentice bard, ready to enter a period of intense study under the tutelage of one or more teachers. I was still a child so I thought my parents knew this. In retrospect, perhaps they did not. Many of my interactions were with servants and teachers, who reported remarkable progress, but my parents must have discounted it as a childish fancy. When my parents argued, they were unaware of my presence nearby. A normal eight-year-old would not have understood their conversations. I certainly did not. But I memorized what they said, and retrieved it later, when I did understand.

Why is this relevant, you ask? I was an eight-year-old with the memorization skills of a much older boy. I spied on my parents, and what I heard went into some dark corner of my mind. Over the years, I came to understand those words, replaying the conversations in my mind. Then I finally understood the events of the year my mother died."

It struck Devavrata that something had changed in Yudhishthira's demeanor. He had entered abruptly, without the usual polite greeting. His eyes frequently darted to the flap over the tent entrance. When they came back to focus on him, they seemed to have lost their brightness. *Was he even listening? Why the sudden agitation?* He would have to solve that puzzle. In the meantime, he did not wish to deviate from his narrative. Whatever Yudhishthira's hurry was, it would have to wait. "May I continue?" he asked.

"Yes, of course." Yudhishthira's forehead furrowed, trying to grasp what Devavrata had said. He summarized in his mind: Devavrata's memorization skills were not public knowledge, and he did not display them. The rulers of Hastinapura no longer trained to be anything other than warriors.

Devavrata went on: "I listened to all the conversations that went on in my house and memorized them. I was young and had not developed the moral yardstick by which to judge a person's actions, whether the person was my parent or my teacher or one of the staff, with whom I spent most of my time. That judgment came later. With the power of memorization, the past is never a closed book; you can retrieve saved memories and learn from them, again and again.

One day, I was about to enter my mother's private chambers. That morning she had gone to the riverside cottage where her father lived. I knew she had returned when one of her maids ran out to moisten the *kusha* grass screen and fetch a fan. I heard my father's voice and stepped back. He seemed to be pleading – he sounded as I did when I wheedled a sweet from the cook. I listened and automatically memorized what was said, though I understood little.

My father said, 'Gangu! Why will you not understand?' I recognized the signs – my father called my mother Gangu only when he was aroused or overwrought. 'We face a crisis! For fifty years, from the time of my grandfather, we have struggled with this problem. We chose to be generous to the refugees when they came here. Everybody agreed to make the sacrifice – that is what makes us great. But we have become poorer and our enemies grow stronger. Every day I hear about some Panchala demagogue wanting to create a new army to liberate our Nagas. We must be practical, pragmatic. You know the Kavi Sangha thought we were being too generous and proposed exiling all refugee families with children, or killing their newborns. That would have encouraged them to go further east.

I disagreed. They would have had to go into a wilderness, with no support from us. I said…we said: *No, we must share the burden,* and softened the law the Kavi Sangha formulated. We ruled that every family would be allowed one child, to replace each adult in the family. We applied this to everyone, even ourselves. We stopped referring to the Nagas as refugees and called them immigrants. We treated them as equals, even though we were the overwhelmed hosts and they the desperate and impoverished guests. We all took a risk. All we need to do now is survive this drought and the threat of famine. And we *will* survive. In a few years, when the crisis is past, we can repeal these laws. If not I in my lifetime, my son Devavrata will in his."

Yudhishthira observed, "Pitamaha, your voice changed and you did not sound like a wounded warrior. Are these truly the words you heard? How can you reproduce them with such fidelity?"

Devavrata replied, "My memory is perfect. That is exactly what he said. But I have often wondered at those words, that I would repeal those laws. You may not realize it, but much is lost in this recitation. Was he proud that I would repeal his laws? Was he chagrined he could not? What else was hidden in those words? I had learned to memorize speech after a single hearing, but teasing out the inner meaning had not figured in that feat. It took time, but I had learned to memorize the intonations, but not the emotions. It was the first time I had put a learned skill to use, and there was something magical and wonderful about it. I stood there memorizing my father's words even as he spoke, full of wonder at my ability.

You ask how this memory works. I don't know but I have an image that provides a metaphor. Perhaps it will help. The sounds come in and are transmuted in my mind into parts of a giant tree, an awe-inspiring banyan tree that provides the framework for that memory. With loving care, the sounds are deposited, one on this leaf, another on that branch. Some make their way onto the hanging roots and cling to them like butterflies. Others flutter about for an absurdly long time, tiny jewelled humming birds, refusing a perch till the right one is found. Then they too, are transmuted into butterflies. As the tree fills with sound that creates a background chorus, the butterflies sparkle and light up, providing hooks for unravelling the chain of a melody. The shortcomings of memory I now complain about are afterthoughts. In hindsight, even the most magical acts become mundane and tiresome. The meaning lies in the melody, and it had to be played, or in this case replayed, to extract its content.

To return to where we were…the beauty of what I imagined overwhelmed the child that I was. It was a long time, years, before I went beyond memorizing the sounds to understanding the words. That required rehearsing the words, and that is what I did. I rehearsed not just this, but many other conversations I had overheard, until I understood them. With understanding they lost the sparkle of wonder.

For a long time I thought I had committed a crime of omission. If only I had allowed myself to understand then the dialogue I had memorized with such pleasure, I might have been able to protect my mother. There were days when I searched desperately through the stock of remembered conversations, rehearsing each one, looking for more evidence of my culpability. Most of them revealed little worth remembering forever. However, I found the mundane exciting for it revealed details of lives that, as Regent, I would never experience for myself. When I was done with a memory, it would return to its assigned spot in the banyan tree of my mind.

Then I recalled a few that pertained to the repeated conflicts between my mother and my father. I had memorized much that could only be retrieved by invoking the feelings of the time. Even as I grasped the meaning of some significant narrative, I discovered that others had become lost and forgotten. The very act of rehearsing can result in forgetting highly charged memories; it is one of the methods for managing memory that the Kavi Sangha calls *nishkamasmaranadharanam*[24]. Luckily, not all had vanished and I stopped rehearsing. The memories were depressing to review, yet there were still days I would return like an addict to rehearse just one more conversation, and then one more and then another, until I hit one between my father and mother. When that memory faded in the act of rehearsing, I would react with self-accusation, vowing never to do it again."

Yudhishthira interrupted the narrative to say, "Pitamaha, are you saying that telling me about your life, risks your memories being lost forever? In that case…"

Devavrata lifted a hand and then let it fall heavily again. "I am dying, my son. Soon these memories will be lost and useless. Let me judge for myself which memories I wish to die with and which to hand over. If you win this war, they could be of some use to you."

"Your death will be a burden I will carry all my days."

[24]*Nishkamasmaranadharanam*, pronounced niche-calm-smur(f)-run-u(h)-thar-run-um, means "holding on to memory without attachment". They were a set of skills to manage memory. This is one of the techniques the Kavi Sangha teaches its bards to enable them to memorize, recall, and forget what they heard.

"Such are the unique burdens that only a ruler carries. If my memories are to be of any use Yudhishthira, you as King must carry this burden."

Yudhishthira took a deep breath. "I would like to understand the past," he said clearly.

And so Devavrata continued. "In any case I listened to the conversation that day. I had three choices. I could leave, but did not have the desire to do so, thinking the conversation revealed secrets I did not know. I could go in and interrupt a quarrel I did not understand. Or I could stay and listen, unseen. Much of what was said was new to me. We had been suffering a crisis since the days of my grandfather Pratipa; I had not known that. There were refugees. I wondered who they were. How did one identify a refugee? What made them different from non-refugees? My father had said, *We…call them immigrants now.* I knew about immigrants; they lived in the immigrant quarter of Hastinapura. I did not know that they did not belong there, that they were not just another Guild that provided a ghetto for its members, but people who were guests at first, but who it was now difficult to feed.

The conversation had even more worrying statements: *We have become poorer. Our enemies grow stronger.* What was this crisis and why did I know nothing about it? The Kavi Sangha had proposed a harsh law. I knew about the Kavi Sangha. They were the intellectual bulwark behind the Kuru family, ever since Guru Vasishtha, founder of the Kavi Sangha, had taught King Samvarana a new way, the way of the warrior. Every day a Kavi Sangha member would be a guest at our dinner ceremony. A brief session with the King would be followed by a recital of poetry. Dinner followed. Occasionally, Vyaasa

Parashara came himself and told stories while the children of the palace ate. Once I had asked him what he did when he was not telling stories. He replied that he wrote poetry. I asked him what the Kavi Sangha did, and he answered that they were especially good at memorizing and repeating stories. Knowing my own ability for memorizing, I had asked him if I could join the Kavi Sangha. My mother frowned but the Vyaasa smiled and said, 'Of course. You will be a great leader who will do great things.'"

Impatient, Yudhishthira interrupted to say, "Pitamaha, our time is short. Did you discover what the law was?"

"You are right, my son, I digress. A much harsher law was proposed, that restricted the immigrants and encouraged them to go east. I knew about 'going east'. That has been the Kaurava mission since the founding of Hastinapura. Every year, at the Spring Festival, the directive of the Name-Giver, Hastin, would be recited. It mentioned the historic role of all descendants of Puru in keeping the Panchnad culture alive; of the Bhaaratas to spread it in all directions; and the particular mission of his own descendants in populating the east.

The only descendants of Hastin who had whole-heartedly accepted this mission were Kuru's descendants, the Kauravas. The others had been killed by the Panchalas, or had abandoned Samvarana, or like my uncle Bahlika, accepted the offer of leadership elsewhere. There were many other directives, but this was the strangest one, for in those days, settling in the east was an unthinkable fantasy. 'The Kauravas cannot go east from here,' was an assertion made by my maternal grandfather, a man who said little, and what he did was difficult to understand. But my father disagreed. Neither the Naga nor the long-term settler could be coerced. But immigrants could be, hence the immigrants had to go east to relieve the burden on Hastinapura. But my father did not know how to make it happen. Yudhishthira, I hesitate to describe this law."

"Pitamaha, you are called Bhishma. What law could be so far beyond the pale that it makes you hesitate?"

"Patience, my son, allow me tell you at my own pace."

In the pause that followed, the only sound was of birds wheeling across the sky and the wounded warrior's shallow breathing. Then Devavrata broke his silence. "The Nagas and the immigrants were a study in contrasts. The Nagas moved often but did not seek to migrate; the immigrants had migrated but did not wish to move. Once a month, the King and I would make a trip to the Naga temple in the center of the city. To get there from the Chief's mansion, we had to ride a bullock cart through the newly formed immigrant quarter, and then the Naga quarter. Sometimes I would sit with the carriage driver, a family fixture named Bakakula. He gave me a pithy description: The immigrant quarter looked like the residents had come to stay, while the Naga quarter looked like the residents were passing through. I don't know whether Bakakula was trying to impress me with his insight or merely repeating a common observation.

At other times I would sit with my father. As we exited the immigrant quarter, he would observe: 'Compare the immigrant quarter to the Nagas. We city dwellers love the immigrants. They keep everything so neat and tidy, unlike the Nagas. Take note, however, that it is the Nagas who go into the forest to hunt, to cultivate crops, no matter how inefficiently. It is the Nagas who forgo neatness and control to settle in the jungle.'

It took me many years to realize that my father and Bakakula were not disagreeing with each other. The Nagas were prepared to settle a new frontier land, while the immigrants hoped to join a developed culture. It made all the difference. At the time their statements left me confused. Who and what did father approve of? He would get upset if the mansion was not maintained meticulously, occasionally calling the house manager in for a lecture on the shortcomings – cobwebs in the corner, dust not swept off the hearth. This in turn upset everybody in the house, beginning with my mother, as it was she who gave orders to the house manager. My father's intervention would lead to a private discussion between them, my mother calling my father's actions unbecoming of a Chief. At these sessions I would be a lamppost, listening, saying nothing, etching the discussions in my memory.

In the conversation I am telling you about, there was a difference. My mother's voice piqued my interest because her words were muffled by weeping. She sounded sad, not angry, and I had rarely seen this. My father's voice was also different, not the low bass he used when talking to his ministers. But the pleading note soon transitioned to an assertive, confident bass. When he mentioned my name, I took it as a cue to enter."

9
Devavrata Is Puzzled

Devavrata said, "I ran in, my chest heaving, as if I had run a long distance. I look back in wonder at my ability, even at that age, for deception. I used to mimic my father talking to his ministers, my audience being Bakakula the cart driver and Sanghamitra the cook. It was but a short stretch from an act, to pretense, to a lie. I stood in my mother's chamber, panting for breath. 'Father, you called for me? Will you play with me now?'

My father did then what he always did when he wanted to distract someone – talk. 'Yes, glorious youth,' he began. You and your generation, Yudhishthira, are used to this kind of speech, but it was a new thing, a style the Panchnad immigrants brought to Hastinapura – complimentary adjectives that meant little but added little flowers of grace to a conversation. I had not yet been taught to speak formally, using the language of the court, but already, in my father's time, fashionable speech had evolved into this elaborate decorative form. My father could never use it with a straight face, so when he addressed me formally, I felt I was being mocked. It made me want to squirm, to scratch an itch that could not be reached. But I had to keep still as he was the King, even though he was my father.

He bowed and smirked. 'Yes, glorious youth, so what is your wish this time?' I wanted my parents to stop arguing; the best way was to draw him away from my mother's quarters. We often played a game in which I would shoot magic *astras* (arrows), as in the stories of gods and demons performed on festival days. I would shoot Agni's *agneyastra,* and father would pretend to put out the fire. I would fire Indra's *indreyastra,* which casts a web of illusion on its target, and father would pretend to be snared in an illusory world. When I wanted to stop playing the game, I would shoot Brahma's *brahmastra*, the weapon that destroyed all of creation, not just the material world of the senses but the immaterial world of consciousness as well. Yudhishthira, you smile…but as a child I wanted to believe even though I knew the weapons were fantasy.

So I said to my father, 'You will be the target, and I'll shoot the *brahmastra* at you. What will happen this time?' I was concerned that this was too transparent an attempt to distract him, but my mother intervened to say, 'Dev, go outside and play.' That decided my father. He said, 'Let him be.' Then, to me, 'I'll fall to the ground and gibber like a monkey.'

Mother's face was set in a frown. She said, 'This is what you do when I talk about my concerns? Do what you wish to your clan, but why kill my sons?' Father said to me, 'Dev, go outside and play.' Taking my hand, he led me into the back garden and pointed to a tree. 'See if you can hit it at fifty paces with your arrow.' Then he went back inside.

I waited a vighati or so, hoping he would return, then sat down on the stoop by the closed door, resting my chin on my fist. That was what Sanghamitra the cook did when he was thinking about a recipe or contemplating a taste. He looked as if he was in deep thought, lost in an ocean of self-realization. It seemed an appropriate pose. I contemplated the *tulsi* bush and listened.

My father's voice came to me quite clearly. 'We have sacrificed a hundred children like them. Do I only kill the daughters of immigrants? That was the Kavi Sangha's recommendation. I rejected that. Was I to say to the people that we would apply such laws only to immigrants? Are we Yavanas, with one law for visitors and another for residents? Are we Mlecchas, who enslave captured women for their entertainment? Are we like the Sumerians, who say that boys are better than girls? Are we?'

That day I did not understand anything. Now I understand everything. What is the use of hearing if one cannot understand? Once said, it can never be repeated with the same meaning. Ah! That startled you, Yudhishthira. It is something to contemplate that if a bard changes a story by as much as a word, and the word for knowledge is memory,[25] if we cannot reproduce the past in speech – it becomes truly lost in time.

My boy, you are impatient of my digressions, I see. But the point of a story is its interpretation, is it not? You shake your head... No matter. Let us go on... What did I understand? That the Kavi Sangha sought to kill all the children. They were speaking of Uncle Vyaasa wanting to kill the children. How could something so frightening be true?

My mother said, 'You counter criticism with a story you made up about these dead children being your nomadic forefathers, the Vasus, re-incarnated to bless your enterprise. Your poets spread the ridiculous idea that every dead child, boy or girl, is a

---

[25]*Shruti* means both "knowledge that has been revealed by hearing" and "memory of orally revealed knowledge." (Revelation was considered to be more like hearing than like seeing.) Such a concept of knowledge would characterize an oral, pre-literate culture (like Panchnad in 2000 B.C.E.).

god or goddess. I have to do something. The banks of the river are dotted with small mounds commemorating dead children. When this is over we will know exactly what it has cost us. I know what it cost me. I would have been happy just to hold them for a few days. My arms long to cradle them, my breasts long for their lips, my eyes long to smile into theirs.' My father replied, 'I can change the law to apply only to daughters.' My mother protested saying, 'No, what if my next children are girls? I would kill myself. I look forward to my next baby, but not with you for husband…'

My mother was going to kill herself? Why? Because of the laws my father had enforced on advice of the Kavi Sangha? That did not make sense. What did she mean? These distracted thoughts almost made me miss the rest of the conversation, but my mind training helped me focus on the words being spoken. My father asked, 'Are you with child?' When my mother told him she was, he replied, 'Let's hope then that it is a girl.' My mother was silent and I heard no more.

After some time it became obvious that my father had forgotten his promise to play with me. I did not want to go in so I left through the outhouse gate and wandered down to the river, where I often spent my free hours."

Yudhishthira said, "Pitamaha, so the law was that each family could have only one son?"

Devavrata nodded. "Yes, and one daughter. More to the point, each person could have one child of his or her own gender to replace himself or herself."

"I see. So that kept the population constant for many years?"

"Yes. Yudhishthira, I tell you this in the hope that you will understand. My earliest memories are colored by this crisis. All our subsequent solutions to that crisis have been traumatic."

"Can we not create our own solutions?" asked Yudhishthira.

Devavrata reflected on his grandnephew's words. Yes, every generation demanded the right to repeat the previous generations' mistakes. It was a fruitless debate. "You are shaking your head; you disagree with me?" he said. "You have a solution? I do not claim to have a solution anymore, nor do I think any solution you may propose will be better." He could feel frustration building within him. He had to be careful not to gesticulate and move the arrowhead. That would kill him. *I must finish the story.*

"Days passed," Devavrata said. "I could not talk to anyone about what I had heard, not Bakakula the cart driver, however close he had become to my father after his long years of service; not Sanghamitra the cook; he would withdraw at the first sign of criticism. I could not talk to my parents. They would be upset to know I had overheard them. I fretted for a few days, watching my mother carefully for signs that she might kill herself. Nothing happened. What was I looking for anyway? Mother was as cheerful with me as always, nor did father change. The words did not increase in meaning when I rehearsed them; rather they became more ordinary and forgettable. A hazard of the bard's profession, as I have told you, is that too much private rehearsal of memorized oral events can cause one to forget them.

My education continued along the same two streams – physical training to be a warrior and mental training in memorizing, calculation, and reporting observations, to work as a trader. The increased emphasis on military training was Guru Vasishtha's contribution. He had taken a trading clan and created warriors of them, ever prepared for battle. The physical training focused on the use of weapons, the effective use of armour, and accuracy with the bow and arrow. We are no longer traders and neither you nor Suyodhana have been trained to trade. But I was."

Devavrata paused. Lomaharshana leaned toward him and held a small earthen jar containing water to his mouth. Devavrata took a sip; the cool water felt sweet on his tongue. Even so, it did not wash away the bitter taste of the memories he was dredging up. *This is another slice of history you do not know, Yudhishthira. Your father is to blame for the appalling way he educated you, failing to understand why the Kauravas bear arms while the rest of the civilized world hires mercenaries.*

Devavrata said, "My mother became ill and was confined to her quarters. I know now that she was with child, but I did not know it then as I was kept in ignorance of her pregnancies. She wanted the child to be a girl. I have learned that the general belief is if a woman does not see a man during her confinement, the baby will be a girl. It does not always work that way, but the failures can be explained away. If the baby is a boy, the mother must have encountered a man during confinement. Do note the ridiculous assumption that what the mother saw established the gender of the child. That is no way to think. A mystery worth solving is how one may determine the gender of a child in the womb."

Yudhishthira frowned. Devavrata looked at him and smiled. "Yes, yes, I see that you do not care for this particular puzzle.

Perhaps it will intrigue you later. Well, days passed and became months. The emotions faded, except for the memorized conversation I could reproduce if asked. Nobody did. My life continued. My mother emerged from her confinement without a child. She behaved as if nothing was amiss, as did my father. So I did not think anything was amiss either."

Devavrata paused. Lomaharshana moistened the old man's lips again. "A little more water," Devavrata said. Lomaharshana looked at the attendant, who shook his head. "I have barely eaten anything. A sip of water will not make me sick," Devavrata said annoyed, a hint of the old tone of command back in his voice. Lomaharshana let him sip water over half a vighati, then took the pot away.

10
Tragedy at the River

Devavrata said, "Over the next few years my mother became pregnant, went into confinement, and emerged without a child, again and again. I realized only later that something was wrong. I was almost twelve then and had gone into mother's garden with some sweets the cook had made, eager to surprise her. She was sitting there, gazing at the river and the winding path that sloped gently down to it, flanked by jasmine and *tulsi* bushes. *Ashoka* trees provided shade with their dense foliage. Further away were mango trees, planted for both shade and their delicious fruit. A small pool had been constructed by the gardeners. An underground canal brought water to it from a rainwater-storage tank. The rainy season had just ended and the world was glistening and green. The river breeze carried the scent of jasmine.

My mother seemed sad, her sorrow incongruous in the verdant setting. 'Why are you crying?' I asked. I have always found it difficult to memorize my own words with any competence. She just shook her head, looking away. 'You look sad. Should I call father?" I asked. She shook her head again. 'No, Dev, do not do anything. I am not feeling well.' Those were her words. I have heard them in my mind many times over the years that followed. I said, 'You have been sick for some time now. Does father know? Has the *bisaj* been in to see you?' She replied,

'I saw the *bisaj* a few days ago, Dev. He cannot help me with this. Your Father is busy. I must decide on my own.'

I asked, 'What did the *bisaj* say?' My mother's eyes glistened with tears. In a calm, low voice she repeated, 'She cannot help me.'

I was at a loss; it was the first time I had seen her like this. I turned to her maid, who had just arrived, holding a small cup in her hand. 'Chaya, did the *bisaj* prescribe anything for my mother?' I asked. She nodded. 'Yes, Prince. She suggested the Queen eat only yoghurt made from fresh goat's milk, for three days. I have just brought her some.'

'Mother! How will that help?' I cried in exasperation. 'The *bisaj* prescribes goat's milk yoghurt for everything! Perhaps father can call another *bisaj*, a better one with more experience. If he does not, I will.' My mother only said, 'No, do not call anyone. Come, let me look at you.' She said nothing more, only pulled me close. Her eyes looked steadily into mine, taking in every detail of my face. I stared back, unblinking. Her gaze was soft but of such intensity that I thought she would weep. I saw unshed tears shimmering in her eyes and felt tears well up in mine. 'Do not cry, son!' she said, her arms around me. Slowly she let me go. 'You are not like him at all. You look like my father.'

I do not know what I was expecting her to say, but that was not it. I blurted the first thing that came to mind. 'Father says I look like *his* father.' She looked away. 'It does not matter. Go play with your bows and arrows. Farewell.'

That was what she said. I would have done as she asked but my legs had turned cold and solid like ice in the northern mountains. My petrified legs would not move. 'Why did you bid me farewell? Are you going somewhere? May I come too?' Questions tumbled out of me. My mind raced but my body stood still. Where were the sweets I had brought to surprise my mother? I must have dropped them without even knowing. My mother smiled faintly, 'Do not worry, my son. I will be with you no matter where I go. Tell your father that. He will take care of you. And you must take care of him too. Now go and play.' Putting her hand on my back, she gently pushed me away.

Those were her last words to me, Yudhishthira, 'go and play'. With that my childhood ended. I left the garden and went to find the cook to get some more sweets to give mother when she was in better spirits. Sanghamitra heard me out and said, 'You go fetch the *bisaj* right away. She is one of the best. I would go but I must prepare the afternoon meal. Take the *bisaj* to the Queen.'

Two ghatis later I was back at the mansion, this time with the *bisaj*. The garden was empty. I could hear the chatter of my mother's maidservants down by the river. The curtain to mother's chamber was pulled aside. We went in and I looked around the unlit chamber. There was no one there. 'Mother! Mother!' I called. 'Chaya, where is the Queen? Mother, I have brought the *bisaj*.' There was no reply. Chaya came in from the garden and said mother had gone to the river. I was puzzled. 'To the river? Why?' I asked. But Chaya only shrugged.

I went out of the garden gate, gesturing to the *bisaj*. 'Come, let's go to the river.' We went down the path. The slope was such that at some turns one could see the river bank, where the path ended. Mother was at the edge of the water. 'Mother! I have brought the *bisaj*,' I shouted.

I cannot say if she heard me. I was only twelve and my voice had yet to break. I was too far to see what my mother was doing, but at the next clear vantage point I stopped, trying to see. Mother had finished whatever she was doing and walked into the river. I stood uncomprehending. Then I turned to the *bisaj*, who was squinting at the river. 'Do you see? Do you see that?' I asked, driven by passionate incomprehension. The *bisaj* stepped back at my vehemence but remained silent. I do not know what, if anything, she made of the situation. But I knew what I wanted him to think. 'She cannot be going for a bath at this time of day. Something is wrong. *Bisaj*, you must come with me.'

The *bisaj* finally said, 'Prince, the Queen may not be happy to see me. I will wait here.' But I was not going to put up with that kind of behavior. 'You come with me right now!' I ordered her. 'Do you not see what my mother is doing? She is walking deeper into the water. It is dangerous.'

The *bisaj* followed me, hesitating at every step. I could not bear to go that slowly, so I ran. 'Mother! What are you doing?' I shouted as I rushed down the path. The gardeners looked up from their work, puzzled. The Queen's maidservants tried to stop me since it was a women's area of the river where men were not allowed. But I was just a boy, not yet a man, so they did not try very hard. I ignored their entreaties and kept running. They followed me.

By the time I got to the river bank, my mother had walked a hundred steps into the water. The riverbed sloped gently, but at that distance it became deeper. I thought I saw her head bobbing up and down, which meant she was trying to keep her head above water. I shouted desperately, 'Mother! Mother! Come back! Somebody help her! Bring her back!'

At that point I understood only one thing. My mother's last words hit me now, her farewell, what she had meant. She had intended to kill herself! I was not going to let that happen. I screamed, 'She's going to die! Bring her back! Bring her back!'

Their faces were blank and they did not move. *Had they not seen the Queen?* Even now, the distant memory brings a lump to my throat. If not for this arrow, I would turn away to hide my sorrow, for what use to you is an old man's tears? You do not need them."

Yudhishthira looked away. *Am I asking too much?* he wondered. His granduncle could die from remembered grief. Memory was a double-edged weapon.

But Devavrata continued. "The inactivity of the maids aroused my fury, and I exploded with a burst of energy. I ran back up the path to the garden and returned with my bow and quiver of arrows. Nobody had moved, further feeding my frenzy. To the left of the beach, the kitchen staff had been constructing a fish weir along a curve in the river. *Sisal* rope, used to make nets in the fish-trap, was wrapped around a roller. I grabbed one end of the rope and tied it to an arrow. I pulled free a long length of the rope. It looked long enough. I shot the arrow out over the water, but the weight of the rope held it back and it only reached halfway to where I had last seen my mother.

I had failed my mother. The memory of a conversation from many years ago echoed in my head and heart: *I will kill myself*. I had known this for so many years and done nothing. I looked around, nobody was moving, no one. It was up to me, only me. I had to keep trying since no one else was.

I beckoned to one of the maidservants who was standing around paralyzed. 'You! Help me with the rope. I must get it to my mother.' The maidservant, a young girl named Usha, said, 'Sir, are you sure you saw the Lady go in?' If I had been the Great God Shiva, she would have been ash right there. My forehead throbbed. 'Yes, I did! It was the Queen!' I was surrounded by fools. 'I don't know, Sir,' she replied. *Why was she so cool about it?* Her lack of urgency enraged me. I raved, I ranted, I pleaded, I cursed. 'I need a boat! Help me find one!' No one moved.

I turned to the *bisaj*. 'Did you see my mother enter the water?' She said, 'I am not sure, Prince. My eyesight is not as keen as yours. If you saw her, it must have been so.' I was aghast at her composure. 'I will swim,' I cried. 'I can save her.' The *bisaj* put a hand on my shoulder. 'Son,' she said, "I know you can swim. That is not enough. Your mother is a grown woman. Unless you are an expert at saving people in the water, you will not be able to bring her back to the shore.'

She was right. I could swim, barely. I berated myself for not having learned to swim earlier and practiced saving drowning people, as the fishermen did. I was to blame if my mother died. I should have been able to save her. I knew, rationally, that this was not a reasonable belief, but that was how I felt. Now you will understand why I insisted that your cousins learned to swim early. If your father had not taken you away, you too, would have learned.

I looked around for support. There was none. All the maidservants shook their heads. A palace guard had arrived on hearing the commotion, but did not enter the women's area of the beach. Watching from afar, he too, looked blank. Where did they imagine my mother was? The *bisaj* tried to pacify me.

If I wanted action, I would have to order it. 'Go fetch a boat to find my mother,' I shouted at the guard. The guard left at a run. Turning, I faced the maidservants. 'If you find her somewhere else, let me know. If you want to stay here, get me a boat. Otherwise, get out.' They gathered together. Muttering, they left.

The *bisaj* shook her head and said, 'Prince, you should not have threatened them. They work for your father; you will need their help.' I was not mollified. 'Do not talk to me of help. *You* were supposed to help her, but all you did was give her weak tea and yogurt!' The *bisaj* looked at me and said, 'She was pregnant. The baby was a boy. On orders of the Kaurava, it was taken away.'

This was news to me. I was oblivious to such things. But it was irrelevant. There was nothing I could do about what had already happened. Right now, I had to rescue my mother. That was it; nothing else was more important. I stared downstream in the direction the guard had gone. I stamped my feet in frustration. Why was it taking so long? Finally a boat appeared around the bend; one of the two rowers was the guard. As they beached the boat, he asked, 'Sir, where did you last see your mother?' As I started to get into the boat, the *bisaj* and guard spoke together, 'Sir, you cannot be in the boat while we conduct the search.' 'If you too, have an accident, your father will have our heads.' I asked the *bisaj*, 'Who will revive my mother when she is found?' and she replied, 'We will. I will go with the guardsman. Point us to where you saw your mother disappear. If she is there, we will find her.'

I watched the boat carrying the *bisaj* reach the spot I had pointed to. They were a little too far to the left, and I signaled with my hands. They seemed to understand. I heard a footfall behind me and turned. It was my father's Chief Minister, Sashidhara, a well-fed man with a smooth, oily brow who listened carefully to my father but did whatever he thought expedient. He bowed low. You could tell a person's rank by the depth of Sashidhara's bow. He said, 'Prince, salutations! I was told you were angry and distressed. I came right away for the gardeners were incoherent and could not explain what had made you so angry.'

'With my own eyes, I saw my mother walk into the deepest part of the river and disappear. No one paid any attention, as though she were invisible,' I said, barely able to control my anger.

He bowed again. 'I will investigate promptly and report to you. Surely the Queen is safe somewhere.'

'You need not investigate anything. What I require from you is an explanation. The *bisaj* tells me my mother delivered a baby boy and my father had it taken away.'

I expected some response but Sashidhara's face and eyes did not change. He waited a moment, as if to understand my question, and then said, 'Yes, the baby was subject to our city laws. I am sure the King and Queen intended to tell you soon. I regret the news came to you from the *bisaj*; he will be chastised. Where is he now?'

'The *bisaj* has gone out in the boat to look for my mother. There! Look the boat has stopped; they are waving.' He peered out over the water. 'They seem to be shouting but I cannot hear clearly. My eyes do not see well. What do you see?' I replied, 'They are pulling something out of the water.'

We watched as time crawled by. The boat headed back. I walked back and forth, pausing to look at the boat, and then going on. As the boat approached the shore, the watchman shouted, 'Prince! It is the Queen. We were too late.'

That was not an answer I could accept. 'Why is the *bisaj* not doing something?' I shouted back. The Chief Minister became solicitous. 'Son of Shantanu, please do not blame the *bisaj*.'

The boat reached the shore. Some of the maidservants had heard the shouting and come running back to the riverside. They collected around my mother's body. It was limp, her wet robe clinging to her body. Lifting her, they carried her ashore.

We heard a commotion behind us. It was my father. The maidservants cleared a path for him. He saw the body and rushed towards it. When he recognized mother, he stopped. They laid her down gently at his feet. The *bisaj* could barely speak, shivering with the wet and the cold. Fear that he would be held accountable for failing to revive the Queen had paralyzed his tongue. My father stood unmoving. When nobody else said anything, he spoke. 'Devavrata! What have you done? Why? Why?' he asked, his voice strangely harsh. I tensed at the strangeness of his charge and replied with equal vehemence. 'You mad King! See what you have done to my mother! She died because of you.' My father turned to his Chief Minister. 'Sashidhara, arrest my son! He will explain himself, even if I have to drag it out of his throat.'

'Everyone leave now!' Sashidhara ordered. 'Take the Queen to her chamber. Leave me with the King and the Prince.' In retrospect, I admire the Chief Minister's skill at being slow in following direct commands and doing something else more expedient. The bustle of activity satisfied my father's need to do something. In a short time the river bank was clear. The Chief Minister addressed my father, saying, 'Sir, do not act in haste. The Prince is not responsible for the Queen's death.' He then turned to me. 'Prince, it is not appropriate to address your royal father in this manner.'

My father said, 'The guards told me the watchman had seen the Prince go mad and drown his mother.' I retorted, 'The guard saw nothing! Nobody believed me when I said mother had walked into the water. He jumped to his own conclusions.' But nobody was obliged to believe a twelve-year-old boy.

I attacked my father with words that day. He, pained that he had wrongly accused me, said little. I accused the Chief Minister of being a liar who would say anything on my father's behalf. I branded the Kavi Sangha as a criminal gang. I called the culture of the Kauravas bankrupt, one that forced people to bow to immoral laws. I do not think my father heard me at all, for all he did was stare at the river, shaking his head while I ranted and raved. The Chief Minister heard me out patiently and responded with soft words, pointing out that my father was grieving and in shock; that the city must see its King and his heir united in grief, that my mother would have wanted us to be together.

His words meant little to me, but his voice, soft and low, gradually doused my anger. He put an arm around my father's shoulder, like a father to his son, and whispered to him until my father too, relaxed. The Chief Minister then went over to the huddled maidservants and held a quiet conversation with them. He came back and, with his arm round my father's shoulders, led him away.

I stayed, staring across the river to the spot I had last seen my mother. Her maids hung about, hesitant to come near me. Nobody spoke. As the evening fell, the breeze from the river became cooler and cooler, until it was uncomfortably cold. I got up to leave. The maids followed, keeping me in sight until I retired for the night."

Devavrata sighed and grew silent, as though he had reached the end of a chapter in his life.

11
Managing a Crisis

Yudhishthira waited in patient silence. A vighati passed. Then another, and another. Devavrata continued to be silent. Worry lines gradually furrowed the brow of the usually quiet, usually tolerant, usually patient Pandava Commander.

"You are sad your mother died when you were a young boy?" Yudhishthira asked. "Is that all there is to this story? Then why tell it to me? Did you try to change your father's policies? Did you oppose the Kavi Sangha? Are you looking for sympathy? I have little time for that. I understand that even after all these years you are not reconciled to the manner of your mother's death and blame your father. So what? I too, have a story of loss, as do my brothers. We lost our father when I was fourteen; you exiled him when I was born. Do I blame you?

My father invited all people – Nagas, Hastinapuris, immigrants, even Rakshasas, to join Indraprastha, the settlement he established on the banks of the Yamuna, along one of its many branches before it had formed a permanent riverbed. When Bhima and I were toddlers, running through the settlement, father barely found the time to hug us; he was away, dealing with crises every day. Then Arjuna was born and miraculously, the next three years saw a flowering of the settlement as trade along the Yamuna with the Nagas and the Yadavas flourished.

Arjuna played at our father's knee. He knew him as a father. But by then Bhima was too big and I too old to know him in the same way.

When Nakula and Sahadeva were four years old, cracks appeared in the settlement. The relaxed founder and leader vanished and with him the relaxed father. Four troubled years followed, when father tried to keep Indraprastha together. The circumstances of his death were unclear, suspicious even. Arjuna walked around in a mute daze for days. Do I blame you for that? Mother Madri, mother of the twins, died soon after. The settlement broke up with a flood of claims and accusations. Mother Kunti, convinced of a conspiracy, fled with us to Hastinapura, to your shelter. I am, we all are, grateful that you took us in. However, the story of our childhood does not explain the principles we hold dear. So why was the story of your mother's death relevant to the policies you followed?"

"Yudhishthira," Devavrata said, breaking his long silence, "when the Kavi Sangha helped Samvarana, ancestor of the Kuru family, to become the dominant power in Hastinapura, they also established the precedent that the King's decision was the final law of the land. Hastinapura was a trading town and the Nagas and Panchnadis lived alongside peacefully, for they needed each other. Disputes would be negotiated. But after the Panchala invaders were expelled, the Kauravas enforced the King's laws on both the Nagas and the Panchnadis living in Hastinapura territory. It was easy to do this within the city, but beyond the city boundaries, those rules were often ignored. The immigrant Panchnadis accepted that law-making was the prerogative of their host State, so opposition to those laws outside the city bemused them. The city residents, ever-conscious of hostile Panchala, needed the protection of the

King's army. They accepted the constant presence of the army grudgingly, as a short-term option, but became increasingly unhappy as time went by. The Nagas in the city were often the ones who had gone rogue in their own community. Becoming traders in Hastinapura gave them a new and prestigious role in their own culture, and so they too, obeyed the King's laws as an interim solution to the threat.

The death of my baby brothers scarcely caused a ripple; there were so many other child deaths. I do not seek your sympathy as you seem to think; we were raised in different eras. As I grew older, I realize that even if I could not accept the law like an immigrant, I could not react like a city dweller. I was going to be King and the sole law-maker in the new political framework. I had to suppress my anguish, just as my father suppressed his. The law my mother died to protest against was not repealed, but its enforcement weakened. When my father married again, his wife demanded changes. These changes crippled the earlier law and, over time, ended it."

Yudhishthira said, "I see. Let me tell you how my father explained it to me all those years ago. The traditional, consensus-based framework under which families policed themselves in Panchnad no longer held in Hastinapura. Vasishtha and the Kavi Sangha thus created a military State, the first in the region, to ensure Kuru hegemony. This framework was replaced with one wherein the King had absolute power. The clan became powerless and citizens had to directly petition the King, who received too many to consider carefully. The only way to get a petition addressed was to draw attention to it by organizing public support to express outrage. That brought the King's standing army out to maintain order. The army's violence, State-sponsored violence, became an easy option to keep order. This is exactly why my father wanted change, to create a government that was closer to the old Panchnad form. Unlike the Panchnadi towns, your government established and maintained law and order by force.

I have one question though. You mentioned that your brothers were killed to satisfy a law the Kavi Sangha proposed. My father never told me what it was, saying the law was not important. What exactly was that law?"

"The region around Hastinapura is not as easy to cultivate as Panchnad," Devavrata replied. "The Nagas engaged in agriculture while the city dwellers were manufacturers and traders. The standing army, established after Samvarana's return, was a drain on resources. When the immigrants started coming, we had to grow more food or import it. The standing army also grew in response to the increase in population. Importing food was out of the question for everywhere there was drought. We asked the Nagas to increase the forest areas they cleared for planting, for the coming season. We assured them it was for a short time, until the immigrants returned home. That was easier said than done. A Naga band typically managed a plot size right for the number of people in the band and the effort they could muster. There was no quick and simple way to change their age-old practices. We made other attempts to improve food production, both grains and cattle, but failed in the face of the Nagas' inflexibility and the immigrants' reluctance to become full-time farmers.

A few years later, the Kavi Sangha noted that many tracts of land surrounding Hastinapura had become over-tilled. Some forests had become denuded and arid due to the smelting furnaces nearby. The Sangha projected that in just two hundred years, all the arable land would become unusable. There were more and more immigrants coming from Panchnad, and the birth rate had increased. If it continued, the land would become unproductive in sixty years, not two hundred. But if the birth rate could be controlled, they would have a hundred and twenty years to repair the damage. And if immigration could be controlled, it would help.

To address the problem, the Kavi Sangha proposed a rule that a couple could have just one girl child. There were no such limitations on boys. Female children, after the first would be handed over at birth to the State. The Kavi Sangha argued that controlling the number of girls was the most effective way to controlling population growth. Restricting the number of boys would only limit population in one generation, but restricting the number of girls would limit population growth into the next generation as well.

This law was difficult for Shantanu to accept. Most Panchnad cities were still matriarchies, and blatant discrimination against female babies would be opposed. As a trading center, Hastinapura maintained good relations with all settlements as a matter of policy. Shantanu did not want the remaining Panchnad cities, however weak, to consider him an enemy. To forestall opposition, the rule was extended to babies of both genders. Every person could have one child of the same sex as himself or herself, no more. This seemed cruel but fair. However, the military police was often called in to enforce it in Hastinapura.

After I was born, my parents wished for a girl, but my mother delivered only baby boys. King Shantanu set an example by obeying his own law. His children were taken away and handed to the Kavi Sangha. They took care to put the babies to sleep by feeding them sweetened milk mixed with *datura*[26] essence. Death followed. Once a month, they would hold a memorial service for all the babies who had died in this way."

Annals of the Kavi Sangha Appendix A.6: An Archive Saved

When Devavrata realized the Kavi Sangha had an archivist with the Pandava forces, he wondered if they had been playing both sides. Vyaasa Shukla explained how this had come about. From the perspective of the writers of the Annals, twelve hundred years later, it was a miracle.

Yudhishthira looked at him in silence, his face frozen in patent disapproval. Devavrata felt an urge to defend his father, but did not know how. How could he explain to this young man, child of a different time, that Shantanu had not been a monster?

"My father would say the Kavi Sangha was the only organization he knew that was determined in its actions, whether ruthless and cruel or merciful and kind. It was the only organization that could have done it. The Sangha was not a monolith. It consisted of two parts – the bards who performed at festivals and the archivists who documented a reign and maintained histories, both financial and of events. They also

[26]*Datura* is the Indian thorn apple (*Datura metel*), first documented in ancient Sanskrit literature and traditionally used as a painkiller, a narcotic, and a poison.

provided witnesses for contracts and performed other such functions. The bards kept the Kavi Sangha popular. But even in the best of times, performing at festivals did not pay well, for the bard's compensation was at the discretion of the *yajaman*[27], sponsor of the festivities, or the audience. The archivists brought in wealth, for the contract archiving business was critical to running the economy. The result was that the archivists ran the Kavi Sangha, and it was they who performed the culling. The bards could never have done it, but they went along with the practice. The laws were enforced by the archivists. The bards made life bearable with their stories that explained everything."

"I did not know this about the Kavi Sangha," said Yudhishthira. "Perhaps it explains my father's opposition to the Sangha. I understood his reasons for opposing you, but his opposition to the Kavi Sangha puzzled me. So King Shantanu tried to be fair by expanding the law to apply to both boys and girls, and the whole population, not just immigrants?"

"Yes. But that attempt at fairness did not win him any friends. The people watched him apply the law to his own family. But while the immigrants accepted it, the residents did not. Unrest grew, and with it the size of the standing army."

"I understand. I thought you were digressing with the story of your mother's suicide, but the deeper story was the role of the Kavi Sangha. Yet, today you are seen as the foremost supporter of the Kavi Sangha."

---

[27]The *Yajaman* was the sponsor of a ritual sacrifice (*yagna*) – he paid for it, received the *prasad*, and distributed the *prasad* among friends, their families, and other attendees. *Prasad* is the sacrificial items placed on the sacrificial altar and blessed by the ritual. The priest conducting the ritual would give the prasad to the *yajaman*.

"Yudhishthira, my son, it is not so simple. At one time the Kavi Sangha and I were united on all policy issues. Our interests meshed. I was their foremost supporter and they the bulwark of my regency."

"How did that come about? After your mother died, you must have stood opposed to your father and the Kavi Sangha. What changed? I am surprised by King Shantanu's behaviour; it did not befit a ruler. So how did great-grandmother Satyavati get him to repeal the law? What was the Kavi Sangha's reaction?"

Talking about his stepmother had never been easy for Devavrata. This direct question from his grand-nephew about her role choked his voice in his throat. He moved his arm to indicate disagreement. This moved the buried arrowhead and a hundred points of pain attacked him; a hundred long needles plunging deep into his body. He felt faint and closed his eyes.

Yudhishthira became solicitous. "Are you weary?" he asked. "Would you like to rest now?"

Devavrata nodded. He could not speak. The pain had eased but it had left him in a mental fog that slowed his thinking. Speech was impossible. Eyes closed, he hoped the fog would clear.

"I'll come back later," Yudhishthira said. He carefully adjusted the position of his granduncle's arms, turning his head and shoulders a little so the pressure on the arrow eased. In doing so, Devavrata's eyes opened and his gaze fell on the mat Shikhandin's body had lain on. The memory pulled down the corners of his mouth, like a mourner at a funeral.

Yudhishthira, seeing the change of expression and the paleness of his face, said, "I will have the mat moved out. There is no reason for you to see where your enemy lay."

Do not have to do that! Devavrata opened his mouth to speak, but his voice refused his command. He struggled to get the words out, but failed. *I am like a lake after a dam has collapsed.* All his power had drained out like so much water.

Yudhishthira waited for a few vighatis. Devavrata did not want to sleep but the effort to stay awake was exhausting. His eyes closed and his breathing became steady. He was only dimly aware when Yudhishthira rose and left the tent.

12
Devavrata Refuses To Speak

When Devavrata awoke the next day, he found he had been moved. He could no longer see the opening of the tent. He looked around. *Shikhandin was gone.* Everything else was as it had been. Only Shikhandin was absent. The last traces of his presence were gone. Yudhishthira had done as he promised. *My fate,* Devavrata thought. He felt a constriction in his chest that tightened and squeezed his heart. He could not breathe and tears flooded his eyes. *Self-pity! I thought I had conquered it years ago.* He turned his head but gasped at the flash of pain that caused his neck, stomach and legs to spasm, and his heart to thud in his chest. It reminded him of the arrow still embedded in him. He turned and a bolt of lightning slashed from his armpit through his heart to his left abdomen. He fell into darkness.

When he opened his eyes, Yudhishthira was leaning over him. "Pitamaha! Wake up! Wake up! Ah….good…" Yudhishthira and his brothers, raised in exile, had not known what to call him when they were brought to Hastinapura. The memory of their return made him smile. They had called him 'grandfather, which had made Satyavati's courtiers giggle nervously and look around to see if she was around before admonishing them not to do so. He was their granduncle, not their grandfather. Satyavati wanted to make sure they knew that. Over time, they learned to call him Pitamaha, like everyone else.

Yudhishthira must have been waiting for me to wake up. That was another difference between him and his cousin Suyodhana. Yudhishthira behaved as if he cared; Suyodhana as if he was the King and above caring.

The Archivist was sitting a short distance away. Yudhishthira gestured towards him and said, "You have met Lomaharshana, the Archivist." Devavrata nodded. "You are feeling rested? Have you had your morning meal?"

"No," Devavrata said, "but it matters not; I am not hungry."

Yudhishthira frowned at the Archivist. Lomaharshana said, "I will get him something, Sir," and left.

Yudhishthira said, "What I learned from yesterday's narration was that your disagreements with your father began very early. Were they the cause of your father's decision to disinherit you? Why did you agree to his outrageous request? What role did Satyavati play? She was young, a girl, barely a woman, how did she manage to convince King Shantanu to disinherit you and make her son the *Yuvaraja?"*

The tent flap was blowing in the wind, creating a steady beat. The season of cold winds from the Himalayas had begun. The sound of the flap merged with the beating of his heart. *Why do I have to tell this story?* He wondered wearily.

"No, my son, there was no estrangement between my father and me on policy. The policy I implemented in later years was the policy he and I agreed on."

"He still demoted you and denied you the kingdom. Why?"

"It was not over policy. I do not wish to talk about it."

"This action by your father was the most controversial of his reign. People still talk about it; about the injustice he did you. They even claim it is the cause of Hastinapura's downfall. We are all being punished for the injustice done to you."

"Yudhishthira! I do not wish to discuss it."

"It is possible your father had good reason, of which I am ignorant? I cannot believe it was a whim. Why not tell the world your side of the story?"

Devavrata could feel his heart beating faster, much faster than the fluttering of the tent flap. *Why was Yudhishthira persisting with these questions?* He tried to turn his face away but his shoulders would not move; darts of pain shot through his body. He closed his eyes.

"If not policy, what was it?" Yudhishthira asked.

Devavrata's eyes remained closed. The Archivist returned with an earthen bowl of soup and a leaf of seasoned rice and yoghurt. He looked from the silent Devavrata to Yudhishthira, frowning and asked, "Has something happened, Sir?"

"He just stopped talking and closed his eyes, not wishing to answer my question."

"Question?"

"Why he gave up the kingdom to Satyavati's children."

"Hmm…" Lomaharshana put the food down near Devavrata. He walked out of the tent, gesturing to Yudhishthira to follow. When they were both outside, he whispered, "The Vyaasa is coming this afternoon, ask him."

"The Vyaasa? Why have I not been told of his visit?"

"It is not a public visit. He does not want the news broadcast. I do not know if he can answer to your question, but of all the people alive today, he may."

Yudhishthira squinted into the sunlight. "Hmm…I must have angered the Regent. You are right. The Vyaasa should know, if anybody does. I would be chagrined if the Regent stopped talking because of me."

"I will see what I can do, Sir."

"When the Vyaasa comes, he may be able to talk to him as a friend." So saying, Yudhishthira left.

Lomaharshana went back into the tent. Devavrata looked away when the flap swung open; he did not give the Archivist a chance to speak, but said, "I am tired today. Leave me alone."

"The Vyaasa will be visiting us today. He expressed a desire to see you."

Shukla and Devavrata were old friends, but communication between them had become infrequent. As Shukla became more influential in the Kavi Sangha, finally becoming its Head, it had become harder to meet as they once had. Every meeting was fraught with meaning for the people around them. *It will be good to meet without all that.* But there was a hitch. What was Shukla doing here in the enemy camp? The Kavi Sangha had supported Devavrata's plan. *Or had that changed? Were they double dealing?*

"Shukla? Here?" When the Archivist nodded, he said, "It will be good to see him. Wake me if he wishes to see me."

"Yes, Sir." Lomaharshana stood up and bowed, his palms joined respectfully. "By your leave, Sir, I will leave now."

Shukla's Visit

13

Shukla's Reassurances

Lomaharshana could not be still. He stood in the shade of the banyan tree at the northern end of the camp. The entrance to the camp was through the hanging roots. It was mid-afternoon and he had been waiting for the Vyaasa since morning. The Regent refused to listen or talk. The guards occasionally glanced at Lomaharshana as he paced around the tree. They knew who he was, that he was harmless.

What he was planning to do broke protocol. The King expected to be the first person to meet the Vyaasa, who was not just another Head of Guild. As the Head of the Kavi Sangha, he wielded tremendous influence in the marketplace, and as the intellectual descendant of Vasishtha, he was Chief Advisor to the rulers of Hastinapura. The Vyaasa was close to the Regent, perhaps his only friend. The capture of the Regent could change many things. *Why had the Vyaasa sent word, offering to cooperate with the King?* It was the first time the Vyaasa had used the renegade group of kavis in the Pandava camp, and that could be interpreted as approval. From that point of view, the Regent's refusal to talk was a disaster. *Did I make a mistake in leaving the King alone with the Regent? What happened while I was gone? The Vyaasa will hold me responsible. He could withdraw his tentative approval of our work.* Lomaharshana had decided he must talk to him first.

There was a flurry of movement as the guards held aside the dangling roots of the banyan. The Vyaasa appeared. Lomaharshana had expected the usual entourage of helpers and onagers[28] drawing carts; the circus of guards inspecting everything while chatting with the driver and the cook. It would have given Lomaharshana the opportunity to speak to the Vyaasa without being interrupted. But the Vyaasa appeared to have come by himself. *Had he walked all the way from Hastinapura?* Lomaharshana wondered. *No circus. He would not have much time to present his problem.*

Lomaharshana went up to the Vyaasa and bowed, his palms joined. "Welcome, Sir!"

"Ah, Lomaharshana! It is a pleasure to be welcomed by you. Is the King not well?"

Lomaharshana looked towards the leader's tent and his face darkened, the King himself was coming towards them. There was no time to explain.

The Vyaasa saw Lomaharshana's quick look and said, "Difficulties with the King?" Lomaharshana nodded.

---

[28]The onager is the Asian wild ass, of the equid family, larger than a donkey and smaller than a horse. Its range extends from West Asia to India. It was one of the first equids domesticated for hauling and may have been the preferred mode of transport from 3000 BCE to about 1500 BCE after which it was largely replaced by horses and oxen. The Indian onager is a subspecies that is easier to tame than the other members of the family.

The Vyaasa smiled as Yudhishthira came up to him and said, "Welcome, Sir! You visit us after a long time. We are grateful for your years of advice and support. The Council awaits you."

"I accept your welcome, my boy but I would like a quiet visit without public acknowledgement. I will meet only a few. I want no ceremony."

Yudhishthira pursed his lips. Worry lines crossed his forehead. He said, "I will give instructions right away, Sir. There will be no public meetings; none have been announced as we did not know you were coming."

"That is excellent," said the Vyaasa, squelching any hopes Yudhishthira might have had that he would change his mind. "I hear the Regent is a prisoner here."

"He is."

"Is he injured?"

"The *bisajs* say it is a fatal wound that will not heal. He cannot move. I will take you to him now if you will."

"It is late; I will see him tomorrow morning."

"We have prepared a tent for you." Yudhishthira led the Vyaasa to an unusually large for one occupant. The floor sloped slightly, from east to west. The entrance, therefore, was at the western end. A rectangular trench, about ten hastas[29] across and eight hastas deep, had been dug. Three rows of poles were

[29]*Hasta* is the same as the cubit, the length of the arm from the elbow to the tip of the middle finger, which is approximately eighteen inches. A more exact definition is needed when the term is used as a standard unit of measurement because each person has a "personal hasta" measure.

embedded into the ground; the outer row in the trench and the two inner rows on slightly higher ground. Crossbars were placed above and tied to the poles, forming a roof that sloped to the back. In addition, sisal ropes from the middle row of poles to the outer ones and the cross ropes, created a web. This was overlaid with large felted cotton squares, tied to the ropes. The walls were cloth. The floor was rammed earth, a luxury made possible by the fact that this camp had been occupied for many weeks; a temporary tent would not have such a floor.

The Vyaasa's Tent

The details of the Vyaasa's tent are based on examples of housing from the Sarasvati-Sindhu Culture as well as other Bronze Age cultures. Permanent settlements often follow the layout of temporary housing used by nomads, so the design of Vyaasa's luxury tent has been reconstructed from the design of housing in the Sarasvati-Sindhu Culture in places like Harappa, Lothal, and Kalibangan. The walls would have been cotton felt for short-term camps and wattle-and-daub for more permanent camps; the floor would have been rammed earth, and the ceiling would have been cotton felt. Cotton and cotton felt were used extensively in the SSC as it is cheaper than woven cloth. The toilet and the sewage trench are based on the permanent structures of SSC housing. Rain except during the monsoon months is rare in South Asia, and nobody went to war during the rains, so tents often did not have ceilings and drainage ditches did not have to double as storm drains. Seats would have been constructed from tree trunks before the invention of multi-legged chairs, and pillows would have consisted of pieces of waste cotton and felt rolled up inside a larger piece of felt and the corners tied off. Tables would have been made from tree-trunks. A raised bed with a mattress would have been an expensive luxury. The mattress itself may have been constructed by tying pillows into a "raft," or coiled like a snake (possibly the source of the image of the god Vishnu lounging or resting on the coils of the Naga Adisesha).

The tent was covered with felt, a luxury offered to the Vyaasa. The trench was a traditional feature of permanent structures, also put in for his convenience. The brick houses in Panchnad had similar trenches for sewage. It was useful in the odd rainstorm as well. The trench was not intended to be rain proof as it was customary to desist from war during the rainy season. One corner of the tent served as a toilet. A hole had been dug in the ground and a ceramic pot with drainage holes in the bottom, placed in the hole. The dug out soil was mounded to the side, and had a small wooden paddle stuck into it, to be used as a scoop to cover sewage and trash. A small bucket of water stood nearby, with a flat rounded stone for washing the face, hands and feet. The water drained from the stone into the trench. Another luxury prepared for the Vyaasa was a low bench with a tile top that covered the hole. This was short-term accommodation. If they broke camp in an orderly manner, the pot would be removed and emptied into a field trench, and the hole refilled. The trench around the tent would also be filled. The tent contained a sleeping area along the side furthest from the toilet area. It had a few more pieces of felt. A roll made of cotton, sewn along the long edge and stuffed with cotton, served as a pillow. The Vyaasa's tent had a wooden slab cut from the trunk of a tree, approximately two cubits in diameter and polished on both sides. This served as a seat or a table.

The Vyaasa took in all the effort that had been made for his comfort. He washed his face, hands and feet at the stone and then lay down to rest. But rest eluded him. He had first heard that Devavrata Bhishma had been grievously wounded and was dead. Then he had heard that he was alive but on his deathbed. And then again that he was dead. In his mind, his friend was not a single person but two. He had come here in the hope that he could confirm Devavrata was alive. But he could not shake the thought that Bhishma's death could be convenient. In his heart he wanted Devavrata alive, but what of Bhishma? Did he want Bhishma dead? Bhishma's death would free the Vyaasa of the debts he owed Devavrata; debts he could not ignore.

Yudhishthira had said Devavrata was still alive but fatally wounded, not likely to last more than a few days. That Devavrata was still alive meant the Vyaasa could see him one last time. In recent years their interactions had become formal, and he missed the informality they had enjoyed as young men. He could share this feeling with Devavrata, however much he may have become Bhishma. It was not that they did not have strategic issues to discuss. His last interaction with Suyodhana and Karna had been wasted effort – the two behaved like hunting dogs that had cornered an injured doe and would not be pulled away. If Devavrata was no longer around, Shukla would feel less of an obligation to Hastinapura. He owed much to the Regent of Hastinapura, but little to Indraprastha and its allies.

Lomaharshana, the Chief Archivist for Indraprastha and leader of the small group of bards in the Pandava camp, had broken protocol to talk to him. He had been worried and needed reassurance, some guidance, and if possible, direction. The group of kavis was an unexpected treasure that was paying strategic dividends at no cost. If Hastinapura lost this unnecessary war, the Kavi Sangha would survive as Advisors to the Pandavas. If the Kavi Sangha survived this war, it would need leaders like Lomaharshana. All they had to do was survive.

After a fitful sleep Shukla felt barely rested when he woke to the sound of bells outside his tent. But as was usual with him, he sat up fully awake.

The bells announced Yudhishthira.

"It is I, Yudhishthira."

Shukla said, "Come in, my son, come in."

Yudhishthira entered with joined palms, "Jaya! We seek your blessings, honored Guru."

"Live long, my son. You have my blessings a thousand-fold."

"Are you comfortable? Is there anything I can do for you?"

"You have done very well, Yudhishthira. My needs are few. There is nothing more that I require. I have not seen your brothers. Are they well? What news of your wife, the Queen of Panchala? How is she?"

"Honored Guru, your concern for my brothers and wife is appreciated. My brothers are doing well; they wish to see you if possible. Panchali, of course, has her responsibilities in Panchala. We send messages to Kampilya[30], past Suyodhana's troops and Sushasana's spies. They patrol all the paths leading from the old city towards us. Please share your news with us. How is it with you and your sister, my grandmother Queen Satyavati? Tell me how my mother fares? And my uncles Dhritarashtra and Dharmateja Vidura – are they well?"

"I am glad to hear you are all well. Come closer, Yudhishthira; do not stand so far away. Sit near me so that I need not speak so loudly. I speak to you as an advisor, not your master. I am not the King; you are."

Yudhishthira moved closer and sat down facing the Vyaasa.

[30] Kampilya was the capital of Panchala.

"Now tell me what this is about?" the Vyaasa asked.

"It is about Granduncle Devavrata. He agreed to work with the Archivist to record his story. Then, when I asked him about something, he stopped and has refused to speak since."

"What did you ask?"

"How did his stepmother convince his father to disinherit him? Why did he accept the decision? Were there differences over policy? He said there were none but refused to explain any further. His answers were terse, his attitude brusque. Finally, he refused to answer at all. When I insisted, he told the Archivist to come back the next day."

"Hmm… why did you insist?"

"There are so many questions to which only he can provide answers. What was King Shantanu's plan, and how did it differ from Devavrata's actions? Did the crown make a difference? If Devavrata had become King, would he have followed different policies? What was my father's disagreement with the Regent that caused him to give up the crown and exile himself? These differences and what they meant – we must understand them."

Annals of the Kavi Sangha

The future King asked the Vyaasa a number of questions about the details of the events that led to Devavrata's vow. Shukla's answer is recorded in the Annals.

Appendix A.7: The Disaster

Yudhishthira wanted to know why and how the Disaster happened. The Annals only know what happened and how the people made it worse!

Appendix A.8: The Panchnad Migration

The Annals describe how the Migration proceeded – who went where, who was displaced, and what were the consequences.

Appendix A.9: The Refugees in Hastinapura

The Annals answer Yudhishthira's questions about what the refugees from Panchnad expected when they came to Hastinapura.

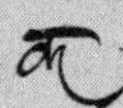

Appendix A.10: Panchnad Fails to Come Together

The Annals explain how and why the cooperation that the Panchnad settlements had been famous for broke down in the period after the Disaster.

"I can give you the answers you want."

"Answers without context are useless, Sir."

"You are right. Your father's differences with Devavrata were many and deep, but they occurred before I became the Vyaasa. I spent much of that time in Takshashila. But I can assure you there were no differences on policy matters between King Shantanu and Prince Devavrata, not even when Devavrata became Regent after Shantanu died."

"How do you know, Gurudeva?

"I was there. Satyavati is, after all, my sister. Devavrata and I became friends when she married Shantanu. I know why he declined the crown. I had a small, if unfortunate, part in it. I could have kept aloof, instead I stirred the pot and made complex what might have been simple and uncomplicated. I am not proud of my role."

"The reasons he declined the crown – how did they influence policy, if they did?"

"They did, but not in the way you would expect. My advice to you is to avoid raising this matter with the Regent."

"And skip the story of his disinheritance completely?"

"No, you do not have to do that. Just do not ask Devavrata. I will tell you. The Archivist can listen and include it in his archive. Let me get ready. Ask the Archivist to come here. I would like to speak to him."

Yudhishthira sent a guard to summon Lomaharshana who arrived half a ghati later.

The Vyaasa came directly to the point. "The Regent will not willingly tell you what led to his vow and Queen Satyavati's marriage to his father. I played a small part, so I am familiar with it. Certainly it would have been best if the Regent's story had been told in his own words, but I do not expect he will do so. Supplement the Regent's narrative with this story I narrate."

"Where does it fit, Sir?" asked the Archivist.

"It pertains to the marriage of Satyavati and Shantanu, and Devavrata's vow."

"I am ready, Sir. When should we begin?"

"Shortly. I must attend a meeting with the King's closest Councilors first. I expect it will last most of the afternoon. We can begin two ghatis before the evening meal."

Lomaharshana bowed and turned to leave. As he was stepping out of the tent, the Vyaasa said, "You have done well, Lomaharshana, and your team."

Lomaharshana turned, bowed, and left. *Praise from the Vyaasa was rare.* He felt a heavy burden had been lifted from his shoulders.

When the Vyaasa returned from the meeting, he found Lomaharshana waiting for him. A bowl of fruit, lightly mashed with mead, lime and water, sent from the camp kitchen, sat by the bed. Lomaharshana waited as the Vyaasa carefully picked out the bobbing crab apples and placed them to one side.

"Lomaharshana, you will taste real apples when you are sent to Takshashila. That is if this war ever ends. Those apples almost rival the mango in taste, though they are very different experiences. For now, enjoy these smaller tart cousins."

A kitchen attendant arrived with their evening repast. It was a traditional light meal of rice and salty buttermilk. They ate in silence and then sat outside the Vyaasa's tent as the sky turned dark. A bright band of stars spanned the sky. It was the eleventh day after the full moon. It would be a dark night, one for reflecting on the stars. An attendant came and lit a small fire in a pit a few feet from the tent, sprinkling a little citrus oil to keep the insects away.

Soon Yudhishthira came by. "Lomaharshana tells me you will be narrating the story of Devavrata's renunciation. I would like to hear it first-hand."

"And you shall" said Vyaasa Shukla.

14
THE RENUNCIATION

"*I renounce my right to Kingship…I will not marry. I will not have children. I will know no woman.* With those words," Vyaasa Shukla said, "Devavrata created the world we know; he set in motion the chain of events that has led to this war. The fire of his anger was stoked by a woman and a King – his father Shantanu, and his stepmother-to-be, Satyavati. The public cause was the King's willingness to circumvent his own laws to satisfy his desire for Satyavati. Of private causes, there were many. It is likely that if the King had not made those laws, none of the consequences we faced would have come about."

"Gurudeva, I do not understand," Yudhishthira said. "What did the King's laws have to do with the renunciation?"

"Everything. That is what I will explain."

"If the laws were responsible for everything, I must know what they were and why they were made in the first place. Without that the narrative is incomplete."

Shukla nodded slowly. "I hoped to finish in two ghatis, but the story of the laws is long, for it is the story of the Disaster. We will need most of the day tomorrow to satisfy your request."

"That is acceptable. Pray begin."

Thus Shukla narrated the history of the Disaster and the resulting Migration.

15
Shukla's World

Shukla took a deep breath and exhaled slowly. "Satyavati and I come from a family of Meena-Nagas, called Matsya by the Panchnadis,[31]" he began. "You look surprised. Yes, I am a Naga, and so is Satyavati. Lomaharshana, you too are a Naga, but not a Meena-Naga. We Meenas are different, even though we are all Nagas. The last fifty years have seen much change for the Nagas as well as the Meenas. I will try to describe the world my sister and I came from.

My father's sister was the Matriarch of our small band of five families. He, the Matriarch's elder brother, was head of the band's fighters. That made us part of the ruling family, but with no expectation of ever being the Chief or Matriarch. Unlike Panchnad, we had no guilds. Nor do we share with the Panchnadis an obsession with the number five. You have seen often enough how the Nagas like to see groups of five. It is considered a lucky number. The size of a band could vary but number of families comprising a band would always be a multiple of five; large bands were often composed of five smaller bands similarly structured. We have had bands with over a hundred families.

Unlike other Nagas, the Meenas do not migrate for land – we migrate for water. We establish our settlements on the edge of

[31]*Meena* was the Naga word for "fish", while *Matsya* was the Panchnadi word.

the river at a place where a small pond or lake can be made. Such lakes are often created naturally at a bend in a river. But if the downstream channel silts up, followed by the upstream channel, the depression is cut off from the river and the lake dries up. The Meena-Nagas specialized in restoring such lakes. The depression had to be small, but not too small. It had to be large enough and not too far from the changed course of the river. A number of Meena-Naga bands would get together to dig a new short channel from the river to the depression and a longer straight channel downstream back to the main flow. The channels were designed to cut the speed of the swiftly flowing river, which reduced soil erosion. It was hard work, but when ready, such a lake would support many Naga bands.

The Meena bands could not settle immediately after digging the channels. It took a few years for grasses and other plants to grow near the lake, followed by the appearance of insects and tadpoles. The next season, small fish would appear, followed by bigger fish. Finally, the river dolphins would enter the lake. They are vehicles of the Goddess, signalling plenty and giving us permission to settle on the lake. The calm lake thus provided a home for fish, including river dolphin and trout. The construction of such a lake was a major investment and we did not easily abandon a lake. A fish weir could be constructed, though we only did that in preparation for hosting the clan's *potlatch*[32]. The houses by the water were often built on platforms held up by stilts, while the houses further back would be on the ground. Once a band settled down, it would establish a garden for root vegetables and herbs close by.

[32]The word "potlatch" comes from the name of a redistributive feast held by the Trobriand Islanders of New Guinea.

Our band settled on the banks of such a lake, near the southern border of Hastinapura. The city-dwellers had occupied land the Nagas had left fallow, using it for their ceramic and metal furnaces. The Naga bands grumbled about this, but as no bands were occupying that land, there was no one to actively protest. In those years the Nagas avoided conflict by moving elsewhere. They did that for many, many years. The Naga Chiefs were sensitive to the changed balance of power created by Samvarana's return. Hastinapura became a militarized capital city, not just a trading entrepôt. The Hastinapuris abandoned their foundries when the chaos of the immigration crisis cut the eastern ore trade. The land to the north was left a sorry, blighted stretch. But we assumed this was how city-dwellers left land fallow; that they would return when it was productive again.

I was fascinated by the Hastinapuris and spent much time with them. Noticing my interest, Parashara adopted me as his protégé. This was before he became the Vyaasa. He had come to our settlement to assess how the city-dwellers and the Nagas could cooperate rather than fight each other. Refugees were coming in from the west in steadily increasing numbers. The Kavi Sangha hoped to establish them in new settlements rather than overwhelm Hastinapura. The Nagas' cooperation was essential. The immigrants could learn from the Nagas and the Meenas how to live off the land and river.

Parashara spent a lot of time with us. He was freely available to me as a teacher. I did not know then the reason for his frequent visits, but at that time I was excited about city life. My life by the lake seemed monotonous and boring in comparison, and I felt useless. Parashara sponsored me into the Kavi Sangha and enrolled me in the school of bards, even though, at ten, I was much older than the six-year-olds around me. I was excited and engaged. I did very well, so much so that in less than two years I caught up and was counted among the bards of my age who were the most skilled at memorization and storytelling. In those skills I was the equal of Devavrata, who had established extraordinary performance records when he had studied with the Kavi Sangha apprentices.

In the meantime, my sister Satyavati, a few years older than me, became pregnant. A pregnancy unacknowledged by the father was not considered remarkable among the Nagas. The same held true in ancient matriarchal Panchnad. When Samvarana regained Hastinapura, it should have become a matriarchal settlement like the others in Panchnad, but it did not. It was ruled by a Head Trader, with the line of succession as the Trader's son. Paternity became important. The Kavi Sangha thought it knew everything about fatherhood. They had rationalized change as being in line with local hegemony enforced by a standing army. In recent years, the focus on paternity has become more intense. I do not know why. Suyodhana and his brothers are particularly obsessed with establishing their paternity, and, as they call it, 'the purity of the mother'.

The situation was not so extreme when Satyavati delivered Parashara's child. Parashara asked us to be circumspect among city folk. We were puzzled but followed his advice. That year, he became the Vyaasa. His visits stopped. Unfortunately for Parashara, the leaders of the Kavi Sangha learned that Parashara had fathered a child with a Naga woman. I should mention that, in ordinary times, this would have barely caused a ripple. But they were not ordinary times. The Vyaasa's credibility as an observer and memorizer of Naga customs and an advisor on policy towards the Nagas, was compromised. His secretiveness made his behavior seem deceitful and unwise.

That the woman's father was the Chief of a Naga band raised more questions – the immigrants did not trust the Nagas, and every action by Shantanu had to appear fair to both groups. The senior members of the Kavi Sangha, its governing body, determined that Parashara should be penalized.

Parashara realized he had compromised his role as an advisor to Hastinapura, the Nagas, and the Panchnadi refugees. From that point of view, his actions had been unwise. He agreed to a penalty. The Kavi Sangha determined that he undertake a two-year vow of silence, a particularly harsh sentence for a bard. Parashara decided to spend his two years of silence on an island near our lake. In Panchnad, his responsibility to his child would have been to ensure acceptance into a guild. He chose to stay close to us. My sister Satyavati, the child's mother, was also upset, first about the secrecy she had been asked to maintain, then about the public disapproval. Faced with the stance of the Kavi Sangha, Parashara's questionable judgment and his fickleness, she decided to raise the boy herself and refused Parashara any significant role. Thus, Parashara's efforts to be near his child came to naught. But he was still my Guru and my mentor within the Kavi Sangha."

Lomaharshana said, "The great Parashara was penalized while he was the Vyaasa?"

Vyaasa Shukla nodded silently.

"But…but…such a punishment is not mentioned in any of our archives."

"The entire episode was kept secret within the highest circles of the Kavi Sangha," Shukla said. "Hastinapuris were given the impression that the vow of silence had been taken by Parashara for personal spiritual reasons. Even Shantanu was not told. It was felt that his trust in the Sangha would be tested. He was not inquisitive by nature and he accepted Parashara's story.

My sister named her child Dvaipaayana[33], acknowledging his obscure parentage. His skin color led to the nickname Krishna[34], partly in contrast to my name, Shukla, as I was so light-skinned. He looked like his mother and had the family hallmark of the full upper lip that curved down. He was a chubby, playful boy whose presence cheered my father.

Mine was a peaceful world for many years. But it was turned upside down by the events I am about to describe. I was not present at the beginning, but my father and sister were. I picked up bits of information that I have woven into a narrative. Even in the days before I had heard of the Kavi Sangha, I delighted in creating and telling stories. I would have been a natural candidate for membership to the Bards' Guild at a young age if I had lived in the city. I have thought over these events many times, in the hope I would discover a prefigured destiny that would give meaning to the rest of my life. This is what happened…"

[33]*Dvaipaayana* means "born on an island."
[34]*Krishna* means "dark," while *Shukla* means "light." In this case, the names described the color of their skin.

Satyavati

16
The King Comes a-Courting

Shukla continued: "It was about a hundred moons[35] after Devavrata's mother had killed herself. One day, my father was outside the house, playing with Krishna Dvaipaayana, who was then forty moons[36] old. Satyavati was sitting on the steps leading to the house, watching them play. I was away collecting wood in the forest and only heard what happened much later from my father.

A stag burst out of the forest to the east of the clearing and stood panting by the river bank. It continued along the river and entered the forest to the west. My father was quick. 'Hunters… Satyavati, go in,' he called in warning. She did so, leaving him alone outside. A few *vighatis* later, four men emerged from the direction the stag had appeared; they were armed with bows and had been following the stag's trail. They stopped when they saw my father. One of the men walked towards him. After some hesitation, two others followed, but the fourth held back.

[35] Almost eight solar years.
[36] About three years.

My father knew the first man – Shantanu, King of Hastinapura, who held out his arms to my father, embraced him and said, 'Rajah! I rejoice to see you. How is your land here? Does your family flourish? Does this mighty river provide enough for you?'

My father was relieved but taken aback by the King's friendliness. He tried to respond with the same enthusiasm. 'You are welcome, brother, to my humble abode. The goddess has treated us well. We flourish in the shadow of your protection. What cause for worry could we have? It has been many years since you came this way. How are your Queens and children?'

Shantanu gestured to the one who had hung back. 'My wife passed away many years ago. This is my only son, Devavrata.'

The young man, of slight build, did not respond, engrossed in shining his bowstring with a piece of leather. One of the other men walked back and nudged him. He looked up, flushed, and stepped forward. He struck my father as being much younger than the others, but his bow was strung more tightly and his quiver had more arrows. Devavrata bowed to my father, who raised his hands in blessing.

Shantanu said, 'How are your children? You had two, as I recall. Are they still with you or have they joined other families?'

'Satyavati and Shukla are still with me.'

Meanwhile, Satyavati had put down baby Krishna inside the house and began rolling up the mats we slept on. Krishna did not like being put down and showed his displeasure by crying loudly. Satyavati went to the door, saying, 'Appa, can you…' She froze when she saw the men. Her eyes scanned all four and stopped at Devavrata. After a moment's hesitation, she looked back at my father and finished her sentence in a voice that was almost inaudible, '…find his toy elephant?'

At the sound of a woman's voice, the men had looked up. Devavrata, who had returned to working on his bow, put it down. All the men stared at Satyavati, as if frozen by a spell. My father picked up the toy from where it had fallen and handed it to her, and she went back into the cottage. The King was the first to come back to reality. He asked my father, 'Is that charming lady your daughter?'

A thousand thoughts went through my father's mind. Ever since Hastinapura had established itself as the dominant power on the strength of its standing army, the Nagas had learned to be cautious around city dwellers, especially armed fighters. Some, like Parashara, were friendly, but there were the arrogant ones, with whom caution was warranted. He therefore hesitated, making up his mind about something before saying, 'It is my daughter, Satyavati, Sir. She is taking care of Guru Parashara's son. As you know, he has retired to a nearby rest house while observing his vow of silence. Nevertheless his wisdom shines through. Please come in and grace my home. Stay for a meal.'

My father hoped that by mentioning Guru Parashara he would mitigate any risk posed by the Hastinapuris. The invitation to eat was a calculated risk. It was not yet time for a meal, and hunters did not usually abandon their prey unless they were hungry. But these men did not look as if they had ever gone hungry.

Shantanu looked at his men, making ready to leave. He said, 'Thank you, but we must resume our hunt; some other day, perhaps. Did you see a stag come this way?' My father pointed to the west. 'It ran past just before you arrived. It went that way.'

Some days later, a royal messenger came with presents from the King. He said the King wanted my father to consider a future for his daughter in the Kuru family. My father thought the message referred to Devavrata. The lad had seemed young and malleable so my father was amenable to the notion of his courting Satyavati. The city-dwellers did not have the same customs as the Nagas, and the city women were less forthcoming than Naga women. But in matters of love, all men and women were similar. He recalled the wandering soma-peddler from a few years ago, who consumed as much of his drug as he sold and was always in a semi-trance. The peddler had claimed to have gained spiritual powers from the spirits in the Himalayas. On seeing Satyavati, he had proclaimed she would be a great Matriarch and her progeny would rule the greatest empire in the land. Everyone had laughed for she had five cousins before her in line to be Matriarch. The only way she could become a matriarch was by spinning off a daughter band. But our band was newly formed and too small for offshoots. Now my father thought the prophecy would make perfect sense if Satyavati married Hastinapura's future King and became Matriarch. Hastinapura was the only large State within a hundred yojanas. So my father's response to Shantanu's request was, 'The boy can come himself and persuade her. Naga women make their own choices.'

Later that day, Devavrata approached my father asking permission to court his daughter. 'I am the King's son and heir. I will be King after him. The people of the city will treat your daughter with the greatest respect. You need have no fear for her wellbeing.'

My father encouraged Devavrata to court Satyavati, saying, 'Naga families do not arrange marriages. Feel free to approach her directly. However, remember that she is as free as you. Any Naga woman would be delighted to be invited to be Matriarch of a band.' My father did not fully understand Kuru customs, and tried to make sense of them in the light of Naga practices. He thought that marrying the King's son would elevate Satyavati to the status of a future Matriarch.

So Devavrata left to find Satyavati. In the meantime the messenger returned to clarify that the King wished to marry Satyavati himself. My father realized there could be trouble, and his family would be in the middle of it. He shouted Satyavati's name, hoping to prevent Devavrata from speaking to her. Only a few words had been exchanged before Satyavati heard father calling her.

I was once again absent from home when these events took place. If I had known what was happening, who knows whether I would have acted as I did. Things may have turned out differently. I discovered later, from her girlfriends, what had transpired. Devavrata had met her in the company of her friends. He had been tongue-tied and awkward, while her friends teased him. He had made hurried excuses and left. The boy had been, she told her friends, very sweet.

When I returned, my father looked at me thoughtfully. I thought he was about to ask me something, but he turned away and said to my sister instead, 'I have something important to discuss with you. The King visited us today. He wants something that is not mine to give. What am I to say? I am troubled by strange dreams and visions. I cannot express what I am feeling and thinking.'

Satyavati smiled and said, 'Do not worry, father. I know what he wants. I hope you told him that with us the boy takes the lead?'

That got my father's attention. 'What did you say to him?'

'Oh father, I know why he came.'

'I cannot tell the King how to behave; he is not a commoner. Nor does he know our customs. It is dangerous to run afoul of the Kauravas, especially a powerful Chief like Shantanu.'

I did not know what my father was talking about, nor did my sister, who said, 'Why are you so worried? It is for me to decide and I see no reason to say no. You know me, father, I will never let you decide for me.'

My father said, 'Satyavati, my child, this has gone beyond my simple powers of explanation and understanding. Let the Kaurava do as he will, and you as you think right.'

We both wondered why he had said 'the Kaurava', as though there was just one. Satyavati said, 'What is the matter, father? You worry needlessly. We have nothing against him. He is an honest, caring, earnest young man. There is nothing to fear.'

My father mumbled when he was confused, and he did so now. 'If only your mother were here. Oh, what am I saying? Even she could not have helped me. How do I explain this to you?'

Satyavati tried again. 'It will be good for Krishna to have a father. You have said so yourself. We are fisher-folk, not city-dwellers with their ridiculous laws. According to our customs, the boy must approach me. That is as it should be. Why worry?'

'The Kauravas are not Nagas, my child. You will not be able to remain here. They will expect you to go with them.'

I listened silently to my father and Satyavati, excited to learn that if Satyavati married a city-dweller, she would live in the city. It would mean that I would have a safe place there to achieve my ambition. I joined the conversation. 'Father, Satya's friend Gauri told me the King came here! You should have called me! You know I want to move to the city. I could have asked him.' They ignored me, looking unhappy; Satyavati's mouth set in a pout, my father mumbling inaudibly. I persisted; this was not an opportunity to be missed. 'Is Satya going to Hastinapura? Perhaps I can go with her and stay in the palace.'

Satyavati eyes narrowed. 'Oh, Shukla, is that all you think about – the city? Maybe you will become a jester in the King's court.'

'I'd like that,' I assured her. 'Father, what is going on? Why are you both looking so upset?'

My father said, 'The King wants to marry Satyavati and take her to Hastinapura.'

'Father is against it, only he won't explain why…' Satyavati began, then stopped abruptly, realizing what he had just said.

'What!' we exclaimed together.

17
Who Is The Groom?

Shukla paused, reliving the moment. Emphasizing each word, he continued, "My father said, 'No, no…I made a mistake, I was just mumbling. It is nothing, nothing at all...'

It made no difference to me as long as I made it to the city so I said, 'You won't be lonely; I will go with you. It will be good!'

But Satyavati gave a shudder. When I think back, I imagine that she must in that moment have felt an ice-cold wind from the northern mountains blow the joy out of her life.

'The King! Marry the King? I will not! Father, tell him no. Why can I not marry Devavrata instead? I will kill myself. How can I be the King's wife?'

My father looked at Satyavati and just said. 'What did you say? How do you know about Devavrata?'

'We exchanged a few words. He was charming but shy. I just thought…'

My father interrupted her. 'What did he say?'

'I know he had come to see me and my friends teased him. We hardly spoke before you were shouting for me. He went away. Perhaps the King comes on his behalf?'

I finally understood what Satyavati's objection was. She did not wish to marry the King, but someone called Devavrata. 'You do not wish to marry the King? Why? Are you worried about your baby? The King can surely be his father. Who is Devavrata, anyway? Sounds like a citified name, not a Naga.'

My father said, turning away, 'The King will have my head.'

'What did you tell him?' Satyavati asked.

I had to make my position known, so I said, 'I hope you agreed?'

Satyavati looked at me, her eyes wide, nose flared, lips pinched together. I did not know what she was accusing me of. Her voice rose to a higher pitch as she said to my father, 'I hope you said no, right away.'

My father and I were familiar with that high pitch, which brooked no opposition. We both spoke up.

My father said, 'We are not a wealthy or powerful band. The King calls me Rajah as a courtesy; he is being polite, for it is merely a courtesy. If I say no, he can destroy us.'

I said, with the single-minded conviction of youth, 'This is my only chance to enter the city as an equal and not a supplicant.'

Satyavati replied, 'I do not care. If my life is to be destroyed, why should I care about you? Father, you must stop this!'

My father held his head in his hands. He was the nominal Chief of the band because his sister was the ruling Matriarch. Avoiding conflict had always been his métier. He said, 'Satyavati, the matter is beyond my control. If you refuse, the Kaurava will destroy us and you will become his property. If you agree, you will reign as Queen, and we will survive.'

I added my perspective. 'I will have a glorious career as Councilor to the great King Shantanu.'

Satyavati said, 'If he knew I wish to marry his son, he might change his mind.'

That was when I finally got it. She loved this fellow Devavrata, but he was not just anybody. Devavrata was the King's son! My voice joined hers in an upper register. 'His son?'

My father replied, 'I cannot do that. He thinks you have never met his son, merely glimpsed him the day the hunters came.'

I got my voice under control but my mind was still flailing to understand. 'His son! Oh…'

Ignoring me, Satyavati said, 'Father, tell the King to ask his son.'

Either way seemed good to me. I said in my priceless wisdom, 'Why would you want to marry the son when you can be Queen? Fine, so you love the son, not the father, if that's what you want, you can be Crown Princess, and I will be famous as Advisor to the glorious Samraat Devavrata.'

Satyavati went and held our father's hands. 'Yes, that is what I want. Do not mention his son, just say I do not wish to be Queen, that I am not trained for it, that I will disgrace him in public and his people will be shamed.'

'Satyavati, I will do as you ask but I expect he will answer your objections. You can be trained. You could never disgrace him. What if he accepts whatever demands you make? Will you then marry him and forget the son?'

'Never. Tell him something else. Shukla, stop thinking about yourself and help me.'

The problem was intriguing. I look back at myself and wonder at my insensibility. I said, 'Hmm…King Devavrata. I wonder what he will do if you marry his father?'

'I don't know. Perhaps he will go away or kill himself. How do I know?'

I said, 'Are you sure? I don't think so. Let me tell you how they do it in the West, in Sumer and Parsaka. Traders tell stories of how heirs, who rebel against their fathers, have to debase themselves in apology under pain of death. The desperate heir is angry not with the king, but the person he blames, often a stepmother, brother or sister, even someone who may have been trying to help him. He exiles himself and bides his time. When the king's successor tries to occupy the throne, the exile returns to fight. If he wins, he kills his rival and anyone else whom he blames for the falling out with his father. Hence most court officials desist from taking sides between father and son as it is a risky business. I feel Devavrata will follow that example. He will go into exile and when the King dies, he will return and become the Chief. Then he will kill you.'

My father said in exasperation, 'Shukla, are you mad? Do not come up with these grotesque tales. Help us come up with a plan. What do we do?'"

18
Shukla's Confession

My response to my father had many consequences. One shameful act by an ambitious young boy made me what I am. It led to Devavrata's renunciation; to my sister's unhappy life. It brought us here."

Lomaharshana frowned. The Vyaasa made these pronouncements as though they were unquestionable. "What do you mean, Sir, which ambitious young boy?"

"I was that foolish youth. And this confession is meant only for your ears, for Yudhishthira, and the archives of the Kavi Sangha," stated Shukla.

"Sir, am I the right person to make such a confession to?" asked Lomaharshana.

"Yes, you are the right person, Archivist. I have lived a long life and do not have much longer. I may not have the time to submit this confession to other senior members of our Sangha, to be judged as my predecessor Parashara was. Nor do I have the courage to accept such punishment."

Lomaharshana replied, "Sir, you are Head of our Sangha. I am merely a fledgling, a child. I ask you once again: Is it appropriate that you confess this to me?"

Shukla said, "My confession must remain secret for my punishment would be as rigorous as Guru Parashara's. I cannot risk it. After the war, perhaps…"

19
SHUKLA'S PLOT

Lomaharshana said, "Sir, let us return to the narrative and leave the confession for last. My task as Archivist takes precedence. You can rest now and continue later if you wish."

Shukla shook his head. He could feel anger building within him at his younger self. *How arrogant, how thoughtless he had been.* Another thought struck him. *If I stop now, I will not have the resolution to complete this part of the story.* There was no alternative. Shukla said, "Lomaharshana, you are right, we should continue with the narration of events. No, I do not need to rest.

I said to my father, 'Demand that your daughter be crowned Matriarch of Hastinapura, with her husband as King. A husband as King is unorthodox for a Panchnad city, but then Hastinapura is not a Panchnad city; there only the King rules. It would be equally unorthodox for Hastinapura to have a Matriarch. Demand that this new practice continue for future generations as well. The Matriarch's eldest daughter will be the next Matriarch, and her daughter's husband will be King. If the Matriarch is unmarried, a Regent, chosen from among the qualified nobles, will perform the King's rituals and duties. Also demand that the laws regarding the number of children one can have, will not apply to Satyavati; her children cannot be killed by the Sangha.'

Satyavati said, 'What are you talking about, Shukla? I do not want children by the King.'

I was ready for that. 'Satya, the King's own law prevents him from having any more sons. It was why his first Queen committed suicide. This way, he will not have to break his own law. His daughter will inherit. However, Devavrata is a danger to this plan; he cannot exile or kill Devavrata. That would lead to civil war because the Crown Prince is popular with the people. What we propose puts pressure on the King to go against the son he loves. Hence the King will have to give you up. Later, after the dust has settled, and he comes to his senses, for you are so much younger than him, his son can marry you.'

'The King could just kill us and take her,' said my father.

'Make the demand in public. Tell him how an astrologer foretold her descendants would be monarchs.'

'You think he will believe that nonsense?' said Satyavati. 'And how does it allow me to marry Devavrata?'

I had come up with the idea on the instant; I could see no flaws in it. I knew how it would work; I knew why it would work. I said, 'The King will give up the idea of marrying you. In a few years, Devavrata will ask to marry you and it will be seen as fulfilment of the sage's prediction. The King will have forgotten his instant infatuation. He will realize how much more suitable you are as a daughter-in-law.'

My father said, 'I do not like this. What will Guru Parashara say?'

'He is observing a vow of silence and I am the only student who understands his signals. I will provide his advice.' But my father's fear of retribution was far greater than his worry about making up a story regarding a prophecy.

Lomaharshana said: "Sir, were you not afraid of Guru Parashara exposing you?"

Shukla replied, "I do not know where I got the gall or deviousness. This is the first I have spoken of it."

For a few vighatis both men were silent. Shukla's shoulders slumped and his eyes were downcast. His hands began to tremble. He brought them together and interlaced the fingers. He glanced briefly at Lomaharshana's face, but it looked blank, almost as if he were practicing the *nishkamkarnarpana* discipline. He could not guess what Lomaharshana was thinking. *Does he not judge me?* Shukla wondered.

In fact, Lomaharshana's mind was whirling. *How am I going to keep this a secret? Why is the Vyaasa confessing at this time? Why to me? I cannot forgive him; that is for his Guru to do.* He fought to keep his emotions from showing on his face; the effort to do so made him involuntarily enter the *nishkamkarnarpana* trance state.

Shukla continued. "We waited half a day for a reply from Shantanu. My father did not attend to his routine tasks. The fish line was not pulled up nor the fish harvested. He did not go to the men's hut where he was expected. Satyavati also hung around doing nothing, her eyes listless, her face thin and drawn. Nobody ate. I asked my father what had happened earlier, and that is how I learned the details.

Shantanu's messenger returned eight ghatis later. I went out and offered him some food, but he said, 'I am in a hurry. King Shantanu awaits a reply.'

I replied on my father's behalf: 'My father says: To my brother and great King, Shantanu, greetings. Be assured of my deepest respect and regard. Your offer does my daughter great honor. It does me and my family great honor. We are greatly indebted to you. That my daughter Satyavati came to your attention is surely a sign of a great and good future. However, she is concerned, as am I, about the abyss that lies between our customs and yours. We are different people, who live different lives. Far be it from me to judge what is best for your people, your family, or for yourself, O King. My daughter was born to be a great queen, so said Guru Parashara when he first beheld her. Among the Meenas, she could become a great Matriarch of an influential band. But what would she be among your people? There is no Matriarch in Hastinapura. She will just be another of your wives. Will that fulfil her destiny to be a great Queen? The fortune-tellers have said that from her womb will be born a dynasty of great rulers. How can that come about when, according to Hastinapuri custom, your older children will take precedence over hers? Your son, Prince Devavrata, is the *Yuvaraja*, next in line to be King. Your laws limit every family to one boy and one girl. You already have a son. Hence any sons born to Satyavati will be surrendered and killed. Only one daughter will be allowed to live. If she bears no daughter but is not permitted to have sons, she cannot establish a dynasty with you. She cannot accept marriage under these conditions.

As Satyavati's father, I do not intend to bar the fulfilment of your mutual desire, so these are my conditions: Satyavati will be your only wife and Matriarch of Hastinapura. All of Satyavati's children must be allowed to live. Her eldest daughter, if she has one, and only her daughter, will be next Matriarch of

Hastinapura. The matriarchy shall continue through her line. If Satyavati bears only sons, one of them, or one their progeny, will be crowned King of Hastinapura. Neither Devavrata, nor any of his descendants, nor any of your progeny not descended from Satyavati, can be King. Satyavati's dynasty cannot die with her. Her promised future must come to be. These are all my conditions for the marriage.'

Shantanu's messenger took this response back to his master."

20
The Chief Minister Reconstructs a Memory

"'This is preposterous! I cannot disinherit my own son!' 'Shantanu's response was immediate. His smile of anticipation turned into a grimace and his face darkened. He walked away.' That is how his Chief Minister, Sashidhara, described Shantanu's reaction to the message. I heard the story from him when I paid him a visit after his retirement," Shukla said. "Sashidhara retired when he became ill with a disease that robbed him of his energy. The *bisajs* had given up on him and Sashidhara was getting bored in retirement, so he was glad I had come. He piqued my interest by saying, 'Everyone gave in to Shantanu's demands. I did too. He charmed us all. I helped him exploit Devavrata's generosity.'

'What do you mean?' I asked.

His eyes lit up. 'It's a long story and I tire easily. I do not know if I can tell it in one sitting.'

I love stories; I always have, so I offered him an inducement. 'If you will tell me the story, I will visit every week.' My duties at the Kavi Sangha were not onerous then. My position as brother of the Queen meant that my movements were not questioned or subject to review. So I paid many visits to the Chief Minister, which enabled me to reconstruct the events that took place after Shantanu received the message from my father.

Sashidhara was an extraordinary story-teller and actor. It was a curious act of fortune that the Chief Minister of Hastinapura came from the Performer's Guild. It went back to Hastin's time, when Nagapura was founded as a caravan site. Caravans go on trips lasting months. Even though every day requires work, the tedium can also be extreme. So all caravans carried one or more performers to provide entertainment. Sometimes a performer even became a close friend of the Head Trader. The Performer's Guild had always been one of Hastinapura's core guilds.

Shantanu had not been trained to be King. He had two older brothers, Devapi and Bahlika. Even if one died, the other would succeed. But destiny had other plans. So when Shantanu became King, he was not ready for the role. He rejected the names suggested as Chief Minister. They were much older than him, close to his brothers, and he felt patronized. But Sashidhara was a friend and he trusted the performer's ability to read people. He insisted Sashidhara attend all meetings and events, alongside him. His friend's presence increased his confidence. Later, Shantanu insisted that Sashidhara be his Chief Minister. Initially, the decision was not a happy one as Sashidhara lacked the essential knowledge of statecraft. But Pratipa's old minister decided it was best to accommodate the King and took charge of Sashidhara's training. It was he who turned him from an actor into a Chief Minister.

Sashidhara was present when Devavrata renounced his inheritance. Despite the passage of time and his illness, he never forgot the events leading to the renunciation. He recalled those long gone events with exceptional clarity, and portrayed with his *abhinaya* skills, the participants' feelings through their posture, behavior, actions, and words. Sashidhara was a gifted actor. He performed for me Shantanu's reaction when he heard the messenger. Then, as he narrated other events, he performed other parts. It was a *tour de force* performance of the *naatya* craft. I felt I was an invisible spectator, watching a play. What I tell you now is Sashidhara's version of events, that he narrated to me.

When the messenger arrived, Shantanu smiled broadly, his eagerness there for all to see. The messenger paused, asking to be forgiven for the message he brought. This prologue was unexpected and Shantanu's smile became strained and his face darkened. When the messenger had finished delivering the message, Shantanu's hands were shaking. His face was grim when he said to Sashidhara, 'This is preposterous! I cannot disinherit my own son! Nor can I change the law to suit me, for I would rightly be condemned as a hypocrite. Send an answer to the Naga-Meena Chief that his message has hurt me.' Having said that, the King walked out of the Council Chamber and entered his own quarters in the mansion. He did not emerge for days.

With the King absent, the Council did not meet. He sent a message to say he was unwell and did not wish to leave his quarters. But Sashidhara did not send the fisher Chief Shantanu's reply. Instead, a few days later, he went to the King's private chambers and said, 'Sire, do not make yourself ill. These requests from Satyavati's father can be addressed without changing anything.'

'You are doing it again,' said the King, 'trying to cheer me up by being optimistic. Well, stop it…' He paused as the meaning of Sashidhara's words registered in his brain. Looking at his Chief Minister and friend, he asked with a sigh, 'How?'

'My Lord,' said Sashidhara, 'I do not offer foolish optimism. All of Satyavati's father's requests can be accommodated, at least for the immediate future. First, you will announce that people can transfer their right to have a child to another person who cannot. Some such transactions have already been reported. We would merely be formalizing what the people already do. I will then arrange for a number of volunteers, both men and women, who are willing to give up their child rights to you.'

Shantanu looked at Sashidhara, uncertainty reflected in his eyes.' Surely that is not enough. What of my son, Devavrata? What of his right to inherit the throne of Hastinapura?'

'Sire, it is your prerogative to name your heir; it is not Devavrata's by right. You can promise Satyavati that Devavrata's rights will be subordinate to those of her son.'

'That does not change the truth; that I will take from Devavrata his birthright.'

'Yes, but the path is strewn with conditions. Satyavati must first give birth to a son, maybe sons, who must then grow up to be crowned. For that matter, Prince Devavrata must survive you. The issue may never need to be settled.'

'I will not lie,' stated the King.

'There is no need for subterfuge. I will talk to the Prince.'

So Sashidhara approached Devavrata with a request, saying, 'Yuvaraja, the King, your father, has a request to make.'

'My father's wishes are paramount, Chief Minister. He has only to ask,' said Devavrata.

'King Shantanu wishes you to relinquish your title of Yuvaraja.'

Devavrata gazed at Sashidhara in amazement. 'Relinquish my title as *heir apparent*? Have I done something? Or not done something? I fail to understand. Is this a punishment? If so, why request? The King has the right to withdraw the title at any time. It is thus not a request but a command and I will comply. But tell me if you can…why?'

Sashidhara said, 'The King wishes to marry again. But the lady has demanded that *her* son be the next King; that her descendants alone will ever rule Hastinapura.'

Lomaharshana was jolted from his trance; he could not understand the proposal and said, "Sir, a moment...I am confused. Satyavati had not made those demands."

Shukla nodded. "Good, good…you get the point. Sashidhara understood the patrilineal mode of inheritance and re-interpreted Satyavati's request, *my request,* in those terms. In his mind, the rule regarding who became the Chief (or King as the Hastinapuris called him) was more important than that about who became the Matriarch. Any Naga would have focused on the matrilineal descent requirements.

I had stipulated that Satyavati's daughter would be Matriarch and therefore, her son would be the next King. Sashidhara and the patrilineal Hastinapuris, focused on the second part of the demand, that Satyavati's son must be King, and ignored the first part. They also ignored the stricture that if my sister had sons but no daughters, her son's daughter would be the next Matriarch, and that daughter's brother would be the next Chief. The sons' rights would always be subordinate to the daughters'. If Satyavati did not have any sons, any son of Shantanu could be the Chief.

Lomaharshana said, "I understand the intent. What happened?"

"I thought I had made it clear," said Shukla. "Unfortunately, I was not understood and there was much confusion. This I had not intended. Some of that confusion has undoubtedly played a part in the disputes of today. Sashidhara thus conveyed the request to Devavrata. A long silence followed. As the vighatis flowed by, Sashidhara wondered if he should have taken a subtler approach. But then Devavrata said, 'This is good news. My father has been lonely and needs a Queen by his side. She will be my mother. My life is hers to command. A title is a little thing; easily given up. Is that all she wants? Is there anything else she requires?'

Sashidhara said, 'That is a true and wise observation, *Yuvaraja*. Yes, that is all she asks. Your father will appreciate your generosity and greatness of heart.'

'Nothing else?' asked Devavrata again.

'Nothing else from you,' replied the Chief Minister.

'Who is she? How long has my father kept his wish a secret?'

'He has not known her long. He has asked that his desire to remarry, as well as the lady's identity, remain a secret for now.'

'If that is his wish, I will certainly obey.'

As Shukla paused, taking a sip of water, Lomaharshana said, "Sir, may I venture an opinion?"

The Vyaasa smiled. "That is not expected of an Archivist. The best archives contain facts, not opinions."

"Sir, it is a Kavi Sangha principle that one person's fact is another's opinion."

"Tell me," said the Vyaasa, "what opinion would you venture?"

"The events you have described have a complex tangle of emotions. How can I convert them into a coherent tale?"

The Vyaasa stared at Lomaharshana. Neither spoke. As the silence lengthened, the fear that he had overstepped his boundaries overpowered Lomaharshana and he began to shiver.

Suddenly the Vyaasa laughed. "Lomaharshana, courage is another attribute of a good Archivist, for falsehood must be confronted. You have done well. I agree that the Chief Minister's story is difficult to understand. Simplify it if you can."

Lomaharshana nodded in silence, so the Vyaasa continued.

"Now, let us return to Sashidhara's narration. My age makes me lose the thread. What was I saying?"

"Sashidhara had just informed Prince Devavrata that his stepmother-to-be wished for her sons to inherit the throne, and the Prince agreed, with barely a moment's thought."

"Ah, yes. The next day Prince Devavrata heard a proclamation in the center of Hastinapura. I asked Sashidhara how he knew Devavrata had heard the proclamation. Sashidhara's eyebrows went up and he stopped talking. It was a silly question. His spies reported the Prince's movements, as well as those of the other members of the ruling family.

Devavrata was in a class at the Kavi Sangha when the announcement was made. The class was conducted under a banyan tree in a small garden off the central square of Hastinapura, and the town crier's voice could be heard in the class loud and clear. One of Sashidhara's spies following Devavrata reported that, at first, Devavrata turned towards the source of the cry and there was a smile on his face.

The crier continued: 'The King has decided to heed the call of his people. A market in which men and women can buy and sell their right to have a child will be established. His son, Prince Devavrata will be the arbiter. The Prince will deal with all questions. He will be personally responsible to the King for his decision on every purchase.'

The spy did not expect what followed. The spies had not been given any specific directions other than to note the Prince's activities, but they were expected to keep the Prince from coming to harm. This time, the Prince's behavior was inexplicable. As the announcement ended and its meaning sank in, the Prince jumped up and shouted, 'No!' It was apparent that the announcement was a surprise for the Prince. The other students and the teacher had turned to him, but he was oblivious to their stares. He looked around as though he was lost, as if he wanted to run away. When he began to walk away, the other students parted to clear a path for him. He sat down hunkered against a tree, his knees drawn against his chest and his head bowed down. Everybody was silent.

Later, the Chief Minister met the teacher and the students to persuade them to remain silent about the Prince's reaction. The teacher, a kavi who had a fondness for simile and metaphor, described the Prince as a man who had walked off a cliff and was desperately flailing his arms and legs seeking support. The teacher and students cooperated, and news of the episode never spread.

Back in the class, ten vighatis passed. Devavrata's head came up. His eyes were dull and seemed to be focused far away. He stood up and without looking at anybody or even acknowledging the teacher, he walked out of the class. The spy followed him. Devavrata went to the council chamber where his father was in a meeting with the Chief Minister. He said, 'Father! Chief Minister! I just heard your town crier announcing the new market for buying child rights. What is this? When did you decide this? When did you decide to name me as the arbiter?'

Sashidhara said, '*Yuvaraja*! Were you not informed? This plan was discussed at an emergency meeting this morning. Your servants told us that you were away by the river.'

Devavrata's eyes were cold and distant as he turned and stared at the Chief Minister, as though his presence was an unfortunate accident. Devavrata said, 'Please do not explain why you did not tell me. I know why you did not tell me. I want to know why you are creating a market for these rights at this time.'

The Chief Minister said, 'Yuvaraja, you know yourself that the law we have created is a harsh law. We need it because of the crisis. The Kavi Sangha expected that the law would discourage the refugees from coming to Hastinapura. We hoped that those who did, would go on to the newer settlements further south along the Ganga where the law would not apply. Within Hastinapura, the law has fallen most heavily on people who are poor and do not have the resources to adjust to the crisis. This has been a source of unrest.'

'We have known this for a long time,' said Devavrata. 'What is the difference now?'

Sashidhara continued, 'In celebration of the King's wedding, we thought that we could soften the law. Every year, some people try to circumvent the law and the result is unhappiness. We could address that problem, for every year a number of childless persons die, forfeiting their right to a child. They could transfer their rights. Some of these people die of illnesses that require special care or for which the only cure is in a foreign land, Takshashila, for instance. If they had some property or other wherewithal, they could arrange with a merchant or trader to take them there in exchange for this right. Their right to have a child is the only valuable property they possess.'

The Prince was not mollified. He said, 'Your spy service needs to be re-trained, if they cannot track all the pregnant women in Hastinapura at any one time.'

'I will certainly deal with that deficiency, Yuvaraja. Your advice is most welcome. Meanwhile, some residents of Hastinapura desire another child. We asked the Kavi Sangha whether it was wise to let such people buy the child-right of another. Initially, the Kavi Sangha opposed such changes. Softening the law would gut it, they felt. During the morning's discussion that you missed, Yuvaraja, the question that came up repeatedly was the seller's reasons for selling the child-right. The Kavi Sangha representative suggested the reasons we came up with. For my part, it felt less than legitimate. One sold one's child-right at the risk of injuring one's ancestors, whose spirits rely for sustenance on the food we eat. The ancestor with no descendant is doomed to starve in the world of ancestral spirits. However, I did not wish to oppose the Vyaasa's counsel.

The Kavi Sangha added one minor condition. They wanted Shantanu to encourage the seller to migrate to one of the frontier settlements where the right to children would be restored. This would encourage younger, more flexible men and women to be pioneers while the older immigrants tried to make their living in the city.'

Devavrata said, 'Kavi Sangha proposals have never been adopted hastily. How was this proposal approved in one short meeting? Was the Vyaasa consulted?'

The Chief Minister said, 'Yuvaraja, you know that Guru Parashara has taken a vow of silence. He does not speak. It had to be this way.'"

The Vyaasa Shukla said to Lomaharshana, "The Chief Minister would recall his slip of the tongue vividly in later years. The only decisions that were described as 'it had to be this way' were ones that the King had already made, ones for which the council approval was *pro forma*. As the head of the Kuru family became increasingly regal, his expressed wishes had become commandments. What followed was a direct consequence."

Shukla continued, "'The Chief Minister reported this as one of the most dramatic confrontations he had seen between Devavrata and his father. Devavrata turned to his father, 'Why now?'

Shantanu could not meet his son's gaze. He looked away, then down. His hands shook and a slight flush crept up his face. 'It had to be now.'

Devavrata said, 'Your new wife wants children and does not want to be bound by your laws!'

The King's voice was a whisper. 'Yes.'

'You have already asked me to give up my right to the crown. Why did you not ask me to give up my right to a son so that you and the Queen can have a boy as well as a girl child?'

Shantanu's eyes scrutinized a spot on the ground. He said, 'Err... I am sure we would not want that...'

The Chief Minister said, 'We know, *Yuvaraja*, how devoted you are to your father. I advised the King to be cautious. There are so many problems. The new Queen may be barren. She may only have daughters. Who but you could be King?'

Devavrata looked at his father and then at the Chief Minister. As the implications of the Chief Minister's statements dawned on him, his face changed. Anger had turned it red; shock drained it of color. His eyes had sparkled with rage but now became hooded and dull. His full cheeks lost their tone and turned grey like unpolished granite."

Vyaasa Shukla said, "Recalling how Devavrata changed color, the old Chief Minister's voice shook and became a whisper. I had to lean very close to hear him.

The Chief Minister told me, 'That was one of the times that I watched the Prince closely, and I felt I was looking into a soul in pain. He resembled his father in so many ways, except this one – the King never seemed to have suffered any kind of deep hurt. The manner in which Devavrata conducted himself was also revealing. He was a young man with a well-toned physique and was impressive when he held himself straight. His father had looked like that when he was twenty. Devavrata's neck turned pink and if his *angavastram* had not covered his upper body, we would have seen it spreading down his chest. I watched as his face regained its color. His fingers were shaking. If he was anything like his father, he was going to explode with anger. I signed to the guard, for prince or no prince, he could not be allowed to injure the King. Devavrata finally spoke, in a low bass voice from lips curled in bitterness, with the nose flaring with every word.' I was struck at the vividness of the old man's memory and applied all my skills to memorize his exact words. He continued with his narrative:

"Then the Prince said, 'Is this how you begin your new marriage – with a lie and a promise? You tell her that her children will be King, that she can have as many as she pleases. My mother died for your plans. My brothers were killed as babies. Now you want me to arrange the buying and selling of child-rights for your new love?'

The King looked up briefly and was about to say something. Sashidhara thought it would not be wise, no matter what the King said. So he made downward motions with his palm, signaling the need for patience. Fortunately, he said, the King saw the gesture and remained quiet, not saying whatever he had intended to say. He let his eyes drift back to the ground.

Devavrata did not stop his rant and the words poured out. 'You did not want to ask me to offer the logical sacrifice now. If there are no sons, there would be no need to deliver on the promise you would have demanded of me. You even created a new role for me – chief broker for buying and selling children.'

Sashidhara tried to intervene – he said, '*Yuvaraja*…'

Devavrata turned to him, his face livid, 'Don't call me *Yuvaraja!* I am done with that title. You chose this… this is your solution.'

That was the last time the Chief Minister called him by that title. He said, 'You make it sound complicated.'

Shantanu's face sagged and looked grey. He said, 'Son, please do not be angry. I want her to be my Queen. I think of her constantly, and I am unable to do anything else until I have her.'

Devavrata's voice did not change. 'Take me to this paragon. I will renounce my rights to the crown before her.'"

21
Renouncing The Crown

Shukla continued with Sashidhara's story. 'I will renounce my right to the crown in the presence of the future Queen,' Devavrata said in a flat voice that carried no emotion. Nevertheless, it froze the King and Chief Minister, who stood unmoving, like blocks of ice cut from the eternal white heights of the Himalayas. Sashidhara wanted to suggest a quiet meeting in a private location, but Devavrata forestalled him, saying to the guard at the door, 'Call Bakakula!' He did not wish to wait.

Later, Sashidhara often wondered what would have happened if he had succeeded in preventing the ensuing drama. The world might have been a different place today. He heard the King say, 'Stop! Don't do this!', but the words came out as a gruff mumble. Sashidhara hesitated, but when the cart came, they followed Devavrata into it silently.

Devavrata said, 'Please direct Bakakula where to go.'

The Chief Minister looked at the King, but received no help. Shantanu seemed to have been struck dumb, bewitched. So the Chief Minister said to Bakakula, 'Take us to the fishing village. You know the house.' Bakakula nodded and they set off. No one spoke.

As they rode past the village, I saw them. The awkward way they sat in the cart struck me. Though I did not know what to make of it, I knew their presence concerned my sister, so I followed right behind, to my father's house. Sashidhara looked at me but I was just another Naga boy then; he did not even recall it later. Devavrata had sat unmoving, seemingly oblivious to everything around him. When the cart stopped, his forehead furrowed. I heard him ask the driver, 'What are we doing here?' Bakakula replied, 'This is the lady's house, Sir.' Devavrata shook his head in denial and disbelief, making no move to get down.

My father must have heard them for he came out of the house. I could see he was nervous. He rushed down the steps and stood before the cart, unsure what to expect. He saw me and waved, indicating I should go away. But I did not obey. He was not smiling; his mouth grim, instead of welcoming. In all my young life I had not seen him act as strangely as he did that day. The Chief Minister whispered something to the King, but Shantanu's countenance did not change, showing no sign he had heard or understood. Later, the Chief Minister told me his words had been: *Be careful; he looks like a frightened man and in his fear he may go berserk. We should act to reassure him.*

I think the Chief Minister's reading of my father was wrong. My father frowned at me. He did not wish me to be present. I did not move. He waved his hands in the *reversed pataka* sign, used to warn people of a deadly predator, such as a tiger. I did not leave. He frowned but was compelled to attend to his august visitors. Later, he told me he had been concerned that the King might attempt to kidnap Satyavati, killing anyone who tried to stop him. He was worried I would act in defence of my sister.

My father said, 'Welcome, Sirs. We are overjoyed at your visit to this humble house. We cannot offer you much, but please accept our hospitality.'

The King and the Prince were silent, gazing into the distance. So the Chief Minister said, 'The King and his son wish to see your daughter, Satyavati.' Devavrata turned sharply at the name. A glow returned to his eyes even as his brow furrowed.

'My daughter is within and will be delighted to see you. Pray come in.'

The King and Chief Minister climbed out of the cart. Devavrata remained motionless for a vighati before dismounting. They all went into the cottage. I followed despite another frown from my father. The baby was in a hammock hanging from the ceiling, near the door. Satyavati sat rocking the baby. Clean banana leaves had been laid in front of seating pads, ready for the mid-day meal. When the visitors entered, Satyavati rose quickly with palms joined, 'We are honored you have come to our simple house. Please sit here,' she said, pointing to a low seat.

The Chief Minister replied, 'Namaskar, Satyavati. The King wishes to speak to you.'

Satyavati's eyes went wide but she smiled, perfectly composed. I knew her mind was in turmoil. How she appeared so calm I do not know. I saw the lines of anger on Devavrata's face disappear as he drank in her soft brown eyes and a reflected smile began to form in his eyes, on his lips. I think that was when the significance of the Chief Minister's words hit him, for the smile suddenly vanished. The strangeness of the situation, his father's presence, the exchanges with the Chief Minister, all conspired to drag that smile away. His eyes became thin slits, his forehead wrinkled. I could see his throat muscles move as he swallowed.

Satyavati had been looking at him, but she now turned to the Chief Minister and said, 'Speak to me?'

Shantanu seemed to be having second thoughts. When he spoke, he asked her father a strange question. 'Is it true that an astrologer predicted a bright future for your descendants?' Sashidhara and Devavrata's faces were studies in puzzlement, their brows furrowed, eyes moving from person to person.

Satyavati said, 'I do not know, Sir, that is what some people say.'

Her father said, 'Sir, forgive a foolish man's credulity. I should have known better than to tell others of the astrologer's ravings.'

'No matter,' said the King. The exchange had given him time to compose himself. Now he spoke plainly. 'You have demanded that I marry only one wife, namely yourself. This I assent to. You have also said you will marry me only if the law of one-person-one-child does not apply to your children, and also that your son become King on my demise. Both these are difficult demands. Tell me, are these your wishes?'

Devavrata was standing aloof from his father. His head snapped up at his father's words. His eyes held a faraway look and he swayed slightly. He must have felt the ground disappearing from beneath his feet. I had not anticipated this conversation. I did not know where it would lead. My sister was on her own, she would have to navigate her own path.

Satyavati said, 'Yes, Sir. Those are my conditions.'

Don't say that, I wanted to whisper, but 'No' led into a fog of uncertainty as well.

Shantanu replied, 'Your demands have created a storm in my family.'

Satyavati glanced at Devavrata before looking away. When Sashidhara narrated this to me all those years later, I told him what had transpired between Devavrata and my sister. It was the first he had heard of their mutual infatuation. He said he believed she had been waiting for Devavrata to say something. As for me, I was too inexperienced then; I do not know that I could have done anything to help her. Neither Devavrata nor Satyavati said anything. I regret now that they did not – if only they had…if only they had… I regret I did not do something, anything, to stop what happened. My father had spent the whole day worrying about what to do and say. But faced with the King, he remained silent."

Shukla stopped. Turning his face away from Lomaharshana, he stared into the far corner of the tent. The wrinkles on his forehead deepened and his eyes retreated into the shadow of his brow. Lomaharshana waited. *There is no hurry,* he thought. *This story has been simmering for a long time, and we can wait a little longer.*

Shukla turned his head and stared at the Archivist. *I hope he survives this test of faith. The war between the Pandavas and Kauravas has done much damage to the Kavi Sangha. Now I have laid out my contribution, my corruption, my regrets… But there is more.*

Lomaharshana said, "Are you feeling ill, Sir? We can continue some other time."

Shukla replied, "Thank you for your patience. I have much to atone for and would much rather finish the story now."

"As you wish, Sir. I am ready if you wish to continue."

Shukla said, "After that exchange between the King and my sister, everyone was quiet. The King, Devavrata, Satyavati, my father, and Sashidhara, all stood like statues carved from stone. Nobody paid any attention to me. The silence went on and on. Satyavati did not look at Devavrata. I glanced at him; his head must have been spinning.

The ensuing vighatis felt like an eternity before Satyavati said, 'My conditions are just and honorable. My children would not be killed if I married a Naga. Why should they be subjected to your arbitrary culling? As a mother, I would want my children to prosper; not be subject to Hastinapuri laws. My descendants must be free to rule. It would be dishonorable to place conditions after we are married, I make them clear now.'

Silence followed. Then Shantanu spoke. Nobody looked at Shantanu, but everybody heard him.

'I accept your conditions.' Pointing to Devavrata, he said, 'This is my only son, Devavrata.'

Satyavati's head snapped around to look at Devavrata, who stood with his gaze rooted on the ground, no doubt wishing it would open and swallow him whole.

Shantanu continued, 'He has been my heir since he came of age, expected to rule after me. But he has renounced this inheritance, on the condition that he do so before you, and hear your wishes directly from you.'

My memory of that moment is of unmoving statues, but Sashidhara's version was more dramatic, especially after he learned of Devavrata's nascent feelings for Satyavati. The walls imprisoning Devavrata could have collapsed at the King's words! But Devavrata did nothing to breach them. He raised his head to look at Satyavati, but could not meet her eyes. I think he lost hope, unable to imagine that she preferred him to his father, and that held him back from speaking. He hung his head, his eyes dull like those of a prisoner. Devavrata must have seen only boundaries and restrictions wherever he looked.

But then, breaking all the rules Sashidhara believed governed social behavior, Devavrata raised his head and stared directly at Satyavati. Satyavati flushed at the implied challenge. Anger flared within her at the position she had been placed in. I looked at my father, waiting for him to say something. The King's words seemed to have flown past him, never touching him. Silence held him in thrall.

Satyavati said, her rage barely contained, 'I am touched by your son's desire to satisfy his father at the cost of his own interests. The Prince is welcome to visit me and to ask me anything.' My father looked at Satyavati, his face colorless, his eyes those of a mouse transfixed by a swaying cobra.

Shantanu glanced at his son, trying to understand what was in his mind. Devavrata continued to stare at Satyavati, as if trying to read her innermost thoughts. Satyavati looked away, her eyes dull and blank. Sashidhara enacted all this for me during his narration, showing a man who felt betrayed to the core, and a woman who had lost faith that her life could be salvaged, that anyone could stop a runaway cart. They were all silent. The silence stretched for one vighati, then another, then a third. Finally, the Chief Minister coughed.

Devavrata stirred. Looking out of the door into the distance, he said, 'My father has decided I will manage a market in which people can buy and sell their child rights. He expects to be able to buy as many child rights for you as you desire. I am no longer his heir but Supervisor of this barter of children.'

Shocked, Satyavati said, 'That is not what I asked for.'

Devavrata went on. 'But I will not be party to such trades. My father desires you, and you wish for your children to rule. Your demands…your wishes…shall be met. I hereby renounce my rights to have children, and give them to my father.'

Shantanu said, 'Devavrata, what are you saying?'

Devavrata bowed deeply to his father, palms joined, 'Father, our ancestor Yayati demanded a year of youth from his son, Puru. With the help of the gods that was possible. As it was for Yayati, so it will be for you. Your desires too, must be satisfied. To you I yield my birthright. And you, Satyavati, wish to be the mother of Kings. My mother made me promise I would take care of my father. I see no way to stop this lunacy without violating that promise and thereby causing pain to you and my father. You do not need to create a market to trade child rights. I vow I will not marry; I will not have children; I will not know any woman. My King, my father…my right to father a male child is hereby given to you. Welcome, my Queen, to the Kaurava clan.'

Tears rushed unbidden to my sister's eyes. 'But…' she said, and then stopped, for Devavrata had turned away and was walking to the door. Shantanu followed his son, and the Chief Minister followed the King. Satyavati followed them, I close behind.

Shantanu said, 'Son! Why did you do that? You need swear no oath, aah…such a terrible one! Chief Minister, stop him. Bring him back. What a terrible vow!'

The Chief Minister said in a whisper, 'Do not worry, my friend, this storm will pass. You have what you came for.'

The King continued to plead with Devavrata, his voice slowly losing strength and conviction. Finally, Shantanu stopped and turned back to Satyavati and said, 'Satyavati, your demands have been met. I assure you I will ensure your children live. Your son shall be King after me.'

Satyavati stared after Devavrata, walking away towards the hunting trail. Tears choked her throat and she could not speak, only shake her head mutely. The Chief Minister said, 'Great lady, I take your leave. Your father should prepare for the wedding.' With those words he followed the King out. The climactic scene ended as the King and Chief Minister drove away and Devavrata walked off into the forest

My father came back to life once they had left. He said, 'Satyavati, what have you done?'

Satyavati said, 'I am lost, father.'

When I remember those words now my heart fills with sorrow. But that day my reactions were unforgivable."

Lomaharshana said, "So the most dramatic moments in this story are the imaginings of an actor?"

Shukla smiled. "Shush, boy…I was there. Sashidhara's narrative differs only in emphasis. His memory of the conversation matches mine exactly. I have had some training in the Kavi Sangha school, so I am confident I remember it as it happened."

Shukla continued, "I kept quiet till the visitors had disappeared from view, then I ran to my sister and hugged her in delight, saying, 'You did it! You did it!' while she stood stiff as a tree trunk. Even now, after so many years have passed, I can still feel the smile on my face. I said, 'You are to be Queen of Hastinapura! That is the best thing that could have happened.' I looked at my father, who stood silent and dejected. *What's the matter? Why aren't they happy?* I wondered.

Satyavati said, 'I am lost. I will kill myself.'

My father turned to me. 'Shukla, see what your mad plan has done! The King has agreed to all her demands. Now she must marry Shantanu.'

I had watched the Prince when he had approached my sister and now I had witnessed his acceptance of the King's extraordinary demands. *What kind of man gave up so easily? He is a weakling, not one to create an empire. If there is any truth to the fortune teller's predictions, he is not fit to be her husband.* Now when I recall that caustic judgement of youth, and how wrong it was, how ignorant and arrogant, the memory serves to curb groundless enthusiasms.

I said, 'This is the best outcome! The Prince is a young man who does not know his own mind. He loves her now, but that can change with the next beautiful woman he sees. Now she will be Queen, and our band will gain protection from the city.'

'I'll be Queen…the dead Queen.'

Our father said, 'Satyavati! Please do not speak like that.'

'It does not matter,' she sighed. 'I might as well be dead.'

'If you kill yourself, our band and the other Meena bands, will suffer at the hands of the King. You cannot do this.'

'I might as well be dead,' Satyavati said again."

Lomaharshana looked increasingly confused and uncomfortable. The Vyaasa said to him, 'What is the matter, my son?'

Lomaharshana replied, 'Sir, I understand the Queen Mother's reaction. But the King leaving in a cart and the Prince walking off into the forest makes no sense."

The Vyaasa grimaced and said, "Lomaharshana, I am narrating the Chief Minister's memory of an old conversation. I was there, but all I remember are the words, not the feelings. I did not know Devavrata in those days, and even though we became friends later, there were certain subjects we never spoke of. I do not think he thought I knew of his loss. Nor did I know then why and how his mother died; what he had felt. He should have hated his father, but he did not. He was in his late teens, I a few years younger. When we were together, we were occupied with other things; I was not privy to his innermost thoughts."

22
Satyavati's Decision

"'I might as well be dead.' Satyavati's pronouncement resounded like a gong of lead," Vyaasa Shukla said, continuing his narration of Satyavati's desperate response to the sudden turn of events. "My sister thus announced her indifference to life. My father and I were familiar with Satyavati's passionate proclamations, but there had never been anything as unusual as this situation or an announcement as extreme as this one. *I might as well be dead.*

I recall thinking, 'Yes, the situation has got out of hand, but she is going to be the Queen! Why did it matter who she married?' I look back at the young Shukla and am appalled at my insensitivity and selfishness. Was that really me? Are all children like that at that age? I could not imagine why my sister would wish herself dead over a marriage. After all, there had been no drama when, at the age of fifteen, she had welcomed Parashara to her bed. He had been handsome, clever, fit and devoted to her. I had been barely ten years old and paid little attention to most of the social interactions around me, romantic or otherwise. Unfortunately, he was even more devoted to the Kavi Sangha. When he asked to keep Krishna Dvaipaayana's parentage a secret, Satyavati had gone along and told us to honor the request. There had been no drama, no morbid resignation. She finally told him he was not welcome in our house any more, but it had been a calm and reasoned decision.

However, Parashara's request showed how different we Nagas were from the Hastinapuris. Parashara believed Krishna Dvaipaayana was his son, but told Satyavati he had to stop visiting her as he was going to be the Vyaasa. She was unhappy but accepted his decision. The Nagas allowed both men and women the right to make such decisions. When he returned as Leader of the Kavi Sangha, punished with a vow of silence, she found he was no longer the man she wanted but a stranger and she did not receive him again.

After her startling statement, my father and I were worried what she might do and tiptoed around her, keeping watch. Fortunately my sister did not commit suicide. She did not even make the attempt."

23
Parashara's Blessing

Shukla said, "There is an additional vignette to narrate. Following Kaurava practice, Shantanu visited Parashara, the Head of the Kavi Sangha, to obtain his blessings for the marriage. My father stayed away, saying that he was not well. My sister pleaded the malady of women. So I went as the only person who could interpret the Vyaasa's mute signs. Sashidhara did not know of the expedition. I suspect he would not have been as easily deceived as the King.

Shantanu was unaware that the baby in our house was Satyavati's son by Parashara. Children in Naga bands had many caretakers, and he had assumed that baby Krishna was just some child in the band. He did not know that Parashara had once been my sister's lover.

Annals of the Kavi Sangha Appendix A.11: Satyavati's Ambition

The Annals of the Kavi Sangha do not provide answers to questions regarding Satyavati's real ambitions. What did she want and how did she try to get it? Despite her brother Shukla's rise to the role of Vyaasa, it is generally believed that he was too close to her to be objective.

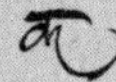

Shantanu told Parashara of the proposed marriage and asked for the Kavi Sangha's blessing. I could see inner conflict in Parashara's eyes, but he controlled his feelings and gave his blessing. If only Shantanu had stopped there, I would not have this guilt hanging over me. But he saw fit to ask about the prediction that Satyavati would be the mother of great kings ruling an empire. Over the years, despite my father's feeble attempts to correct it, the prediction by a wandering traveller had become ascribed to Parashara, just before he stopped speaking. So Shantanu asked him about the prediction.

Parashara signed that he knew nothing of such a prediction. I kept my voice low as I translated for the King that the prediction was real. Parashara had taken a vow of silence, but his hearing was acute. He signed now, demanding that I tell the truth. I translated these new signs, constructing a revised version of the prediction. Parashara became increasingly disturbed and tried once more. I continued my dissimulation.

Lomaharshana, you may wonder at my younger self's actions. I was playing a dangerous game, one that hung by gossamer threads. I prayed Parashara would not break his oath; I had seen him accept in silence my sister's decision to exile him. I also relied on Shantanu's infatuation with my sister. The King would be angry if my duplicity was exposed, but he would stay his hand for my sister's sake. Parashara hesitated, then stopped signing. To my relief, he did nothing. He sat still for a few vighatis, signed again, and then left abruptly.

'What did he say?' asked the King.

I had to say something. 'He warned me to stay close to my sister for she will need my protection as well as yours.'

In this manner I assured myself a permanent place in the entourage of the ruling family."

24
Devavrata's Life

Shukla said, "Devavrata disappeared. First he secluded himself, and then one day, before the wedding, he left Hastinapura and walked to the site of the first settlement he had created – Varanavata – named after his ancestor, Samvarana. He did not attend the royal wedding. Shantanu took this to mean that his son was not reconciled to the loss of his status as heir apparent. The rumor mills of the city churned with the news of an imminent rebellion. It came as a surprise to most people when Devavrata returned to Hastinapura a few months later. Only three people knew the nature of his loss – my father, Satyavati, and I.

Do not judge Satyavati by the standards of Hastinapura. The Kauravas had already started down the path of walling women away from power. Satyavati was, and is, a Naga woman. If she had remained with the Nagas, she would have eventually founded a band as Matriarch. She would have been a powerful mother-ruler, caring and terrifying to her children. She did not know the system she was marrying into when she married Shantanu. For that matter, neither did I. We did not understand how patriarchy worked and how it had changed the Kauravas. When the trader Samvarana returned to Hastinapura as a King leading an army, the core leadership of the kingdom passed to the warriors. Kuru, who came immediately after Samvarana, was a hybrid – a trader and a warrior. But he was still a trader first and a warrior second. That changed. Even though the city was renamed after Hastin, a trader, and the ruling family took Kuru as their dynast, the later generations trained to be warriors first and traders second. This was the society Satyavati entered.

Devavrata's vow became publicly known in a modified form. His mother's suicide was believed to have been a protest against the one-person-one-child law, and she was revered as Goddess Ganga, to whom the culled children had been consigned. Devavrata's renunciation of his birthright on the occasion of his father's marriage gave notice that his mother had not been forgotten and that her pain remained his pain. Some people called him *Gangaputra*[37]. When Shantanu finally repealed the law as a failed enterprise, Devavrata was credited with the change, though it was Satyavati's demands that were instrumental in persuading Shantanu.

I discovered that life in the palace was mostly tedious and only the Kavi Sangha's meeting halls provided a stimulating environment. Devavrata was there too, and I was only a little younger than he was. I think Devavrata welcomed the loss of kingship. In those early meetings at the Kavi Sangha, he questioned the Kavi Sangha's wisdom, which he had not been free to do as Crown Prince. He was still a Prince, but he was not a guild member, which meant he could not be pressured into agreement.

There are two parts to the puzzle of Yuvaraja Devavrata, as he was then known. Only he knows what happened between him and his father in the years following his mother's death.

---

[37] Gangaputra means "Son of Ganga."

He had blamed Shantanu and the Kavi Sangha for that death. The Chief Minister, reminiscing all those years later, said he had taken the young Devavrata under his wing. Being empathetic, he allowed Devavrata great latitude to express his feelings about his mother's death and find his own way to deal with it. He pointed out how dependent his father was on the Kavi Sangha, and how the Kavi Sangha used the King to execute its plans. In the ordinary scheme of things, the Bard's Guild was a useful organization, but it had acquired great power and potential for evil. The Vyaasa was directly responsible for using this power.

The young Devavrata was convinced his father was weak and that a powerful Vyaasa had manipulated him. The Kavi Sangha archives reveal how often this had indeed happened, from Samvarana onwards. Vyaasas do sometimes bite off more than they can chew. Even Vasishtha, Founder of the Sangha, could be said to have overplayed his hand when he established a standing army. Vyaasa Bharadvaja[38], who proposed the one-person-one-child law, was the Vyaasa when his mother Ganga died. He passed away a few years later and Parashara became the next Vyaasa. One of Parashara's first acts as Vyaasa was to express to Devavrata his sorrow for the death of his mother. He also promised to work at changing the law. But before he could do so, he became surrounded by controversy and sentenced to a vow of silence. Parashara's intervention enabled Devavrata to grudgingly accept that his father was not responsible for his mother's death. He recollected the many conversations in which his father had expressed sorrow and contrition over what

[38] I have imagined *Bharadvaja* as a complete rationalist and pragmatist, taking this assessment from Kauṭilya's *Arthashāstra* in which many amoral, if pragmatic and rational, policies are ascribed to a predecessor named Bharadvaja.

had been done. Vyaasa Bharadvaja, inclined to be manipulative, could be blamed for some of these extreme policies. The Chief Minister considered the reconciliation between Devavrata and Shantanu as his greatest achievement.

With Sashidhara in a nostalgic mood, the floodgates of reminiscences opened when I told him of Devavrata's feelings for Satyavati. It explained so much that had puzzled him. In his opinion, Devavrata forgave his father for falling in love with Satyavati; it was human nature. Satyavati was beautiful, his father was weak; a man who gave in easily to his desires. But Devavrata did not extend that forgiveness to Satyavati. Her actions were not a result of a Kavi Sangha plot gone awry, but of a deceitful and dishonest person. She had deceived him. The demands she had made of the King showed her for the ambitious woman she was, determined to be Queen and Matriarch of a dynasty. He suspected even the Chief Minister, who had tricked Devavrata into giving up the throne. The Kaurava family had become rotten at its core. The thought of a market to buy and sell child bearing rights, of being in charge of it, must have made Devavrata feel he was sinking in sewage and putrefying matter. He must have felt relieved to forestall the rot through his vow of celibacy. If Satyavati had suffered because of his vow, she deserved it. Everyone around him was flawed. Only he, Devavrata had held to the truth. He had gladly given up the throne to make his father happy. He would have been happier still if his father was released from the deadly embrace of the Kavi Sangha.

I questioned the Chief Minister closely about this interpretation of events. 'Experience is the mother of all knowledge,' he said. 'I understood Devavrata here,' he said, pointing to his gut. 'He was quick to judge; quick to act; quick to forgive.'

Accurate or not, this assessment of Devavrata did not describe his actions with regard to Satyavati. He judged her in the blink of an eye; the vows made the next instant. There was no forgiveness for my sister and Satyavati became the cup-bearer of all Devavrata's anger – over his mother's death, at the Kavi Sangha's wrongdoings, and my sister's ambitions, as he saw it. I could not tell him of my role in devising the disastrous strategy. Nor could she, for he so clearly lusted for her, perhaps even loved her, but could never have her. I observed him closely in the days following the dramatic vow. If he was angry, he did not show it. He avoided the subject of his new stepmother. He avoided her. If she was in the palace, he would be out of it. If she was in the city, he would go hunting in the forest. The only subject he seemed to care about was the refugee crisis and how it could be managed."

25
Shukla's Life

Shukla said, "I visited my sister often. I was a few years younger than Satyavati and still considered a boy. My time with Parashara had made me eager to live in the city, and I was ready to abandon Naga constraints. I was already studying with the Kavi Sangha. That, and my sister's place in the ruling family of Hastinapura, allowed me to enter the most powerful cliques. I knew I could never be Chief of my own band (my father's sister was the Matriarch, so her daughter would be the next Matriarch and her son, if any, the next Chief). I now regret not completing the adult initiation ceremony to join the fraternity of Naga men. Without it I cannot be considered a true Naga.

Occasionally, if a Naga Matriarch had no brothers, a band would look for a Chief directly related to her, such as male progeny born to her sisters. If the Chief died, his brothers were next in line. If he had no brothers and no acceptable cousins, the band looked for a trusted Chief outside the band, who was not directly related. But this was rare. If Satyavati had founded a Naga band, I would have been her obvious choice for Chief, but when she left for Hastinapura, she expected me to accompany her. I wanted the city life so it was an easy decision.

But I was in constant terror that Parashara would denounce me when he returned at the end of his penal term. I could not tolerate the thought. So one day I went to Parashara and apologized profusely. I do not know what I was looking for, but Parashara's countenance did not change. I cried. I demanded to be punished. I vowed that, like Devavrata, I would give up all pleasures. But Parashara maintained a stony visage. A few months later, Parashara died, still observing his vow of silence. That is when I understood what he had intended to convey – that he had come to the end of his time on earth and he no longer cared about the success or failure of the Sangha.

The court I had so longed to join was a meaningless façade for power games, and I a mere spectator, its inner workings unknown to me. There were daily reports of disorder in the refugee camps, rumors about Panchala. Where, I wondered, was the imagined heart of the kingdom, where powerful individuals congregated in animated discourse over important issues? The most excitement generated was when a caravan arrived with news of the Western world, evoking memories of the stories Parashara had told the children of our band – stories about the grand courts of the Kings of Parsaka and Sumer. These were the stories that had fired my imagination. I now realized that some of the stories had been made up.

One of the more amazing tales was about the Sumerians, who claimed to be inheritors of an ancient world with a single culture and language, which had perished when they constructed a giant brass needle to pierce the veil of heaven.[39] Why would such an advanced people have imported the tiny bronze figurines from Panchnad or the cotton textiles the Yadavas specialized in? Other stories, which mentioned gigantic buildings that rose high and from whose top the

[39] I've imagined what a Panchnadi might make of the story of the Tower of Babel.

Great Father[40] could survey his whole empire and command obedience, underlined the difference between us and the rest of the known world. Nobody in Panchnad would dream of constructing such a thing.

I began spending more and more time with the Kavi Sangha. As a Naga, I was not raised to be a member of any of the Panchnad guilds. I was not required to join one, but I participated in all the lessons of the Bard's Guild. Despite my late start, I did well. So my life became entwined with Devavrata's, for he too, had begun to spend more and more time with the Kavi Sangha. In Devavrata's case, he did so to avoid Satyavati. He stayed away from the areas of the palace she used. By not joining the court, he did not have to see her sitting next to his father. Like me, he found his vocation in the Kavi Sangha.

In the beginning, this made Satyavati unhappy and angry. Matriarchs of Naga bands learn a style of speech, a commanding voice used to control and manage the men of the band, whether they are born into it or received as adults visiting women of the band. The men learn to obey the Matriarch's voice of command. But it did not work that way in Hastinapura. Satyavati expected me to obey her, and I did. It was a habit for both of us, and to this day she commands me to perform trivial chores. 'Bring me that pillow,' she says, and I do it. It is only complex demands that are deliberated over. So she expected others too, would obey her, and they did, but not because of her command voice. They obeyed her husband with greater alacrity.

Satyavati also found that, unlike Naga Matriarchs who worked just like other women, except in a formal role, she had very

[40]*Great Father was* one of the titles of the ruler of *Pitr-vihaara-naadu* (Land of the Temple of the Ancestors, i.e., Egypt), the greatest of the western lands.

little to do as Queen of Hastinapura. When she tried to do something, one maidservant or another would jump up to do it for her. Her role in court was to sit next to Shantanu on formal occasions. He tried to dissuade her from attending private meetings with him. When he finally relented, Satyavati found that Hastinapura was, all said and done, still a trading town and much of the private discussions were about shares in caravans, dangers to be avoided during trips to Laghu Nagapura, the dramatic drop in trade since the refugee crisis began, and other such matters. This was in stark contrast to the life of a Naga Matriarch, who was treated as any other member of the band in daily life, but the ritual Head during twelve festival days in the year. The twelve festivals were the first day of spring, the feast of the mango, the feast of the burnt sacrifice, the ceremony of planting, the blessing of the waters, the day of waiting, the ceremony of the first harvest, the ceremony of closing the harvest, the day of decorating the earth, the return of the sun, the hunting ceremony, and the gleaner's day. For four of these, the Matriarch was the focus of celebration. The Kuru traders had nothing like this. Their observances were centered on the safety of the caravan. In a ritual sense, Hastinapura was still a caravan led by men, and women had only a small part to play.

Satyavati found a mission she could lead – the establishment of community festivals and traditions that would make Hastinapura a city of people rather than traders and warriors. It was a gallant effort and, over many years, she created a meaningful way of life for the community; a cycle of annual celebrations that gave meaning to daily life. But the Great War had brought ordinary life to a halt. It threatened to undo all she has done."

Shukla stopped. For a few vighatis he was silent, with eyes closed. Lomaharshana offered him a bowl of water. Shukla drank, almost absent-mindedly. Lomaharshana pursed his lips and frowned. *Has he fallen asleep? Dare I interrupt his train of thought?*

Shukla stirred and focused on Lomaharshana. "I wanted forgiveness from Parashara, but did not receive it, for he despised me. I wanted forgiveness from Devavrata, but never asked for it. I wanted my sister's forgiveness, but she refused to think back on the events of that day. My father, who died of a broken heart soon after Satyavati left our house, forgave me on condition that I stayed around to look after my sister. That condition constrained my choices but I still did my best to take care of her.

Lomaharshana, Satyavati's actions and achievements, both good and evil, deserve their own space in the annals. The changes she introduced made her ubiquitous and Devavrata felt haunted by her presence. He wished to leave Hastinapura, but Shantanu would not hear of it. The King was cautious, as most Kings with adult heirs are. Even though Devavrata seemed loyal, he could change, regretting his sacrifice.

Our activities in the Kavi Sangha had proceeded in parallel and we were companions through much of our education. Devavrata appeared uninterested in Satyavati. Maybe he was, but he would always ask to see me after my visits to my sister, though he never asked about her. We became friends. Together, we came

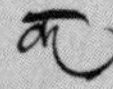

Annals of the Kavi Sangha
Appendix A.12: Policy Changes

The Annals of the Kavi Sangha are incomplete when discussing the changes of policy under Shantanu. The Kavi Sangha went through some difficult leadership transitions and failed to record the archives completely.

to understand the Kavi Sangha and its projects, to appreciate its thinking. Despite this improved understanding, in his heart he could never reconcile the logic of empire-building with the sacrifice of his infant brothers. After Parashara died, Devavrata persuaded the next Vyaasa that the one-person-one-child policy had been ill-advised. It had not taken into account the response of the common people, and Shantanu's small modifications had not made it any better.

This is then the story Devavrata never revealed to anyone. I know it because I witnessed the events and saw what happened to him. He did not know of my shame and regret over the advice I gave Satyavati, that caused so much unhappiness to them both. We never talked about those days, no matter how deep our friendship."

The bell at the entrance to the tent rang to announce Yudhishthira. He came in and said, "Gurudeva, how is the narration proceeding? I am finally free to listen to you, if only for a couple of days. I must urgently talk to the Pitamaha. I am concerned that his strength is fading fast."

The Vyaasa said, "Yudhishthira, my son, Lomaharshana can narrate his composition to you. It will answer your question about the policies of the Kavi Sangha and how they changed as a result of the events leading to the marriage of Shantanu and Satyavati. When you understand your Pitamaha, you can speak to him. If he is not pressed on this particular matter, he will answer your questions. I will visit Devavrata tomorrow before I leave. We shall see."

Yudhishthira said, "Gurudeva, I am deeply indebted to you. I will come to see you tomorrow."

26
Swapping Tales

The next day, the Vyaasa Shukla was up early. He stepped out of his tent and looked east. The sun had not yet risen and a slight fog had crept up overnight from the river. The campsite was on a slight rise north of the Yamuna. As Shukla gazed over the river, dawn appeared to the east. As the sky grew lighter and the fog dissipated, the river emerged out of the haze, moving swiftly past the camp, white eddies marking where it flowed over rocks near the bank. Shukla felt at peace. It was nothing like the placid lake of his childhood, nor was it the Ganga at Hastinapura. *In the many years I spent there, I have never felt peace like this*, he thought. Relating the story of his sister's unfortunate demands had made him think of her as he fell asleep. He had woken still thinking of her. She had been a victim of his own ambitions. Now he had to convince Devavrata, another victim, to plunge into that painful past… *To retrieve what? What will he find in that desolate land of lost time?*

The camp had been stirring for some time. As Shukla prepared himself for the day, a bearer from the kitchen brought a warm cup of almond milk, yellow with turmeric, and slices of guava, sprinkled lightly with salt and pepper. The frugal repast satisfied him. As he finished, Yudhishthira and Lomaharshana arrived to escort him to Devavrata's tent.

Yudhishthira said, "Gurudeva, we will be outside until you ask us to enter. Our ears will be deaf to anything said till then."

Shukla nodded his assent and rang the small bell at the entrance before he stepped into the tent.

"Devavrata, my friend…" The familiar voice cut through the fog Devavrata had lost himself in. *It was a bad dream,* he thought, opening his eyes. But he was still in the tent, his legs and one arm tied to support poles. *Do they think I will attempt to escape?* he wondered. But it was not a dream, and he was not free. His shoulder hurt. He remembered he was mortally injured. He had heard Shukla's voice. *But what is Shukla doing here? I left him in Hastinapura.* Perhaps, on the brink of death, he was imagining a visit from an old friend. *Is this how I will die, with my friends flashing before my eyes?* He was lucky he had so few friends, he thought; he would die quickly.

He turned his head but stopped when the flashes in his shoulder became a continuous river of pain. He was determined not to let the pain control him. He closed his eyes, his face set in a grimace that betrayed him, but opened them again to look at his friend. "Shukla, my brother," he said. "What are you doing in the enemy camp?"

It had been over a year since Devavrata had met with the Vyaasa in private. Public meetings in Suyodhana's court had become exercises in formality once war broke out with the Pandavas. Suyodhana did not trust the Kavi Sangha. Though the Sangha supported Hastinapura, and had done so for many generations, though the Vyaasa had called for the Pandavas to make peace on Suyodhana's terms, though there was no reason for the Sangha to change its mind, Suyodhana remained suspicious of its activities. The Kavi Sangha had told him to be generous to the Pandavas if they surrendered.

Now, Shukla said, "I too, am a prisoner at home."

"Are you? I have met the Archivist. He says your whereabouts are secret."

"Ah…yes."

"He predicted yesterday that you would come today. Keep him close; he seems to know when you are not in your prison."

Shukla laughed. "There is no need for sarcasm. The Kavi Sangha has its methods of communication. It is not an army that imprisons me. It is my body that betrays and holds me captive."

"As does mine. I have an arrowhead in my lung. I will die."

"My *bisaj* says I too, will die soon, he just cannot say when."

"What does the *bisaj* know, Shukla?"

"He says my urine is a sweet dish for the ants. My waning eyesight is a warning sign. The aches and pains in my arms and legs are a prelude to the final crossing."

"Is that why you came…to sit beside my deathbed?"

"No. I came for many reasons. I had hoped to archive your memoirs of Hastinapura in more pleasant circumstances. Now that will not be possible. So I ask you to work with the

Archivist. Before your capture, a Hastinapura victory in this unfortunate war, was inevitable; now it is not. Suyodhana and Karna are impetuous, strong-willed and stubborn. Only you could have restrained them and focused their efforts. You knew that, too. I was not in Hastinapura when you decided on this expedition. You are the senior-most Commander. What could have possibly tempted you down this foolhardy path?"

Devavrata grimaced. "Shikhandin offered us a chance…"

"Shikhandin? Of Panchala?"

"Yes, you know of him? He came to Hastinapura on a secret mission, with a proposal from the disaffected leaders of clans within Panchala."

"And he convinced you?"

"More or less."

"How did he manage to do that?"

"I know now what I did not know then. But I was inclined to believe him. He revived old memories."

"Amba?" Shukla asked, his voice low.

"You knew?"

"Did I suspect? Yes. Not with any certainty though. Some Kavi Sangha members visiting Panchala returned with disquieting news. I had asked them to assess Panchala's preparedness for war. You recall how Chief Drupada would issue challenges to Hastinapura every few years, to meet Panchala on the field of blood? The Sangha members reported that no one was preparing for war. The spear and arrow makers were idle, and the smiths were preparing for the harvest festival. The challenges were just bluster.

"I see. Does it mean that you have suspected all these years that Amba was alive?"

"All these years? No. I learned of it a few years ago."

Devavrata tried to raise himself but fell back. "Tell me more," he said, sighing.

"I will. But I wish to trade your memories for mine."

"Why now? The great river beckons me to the other side."

"I told you. I am old. I will not have many more chances to reconcile the warring factions. Consider it a final plea."

"Do you know what they want me to remember?"

"Yes. I have relieved you of a painful narration. I have told Yudhishthira and the Archivist about your first meeting with Satyavati. You need not recount it again. Go beyond, start with the death of your father, King Shantanu."

"Why is all this a part of your archives? I am not convinced that what I felt or what happened to me, matters. Can I not take my private sorrow with me, to be forgotten? You already know how the world has changed. Make that your story."

"Let the Kavi Sangha be the judge of what is relevant, Devavrata. There is more to a culture than dynastic family trees and an inventory of monuments or even tales of victory."

Devavrata sighed. *Why did the story of his life have to be added to the history of our culture?* "You think that the 'more' is the story of my life?"

"Among others, yes. I plan to interview Dhritarashtra, Kutaja Drona, Kunti, even Suyodhana and Yudhishthira, young though they are. I will wait for them just as I waited for you. And if I can get to them, I will even listen to the Queen of Panchala, Krishna the Yadava, and others too."

A few vighatis passed in silence. Shukla closed his eyes.

"How long will you wait here?" Devavrata asked.

Shukla opened his eyes. "Until you agree," he said.

"Hmm…what if I refuse?"

"Then I will wait."

"I could choose to die."

"Then you will never know what happened to Amba."

Amba's story…the only one he yearned to hear! *Shukla's words implied a threat: Tell us what you know or you will die in ignorance of what happened with Amba.* A sinking feeling of despair engulfed him when he thought of Amba. He had failed her, and he was desperate to know the extent of her suffering. He wanted to mourn her lost life; he needed absolution. He had been responsible for Amba's pain. She had raised Shikhandin on her own. And yet Shikhandin had died in his arms. He wanted to tell Amba that her son had felt his father's touch at least once in his short life. But how could he tell her he understood her pain if he did not know what it was? For her suffering to be his suffering, he had to know what her life had been like. Even the bare bones of her story would be better than nothing. But what was Shukla offering? He would take their private story and make it public. It would become another story to titillate the public, stories about great men with feet of clay.

"The Kavi Sangha performs historical story-telling every year at festivals in Hastinapura and Panchnad. Will this memoir be part of such recitals?" Devavrata asked.

Shukla smiled. "Do not worry. There will be no performances based on this archive for many years. The Kavi Sangha recites archival histories only after seven generations have passed. All persons in these histories will be dead before the stories are made public. Not every story makes it to a recital. The stories that do are always more than entertainment."

Devavrata considered this assertion. Was it good enough? *I do not want to be reassured; I want a commitment I can believe.* "What about him?" Devavrata asked, indicating with a glance the Archivist standing quietly outside.

"You know the rules of the Kavi Sangha," Shukla said. "You considered becoming an archivist yourself when your position in the city seemed precarious and you thought it possible that your brother, the King, would imprison, if not kill, you. Joining the Kavi Sangha would have saved your life."

"You mean Chitrangada, Shantanu and Satyavati's son?" Devavrata's voice was almost inaudible.

"Tell me about him," Shukla said. "Tell me how he died. Satyavati says a gandharva killed him; that you were there when he was killed but were too cowardly to bring his body back.

Did you tell her that? What was the truth? Gandharvas, magical beings who sing as they fly, do not exist."

Devavrata had made up a story to save Satyavati grief, but the lie had not satisfied her. And now it had caught up with him. A hastily conceived lie, built on memories of the stories an imaginative twelve-year-old Chitrangada told his five-year-old brother Vichitravirya, stories of a king with magical powers. Now Satyavati's brother was asking for the truth. *Can I trust him?* The answer would have been clear if Satyavati had been anyone but Shukla's sister. As it was, the question was not easily answered. Shukla was neither a trader nor a warrior. A trader habitually kept secrets; a warrior learnt not to obsess over scenes from a battlefield. *Is the value of telling the truth about Chitrangada's death greater than letting it die with me?* Such questions clouded Devavrata's mind. *It is a good thing I am dying,* he thought. He had never bothered to learn Satyavati's side of the story. He did not want to know now. *We remained aloof for so long. What was the point of cutting open an old wound to see if it had healed?*

The story of his life after Shantanu and Satyavati were married, had been told and retold many times; it had captured public imagination. Devavrata had devoted himself to projects that took him away from Hastinapura. Two years passed. Satyavati had a son, Chitrangada. When Chitrangada was seven, his brother Vichitravirya was born. Whenever Devavrata came to Hastinapura, he saw Shantanu playing with Chitrangada. The toddler looked like his father, a miniature Shantanu, except for his eyes and the pouting mouth, which opened in a broad smile when he saw Devavrata. *Anna,* he would scream and run to him. Shantanu was almost fifty years old then and not inclined to play on the floor with his son, but Devavrata could. Chitrangada would copy Devavrata's every move. He would run when Devavrata pretended to be angry, chasing him round and round without catching him. Chitrangada would climb onto Devavrata's shoulders and then jump into his outstretched arms. As Vichitravirya grew older, he too, joined in their games. But the bond between Devavrata and Chitrangada remained the strongest. Despite the hint of Satyavati in Chitrangada's features, or perhaps because of it, Devavrata grew to love his brothers.

The relationship between Chitrangada and Devavrata did not, however, overcome the strain between Satyavati and Devavrata. Occasionally, Devavrata noticed his father's puzzlement while observing the stilted interactions between his son and his wife. But for the most part he was oblivious to the tension. It was possible that he sensed the truth but chose to ignore it. It took many years but Devavrata and Satyavati gradually settled into a routine that allowed them to appear next to Shantanu in public. In private, they avoided each other.

Shortly after Shantanu's death, Shukla persuaded Satyavati and Devavrata to meet in his presence to resolve a particular conflict. It had been an awkward and disastrous meeting, where both proved incapable of initiating a discussion or following Shukla's leads. *It was good advice, just premature,* Devavrata thought. Unwilling to try again, they never did. Then Chitrangada went on a fateful expedition. Devavrata had arrived too late to save him. He had fabricated a tale to spare Satyavati the details of her son's end.

Devavrata was silent again. *Everything I love turns to dust. Such old memories and they still make me sad.*

A few vighatis passed. Shukla looked at Devavrata with concern, "Are you alright? You are silent, and your eyes look far away."

"I was thinking about Chitrangada's life and coronation."

"His coronation?"

"Yes. A lot started with that coronation."

"I want to know about his death."

I am a trader and here I am, freely giving away this story. Devavrata laughed at the thought of payment. He stopped as the shoulder shot its agonizing message across his chest. *I can get stories out of Shukla! A bard habitually tells stories.* He returned to his earlier question. "Do you really know what happened to Amba?"

Shukla slowly turned his head away, but not before Devavrata saw his eyes lose focus. He waited for three vighatis and then tapped the tent pole with his feet to get his friend's attention. The tent shook but it did not seem to affect Shukla. Finally, the Vyaasa turned back to him. "Are you alright?" Devavrata asked. "Am I not permitted to ask you questions?"

Shukla smiled. "You want to know about Amba, so let's play your game and trade. You tell me about Chitrangada's death, and I will tell you about the events following Vichitravirya's death."

He does not want to talk about Amba. Why? Every reason for secrecy has disappeared in the last few days. Were there more perhaps? The questions multiplied in Devavrata's mind.

"Can the Archivist memorize all we say?"

"Oh, far more than that."

"Amba's story has three parts," Devavrata said. "The first part I know and will tell you. It is the story of how I met her. The second part I do not know: Why she left and what she did afterward. Do you know that part? The third part I think you know: What happened to her; how she ended up in Panchala, and how she raised Shikhandin as a warrior?"

"I do not know everything. How you met her, how you bonded with her, is still a mystery. If you tell that story, I will have the boy recite how and why Amba escaped Hastinapura and hid from you. I will tell you what I know of Shikhandin and how he was raised. But I do not exactly know how Amba ended up in Panchala."

Devavrata was struck by the words. Once again Shukla had said that Amba had escaped! Escaped from what? Perhaps from someone? Shukla's offer seemed a fair exchange. Devavrata felt exhausted and needed to rest. *Not now*, he thought wearily. *I cannot take this in now.* "I am tired," he said. "I will start with Shantanu's death and how Satyavati and I became co-Regents. Then the story of Chitrangada's northern misadventure. Finally, I will tell you the truth about Amba. You will then tell me of Vichitravirya's death and what happened to Amba after she disappeared from Hastinapura."

"Yes, but only what I know."

"No drama then. Now go away and let me rest."

"Stay strong, old friend," Shukla said and left on silent feet.

Devavrata fell asleep. The narration was not physically tiring, but with every word that he uttered he felt he was losing something of his soul. That was emotionally exhausting. Some memories rang with joy but many were dark monsoon clouds obscuring the sun and inducing gloom. Some memories he had worked hard to forget were returning, an alarming occurrence for one trained to remember and trained to forget.

He woke later that morning with Satyavati's words, *He is going to kill me and then my children*, echoing in his mind. *It was only a dream*, he thought, and then realized it was a true memory, not a dream. Shantanu had died, and Satyavati had barely waited for the funeral ceremonies to be completed before she rushed off with her children to Varanavata. This was what he had to tell Shukla and Yudhishthira – about his father's death, his stepmother's panic, his own deep conviction that he should not be the ruler; the co-Regency and how it worked. It had happened and Shukla was coming with Yudhishthira to hear his version of events.

The sounds of the camp grew louder for the mid-day meal. An attendant was required to take care of his every need, and Devavrata found that awkward. In any case he had lost his appetite and ate only a few mouthfuls. But he needed the occasional drink of water as he talked. The water fell into his empty stomach, making gurgling sounds. He felt no hunger. Every trader and every warrior encountered times when meals became irregular. A day or two could pass without food, due to an error of judgement, such as taking the wrong turn at a fork in the road or hastily shooting off an unsteady bow and missing the quarry. No, hunger was not the problem. Thinking about food made him queasy and he waited uneasily for the meal-time sounds to cease.

Shukla came in with Yudhishthira and the Archivist. Shukla told him he still looked powerful and healthy despite his injuries.

Did they have to be so unrelentingly positive? Devavrata thought. It only reminded him of the pain he was trying to ignore. Then his visitors insisted on pointing to the elephant in the room.

Shukla said, "Devavrata, let's get started."

He and Yudhishthira sat cross-legged, facing Devavrata, while the Archivist took his place behind Devavrata's head so he could not be seen. *That was a good idea.* Devavrata considered asking Yudhishthira to position himself similarly, out of sight. But one could not make such a request of one's jailor. *It would be easier talking about these events if Yudhishthira was not here.* What could the story of Amba, of Chitrangada's death, or a host of other Kuru family secrets, mean to Yudhishthira, who had been a stranger to the family for much of his life?

Yudhishthira spoke first. "The Vyaasa tells me you have much to say. And there is much I wish to know. If my duties call, I must leave. But the Vyaasa assures me the Archivist will reproduce all that you say without error, and I can listen to him later. Meanwhile I am here."

Shukla felt cheerful. He enjoyed the rare experience of listening to fresh stories and anecdotes he did not already know. Usually it was he who was expected to be the originator of narratives. The other source of pleasure was this private meeting with Devavrata. It had been difficult for them to meet in Hastinapura. A meeting between the Regent and the Vyaasa of the Kavi Sangha was a political event, fraught with consequences. Suyodhana would have questioned it, and not found the answers acceptable. Under political watch, his friendship with Devavrata had threatened to disintegrate, the bond becoming as frail as a spider's web. A meeting between them was long overdue. It was a pity they had waited till they were both ready to leave this world.

Shantanu's Sunset

27
Shantanu's Death

So Devavrata continued with his narration. "'*He is going to kill me, and then my children.*' With these words, Satyavati gathered her sons and made her way overnight to the town of Varanavata."

Shukla said, "I was absent when Shantanu died. What led to his death so soon after the birth of his sons?"

Devavrata said, "A few years after the birth of Vichitravirya, my father fell ill. The right side of his body became paralyzed. Then his organs failed. He complained of headaches, mild at first, but increasing in severity despite the *bisaj's* ministrations. Then one morning he could not get out of bed. I was visiting Hastinapura from the extended waterworks projects that kept me busy and out of town. I had asked to meet my father and Vyaasa Jaimini, regarding the problems posed by the Meena-Nagas, Satyavati's people, who were expanding their range up the Yamuna into the land called Khandavaprastha. But the

King's illness precluded this discussion, but at the Vyaasa's insistence, I stayed on in Hastinapura.

I spent my time playing with my brothers. There was no one else at court that I wished to meet, and of course, no one wanted to be seen with me, for that could arouse Satyavati's wrath. My father was still in his early fifties. Chitrangada was eleven, and Vichitravirya about four. I was in my early thirties. No one expected my father to die so young, but he grew weaker and weaker. Some days he was delirious, living a different life in some other world. He talked to my mother, calling her Gangu, as he had done many years ago. He would become animated whenever I went to his sickbed and spoke to him. He recognized my voice and tried to sit up and respond. He spoke clearly, but his words made little sense. If there was a theme to the delirious ramblings, it was guilt and sorrow. Some of the more comprehensible statements regarded the one-person-one child policy. *They welcomed me into their midst. 'Who are you?' I asked. 'The children you killed,' they said. 'Now we are immortal. Come join us.' There were so many*… If I were asked to explain, I would have said he was describing being surrounded by dead children.

Another discernible and guilt-ridden statement was that he had deprived me. *I failed you. Gangu was supposed to kill all of you.* This was strange, given that the order to kill the babies had come from him and my mother had nothing to do with it. He went on to say that I could have been in heaven like my dead brothers, but had to suffer here. He offered to release me from mortal suffering so that I could join them. *I can make you immortal, just like me. From heaven, all is possible.* Of that which he truly deprived me, there was not a word.

He also conversed with his absent brother, Bahlika. He said, 'Bahlika, come back to Hastinapura. We will honor and welcome you.' My uncle had left with his family long before my father became King, intending to go as far west as he could. My father seemed to believe that Bahlika's children had died. It is said that men who died without living progeny suffer eternal hunger. He may have believed that his brother was in torment, which added to his hallucinations.

He dreamt that his second brother, Devapi, was dead. *Devapi, my brother! Forgive me for making you leave. I should have stopped you that day.* Devapi had discarded his royal robes at the edge of the forest and was believed to have entered the woods, leaving behind his wife, but no children. *Shantanu had seen Devapi leave?* It was the first time I heard that my father could have stopped Devapi. The dead Devapi also had other concerns in my father's imaginings. '*Where are my children?*' he asked.

If Devapi had children, they would have been the rulers of Hastinapura. But Devapi had had no progeny; his wife barren. She continued to live in Hastinapura, a sad, invisible ghost, till her death. Shantanu dreamt that he had been very clever in convincing his brother that he was cursed by the gods because he could not have progeny, and should thus abdicate. But he had not expected Devapi to go away, perhaps kill himself. Now Shantanu felt guilty that he had not tried to find Devapi. At first, he had not wished to do so; later, he thought that it would make relations with Satyavati even more fraught if Shantanu's brother was to return.

It was news to me that Shantanu and Satyavati were unhappy. He called it his *karma*, that his actions in depriving Devapi of his birthright were the cause of Satyavati forcing him to deprive his son of his. My father was sorry he had made me give up my birthright and gave me a boon: *You can choose the time of your death.* It was a strange boon from a delirious man. But the idea that Devapi had children was disconcerting. If it was not some delirium-induced rambling, it would serve to make the chaos surrounding us worse. I took the possibility seriously and sent trained searchers to look for Devapi, all the way to Laghu Nagapura. But they found nothing.

Shantanu ignored most visitors but for some he roused himself. Satyavati would come, with Chitrangada and Vichitravirya. I would leave when I was informed of her coming, so I never learned what was spoken between them. A few days later, I thought he was getting better and said so to the *bisaj*. But he shook his head saying, ‘He smells sour; I cannot change that. This disease mimics health shortly before death. I have seen it often and caregivers are often fooled.’

The pronouncement left me puzzled. What did the *bisaj* mean that the patient smelled sour? Why would the odour, probably caused by drinking spoilt milk, indicate disease? The *bisaj* had no real explanation and only said that the smell was indicative of the body consuming itself; of a disease without cure. He did not have a name for it. There would be periods when the King appeared to get better. He appeared more active and the delirium stopped. He was more in control of his mind, if not his body. One side remained paralyzed. But his mind was clear.

The *bisaj* was proved right. One morning I went to consult my father about Vyaasa Jaimini’s proposal to stop using the army for civil construction. Jaimini had become the Vyaasa just before Chitrangada was born, and had worked at creating alternatives to the plan developed when Bharadvaja was the Vyaasa. Bharadvaja's plan had entailed the use of the army to suppress opposition. Lakes and waterworks were to be constructed and owned by the state. Immigrants would settle newly irrigated lands. The Nagas would not be allowed to return to their slash-and-burn practices. With the immigrants as the vanguard, the empire would expand southwards, using a sequence of waterworks to define the boundary; creeping further south with every new generation; gradually eliminating the Nagas from their current range.

When Parashara became the Vyaasa, he wished to change the emphasis from exclusion to inclusion. The sentencing to a vow of silence cost him influence; subsequently, death cut short his tenure. His inclusive policy was never put into effect. Jaimini, who followed Parashara, was not a revolutionary, nor was he enamored of Bharadvaja's imperial solutions. He did not support a waterworks empire that catered to one group while destroying another. I agreed with him, but knew that he lacked pragmatism. In his search for the fairest solution, he ignored what was happening on the ground with the help of the army. So slowly but steadily, the boundary between Hastinapura-irrigated land and Naga territory moved south.

We were in the King's chamber, discussing Vyaasa Jaimini's proposal to withdraw the army from the frontier construction projects. Shantanu was walking around slowly; he felt that exercise would keep his legs healthy. Suddenly he stopped pacing and closed his eyes, bending his head; he complained of excruciating pain in his left arm. He sat down, his mouth set in a grimace. Even as the Vyaasa Jaimini and I considered calling the *bisaj*, Shantanu said that his chest hurt and collapsed. We picked him up. He had lost consciousness and felt limp in our arms. We laid him on the bed. As we waited for the *bisaj*, I listened for a heartbeat, but could not find one. Just as the *bisaj* entered, the smell of urine and waste filled the room. The King was dead.

A messenger was immediately sent to Satyavati. She came quickly, her children in tow. I could not bear to meet and commiserate with her, so I left the death chamber and retired to my quarters.

The Chief Minister came to see me that night. He said, 'You must take charge, Prince Devavrata. There is much confusion all over the city.'

'Why?' I asked. 'The Queen is in charge. I will support whatever action she wishes to take.'

'She has left with the Princes for Varanavata. She was heard to say, *He is going to kill me and then my children*. It appears that she is uncertain of your intentions.'

I did not wish to rule. I had said so. But the statement had seemed mere talk to others. Even the Chief Minister, Sashidhara, seemed uncertain of what I would do. *He has known me since I was a child. But he too, is skeptical. After all these years, I am not trusted or understood.* In the few days before my father's death, I had begun to think that he would agree with me about the imperial plan. *Was that a delusion too?* Why did the Chief Minister not read me correctly? Why had he not responded appropriately to Satyavati's fears? A loyal and knowledgeable minister, concerned for the succession, would have reassured her that I had no intention of harming either her or her children. It was because he himself was uncertain of my intentions that he had stayed silent.

I know now that I was naïve. In Panchnad, the Queen's Council made decisions jointly. In Hastinapura, the King made the final decision, often based on many streams of information that could seem opaque, even surprising, to an observer, who only knew some part of such information. This was normal. This was why, even when following the policy suggested by the Kavi Sangha, King Shantanu had appeared unpredictable to some of the participants in the process.

Looking back, I think the Chief Minister was being properly cautious in not responding to Satyavati's fears. If I had intended to get rid of my brothers, his loyalty to the Princes would have made him suspect. And if I had intended to support them, any encouragement of Satyavati's fears would also have made him suspect. However, at the time, his extreme caution made me question his own intentions. I decided that my father had left the task of implementing the policy concerning the immigrants to me. The King and I had had no major disagreements about it.

From then on, I was treated as the King. I found myself receiving the information that usually only went to my father. It helped me understand. My father could, and did, partition the implementation of the immigrant policy from his personal life. I could not. After the trauma of my mother's death, my father maintained a strict separation between his own wishes and the Kavi Sangha policies he implemented. I could not. When I gave up the kingdom, it had been with the expectation that I would never rule nor have to face the dilemmas my father encountered. That was not to be. I was often required to shoulder the burdens of kingship. As I waited for the flurry of activity caused by the King's death to subside, I considered the nebulous idea of withdrawing from public life and leaving my brother Chitrangada, to implement Shantanu and the Kavi Sangha's long-term agenda. But my brothers were too young to understand why I would do such a thing. I would have to reassure Satyavati. I would have to meet her. Nor could it be a public discussion. But I did not wish to meet her in private."

Yudhishthira came in silently. The Vyaasa and the Archivist were in the *nishkamakarnarpana* state. The Archivist did not move. The Vyaasa had formed the *jalampurayatu* mudra with his right palm. The King picked up the small clay pot containing water and held it to Devavrata's lips. Devavrata drank, swallowing slowly. Yudhishthira put the pot to one side and sat down.

The three men waited in silence for Devavrata to continue his narration.

28
Satyavati's Return

Devavrata continued, "Rather than face Satyavati, I postponed meeting her. Instead, I met the King's Council in her absence. When I entered the Council chamber, I could feel the excitement ripple through it, like a warm summer breeze blowing in from the river in the late afternoon. The Council Members and attending citizens bowed low to me, as if my face was too bright to behold. The Chief Minister seemed to have lost his luster. The smiling group that usually clustered around him stood just a little away from him, their faces serious. The Chief Minister himself stood erect and tense, a posture I had never seen him adopt in Council.

I realized they were expecting me to declare myself King. I walked in slowly, glancing at every one of them as I walked by. No one met my gaze. Instead, they looked at the ground and bowed. I wanted to admonish them, but said nothing as I walked past. The throne stood on a platform reached by three steps. It was made of a ficus tree trunk, about four feet in diameter, about a *hasta* tall, its top covered with cotton padding. On the throne was a cushion. My usual place was on the floor, to the left of the throne, marked by a single pillow. To the right of the throne was a place similarly marked by a pillow, where Satyavati had sat. As I sat down in my usual place, I heard sighs ripple through the chamber.

In the past, when the King had been absent, Satyavati would call the meeting to order. That day, I initiated the meeting, even though I did not wish to. The people present acted as if this was perfectly normal and it was merely a matter of time before I moved to the throne. I asked the ministers to report on what had been done that year in their departments, and what remained to be done. They responded with great alacrity and little substance, making no attempt to provide the summary I had asked for, or describe the status of their responsibilities. Instead, they devoted their time to extolling my virtues. *They had always been impressed by my deep understanding of discussions. I had brought reasoned thought and a keen intellect to the discussions. They were awed by the wisdom I had shown even as a young boy.* In the past they had looked to Shantanu and Satyavati for direction and my ideas had received only the respect my father chose to bestow on them in public. '*Now we see how right you have been, Sir,*' they said. I wondered if my father had felt as repelled by this false praise as I did. I wished I had not called the meeting.

After half a dozen hagiographic reports, I stopped the speaker and said, 'The next one who avoids presenting a report and uses the time to praise me, will be expelled from the Council and from his post.' There was complete silence. All the little sounds, the ripples if you will, that mark a group of living people, died. The unfortunate Councillor, a polished and sophisticated urbanite, an early immigrant from Panchnad, stumbled through his abbreviated presentation and returned to his seat. The session moved quickly after that.

Then it was my turn. By now some life had returned to the group, for I had not punished anyone. I said, 'My brother Chitrangada was anointed as Yuvaraja by my respected father. His wishes were clear. In accordance with those wishes, Chitrangada will be crowned King when he comes of age. In the meantime, the Queen Mother Satyavati, will be Regent.' I said I would go to Varanavata to bring the Queen Mother-Regent, and my brothers, back to Hastinapura, for the formal investiture.

The silence that followed this announcement was absolute. No one moved. I could almost read their minds: *Is this a trick?* I wanted to shout from the highest mound: *This is what I want!* I do not think anything I said would have been credible. Some of my auditors glanced at each other, then smiled and bowed even deeper than before, when I passed them. *Had they expected this?* The announcement should have been a stunning revelation, but they acted as though it was a routine announcement. They had interpreted my statements for deeper meaning, and found what they were looking for. I wondered what I could have said that could not have been twisted on reinterpretation.

Satyavati received reports of this meeting and I received reports of the reports sent to her: *Your step-son Devavrata pretended to obey his father's wishes. His speech was a transparent attempt to convince the Councilors of his intentions, but no one was fooled.* The report inserted implied threats into every sentence I had used. So, when I went to Varanavata and requested a private meeting, Satyavati refused, sending a message to say: *Come to my public hall ten ghatis after sunrise. There will be others asking for audience. There, in public, I will certainly listen to you. I will hold you to your oaths.*

I had decided I would do as she requested, no matter what it was. I had promised to ensure that Satyavati's children inherited the kingdom. When that oath had been asked of me, my first impulse had been to refuse. But if I had, my father would have been humiliated. To avoid conflict I would have left Hastinapura. It does not take much to insult a King. Nor can a King swallow insults. This was another difference between the old Panchnad cities and Hastinapura. A Matriarch's rule is not threatened when someone refuses to obey. A King's rule cannot survive if such disobedience is tolerated. At that point I felt a deep empathy for my uncle Devapi's decision to abdicate and disappear. But my vows prevented me from doing the same, compelling me to stay and create the institutions that would establish Hastinapura's control over the land. If I walked away, I a usurper could eliminate my young brothers and their mother. That would have broken my promise."

Shukla said, "I was there and recall your actions distinctly. Satyavati left for Varanavata without waiting for me to arrive in Hastinapura. I followed her to Varanavata but events had already taken their own course."

Devavrata said, "I did as Satyavati asked. I went to her public hall as a supplicant. I beseeched her to return to Hastinapura as Queen Mother and Regent to the future King Chitrangada. I do not believe Satyavati expected this. Her eyes betrayed her apprehension that it was a trap. I saw her fear. *She is driven by fear,* I thought. *I must reassure her now or this fear of me will remain forever."*

Shukla said, "Satyavati described this meeting to me in her own style, one she had developed during her years with Shantanu. She said, 'I looked into Devavrata's eyes and saw the cold, hard calculation of a man plotting the best time to take revenge.' My sister has a talent for dramatic expression."

Devavrata smiled and then continued. "You, Shukla, were not the Vyaasa then. You advised Satyavati. I was grateful for that. On his suggestion, Satyavati made a counter offer. She and I would be joint Regents. She would keep control of the city and any part of the army within the city, and I would administer the rest of Kururashtra. She would enter the city after I had left it. She would announce that she had invited me to be co-Regent. The co-Regency was my reward for my loyalty to my father and to her. But she had rules I was required to follow: I could only return to the city after she had taken control of the army; she would make any other rules as and when they became necessary and let me know. She explained her purpose in doing this – the safety of her son, Shantanu's true heir. She also wished me to repeat my oath that one of my brothers would become the future ruler of Hastinapura. Thus she and I would bring peace to a city on the brink of civil war, between her supporters and the malcontents who were against her because of her Naga descent.

I accepted her proposal. I would have accepted anything that would have erased her fear of me. I finally recognized that Satyavati was afraid of me. But she was even more afraid that the people of Hastinapura would not accept a Regent of Naga origin. No one would think to question my Regency, so I was her shield against public outcry. There were still those who were angry over the conditions she had imposed before her marriage. If they rebelled, I could have made common cause with them. In sharing power, she had made a calculated decision to ensure I would support her.

Satyavati did not return immediately to Hastinapura. Her absence, coupled with disbelief over my announcements, began to weigh on the various families that had settled in Hastinapura, along with the Kauravas. A second public embassy, led by you, was sent to invite her to return. When she finally did, it was to a grand welcome I organized, leaving the city before she set foot in it as Regent.

This was the problem. My avoidance of Satyavati was not conducive to building trust. She feared me, and even though I had abased myself and begged her to return, she continued to fear and distrust me. Our agreement, that I would remain outside the city while she stayed inside it, was unworkable. She needed to go out of the city, if only for pleasure, and I had to enter it for meetings with administrative officials and ministers. We modified the agreement, but it continued to be difficult to manage. It was stressful and irritating to me that I had to constantly monitor my actions so as not to violate some element of the agreement. But the core of the agreement held. Satyavati became co-Regent and Queen Mother; she took care of her children, Chitrangada and Vichitravirya. I, as co-Regent, managed the internal affairs of Kururashtra. We shared responsibility for collecting taxes and authorizing expenditures. The Panchnadi model that mandated standard taxes and expenditures, was already in place and did not change.

Monarchies spend to glorify the ruler. In the absence of a ruler, the revenues could support minor luxuries for the principal family. Satyavati raised her boys, not denying them anything. They were self-willed and stubborn, but no one chided them. Left to their mother, they would have learned nothing of kingship and kingly conduct. So I worked with the Kavi Sangha to arrange teachers for them in history, economics, trade, martial arts, and strategy.

Meanwhile, the Kavi Sangha and Vyaasa Jaimini worked to create a State that maintained order in the face of chaos, while preserving the best in the abandoned cities of Panchnad. The Kavi Sangha could preserve knowledge as long as the rest of the world functioned, for destruction of knowledge was threatened in every riot, every clash between immigrant and Naga, every conflict over scarce resources.

Chaos was unavoidable; it streamed in steadily from outside our borders. The solution was to channel the energy. During the last years of Shantanu's reign, I had begun building dams to create small lakes and ponds along the Ganga and the Yamuna. The Kavi Sangha suggested, and I agreed with their assessment, that the settlement of Varanavata would be the model for all new settlements. Varanavata was where Samvarana had spent his years of exile. It was located on the banks of a constructed lake on the Yamuna, and over the years it had become a prosperous agricultural community. Canals and irrigation channels brought water to the fields. The plan was to create more agricultural settlements in the land between the two rivers, north of the ridge where the Yamuna changed direction. The Nagas had only expanded slightly in that direction. Hence there were only a few bands to deal with. Immigrants could settle in this land. Rainfall was meagre so water had to come from the two rivers.

By the time of King Shantanu's death, we had stopped enforcing the limit on the number of children in a family. Such a law was easier to enforce in an urban setting; far less so in the rural heartland. The need to limit the population did not go away, however. We were left with only two ways of managing the growth – not allowing any more immigrants in, or moving them to the outskirts of the land we controlled. We were not prepared to turn back the refugees, at least not yet. We settled new refugees near the border, where they would have to farm the land. The massive dislocation of people had made the trading network unreliable, so they would first have to produce the food they needed before producing more for export. The fine pottery and ceramics for which Panchnad had been famous, could no longer be made and exports to the West ceased.

Knowledge in an Urban Culture

Vyaasa Bharadvaja convinced Shantanu to allow Panchnadis into Hastinapura in order to preserve their advanced knowledge. Chaos destroyed knowledge even when it did not kill the bearer. *'Knowledge,'* he said, *'in an urban civilisation like Panchnad did not just reside in the minds and bodies of individuals – it also resided in the relationships between people that characterised urban life. Knowledge was lost when the smith who knew how to smelt metals went south while the craftsman who knew how to construct the moulds for a graded sequence of cast weights went north – the system of standard weights that supported an honest oral trading infrastructure would be lost. Similarly, if the last brick-maker who could make high-quality bricks of a fixed shape, size, and strength was lost, the engineer who knew how to make buildings with those bricks would no longer make solid structures. The bricklayer would struggle to lay irregularly shaped bricks and would create a pastiche wall, ugly to view. In an urban civilisation, knowledge nestled in all kinds of niches, waiting to be exploited.*

In Panchnad, the land to the south had been extremely fertile while the land to the north had been suitable for cultivation only in narrow strips, along either bank of the river. As a result, Panchnad had two kinds of towns – the northern towns that specialized in manufacture and the southern ones that produced food. This model was impossible to reproduce in the new border settlements. Among the immigrants there were many northerners and only a few southerners as most Panchnadi southerners had moved into the unknown territory of the southern peninsula. Because our border settlements needed farmers, we tried to make the Nagas our 'southerners', but that was misconceived. Every lesson we learned consumed our best efforts, but took years to absorb. Meanwhile, we kept sending the refugees to these half-built, half-baked northern settlements."

Devavrata paused. Yudhishthira brought him water in a clay pot. The sun had disappeared a ghati earlier, and dusk stole into the tent. Shukla and Lomaharshana dropped their listening pose.

Yudhishthira said, "We will continue tomorrow."

And with those words, they adjourned for the day.

29
King Chitrangada

The next day, following the morning meal, King Yudhishthira, Vyaasa Shukla, and the Archivist Lomaharshana, arrived at Devavrata's tent together. The entrance was closed with a curtain of felted cotton. The attendant emerged to say to the King, "Sir, forgive the delay; the Regent is not yet ready."

After a ghati, the attendant reappeared and invited them in. Devavrata was lying on his side, his eyes closed, his mouth set in a thin line. As they entered, he opened his eyes and said, "Come in. I regret to say I can no longer control my body. Give me death."

The King said, "Pitamaha, we regret to trouble you in this manner. We cannot heal your wound, nor can we end your life."

Devavrata replied, "Perhaps I can attack someone or strive to escape. Then you can kill me."

Yudhishthira said, "I value your life and everyone in this camp knows it. In any case we would not kill a wounded soldier without certain cause."

Devavrata said, "So you do not hold out any hope for me? Am I to continue in this undignified manner?"

"I have ordered that you to be treated with respect."

"You are here for your own purposes. Why should I care?"

"Because we have the same goal – to create a kingdom that benefits its people. The Kavi Sangha wishes to record your life. We both seek to honor your life and your work. You have done much, and even if I do not agree with all you have done, I still wish to understand, if only to avoid repeating your mistakes."

"Is this the consolation you offer me – that you will remember my errors?"

Shukla intervened. "Devavrata, my friend, we have known each other for a long time. You will die soon. I too, will die soon after. You can be remembered for all you have done, both successes and failures, errors if you will. Alternatively, you can be forgotten completely. Which would you prefer? That choice I can offer you as the Vyaasa. Forgive Yudhishthira. The ghost of his father, your nephew, drives him. Tell him what he wants to hear, so your brother's son can rest in peace."

The men contemplated each other in silence. Devavrata considered what had been said. He had given up so much in his life. Was this to be the ultimate fruit of his sacrifices? He had killed his own son; Amba had attempted to kill him; the people he had sworn to protect had died – his brother Chitrangada, his nephew Mahendra Pandu, and many others who had opposed him. Shukla offered him oblivion or fame; he cared for neither. The only person who had expressed sorrow at his present condition was Yudhishthira, who had little reason to be kind to him. If he owed anything to anyone, it was to Yudhishthira. Yudhishthira had empathised with him in a way that no one had for many years. It would be an act of kindness to satisfy his request, and it was the only thing within his power to grant.

"Yudhishthira, my child, I will do as you wish. Archivist, come sit near me and listen to an old man talk. Yudhishthira, is there any question you wish me to answer?"

Yudhishthira said, "Lomaharshana ended yesterday by saying the refugees were directed south into hastily made homes in territory the Nagas had left fallow. What was the reason for that?"

Devavrata stared silently at the central pole of the tent. He was about to say something but stopped, continuing to stare. They waited for ten vighatis. Then Devavrata closed his eyes. Yudhishthira did not move.

Lomaharshana could not wait and said, "Forgive me, my Lord, but could you continue with your narrative?"

Devavrata's eyes opened. He looked at Lomaharshana. So did Yudhishthira and the Vyaasa, causing the young man to cringe.

"I will, my son, I will…" said Devavrata. He looked at Yudhishthira. Shantanu used to have the same stubborn look of conviction. *We lose ourselves in memories that are in turn lost in time.* Yudhishthira was looking at him with the same concern he had shown the day before, and the day before that.

Devavrata said, "Yudhishthira, I will answer your questions in time. Now I speak of Hastinapura after my father married Satyavati. As I said yesterday, she and I established the co-Regency. A few years passed; Chitrangada came of age and was crowned King. He died fighting Shakas in the north."

Shukla said, "This is a point that has created much debate. My sister was told that a gandharva, also named Chitrangada, challenged him. Well…we know that gandharvas are imaginary beings and do not exist. Whoever told Satyavati did not tell the truth. Now you say Shakas killed him?"

"What exactly was the Queen Mother told?" Yudhishthira asked.

The Vyaasa said: "I learned from her that Chitrangada had set out on an expedition to the northern border and that Devavrata had followed, to stop him. Devavrata's men returned with the story of a gandharva having killed Chitrangada. At the time I investigated the death on my sister's behalf. I questioned Devavrata's soldiers and they all had the same story; that Chitrangada was already dead when they arrived. The gandharvas had vanished, leaving behind a small contingent of allies – the Shakas. The ensuing battle with the Shakas lasted longer than anticipated and there were more casualties than expected, but Devavrata's army finally prevailed. Many Shakas were captured and following their own practice, were enslaved. The Panchnad settlements did not have slaves, but slaves could be easily sold to the western countries that clamored for them. The Shaka prisoners were shipped to the port of Tripura on the Sindhu delta, from where they were taken to the West for sale. Chitrangada's body was cremated as it had begun to decompose and could not be carried to Hastinapura."

Devavrata said, "No, gandharvas do not exist. I made up that story to spare Satyavati the details of her son's death. I also wanted to spare the people of Hastinapura."

Shukla said, “A bard reciting a story knows what to include and what to exclude, for the audience dictates the telling. However, the bard must know the whole story so that he can make the choice at the time of the telling. You have told us of the death of your father and about the co-Regency you set up with Queen Mother Satyavati. What happened after that? What led to your brother’s death and another co-Regency?”

Devavrata said, “I will come to that. Recall that my second step-brother, your grandfather Vichitravirya, became King after Chitrangada. He too, died some years later, leaving two Queens pregnant with Mahendra Pandu and Dhritarashtra. That was the third co-Regency. Later, when Mahendra exiled himself, he left behind his blind half-brother Dhritarashtra. But a blind person cannot be crowned King, so Satyavati, Dhritarashtra and I formed the fourth co-Regency. For whom were we holding the throne?

When your father died, one faction wanted you, Yudhishthira, son of King Mahendra, to be crowned King. Dhritarashtra remained silent but it was clear that the suggestion to overlook him because of his blindness had offended him. He supported a second faction that wanted his son Suyodhana to be the King. This was considered radical and against custom. The tradition among caravan masters was that a son could supplant his father as Master only if his father had died or was mentally incapable. This was intended to prevent a caravan from being hijacked by a coup. Hastinapura had never been a matrilineal matriarchy and the Master was called King. Suyodhana could not be King while his father was alive and in possession of his senses. But Yudhishthira, since your father was dead, you *could* be King, if we agreed.

A compromise was reached. Dhritarashtra gifted your father's forest back to you. When you accepted the offer, you gave up your legitimate claim to be King of Hastinapura. We mutually agreed to call Dhritarashtra the King, for it pleased him and did not change anything.

But sending you away did not resolve Suyodhana's problem. He still could not be the King. Nor could he kill his father; that would not have sat well with Queen Satyavati or, for that matter, me. He could declare his father incompetent and prove it by a public demonstration of his father's dementia. But Satyavati would not have countenanced such an act; nor would I have. However, Suyodhana's faction dominated the Council and the city and he ruled in the name of his father, the co-Regent. Though Queen Satyavati and I were the other co-Regents, almost every one obeyed Suyodhana's dictates, as though he was indeed the King."

Yudhishthira said, "You have been co-Regent for Hastinapura many times. Tell us about these co-Regencies, and what you accomplished during that period."

Devavrata said, "I have talked about the death of my father and the establishment of the first co-Regency with Queen-Mother Satyavati. I will now tell you about the short reign of my brother Chitrangada, his northern misadventure, and his death…"

Yudhishthira said, "Excuse me, Pitamaha. Another time I would have urged you to tell me about my granduncles, but today I wish to know about the forces that motivated your imperial decisions. Granduncle Chitrangada ruled for a very short time. I have heard that Grandfather Vichitravirya showed little interest in governing. Neither could have affected policy in any significant manner. As co-Regent, you ran the country. What does the foolhardy death of my granduncle Chitrangada matter if it did not affect your imperial plans?"

Devavrata pursed his lips. His brother's death in itself meant nothing, but the chain of consequences was significant. Chitrangada had been suspicious of the Kavi Sangha, a suspicion he derived from Satyavati, who considered the Sangha evil, even though she used its volunteers to do things she wanted done. Chitrangada suspended all cooperation with the Kavi Sangha. His death therefore restored the Regency and reinstated the agenda of the Kavi Sangha.

Devavrata said, "My son, Chitrangada's reign and his death forced the Kavi Sangha, and me, to change; to expand substantially the scope of our imperial plans. His brother Vichitravirya was too young and had not been raised to rule. He showed no desire to be King, doing so only on his mother's behest. Vichitravirya enjoyed life with his two wives and neglected the office of King. His unexpected death and the subsequent late birth of his children, allowed the Kavi Sangha and me to collaborate with Satyavati, to put in place many irreversible changes. Chitrangada's death thus changed many things; it was a turning point. The co-Regency after Vichitravirya's death lasted eighteen years, until Mahendra Pandu ascended the throne."

Devavrata paused. *Only I know how my brother died. Amba does, too. That was how I met Amba.* These thoughts added to his melancholy. He said, "Shukla, my friend, I have one wish, that you too, tell me what you know. You said you knew how Amba reached Panchala, of her life there, of her son Shikhandin. That is all I wish to know. Tell me about Amba's life."

Yudhishthira said, "Does this need to be part of the archive?"

Silently, Shukla considered. *Why was Yudhishthira, so solicitous earlier, now showing signs of impatience?* His father Mahendra Pandu had disagreed with Devavrata over policies. As a result, Mahendra Pandu had deliberately withdrawn into self-exile. Telling the story of Devavrata's life in such detail postponed the explanation of that decision. Given Devavrata's condition, he might never get to that point in the story. Devavrata's life outlined the framework on which Hastinapura had tried to address the crisis created by the refugees from Panchnad. Some key events in Devavrata's life corresponded to the shifts in policy. His mother's death had resulted from Shantanu's first attempt to limit the population of Hastinapura. Shantanu's marriage to Satyavati had heralded a change in policy, and Devavrata was left to develop it. Shantanu's death and the terms of the co-Regency took Devavrata out of the city. Chitrangada's death then led to an alliance against the Shakas. Vichitravirya's death gave Devavrata sole control of policy. It was not until Yudhishthira's father came of age that Devavrata's power began to diminish. Yudhishthira probably considered the story of Amba and Shikhandin a distraction, postponing an explanation of the differences between his father and Devavrata.

The silence dragged on. Finally Devavrata said, "I care not whether Amba's story is included in the archives. But if you do not tell me what happened to her, I have nothing more to say."

Shukla said, "Yudhishthira, the archive is not solely a repository of how the city was governed. By creating stories that can be recited to hold an audience's attention, we keep alive the history of the city. Perhaps you wish to get to the causes of your father's self-exile. I promise that we will."

It was Yudhishthira's turn to ponder. Then he said, "So be it. I shall be patient."

The bell at the entrance to the tent rang. A Panchalan soldier came in, bowed to the King and said, "Sir! The night's reconnaissance teams have just come in. They have requested a meeting with you and your brothers."

Yudhishthira grimaced. They had successfully executed the ambush and captured the Regent, but the war would not end so easily. If the night patrol had seen troop movement by Hastinapura, the Vyaasa's opinion would be valuable. Meanwhile, Devavrata was working well with the Archivist, recounting what Yudhishthira wished to know. That should continue.

Shukla said, "Yudhishthira, Lomaharshana is a master of memorization and archiving. He will do a perfectly good job even without our presence."

"Gurudeva, I do not question Lomaharshana's skills. The Regent wishes to narrate the events that led to the deaths of my grandfather Vichitravirya and his brother Chitrangada. Your presence and mine are the only guarantees that the Regent will narrate the histories we wish to know. You and I are the ones who can decide if a digression should be pursued or dropped. How can Lomaharshana make that decision?"

"You are right," Shukla said. "You are the best person to elicit the knowledge you seek from the Regent. However, we both know you cannot be here constantly. You could tell Lomaharshana what you are looking for and I will have him summarize the narration for you in the evening. He can get any missing details the next day, while the memories are still fresh."

Yudhishthira hesitated. *I am the King,* he thought. *I should... but there are many other matters to be addressed.* He knew what he had to do. Yudhishthira said, "Lomaharshana…Pitamaha, this is what I seek. My granduncles Chitrangada and Vichitravirya ruled briefly, yet you seem to place great importance on their short lives. Why? Battles were rare in those times. It had been over two thousand moons[41] since Samvarana had been restored through violence. Yet Chitrangada died in battle. My grandfather Vichitravirya became ruler at a young age and died young. I am told he died before his sons were born; their births were described as miracles. I am eager to hear of them, even though my mind is pre-occupied with this war. What was grandfather's life like? What did he accomplish? His death must have been a shock to Queen Mother Satyavati."

Devavrata said, "Yudhishthira, your granduncle, my half-brother Chitrangada, was eager to show off his skills as a warrior. I had trained him myself and I believe he wished to impress me, even though he charged me with treason for not handing over full command of the army. His mother had handed over control of the troops in the city to him, but Chitrangada wanted to command all the troops, including the ones protecting what I had been building – dams, canals, roads and settlements."

"Why did you withhold complete command of the army?"

"He was impetuous, inclined to quick action without thinking through the consequences. I asked him to command the army through me, but he soon realized I was slow to respond to demands for urgent action. He could not see how often a

---

[41]About one hundred and sixty years.

looming crisis would pass, if one just waited. Unfortunately, he did not learn the futility of hurried action from these episodes.

I also kept control of the secret service. I told him this was the traditional practice so the King's reputation and character were not sullied by contact with those low and despicable persons who were only fit to be spies and provocateurs. After that bit of dissimulation, it was a relief that he never found out about his mother's secret agents; he might have confined her to her home to prevent further damage to her reputation.

Despite my best efforts, I was compelled to hand over control of the army to the King. I retained my personal guard, almost a hundred men, but did not use them to guard me. They guarded my projects throughout the region. I also created a border police force to augment the guards inside the city. They would help manage the flow of immigrants and keep them from coming into conflict with the Nagas."

Yudhishthira said, "You told us earlier that the official story of Chitrangada's death was false. Do you know the real story?"

"To the best of my knowledge, there are no gandharvas; they are mythical beings. Yes, I do know the manner of Chitrangada's death. I have kept it secret for all these years. I used to think the secret would die with me for even the Kavi Sangha's archives do not contain that particular truth"

Yudhishthira said, "But it is not appropriate that no one in the family knows the truth about his death. As long as you lived, someone knew the truth. It is incumbent on you to tell the story now. If there is cause to keep it secret, let that burden be mine. Lomaharshana, do you understand?"

The Archivist replied, "Sir, the best way I, as Gurudeva said, for me to memorize and compose a narrative, then give you the chance to review it. I am open to correction."

Shukla and Yudhishthira then rose and departed in silence.

Lomaharshana turned to the Regent Devavrata and said, "Sir, pray continue."

THE FIRST CO-REGENCY

30
CHITRANGADA'S WAR

Lomaharshana said, "Sir, you have heard the guidelines I have been asked to establish in your narrative. Will you be able to tell me everything without tiring yourself?"

Devavrata said, "It is not easy to tell you this story. No, it does not deviate from your directions but even thinking about it creates a knot deep in my chest. As recently as three days ago, I would have claimed this had nothing to do with history, but my encounter with Shikhandin altered that belief. The knot in my chest has three strands, one of which leads unerringly to the man I just killed.

Killing Shikhandin completed the story of my killing of Chitrangada. I will hide it no more – I killed Chitrangada. It had to be done but doing so created the first strand of the knot that now threatens to choke me. It also earned me the name *Bhishma* (The Terrible). Not Devavrata the Terrible, just *The Terrible*. Am I *adhvaya*, alone, one of a kind – the *terrible* kind?

But killing Chitrangada brought Amba into my life. When I lost her, the second strand of the knot was formed. I had given her up for dead but Shukla now says that she left me for Drupada. Drupada? That bombastic hothead from Panchala? No, that makes no sense. Shukla says she has lived in hiding all these years. That does not make any sense either. Her actions created the third strand, hidden from me until revealed by Shikhandin. These three strands, let me call them *Chitrangada-Amba-Shikhandin*, independent though they may seem, are entwined tightly, each born of the previous one.

Why did I kill Chitrangada? The easy answer is that I saved him from a terrible fate. When I decided to kill him my mind was clear, without any doubt. But even as I acted on that decision, my thoughts whirled and became muddled; the purity of the initial intention was compromised, for I always wondered how things would have been different if I had been the King.

When Chitrangada became the ruler of Hastinapura, many of the citizens rejoiced that they would no longer be subject to a Regent's rule. Chitrangada was just a boy, sixteen years old, but with Satyavati's encouragement, he was confident of his ability to rule. And I had trained him to be a warrior. He was good at the business of war; he would have made an excellent Commander of a battalion or even a division. But that was not good enough for him. He considered himself a warrior in the tradition of Samvarana, father of our dynast Kuru. Shukla, who knew Chitrangada well, can tell you how ridiculous that ambition was. My ancestor Samvarana became a warrior under the personal tutelage of the great Vasishtha, founder of the Kavi Sangha, to regain Hastinapura. From the emptying cities of the West, leaders hired mercenaries who guarded the trading caravans. Now they guarded the leaders, maintained order, and prevented riots when the poorest felt unfairly treated. The mercenaries were the only ones trained to fight.

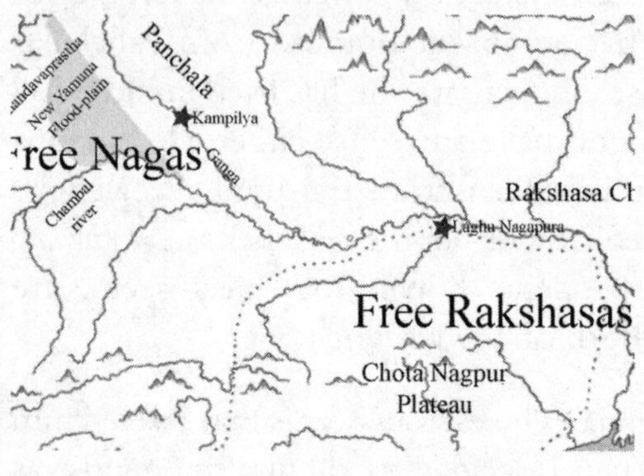

Since the time of Samvarana and Kuru, Hastinapura had defended itself from the Nagas of Panchala and defended Laghu Nagapura from the attacks of Rakshasas[42]. In Hastinapura, we did not use mercenaries but fought to protect ourselves. We kept our trade secrets. My father and I established an internal security force to manage the influx of immigrants and the resulting conflicts with the Nagas. They also enforced his restrictive laws about children. The Kavi Sangha supported him. But mercenaries do not make a good standing army. They only know how to make war and enforce martial law. They do not know how to enforce civil laws. They could not take a child away from its parents without killing them.

My army was not made up of great warriors. If we had ever faced a mercenary army, we would have lost. But mercenaries no longer exist and the guild has vanished. The mercenaries had no employment as the caravans no longer travelled west through dangerous lands. And with the disappearance of the Panchnad cities, there was no need for champions to fight on

[42]The Rakshasas ("protectors" in the Naga language) occupied much of the Southern Peninsula of South Asia, the plateau south of Laghu Nagapura, and both sides of the Ganga to the east of Laghu Nagapura.

their behalf. Better opportunities arose as guards in the west, so the east was abandoned.

After my father's death it was a simple step for me to create an armed militia. I needed them to protect the dams I had built upstream from the northern boundary of Panchala. The Panchalas could have easily destroyed them. South and west of the Ganga, the wayward Yamuna had made the watershed unstable, and new waterworks had to be built to control the old monsoon-fed rivers. The army came in useful to coordinate the design between towns and villages and to direct the construction of dams, canals, and ponds by local work groups. By the time Chitrangada was crowned, we had a small construction corps that could be used for projects.

A ruler with an army itches to fight. Chitrangada's first wish on being crowned was to use our army – *my* army, my *small* army – to attack Panchala and avenge Samvarana's humiliation. *He felt that though Samvarana had re-taken Hastinapura, the Panchalas had to be taught a lesson.* Satyavati and I rarely agreed, but on that occasion we jointly dissuaded Chitrangada by pointing out the difficulty of launching an attack across the river. Unfortunately, I also raised the possibility that we might not have the full support of the Nagas. Once this sank in, it colored Chitrangada's attitude to the Nagas; he in turn influenced Vichitravirya, and the brothers distrusted the Nagas ever after. This distrust was a disease difficult to cure. Even though Queen-Mother Satyavati was a Naga, both Dhritarashtra and Suyodhana were infected.

Chitrangada longed for recognition as a warrior. We checked that ambition then, but it never died. The result was tragedy.

I continued my project of creating dams and canals wherever it was feasible. One of my greatest successes was restoring Varanavata, Samvarana's old abode of exile, located on the edge of Khandavaprastha, at a point where the recently diverted Yamuna exited the forest. A monsoon stream ran through the shallow valley and its channel now overflowed with the waters of the Yamuna. My engineers had designed a series of crescent-shaped ponds that channeled the river, making it flow faster and deepening its median channel. The result was a river that flooded less. Canals led from the crescent ponds to Varanavata's fields much further away. Hence the town prospered and slowly filled with immigrants.

I was visiting Varanavata when I received an urgent message from Hastinapura. Chitrangada had heard of an incursion into Hastinapura territory at its northern extremity, close to one of the branches of the Sindhu. I had learned of this incursion some weeks earlier and had decided not to do anything about it. The Panchnad people claimed suzerainty over Jambudvipa, but it was a formulaic suzerainty. Nobody enforced it. The incursions had become an annual event over the last twenty years. Some Naga bands had settled near there, and I expected the intruders to go back as they usually did. But I did not anticipate Chitrangada's reaction.

Who were these intruders, you ask? They were from a nomadic collection of uncivilized tribes that called themselves 'Shaka[43],' and they came from the open plains north-east of the plateau of the Parsakas. The mountainous and forested lands we

[43]*Shaka* refers to Scythians (as named by the Greeks) who roamed over much of the steppes of Eurasia.

inhabited were useless to them and they usually left after a few weeks. *Why did they come?* They came to trade. They came with lapis and agate, both polished and rough. They brought partially tanned skins of many animals, large and small. Occasionally they had a small collection of yellow nuggets of pure gold. In the days before the disaster, Hastinapura viewed them as competition.

How did they come? This was the most interesting aspect of their visit and the reason I did not try to eject them post-haste. They travelled in carts pulled by small horses. Not onagers like we had, but horses. They did not behave like most traders. For instance, they did not bring their goods directly to the market. Instead, they would set up a camp in a secluded defensible place and come to the market with their goods on their backs or in small handcarts. Thus they never brought their horses to the trading site. I even invited them to come on their horses for an evening meal. They refused, citing cultural prohibitions that prevented them from eating with non-Shakas. What I did not realize till much later, was that they had started coming after I built a dam across the Yamuna ravine, within the mountains. Previously it had been difficult to cross with carts and supplies, now the dam provided a path. I would pay for my failure to anticipate this.

I had sent spies to keep track of the intruders and received reports regularly. When I was not in Hastinapura, the messenger would be re-directed to wherever I was. But the last messenger had gone to King Chitrangada's council-room. He attempted to withdraw when he realized I was not present. But before he could retreat, the King commanded him to deliver his message. Having heard about the incursions, Chitrangada expressed to his mother his dissatisfaction with my decisions and his shock that I had put the country at risk. He decided to take our army – *my* army – and teach the intruders a lesson.

I received a confused message from Satyavati and rushed to Hastinapura. But it still took a few days. When I arrived, I found Satyavati agitated. First, she urged me to leave immediately to help Chitrangada. Then, she fretted that I would steal from her son the credit for repelling the invaders and urged me to stay away. Then she wondered if the people would protect the King or if it was a plot against him? I remained silent during her vacillations and crying fits. What could I say? *It is my army he has taken – the five hundred trained fighters I gave up to him – leaving only a small force of a hundred boys-in-training to protect the city.* Such a statement would have only stoked the flames of her anger and made her more suspicious.

I departed as soon as I could, with fifty of my personal band. Chitrangada had left me with only a hundred men and I left half of them behind to supplement the hundred men of his army protecting Hastinapura.

Our onagers were not built for speed. The Shaka were trained horsemen; they used horses for everything. It was a mystery to us how the Shaka can ride in such a carefree manner. Many years ago, a trader had brought a wild horse in a cage. An angry horse is a terrifying sight. He showed us how the animal refused to submit to a yoke, and even with a yoke, it had uncontrollable power. Only the Shakas had mastered the secret of taming the horse. They did not impart that knowledge to anyone. Anyway, using onagers for transport, I travelled as fast as I could.

31
Devavrata to the Rescue

Devavrata continued, "We had loaded our supplies onto a dozen carts. Onagers are stubborn wilful creatures, but when harnessed with other onagers, they pulled the carts. We needed to make speed, so we harnessed two animals to each cart, while two spare ones walked alongside to replace them at need. People listening to bards tell of past battles, do not realize what it takes to move an army. Even my small squad of fifty fighters needed sixty onagers and fifteen carts for transport. Forty-five of the fifty men were divided into three squads, responsible for driving the carts.

The day began with a meal, followed by harnessing the onagers and travelling for twelve ghatis. There was a break for a mid-day meal of flatbread and salted meat. In a more traditional campaign, we would have stopped to hunt for meat if the game looked promising, and bartered our salted meat for hot cooked meals at local towns and villages. But we were in a hurry and we ate what we carried. After the meal break we would change the onagers and go for another twelve ghatis or until the sun began to set. Then we would settle down for the night after a light meal of the same flatbread and salted meat.

Our fifteen carts were loaded with three or four men each, their arms and armour, food, as well as forage for the draft animals. Each cart selected one man to stay awake the first half of the night and a second man to keep watch during the second half. My primary worry was wild animals such as tigers tempted by the onagers as easy prey. In a small squad like this, the onagers of the carts on the outside could be attacked by wolf packs if they looked vulnerable. Tigers and wolves were the most dangerous as they were not easily frightened away.

My second worry was the *kapi*[44] that roamed in bands, making trouble. I have been told these monkeys can be used as spies. That may be possible but I have only found them to be nuisances. If a cart was not constantly protected, it could be ransacked. The onagers were tied to each cart on opposite sides so that, if startled in the night and they panicked, they would pull in opposite directions and not be able to run away with the carts and be lost. Far more destruction has been caused in camps by distraught onagers than by even the fiercest enemy.

If the destination was far and speed essential, each onager would be spelled by a second onager that walked unburdened. That doubled the distance we could travel in a day. But our haste added to our problems. We had to carry twice the hay and grain for feeding the relief onagers, while cutting the number of soldiers and including one or more handlers for the additional onagers. The point is that moving an army, even a small army, is not an easy task.

I knew Chitrangada had left in a hurry without enough draft animals and would have had to slow down to a sustainable pace. He had a lead of seven days over us but he would have had to move slowly, with almost five hundred men and a couple of hundred followers who provided support. Instead of the four days we would take, he would have needed six or seven to reach

[44]*Kapi* refers to the Indian rhesus monkey.

the intrusion point. We had had some experience of unexpected confrontations with the Nagas of Panchala. It usually took a few days of maneuvering and observation before it became clear who had the upper hand. Against a Panchala corps, the smaller group would configure itself in a defensive formation and send for reinforcements. The bigger group would assess its chances of total victory before those reinforcements came and configure in an offensive formation. We inherited these forms of maneuvering, called *vyuhadyuta*[45], from Panchnad. It was rare for such a procedure to guarantee victory for the larger group; so much of the time nothing happened. A great superiority in numbers was needed before the larger group attacked. When reinforcements arrived, the forces might be equal or the relative strength reversed. The strategic implications of their relative strength led to reconfigured formations. Unless there was an overwhelming advantage for one group over the other, these maneuvers ended in a stalemate. Both groups would withdraw, and sometimes both declared victory. Sometimes the groups engaged in battle. This happened for various reasons – the personalities of the leaders, or an error of judgement by one side or the other, or even a momentary lapse in attention that allowed one side to gain an advantage over the other.

As I mentioned earlier, in the past I would arrange to monitor the Shaka 'visitors' but not engage them in battle. The pattern was that after a few weeks they would leave. They were not used to the never-ending forest and were a noisy bunch, especially when they rode their horses. I had a spy once who followed the Shaka back to their homeland and spent a few years with them. He returned in bad shape – a nervous wreck, voice pitched higher than before, slurring words as though he might lose

[45]*Vyuhadyuta* means a shadow duel of opposing battle formations.

them if he slowed down, eyes staring down and constantly moving. When he delivered the report of his two years on the road, he spoke quickly and I had to slow him down. He gave me useful information about the Shaka. Unlike their peaceful behavior when they visited us, they were extremely warlike in their own land. Every would-be warrior had a horse; the team of horse and warrior can be terrifying when confronted on an open field.

My spy described a battle he had seen when a Shaka band had attacked a caravan on the Parsaka border. The guards protecting the caravan had formed a defensive perimeter when the Shakas were sighted. A Shaka warrior galloped past the line, in arrow range, firing constantly. Arrows shot and spears thrown at the Shaka missed as they moved unpredictably on their horses. If the line of guards wavered, the horseman went in closer. Once an injury to a captain had distracted the soldiers near him and a horseman managed to get in among the defenders. He had inflicted terrible damage with a heavy sword while the guards struggled to organize themselves. As soon as they had regrouped, the horseman rode away, with barely a scratch. The Shaka strategy was to make the defenders use up their arrows and lose spears thrown in haste.

After a few days of this, the defenders became desperate and made overtures, offering tribute. The Shaka accepted the offer and came to collect it. Once in the camp, they rampaged through it on their horses, attacking the lightly armed guards and the defenseless traders and workers. It had been a terrifying sight – a man on a horse charging down a narrow path, slicing walkers as they scattered left and right. They then proceeded to ransack the camp and kill most of the fighters. The few women in the caravan were taken as captives. They tortured the men for amusement, killing most of them in the process and leaving the rest maimed and injured.

My spy had been one of the tortured ones who survived. He shook uncontrollably as he tried to describe what had happened to him but became incoherent when I pressed him for details. I learned later that castration was a part of the torture. I retired him to a home where he was taken care of for the rest of his life. His return to me to report had been an act of perseverance and loyalty. I wish I could have done more but the *bisajs* shook their heads and could do little for him.

I understood then that as long as the Shakas were far from their own land and faced a land or people they could not conquer, they would be peaceful. If they sensed an opportunity to deploy their preferred mode of warfare, on open fields, mounted on horses and dominated by the use of the bow and arrow, they would win every encounter against foot soldiers. Our Shaka traders had been peaceful because the Nagas lived in forested areas and the traders had come over the mountain passes with only a few horses, pulling carts. But something had changed now and this time they were behaving differently.

As I said before, we tried using horses to pull carts with no success. In recent years we have managed to use some young female horses to pull light chariots, but it is a difficult task. These young horses are fragile, temperamental creatures that need a lot of care. Maybe Shaka horses are more docile. The hooves of our horses become tender and inflamed, the horses become lame, and they are easily startled. Unlike our onagers, that are placid. They do nothing that will damage their hooves, like galloping. Only the most fearsome predator can startle an onager. But it is not possible to ride an onager. I know, for I have tried.

The Shakas use horses to make war. We have no experience of such wars. In the world of the Panchnad cities, war was rare and conducted by mercenaries as a game. Samvarana's eviction from Hastinapura and return to it was the only real war in our recent history. A smaller force was trapped by a siege and lost. An onager could not race past a line of infantry like a horse; the very idea was farcical.

Horses are not useful everywhere. A forest is no place to ride an animal like a horse. We cut paths and create trails for people and carts, not animals. The trails cut by Nagas in the forest did not support even an onager-drawn cart. A small horse could probably make its way through the forest. But a bigger one or one with a man on it, would be blocked by branches that would have to be pushed aside – a slow and noisy progression. A troop of horses would have to go single file, making them vulnerable to attack by an enemy. That thought made me confident that we had nothing to fear from the Shakas. In case of conflict, we could deal with them in the forests and not on a battlefield. I instructed my observers to avoid confronting the Shakas as far as possible. I did not want to fight the Shakas. Everything worked out well. There is no predicting what would happen in a battle, and the stakes were too small to be worth the risk.

32
Shaka Attack

Devavrata continued: "Two days after we left Hastinapura, we were met by one of my observers, returning with a message and a head in his cart. The head was that of one of my captains. The news stunned me. The King was missing. The Shakas had attacked us.

My spy gave me some of the details. Chitrangada had planned to camp near the village of Seshanagaram, a Naga village that was a few yojanas from the Shaka camp. The village of Gandhanagaram was much closer, less than a yojana, and would be an observation post for his scouts. Just as they began the tedious task of setting up tents and lean-tos, a small group of women and children came streaming out of the forest.

Gandhanagaram had been attacked. Many of the adult men had been killed. It was the season for planting seed. As was Naga practice, the women had gone into the forest with their children to gather firewood and gather fruit. The able-bodied men were preparing the fields for planting, which involved dragging a large wooden wedge to create a furrow. They would make the furrows for the planting at right angles to the furrows of the previous crop, so the soil was evenly used. But this practice made it harder to drag the wedge. The job required strength and only men were considered suitable. That left only a few older men and women who were relaxing in the central quadrangle of the living area of the village.

The Shaka horsemen had come along the trail that led to the river. The trail was narrow, not cut for horses, and it must have been rough going. But that did not deter them. As they emerged from the trail, the horsemen spread out along the perimeter of the field. They were quiet, but it was the middle of the day and they were quite visible. They did not announce their intention, but they did not have to. There were about twenty Shakas. The Nagas were unfamiliar with the use of horses in warfare, but the armor and weapons told them what the Shakas planned. The men in the fields began to run towards the center to get to their weapons. The women who had not gone to the forest, ran into their huts. The elderly took refuge in the central hut. As soon as the running began, the horses started in towards the center. They gathered speed and quickly caught up with the fleeing men who were closest. The Nagas had no chance. The riders wielded bronze swords that they used expertly to kill or disable.

It was fate, or perhaps ill luck, that Chitrangada had just arrived at the campsite south of the Naga village when the Naga women, who had seen the assault from the forest, had run there for help. Quick response is what I had trained my men for and within a half-ghati a squad of twenty men were ready for battle. A ghati later, the Shakas watched the armored and armed band make its way into the village clearing. Following the same tactic they had used with the Nagas, the horsemen charged the soldiers, who were armed with spears and carried leather shields.

Riding bare back, the Shaka warrior looked part of his horse, a second torso with a human head rising above the horse's shoulders. The horses came at our soldiers with terrifying speed. Chitrangada's men (*my* soldiers), were unfamiliar with such attacks. To them it seemed they were about to be trampled. They sidestepped the horses. As the horses flashed by, the riders slashed at them with swords. Spears protected my men from the first assault but the horses thundering past unbalanced them and many fell to the ground. The horses stopped and turned, to run at them, but more slowly this time. Some of my soldiers had time to retrieve their spears and succeeded in wounding the Shakas as they returned. Some Shakas fell off their horses and, though they landed nimbly, a few were killed – perhaps five or six. Ten of our soldiers died and two others were wounded.

In the meantime a second squad of soldiers had come into the opening. The Shakas realized they were outnumbered. They could not afford to lose so many fighters. One of the Shakas shouted and all the others still on horses wheeled round and galloped back to the trail they had come by. The remaining Shakas fought to the death. There were no captives.

The reinforced squad of soldiers did not chase the horse-riding Shakas. This may have been a tactical error for they would have had the advantage with the horses slowed by the narrow trail. Such possibilities reveal themselves only in hindsight. Instead, our soldiers stopped and helped move the wounded and the dead to Chitrangada's camp. All the Naga men who had been preparing the fields for planting were dead. With the departure of the Shakas the women came out of the forest. The old men and women of the Naga village, hiding in the innermost hut, had been saved only because the soldiers had arrived so promptly. A number of Naga women were missing. They had been foraging in the forest along the trail to the Shaka camp.

Chitrangada was furious. No Shaka had been captured to be questioned; they had fought to the death. He had lost more men than they. Chitrangada questioned the competence of the troops I had trained. The captains tried to calm him and finally Chitrangada called the officers into a quickly erected tent to decide on strategy. That was when Chitrangada decided that more information had to be obtained about the Shakas. It was a fateful decision. The villagers knew nothing. Nobody knew how many Shakas had come or how many were warriors. *Were there any traders among them, or was this a raid presaging more raids?* There were no answers.

One of the spies said he had seen women and children in the camp, but that report never reached the King. His captains were cautious; I had trained them well. Until they knew more about the enemy they took on a defensive posture. But the King was furious. *How could they get this information?* They replied: *Slowly. Spies will observe from hidden vantage points.* That was what I would have done. The King disagreed. *Just capture one and we will wring the information out of him.* The captains demurred politely. *We would have to send a squad and that would attract attention. Until we know more we should avoid exposing our warriors. We only have sixty trained soldiers; the rest are fresh recruits in training.* The King was livid. *Cowards!* he shouted and stormed out of the tent.

The captains conferred amongst themselves and proposed a compromise to satisfy the King. A small squad would go out that night while the Shakas were still tending their wounds. They would proceed silently. The goal was to capture one of the enemy and bring him back. As far as possible they would not engage with the Shakas in any other way. It was an unwise plan, made to appease the King, so as not to oppose his wishes.

When the captains' proposal was put to Chitrangada, he assented with a qualification; he himself would lead the squad. There was no changing his mind. Thus the squad led by the King left that night and were expected to return by daybreak. They had not.

Late that evening a second team consisting of two Naga army men, was sent to discover what had happened. They were to return before nightfall. Moving quickly through the forest they arrived near the Shaka encampment. They had seen no sign of passage by the King's squad, though there were many signs of Shakas on horses. The Shakas are not silent. The observers were about to turn back and report failure when they came across signs of fighting in a small clearing. Some of the trees still had arrows stuck in them. Other trees showed signs of damage from swords. Freshly broken branches lay around. There they found the head of the squad's captain. It seemed obvious that the Shaka had fought the squad in the clearing. Night was falling and the spies had little time to look around. The forest would be completely dark until the moon rose. They could not wait. While it was apparent the King had lost the battle, it was not known whether he was dead or a prisoner.

The news of the King's capture or death created turmoil in the camp. The captains could not agree on a course of action. Unlike my usual practice, the King had not included them as councillors and consequently they knew little of what he wanted to accomplish and how they were expected to support him. *Where was the King? Where were the soldiers who had gone with him?* Another squad of spies was sent at moonrise, around midnight. But they could not go far as the Shakas were working on rearranging their campsite and strengthening its defenses. The squad returned and reported no sign of the King or the squad.

The officers-in-charge could not agree on a course of action. They were too few to defeat the Shakas on horses, but they had to provide the Naga villages with some security. They had learned this from our past encounters with Panchala, when I guaranteed the safety of the Naga villages or towns we passed and was rewarded with help and loyalty. The captains needed reinforcements if they were to get the King back, so they sent me a messenger, with the head they had found, as a way of impressing on Hastinapura the urgency of the matter. Then they deployed their troops in a defensive formation around the Naga village and waited for events to unfold.

They did not know what to expect. The normal practice among the mercenaries of Panchnad was to propose exchanges of equivalent prisoners or demand a ransom. This was usually a simple exchange, except when a leading officer was captured; that required more bargaining. The released men then promised not to participate in the war. Dead bodies would also be exchanged in a similar way. My men knew this and waited for a message from the Shakas. And waited…there was no overture. Nothing happened.

With a sinking feeling in the pit of my stomach I roused my group and we set out as fast as we could. Without a leader and missing a captain or maybe more, my five hundred would be massacred. We got to the campsite that night. At first I was pleased. A defensive perimeter had been set up. But inside it there was chaos. There were some areas of furious activity and other of complete inactivity, with soldiers lounging around. There was commotion at the eastern end of the campsite, where we usually placed a gate. People were rushing back and forth, looking for something. A few were carrying buckets of water. Nobody recognized me until I was well inside and saw one of my captains, who took one look at me and shouted, 'It's the Regent! Regent Devavrata has arrived!'

The news of my coming spread like ripples created by a stone thrown into a pond. Soon my captains and a group of soldiers and helpers had gathered around me. The source of the commotion was a band of unfamiliar people – Nagas – mostly old men and women and children. They looked like they had been through a forest of thorns, with blood on their clothing, arms, legs and faces. Some had hands hanging useless by their sides, barely connected to their arms. There were a few younger men too, but they seemed to have suffered battle injuries. One had his right eye covered with a bloody cloth while another had been laid on the ground, his legs covered in gore.

There were two *bisajs* with the Hastinapura army, and the Naga villages had their herbalist and physician. I could do nothing for these victims of the Shaka attack. The captains had given up hope of a negotiation and expected an attack in the morning. My first concern was that the camp would be targeted as it defended the villages. My second concern was to get news of the King. Had he been killed? Why had the Shakas attacked this Naga village? There was no precedent for it in the past years of their visits. It seemed meaningless. But there is a first time for everything. I would have to ensure it would be the last.

The Nagas from the village the Shakas had attacked made a formal appeal for my help. You know how unusual that is. Nagas help each other unasked only if there is a family connection. Any other request has to be made formally. Some of the Nagas, in frequent contact with us in Hastinapura, were not such sticklers about the custom and had become more like us. There were frequent misunderstandings, situations in which a Hastinapura Naga expected to get help from a bystander unasked, as well as situations where a bystander intervened and was vilified by both parties to the dispute. Here, away from Hastinapura's cultural influence, old Naga practices still ruled. The Nagas appointed a representative, one of the older men who had escaped injury by hiding in the community hut. He asked to see me and said, 'Sir, we, the Nagas of the northern hills, need your help. I am assured that my cousins in the south by the Great River are allied with you. If that is true, I invoke your help.'

I replied 'Yes, indeed! I will help you. I come in search of my brother, the ruler of my city, who may be a captive of the Shakas. You must tell me more about these Shakas. Did you meet any of the traders?'

This was not the first time the villagers had traded with the Shakas. The Naga band that populated this village had moved here fifteen years ago. As usual, they burnt a section of the grove, cleared it of trees and shrubs, and offered sacrifices at the four corners of the clearing to the Mother Goddess. They sowed the first seeds shortly after the spring festival. They then used trees and branches to build permanent homes, wattle-and-daub cabins with roofs made of crossed branches covered with thatch, that would keep them dry during the coming rainy season. This was their age-old practice.

The Naga band encountered the Shakas some months after the rains. They were clearly visitors for they had not been there before the spring planting season and occupied makeshift homes consisting of conical frames covered with leather. The band had ten men and women with their children. They came in covered carts pulled by horses and carried merchandise for trade. They were peaceful. The Nagas and Shakas did not have a common language, but the Shakas had useful and decorative objects that they could barter for grain and vegetables. They wanted bronze but would accept copper.

When the Nagas took the Shaka items to Hastinapura, the merchants, Kuru as well as those from Panchnad and points further west, were impressed by the size of the gemstones. They were awed by the thickness and nap of the bearskins and even the deerskin, so much larger than the native black bear and sambhar deer. They bubbled with excitement at the yellow nuggets. They wanted to know where these were from, but the Nagas kept the Shaka source a secret while the Shakas did not tell the Nagas anything. It was also made clear that the Shakas did not want the Nagas to find out. The Shakas would usually leave when the weather turned warm and the sun began its northward course across the winter sky. Well before winter ended, they would be gone.

This pattern had held for almost fifteen years. The ash layer created in the grove from the old burn had almost drained its fertility and in another year or two, the spot would have to be abandoned. It was time to move on and the band started the process of finding a new grove to burn and settle in. In the typical case it would take a year or two to complete such a move. The Naga band did not wish to lose their exclusive access to the Shakas by moving further away, so they had moved closer to where the Shaka usually camped.

Something had changed this time. The Shaka group was much larger – perhaps fifty men, a larger number of children, and many more horses and carts. They were too many for their old campsite and had instead occupied a cul-de-sac in the side of a small hill, and constructed a thorn fence with a gateway. They worked on their settlement and did not try to contact the Nagas immediately. The Nagas took the initiative and sent a small group to welcome the traders. The Shakas met them at the gate; they were formal and correct, but would not let them in.

A couple of weeks later, the Shakas sent a small group with a cart loaded with goods for barter. This was as expected and the Nagas eagerly welcomed them to their new settlement. It did not take long for disappointment to set in. The Shakas had brought little worthy of barter. Most of the skins were unsaleable as they were old and worn, nothing like the large, furry and well-cured skins of previous years. These skins showed signs of many years of use. In exchange, they asked for the same products – grain and vegetables, copper and bronze – as in previous years. The Nagas were disappointed and refused to take what was offered. The Shakas were insistent. The request to barter became demands, which the Nagas rejected. The demands became unmistakable threats, at which point the Nagas stopped all talk and sat quietly. The Shakas were equally patient or apparently so. They sat for most of that day. The Nagas even offered them meals. In the evening, all the Shakas got up and left silently.

Refusal to barter was unprecedented among the Nagas. It was commonly the case that every place they occupied, every time they moved, new traditions would be created and some old ones dropped. Bartering with the Shakas was now a tradition here. They had been bartering with them ever since the first year of the settlement. Some of the older Nagas had muttered about the bad luck that breaking with tradition would bring. Others pointed out that what the Shakas had brought was itself a break with a much more ancient tradition. The Nagas did not want the Shaka skins and gold for themselves but for trade with other groups, and the products offered could not be traded. Accepting the trade in the name of a tradition here, would cause a break in tradition later. The Shakas were upset. They spoke amongst themselves, glared at the Nagas, and left with their offerings.

This attack then was their response to the Naga refusal to accept substandard products. This was not how a trader would act. Even in the most difficult encounters, traders try to keep the peace. Peace had brought prosperity to the people of Panchnad. The violence of these Shakas showed that they had not come in peace to trade, but to raid or colonize. In either case, they planned to terrorize the local population. *Were the Shakas ever traders? Maybe we were imposing a category we understood on the behavior of strangers.*

'The traders who came to our tents were old men,' the old Naga representative said. 'They did not come riding horses but carried their meagre products in a cart drawn by two of their oldest horses. They looked impoverished and hungry.'

'Does nobody know anything about their camp?'

'Sir, our Chief visited them the first day, to welcome them. He wanted to assure them that we would, as always, engage in fair bartering. He knew they wanted grain, for their land did not produce any. He told them that if they needed grain they should ask, and we would not refuse. He thought this would convey they were welcome visitors. Our Chief's visit was part of tradition, and one of the ways we assess people we trade with.'

This aspect of Naga tradition surprised me. It indicated a level of sophistication in managing trade with strangers that I had not been aware of. 'I need to talk to the Chief,' I said.

'He is dead, Sir.'

A dark shadow crossed my heart – not a monsoon cloud promising rain, but a cloudburst that presaged a raging flood. *Was finding my brother going to prove a lost cause?* I turned away.

'Sir, listen to us!' the Naga pleaded. I turned back to him. 'The Chief went with a small entourage; they were all men except for his oldest daughter.'

'Where are his men?'

"Dead. They were all killed in the raid. But his daughter is still with us.'

The Nagas have some strange customs – strange to us Kauravas, who grew up with Panchnad customs. Among the Nagas, men and women played different roles in daily life. By contrast, in urban Panchnad, there was no cause for differences in roles. Of course, only women gave birth to children and both cultures required women to care for the infants. The Naga women foraged for fruit and nuts and edibles that grew wild and could not be cultivated. The men were farmers and fishermen. They tilled the fields or fished; they called it giving birth to their food.

In Panchnad, a guild, one of seven (not counting the mercenaries), determined the daily life and labor of its members. The only task reserved for men was trading. Few women became traders or participated in the years-long caravan trips. War was not one of the duties divided between men and women; both were equally unprepared to defend themselves or their village. This task was assigned to the Guild of Mercenaries, consisting of mainly men, though a few extraordinary women were members, too.

In recent years, Kuru women have been sequestered away from the public eye. This began when Samvarana sojourned in the forest with Vasishtha, and rebuilt his army. Vasishtha had been insistent that there be no women fighters. It was a new rule previously unheard of. Vasishtha was exploiting the strength advantage a trained man had over a woman of equal training or skill. That rule continues to the present day.

'How old is the Chief's daughter? Is she here?'

'She is a grown woman, Sir, and her name is Amba. She is here in the camp.'

'I wish to speak to her,' I said. 'Please ask her to come here.'

33
Amba

Devavrata paused. His eyes opened wide and for the first time he smiled – a smile that seemed to brighten the darkened tent. It appeared to Lomaharshana that the memory of Amba had blown away the dark monsoon clouds, leaving the ground sparkling with raindrops in the light of the sun.

Devavrata resumed, his voice deep and clear. "That was how Amba came into my life. She was, *dare I say it*, beautiful. My mind struggled for control over my body – my face wanted to turn to her, my lips wanted to smile, my feet wanted to dance, despite the seriousness of the situation. When I first saw her she was wearing a plain wrap that had once been white but was now bloody and torn along the edges. I learned later that she had been attending to the injured. Her dusky complexion made her smile glow – *how many times have I felt a rush of joy at that sight and smiled in response?* Her face was oval, with almond-shaped eyes. She wore a necklace of a single strand of beads – this revealed her age, for older Naga women wore more necklaces with precious beads, reflecting their wealth. To say that I was smitten is to understate it. It had happened to me once before, when I first met Satyavati. My heart raced and it felt as if everybody could hear its drumbeats. I stood still, looking at her, afraid that any movement would betray my feelings.

'You called me, Sir?' she asked, her tone polite. Her eyes caught mine and I felt warmed by her smile. She looked away but not before I saw the hint of acknowledgment. *She knows the effect she has on me.*

My voice came out husky, low-pitched and inaudible. 'You are the Chief's daughter?'

'Sir?' her voice was neutral but her eyes glowed.

'You are the Chief's daughter?' I said, louder than I intended, and immediately berated myself for asking such an inane question.

The glint vanished from her eyes. Her face fell and she became sombre. Her father was dead. 'Y-yes, Sir.'

The smile had gone from her face and like a *soma* addict, I wanted it back. I regretted that I had reminded her of her father. I adopted a matter-of-fact tone that I could barely manage. 'They tell me that you went to the Shaka camp with your father.'

'Yes, Sir.'

'What did you see?'

She did not hesitate. 'They must have come down south along the river bank. It is barren rocky ground that opens out into a flat, grass-covered grove. The soil there is not deep enough for planting, so we do not use the grove. It was their first campsite. The gate faced the trail from the village. Two sides are dense forest and difficult to move through while the back is protected by a rocky ridge. At one corner the trail continues uphill. Their tents face inwards in a circle and block any other entrance to the grove, so you can only go through the gateway they have established. The river runs white over the rocks, but between the rocks it can be deeper than two onager-drawn carts. Inside, they have a central tent. Their wagons are behind that tent. Their horses are corralled further back, so they cannot wander away.'

'Is it a defensible encampment?'

'Yes. The village trail opens out into their grove. They have built a wall across the width of the grove, with trees and branches. There is a small entrance, about five or six hands wide; their horses can come through. You cannot attack from the front. The river is difficult to cross, and on the other side is a steep hill. At the back a rocky path goes uphill to a ridge that runs along the river bank.'

'There is a trail to your village?'

'Yes. The children used to play there.'

She turned to leave. I grasped at a straw. Something. Anything. So I could be with her a while longer.

'Can you guide me and my troops?'

'Yes.'

'At night? Silently? Without light?'

'Yes, even a half-moon is enough. But noise will travel – you must be silent.'

'My troops will not make any noise. We will be ready a little after midnight. The half-moon should be rising.'

She took that as dismissal and walked away. My heart was thumping. I looked around, the camp seemed unreal. It was as if I had spoken to Amba in another world.

We gathered late that night, just as the moon appeared in the east. We prepared fire arrows, with tips wrapped in cotton soaked in pine-oil, and one of my men carried embers covered with ash in a small clay bucket.

Amba led the way from the village where the trail began. The moonlight was just enough for us to walk carefully through the forest. I was proud of how silently my men made the trip from the village. It took us almost five ghatis at a normal walking pace. Running would have been too noisy and too risky on a forest path in the dark. Amba walked carefully but without hesitation, glancing at me from time to time. Her proximity was heady. I wanted to show her all that I could do, but that went beyond the needs of the expedition. When she talked, I became tongue-tied. We skirted the Naga village. Amba pointed out some landmarks in the village – the central hut in which the seniors had hidden and so survived, the granary, and the communal space around which the huts were clustered. We reached the place in the forest that the Shaka had come through on their horses.

'How much further from here?' I asked.

'About three ghatis at this pace.'

The moon was nearing its zenith; we had eight ghatis before sunrise, maybe a little less if the dawn was clear.

'We must move a little faster.'

Amba looked at me. I gazed at her, our eyes trapped.

'We should keep to this pace to prevent accidents,' she said as we both looked away simultaneously.

I grunted, glancing sideways, and saw her smile, her teeth and eyes reflecting the moonlight. We continued walking carefully along the path Amba showed us. A ghati later we heard a rustling in the bushes. I looked at Amba. She understood my question.

'There are no large wild animals here; a lone wolf, perhaps.'

I took my knife out of its scabbard and signaled the men to stop. I wanted to investigate the sound myself. I moved silently towards it. My men knew what I wanted from them; they stopped and waited. Amba followed me. I hesitated, then made a fateful decision – I let her accompany me.

We came to a small clearing. There were a number of bodies lying on the ground. I could not recognize the faces in the dim light but some of the clothing was easily recognizable. These were the men of the King's troop. Chitrangada had followed my example and created uniforms for his men – not the unimpressive grey my men wore, but red and gold. A few ornaments glittered, reflecting the moonlight. Nothing was moved. Then I heard a rustling from the opposite side of the clearing. I went across, Amba following.

There was a body stirring there. The man was still alive. He responded to the sound of our voices by crouching on his hands and knees and trying to stand. But his feet could not support him. I recognized the injury; he had been hamstrung, the tendons in both knees cut. Crouched on the ground he looked up at us. Amba gasped and her hand grasped my upper arm. I do not know if I showed any emotion, but I was overcome by despair and sorrow, for I saw what the Shakas had done to this man. His eye sockets were empty. In the light of the moon they were dark holes reflecting nothing. He moaned, and I could not understand him. That sound would later resonate in my memory and become familiar, the sound made by a mouth from which the tongue had been ripped out. The man's body folded on itself and collapsed.

I took out my knife and stepped up to him, pulled back his head and sliced the throat from ear to ear in a single stroke. I held the thrashing body as warm blood spurted onto my arms and flowed down his chest to the ground. Slowly, the thrashing stopped.

Amba made a strangled sound. I looked up at her. She stood still, staring at me, her eyes shining in the moonlight. I dropped my eyes. I could not bear to link those glistening eyes to this act. *What could I tell her?*

Her words came to my rescue. 'You are a kind man. Is he one of your men?'

'He is my brother.'

I hugged the dead body of Satyavati's son, Chitrangada, King of Hastinapura, then gently lowered it to the ground. I turned him so he faced the earth. There was no reason for our men to see his mutilation. I rose and wiped the blade of my knife clean.

34
Death of a Brother

The Regent looked at Lomaharshana. For a brief moment, the Archivist felt that he had been thrown into the coldest Himalayan stream in the depths of winter. He could not meet the Regent's eyes; to do so would have been to leap into the vast empty chasm that is said to lie between this world of humans and the heaven of the gods. He turned his head and heard a long sigh from the Regent. Then there was silence.

Lomaharshana felt powerless to pierce that silence. *Was it even his task?* In the silence life seemed frozen in a single unmoving moment of time. It was the primal silence preceding the primal scream when the universe had been born of the body of Brahma. Lomaharshana was relieved when the Regent finally stirred and broke his silence.

"Despite all our problems, Chitrangada was my brother and I cared about him. He was born when I was twenty years old. My father continued to be infatuated with Satyavati. After the day's necessary duties were done, he spent his time with her. She left the rearing of her children to maids and wet-nurses. I had withdrawn from all but the most necessary of official duties and did not see my half-brother when he was born, and not for many years after.

The monsoons had been good for a few years. For a brief period the Sarasvati flowed with water again. The refugee stream stopped as the people of Panchnad considered their future to lie in their homeland. We always knew it was blind chance that the river flowed. But hope overwhelmed calculations of chance and the refugee crisis in Hastinapura seemed to abate. Some Panchnad refugees even made plans to return. Those were the good years.

The rains came with their own crises. Once, heavy rains eroded the soil under a boulder that then rolled off and damaged the levee near the women's quarters in Hastinapura – the place I had avoided ever since Satyavati moved there. I now had to inspect the levee with my inspectors to assess the damage. Chitrangada was playing in the courtyard with the women. He must have been about four or five years old. I had not expected to see him, thinking that all the women and children had been moved. I look sufficiently like Shantanu so that Chitrangada thought it was his father. He came running up to me. Some children are unafraid of strangers; that would describe Chitrangada. He paused when he realized that I was not his father, but he came up to me anyway and asked me my name. When he learned I was Devavrata, he said, 'The aunts here say I have a brother by that name.'

'I am that brother,' I said.

Delighted, he shouted, "My brother! My brother!' and ran around me while I stood still, unsure of what to do. Then he stopped and asked, 'Why are you so big? I have another brother but he is tiny and I am not allowed to play with him. Can I play with you?'

It is hard to describe my feelings at that moment. I realized that if I had married Satyavati, this would be my son. I could not touch my half-brother with the flame of my anger at Satyavati. I told him I was busy then but would certainly play with him later. I continued to avoid Satyavati. My bitterness and resentment against her did not go away. But I went to the women's quarters to play with Chitrangada. Later, when Vichitravirya was old enough, the three of us would play together."

At this point, the Regent Devavrata stopped. Lomaharshana was listening and memorizing Devavrata's words mechanically.

"That was my brother. He was only a child," the Regent said, the words forcing themselves out of his mouth. Then he stopped and closed his eyes. Silence again. A few vighatis passed. He leaned back for a moment, forgetting the arrowhead in his chest; immediately his eyes opened wide in pain. He gasped and jerked forward; then his body relaxed in a faint, his eyes closed, turned to one side.

Lomaharshana moved forward and raised the Regent. He was surprisingly light. The Archivist had expected a greater weight in one so large. *He is old. For an old man, he is holding up pretty well.* Lomaharshana called for the attendant, who came in right away. He took one look at the body in Lomaharshana's arms and moved quickly to take over from him. He asked the Archivist to move the bolster and the stuffed mat and laid the Regent down again, making sure the arrowhead did not move. He held the Regent's wrist between thumb and forefinger, and closed his eyes for a vighati. Finally he said, "There is a pulse, but slow. He will live, at least for now. He is a hardy man. What happened?"

"He recalled something that surprised him, and he leaned back against the arrow. I think he forgot it was there."

The attendant left. The Archivist called in a passing messenger and gave him a message for the King, asking him to visit after the mid-day meal, if possible.

Yudhishthira came, the Vyaasa in tow. The Archivist took his place at the foot of Devavrata's cot. The Regent was asleep.

The Vyaasa said, "He is exhausted."

The Archivist replied, "Yes and no. He talked all morning."

"Where did he stop?"

"Just after he had narrated the killing of King Chitrangada. He began explaining how he had first met Chitrangada as a toddler and… I don't think he wished to go on."

The Vyaasa stared at the Archivist. "Did he say that he killed the King himself?"

"Yes, Sir. That is exactly what he said. His last words were 'That was my brother. He was only a child.'"

"That was not the story he told Satyavati or anyone else."

"Is the official story recorded in the archives?"

"Yes. It says: When Devavrata returned, he said that gandharva allies of the Shakas had killed Chitrangada. That did not make any sense, for the gandharvas, even if they existed, have not been known to ally with humans. I questioned the men who had been left behind in the camp, but they did not know how the King had died. The man who found the King's body said he had been ordered not to speak of what he had found. Archivist, did Devavrata speak of it? Did he reveal everything?"

"Enough, Sir."

"I can guess. The Shakas are known for their bestial practices. When Devavrata returned, some of his troops began calling him Bhishma. That was an unusual name for the Commander of an army, but he did not stop them. He said very little about that expedition to me or anyone else."

The Archivist remained quiet. The Vyaasa made a gesture of dismissal. "You may go now. Eat, rest and return. He may awaken and talk some more."

The Archivist left.

The King said, "Gurudeva, I rely on you to keep me informed for I must leave now." So saying, the King too, left.

Shukla was left alone with his sleeping friend. He sat down by Devavrata's side. These were memories from a long time ago. He had to reconstruct as much as recall them. Devavrata had returned with the news of Chitrangada's death, but long before he arrived, a new name for the Regent had spread among the people – *Bhishma.* The story was that the captured Shakas, men, women and children, had been tortured in public. This had changed the people's perception of the Regent. He was no longer the young disinherited heir who had remained loyal to the King despite being pushed aside by the ambitious new wife, but a fearsome, bloodthirsty army chief to be feared and despised. The young man who had vowed celibacy had been a friend if not a kindred spirit. The ambition that had driven Shukla from a fisherman's hut to the leadership of the Kavi Sangha (an often quarrelsome and contentious group), was lacking in Devavrata. He had sublimated his passion in the most down-to-earth projects – building dams, ponds and canals; taking on the problem of feeding the refugees, dealing with runaway rivers, maintaining the trade route for which Hastinapura was the entrepôt, and strengthening relations with the Nagas around Hastinapura. There were failures as well. He failed to establish peace with Panchala; all his overtures to the Rakshasas east of Laghu Nagapura were ignored.

The man who returned from the encounter with the Shakas was a silent man. The memories of his return were lost in the upheaval attendant on the death of the King. *It was before I was the Vyaasa. I was just Shukla, the Queen's brother, just another rising star in the Kavi Sangha.* The old Devavrata would have paid him a visit to describe the events of the encounter and to consider future actions. The new one barely acknowledged his old friend. Shortly thereafter, Shukla had left for the great learning center of Takshashila, in the north-west. It was recognition of his potential to climb up the Kavi Sangha hierarchy.

When he came back a year and a half later, he had expected a joyous reunion with Devavrata. Instead, he found a man who had adapted to the new name, *Bhishma,* the Terrible. This man Bhishma had barely returned his embrace before suggesting Shukla describe his experiences at Takshashila in open court. What had happened to the Devavrata who would have demanded a detailed narration in private between two friends, of all that Shukla had experienced? Shukla's request for a private meeting had been met with a non-committal, *Yes, we should meet*, and had not been followed by any action.

Shukla had questioned his sister. Satyavati was still in mourning for her son Chitrangada. She had been told the official story – that gandharvas had killed him. Devavrata's behaviour, leading to the title *Bhishma,* was inexplicable. Why had he tortured the Shakas? Shukla had thought it was a lie spread by the Regent's enemies.

"Sir," a voice interrupted the Vyaasa's reverie.

The Archivist had returned. Devavrata was still asleep. The Vyaasa motioned for silence and moved outside the tent. He said, "Continue after he has eaten. There is more to come."

"He said he killed his brother. What greater secret is there?" The Archivist stopped. The Vyaasa was staring at him, his eyes burning like coals. "I beg forgiveness, Sir. I will arrange to make him comfortable when he awakens. If he wishes to continue, we will. Later I will come to you."

The Vyaasa nodded. Had he been like this as a youngster? *I know exactly how irritating I was!* That was why he had been sent away to Takshashila to study. "You'll do fine, Lomaharshana. Continue. Get as much of the story as you can."

Lomaharshana the Archivist watched the Vyaasa leave. He breathed a sigh – that had been close. He, at the threshold of his career in the Kavi Sangha, had expressed an opinion and talked back to the Vyaasa, the senior-most member. Though he was the Archivist, and Archivists like him, with a prodigious memory and native skill, came perhaps once or twice in a generation, he was lucky that they had been alone. It would surely have been the end of his career if another good candidate had been available to take his place. He breathed a sigh of relief.

Going over to the cook's tent, the Archivist arranged for the Regent's afternoon meal to be delivered. A soup made of salted roast mutton, rice and herbs was the most he could swallow.

When he returned, Devavrata's eyes were open, staring at the tent opening. It seemed to the Archivist that Devavrata was waiting for him.

"There you are," said Devavrata. "Why did you leave when I was just resting my voice?"

"You fell asleep, Sir. It has been a few ghatis. Do you feel rested?"

"Rested? With this arrow in me?" Though it was a rebuke, his eyes were bright, almost as though he was free of pain.

"My apologies Sir, I misjudged. It has been almost five ghatis, and it is time for a small meal, as recommended by the *bisaj.* Afterwards we can continue if you wish."

"I do. There is little else, I can accomplish here. We must satisfy your master, the Vyaasa."

The Archivist smiled. Making the record was his assigned task, and he was happiest when it made progress.

"Where did I stop? What did I tell you before my nap?"

"You were with a Naga girl, Amba, and you had found your brother maimed by the Shaka and killed him."

Devavrata closed his eyes and took a deep breath. It was as though a monsoon cloud had moved to cover the sun. When he re-opened his eyes, they looked weary, no longer bright. "Must I continue? Of course I must…so let me tell you what happened after I put down my brother's body."

35
Revenge

Devavrata said, "I faced Amba. I could not read her face in the moonlight. Her eyes were wide, her right hand covering her mouth.

'You are a kind man,' she said. 'Is he one of your men?'

'He is my brother.'

She turned her face away from me as I laid down the body and stood up. I could not bear to see her turn away from me. Without thought I grasped her upper arm. Her head jerked back to look at me. Her right hand came up and stroked my cheek, wet with tears. I took her hand in mine and held it to my face. She stood still as my tears flowed onto her fingers.

A brief moment later she said, 'Sir, you must continue.'

She was right. I squeezed her hand lightly and released it. We re-joined the squad.

What is left to report of this expedition is already known. We reached the camp well before sunrise. The Shaka had become careless after two encounters in which they had overwhelmed the Nagas and our troops; they had not posted any look-outs. If they had, we could not have done what we did. While the fire-throwers stayed back, the rest of us crawled to the wall of branches that hid the first row of tents that backed up against the fence they had put up. When we were ready, we signaled with the bark of a fox. The fire-arrows hit the first row of tents. The alarmed sleepers rushed out creating a commotion. That allowed us to breach the fence and move into the tents from the rear. We waited. When the Shakas realized that the fire was not an accident and that they were under attack, they went to their tents for their weapons. We slaughtered them in their own tents. By this time those in the second row of tents had realized the camp was under attack. As they struggled to pick up their weapons, their tents too, caught fire.

Without their horses, and with hastily grabbed weapons, the Shakas were less formidable as enemies. Within two ghatis we had complete control of the campsite, except for the central tent. We surrounded it and I asked those inside to surrender.

A young boy came out, hands held out in front. 'We surrender. Please do not kill us.'

'Who is inside?' asked Amba.

'My aunts, sisters, cousins, my grandfather and two of his friends.'

I kept the boy at my side. 'Ask them to come out slowly and throw their weapons to the side.' I indicated a spot well away from my troops.

When they came out, we counted sixteen prisoners. Two men were fighters, supposed to protect the others, but had decided it was better to live as slaves than die as warriors.

That was not to be. On the way back I made a detour with a chosen few of my men to the clearing where the King and his squad lay. We brought their bodies back to the camp. The next day, we went with the Naga villagers to the site of the Naga massacre. The Naga villagers gathered around us in a big circle. My soldiers formed a barrier to prevent them from coming closer. I lined up the captive Shakas – women, children, and the old men. Then I brought the two fighters to the front.

'I am looking for the King,' I said to the fighters. 'Can you tell us what happened to him?'

One man stood still and silent. The other replied in the language of the Nagas. 'We don't know of any King.' He then whispered to his friend, who nodded his head.

I described Chitrangada – young, haughty, skin the color of the elephant grass that grew by the banks of the Ganga, a small moustache and a stubble of a beard.

The quiet one nodded and whispered to the other, who said, 'Yes, we know the prisoner. He was a tough one.'

'What happened to him?' I asked.

They whispered some more in their own tongue. Then the speaker turned to me. 'Nothing. We just kept him as a prisoner. We did not know he was the King.' He shrugged as he said this.

My eyes narrowed and I felt bile well up in my throat. 'Nothing?'

'Nothing unusual.' That shrug again.

My hands trembled. I struggled to control them. 'Was he tortured?' I asked.

The quiet one turned his head away from me but not before he had caught my eye and averted his gaze. The speaker looked down as he spoke, avoiding my eyes. 'No.' he said.

No shrug this time. The quiet one was now looking straight at me, a sneer lurking at the corner of his lips.

'You must tell me the truth,' I said, 'or I will punish you.'

The speaker looked away to my right. 'He was not tortured,' he said.

I closed my eyes and sighed. They relaxed, thinking I had accepted their information.

'Do you have a wife, children?' I asked.

The speaker shook his head.

'What about your friend here? Are one of these prisoners married to him?'

He hesitated and then, 'No.'

I turned to him, my face livid. I went close and my voice fell to a low whisper. 'You are lying. Both of you were standing next to women. You had two girls by your side, and he had one boy. Tell me the truth, now!'

The speaker backed away from me. I must have looked insane. His companion looked at him and shook his head, but the speaker was not looking at him. Instead, he pointed to one of the women. 'That is his wife.'

I had my soldiers bring the woman over. A boy of about eleven grabbed her hand and pulled her back. My soldiers held on to the woman, who held on to the crying boy.

'Bring him instead,' I said.

They separated the boy from the woman and brought him over. The woman began to scream. More soldiers were needed. It was hard to control the boy, who shouted for his mother. The quiet one looked away; there was nothing he could have done.

Devavrata paused. "I can't go on," he said.

The Archivist asked, "Why, Sir? Are you tired, hungry? Look, the soup has just come."

"No, no, I am not tired. I am…I…how can I tell this story? Come Lomaharshana, pour me some soup. A few sips might soothe my heart and calm me."

The Archivist poured out two small bowls of soup. He held one to Devavrata's lips. The soup was lukewarm. Devavrata took a few sips, then waved it away.

"I cannot drink it. Why don't you have some?"

The Archivist had not intended to drink his soup, but Devavrata's eyes watched him carefully as he emptied the bowl.

The Archivist waited attentively for the Regent to say something. But he lay motionless and silent, his eyes unfocused. Lomaharshana waited. Half a ghati passed and the Regent had not moved. *What should I do?* Lomaharshana thought. His voice low, he said, "Sir, should I come back at a later time?" There was no response. Lomaharshana tried again, louder this time, "Sir!"

Devavrata's eyes focused on him. "Oh! Yes, you are waiting for me. I...I…was recalling what happened. Yes, let me continue from where I stopped." He said, "There was nobody there who could have stopped me. Instead, I was obeyed as I proceeded to do the indefensible. The boy was uncontrollable. I took out my sword and hit him with the flat on the side of his head. He collapsed in a faint and was as quiet as his father.

How can I continue with this narration? What I did that day I did not plan. That day I earned the name *Bhishma*, the Terrible. I had intended to punish only the two men – torture *them* the way they had tortured my brother. It was not hard to contemplate them suffering. But what I wanted I did not get, for them to admit they had tortured the King. I wanted them to acknowledge the justice of the punishment I planned to inflict. That was not to be. In extenuation, I point to those almost invisible shrugs; they goaded me. These are poor excuses for my commands that day, pathetic excuses. I gave the commands. If anyone objected, I did not hear. My men bear no blame. I hope they tried to stop me and I refused to listen. I do not know why they followed my orders, but they did. They too, had seen the King's body, and perhaps the same demon that had gained ascendance over me, ruled them.

By the time I was done, three children and two women lay dead on the ground, hamstrung, blind and mute. *I have been kind.* I told the two men. *Kinder than you were to the King. They were not tortured.* I pointed to the bodies with my foot and turned one over. *See, no signs of torture. They died before they suffered much. Am I not kind? Can you acknowledge my mercy and ask for more?*

The lurking smile and uncaring shrugs had vanished, but the stony faces and fixed eyes did not change. My captains' whispered pleas finally got through to me; my actions could turn the local Nagas against me. I had my men drag the two captives over to me. With careful deliberation I did what I had to do. I did it myself, making sure that each could see what was happening to the other one. They were not dead when I was done, and I laid them next to their families to await death.

The local Nagas watched unmoving from the perimeter where I had placed them. There was no sound from the group. Not then, not later. Amba was present and watched unmoving. I tell myself that Amba's presence had nothing to do with my actions. She had taken part in that night's battle in the Shaka encampment. Perhaps the carnage would have satisfied her. She could not have moderated my rage. Her father and mother were dead – her father's head almost severed from his body. Her mother had run towards her husband. They had not found her body in the field. Later her mutilated remains were discovered in the Shaka camp. The two men in front of me would have been among her desecrators.

Amba had seen the King alive, a young man who cut an impressive figure. She and the Nagas would have put their faith in him. And then she saw his mutilated body, saw why he had to be killed. People like us, raised in the city, are overwhelmed by death. Amba was a Naga, who lived in the forest. She saw death every day. But the manner of death the Shaka had inflicted on her parents would have ignited her anger. I wanted to show her that my anger and resolution equaled hers. She had seen me cry and might think me weak. I wanted to show her that I was strong. But was she among the Nagas who thought I was wrong to order the killing of women and children? Would she turn against me?

I tell myself that I was angry and confused and did the unthinkable because I was not myself that day. Only Amba and the group that had attacked the Shaka encampment knew what I knew – that the King had been tortured the way I tortured the prisoners. The King's men, the other men from Hastinapura, who had come with me, and the surviving Naga villagers, saw a side of me that had never before been seen, maybe had never before existed. As a result I became *Bhishma*, the Terrible. My men gave me the name, and over time, *Devavrata Bhishma* became just *Bhishma*.

I look back and imagine myself not doing what I did. Could a different Devavrata have returned from the campaign, not the Devavrata Bhishma I had become? Could I have been someone liked, not feared? Loved, not just respected. But I became Bhishma, a person to inspire terror. When does the thirst for revenge edge over into insanity? I was insane that day. Later, we reconnoitered the route the Shakas had taken. I discovered they had brought their vehicles and horses over a dam I had constructed some years earlier. I said nothing. In hindsight lies wisdom, I thought. We followed the road and found another Shaka encampment, larger, with mostly older men, women and children, mostly non-warriors. We attacked and killed the ones who resisted, leaving a few wounded survivors to return to their homeland with the message they were not wanted. Those not injured, we enslaved.

On our return we prepared the bodies of the King and his squad so they looked presentable and cremated them *en masse*. The corpses were already stinking and I did not see the point of taking them home. Satyavati would later chastise me about my haste in cremating her son, but I did not wish her to see what had happened to him. Nor did I want to tell her the King's Captains had permitted him leave on a spying expedition with a very small force; heads would have rolled. With the connivance of my troops I invented a story of a pitched battle with an intruding army from Gandhara. This changed in the telling and retelling to the *gandharva* of popular imagination – magical creatures invented by a teller of tales we both know well."

The Archivist frowned. "Do you mean the current Vyaasa?"

Devavrata nodded. "I saw Amba later that day, the day I killed women and children. We were alone and I was certainly deranged. That night, I was subject to no oath. The oath Satyavati so relied on had lost its hold over me. I was not Devavrata, bound by Devavrata's words. I asked Amba to come with me that night. She too, must have been insane. Her father and brothers had been killed; her mother mutilated. She had tasted revenge, but this bloodletting had not quenched the heat of the inferno raging within her.

I must have been insane to think I could keep my relationship with Amba secret from Satyavati. She must have found out quite soon after we returned to Hastinapura, but said nothing. Why did she keep quiet? Maybe by becoming *Bhishma* I had terrified her as well. Perhaps someone had told her the truth behind the name. The old Devavrata had kept his vow for long years, proving his support for what she most cared about – her descendants as rulers of Hastinapura. If she had made a fuss she could have aroused the demon that was Bhishma and Devavrata, the dutiful son of his father, might have disappeared completely. Civil war between my supporters and hers, she knew, had been unthinkable for the old Devavrata, and would have ended her imperial plans. But after Chitrangada's death, exposure was not something Satyavati wished to threaten me with."

36
Love

Devavrata continued: "That night I broke my vow of celibacy. That night I freed myself of Satyavati. Amba came to me willingly. I still had enough of the old Devavrata in me so that I told her of my vow. She did not understand such a vow. To her, it was worse than the monogamy the Shakas required of their women. I could not explain the self-imposed restrictions I had lived with all these years. I abandoned the effort to explain. But she accepted the need for secrecy. We entered the woods silently. There was nothing gentle about our lovemaking. Memories of my brother's dying moments intruded. She responded in kind, possibly driven by what she had seen of her dead father and mother. Our rage found its outlet in sex. It was many weeks before our encounters became tender and loving."

Devavrata paused. He was barely whispering. The Archivist moved closer to hear him. Devavrata shook his head and put out a hand to motion him back. Then he winced and withdrew his hand. But his voice grew stronger as he continued. "The next day I mulled over the problem of what to do about the Naga village. The surviving Nagas – women, some older men, and children of both sexes – could not be a self-sustaining community. Without the men, who would till the fields? Without champions, who would challenge other bands? Their band would lack standing in the six seasonal festivals of the year. Locally related bands, clans related through sisters and mothers, vied for the right to host a festival, for it was a source of prestige and respect for the band. The women formed the heart of a Naga band – the Matriarch and her friends, who took care of the children, were its heart and soul. The women managed the band. The relationship between bands could be competitive. This was displayed at the festival get-togethers.

The men played an important role in these festivals. In most bands the men were charged with organizing the food and other supplies for the festival. The leader convinced the men to help him using a mix of persuasion, charisma and social pressure. The men used their skills to organize and host events that made their band an attractive one to join. But the success of a hosted festival did not accrue just to the men – it bolstered a band's position during negotiations.

If a community lost a few men, it could replace them at the next festival by persuading others to join. The politics of these festivals was a sensitive matter – a band with men born and brought up in other bands could garner support from their parent bands in times of need. A band with a group of men who knew how to build dams could lend these men's services in exchange for other benefits. It was through the medium of festivals that each band displayed its capabilities.

A band whose men were all dead, stood alone. This was the state of Amba's band after the Shaka attack. Such a band had nothing to offer and would be asking for much. It would command little political status or power. To compound the situation, a band that did not have enough men could become prey to wild rogue Nagas – boys and men who had never had a home band or who had been expelled from their communities for some reason, usually an inability to control rage. They lived on the fringes of the Naga world, alone or in small groups. They did not form larger groups, for such men did not know how to cooperate with each other. Sometimes, rarely, an unlikely leader would emerge, who coalesced a few small groups and individuals into a larger gang that would become a source of danger to the Naga bands of the region. Such gangs were dealt with harshly when they were captured, with the leader and most of the older members being killed. Thus, even if the women were strong enough to repel an attack by such a gang, the knowledge that a weak, poorly defended band existed would attract more violent gangs. As a result, on losing all or most of its men, a band would usually disband, unless the Matriarch and her women could attract good men from other bands, sometimes by bartering.

Hastinapura had no place for potlatch festivals, and the festivals of Panchnad did not include communal feasts. Nor did Panchnad settlements exchange men. I could accept these as Naga customs. You now see much less of these festivals because free Naga tribes are disappearing as they succumb to Panchala or come under the protection of Hastinapura.

We stayed in the Naga village for a few weeks after the attack on the second Shaka camp near the dam. We stayed to both prevent and hold off any more Shaka attacks that autumn, and to help the band collect what they could from their settlement and move to another site. No one wished to remain where a massacre had just taken place. The move turned out well, I thought. Some of the Nagas in my army, who had been trained by me and were trusted soldiers, took the opportunity to return to the Naga way of life. They would have been considered wild, for many of them had left their bands at a young age and, failing to find a band, had come to me. Now they returned with the credibility of having worked with me. It meant that I lost a few good men, though they would prove useful later. Their skill in war and organization, and their loyalty to me, provided Hastinapura with a solid bulwark and buffer against further Shaka attacks. The Naga bands they joined are still some of Hastinapura's most faithful Northern allies despite King Suyodhana's disdain for the Nagas. *How do I know that?* Yudhishthira had sent emissaries offering an alliance. They were treated politely but sent back empty-handed. Of course, this was reported to me. All the Nagas in the Hastinapura army come from these bands – collateral descendants of Amba and her sisters.

Amba's aunt, the Matriarch of the band, was not happy with our relationship. The Naga band was grateful for what I had done for them, and grateful for the men who left my army to join them. But my killing of the Shaka prisoners had terrified the peaceable Nagas. Even the Matriarch, otherwise cold-blooded and calculating, who had sent the first emissary asking for my help, shied away from me. The stain rubbed off on Amba – there were no secrets among the Nagas – and her people avoided her. They saw nothing wrong in Amba's taking a sexual partner, just that the partner was a monster. That exclusion from her band was the reason Amba decided to leave with me for Hastinapura. With the death of her mother and father, Amba's response to rejection was further withdrawal. I did not know how this would turn out. Repeatedly I went over the need to maintain appearances, to keep Satyavati and the others from discovering our relationship. Every time I did so, it led to angry words that ended in the urgency of sex.

Amba's sisters – ten-year-old twins Ambika and Ambalika, made a fateful decision to go to Hastinapura just for that winter. They had nothing to do with me and were under no pressure to leave. We Kauravas would have called them orphans and looked for relatives who could take care of them. But in a Naga band, aunts and cousins took care of each other. Later, my enemies, hoping to drive a wedge between my nephews and me, would accuse me of kidnapping the three sisters. Ambika and Ambalika were excited that their sister was going to the city and wanted to go with her. Amba said she would bring back her sisters after the winter, and I believe that was truly her intent.

A sad procession returned to Hastinapura. Two months had passed. The city had been in mourning for the King, and very little government business had gone on while they waited of us. We received daily demands for information from the Queen, along with implied accusations of treachery. I kept her informed with the requested daily reports, but after the first few confusing days, there was nothing to report. I told her nothing of my crazed revenge, but she heard I was now called Bhishma and that I had terrified the Nagas. She did not care to find out why, but found it useful to broadcast my new name. A confused mélange of rumors were also reported in the town – that I had kidnapped three Shaka princesses for my brother to marry; I had been rejected by a Shaka woman and taken a terrible revenge. Among the few people close to the ruling family who knew of my vow, the rumor was that my unnatural celibacy had caused a mental breakdown. Others attributed this breakdown to rejection by Amba. It was also said that I had regretted my pledge to protect Hastinapura and support Satyavati's sons in their claim to the throne. Satyavati and I agreed to suppress the story of the Shaka invasion to avoid panic. My dam-building project had made our northern border porous, and I did not wish that fact to be widely known.

I learned later that an extended period of drought in Shaka-desa (land of the Shakas, well to the north of the Snow Mountains), had occasioned a great migration of the Shakas into Parsaka and Mleccha-desa. My massacre proved to be politically useful in deterring further invasions. I made sure that traders going towards Parsaka and Mleccha-desa were told a lurid and bloody version of the massacre. It has been forty years since the massacre. The sleepless nights, and there have been many, are spent replaying the events that led to it. That I was insane with fury is no excuse. But it is possible that the story of the bloodthirsty ruler of Hastinapura kept away many subsequent invaders. When the invasion comes, as surely it must, it will not be by a small band, but a large and well-equipped army.

I introduced Amba and her sisters as daughters of the Chief of the northern Nagas. I think the Naga residents of Hastinapura understood this was an exaggeration, but the others did not. As the daughters of a Chief, they were welcomed and treated with respect. Satyavati took them under her wing and would have had the younger girls stay with her, but Amba insisted on keeping them with her in separate quarters.

Thus began a winter of subtle gestures, meetings in dark places, sneaking out of my chamber into Amba's. Ambika and Ambalika often slept through these assignations. We explained the need for secrecy and they kept our secret."

The Second Co-Regency

37
Life with Amba

Devavrata woke, the dream of a full moon shining over the lake in Varanavata, formed by the dam he had built, still lurking at the edge of his consciousness. It had been his first and favourite project, completed the same day Vichitravirya died. He recalled gazing into that clear and cold night with the simple thought: *How fortunate he was that he could not be King.* It was a serene time remembered in the dream, and the calm carried over into his waking, in which the sensation of pain in his shoulder was a tolerable anomaly.

The King, the Vyaasa and the Archivist were sitting by the entrance to his tent. They moved closer to him and the Vyaasa said, "Good, you are awake. That was a long sleep. It is almost ten ghatis after sunrise. Are you feeling unwell? Is this effort too exhausting?"

Devavrata's mind was clear and, but for the pain he felt, as rested as the Regent of Hastinapura could ever hope to be. He said, "That is late indeed. I feel fine. If not for the arrow, I would be out of my bed to face the day."

"The attendant has brought you fruit pulp."

"I do not feel hungry. I can do nothing lying here, so why not continue with the record of the past?"

Despite the Regent's denial, the attendant extended a small copper bowl containing the slightly fermented mash, and Devavrata slurped at it. The smell of the fermenting fruit revived memories of his mother – fermented honey had been her favorite drink, but she would never let him drink it. He had stolen a sip once and spent the rest of the day trying to wash the taste off his tongue. The memory made him smile. After one more slurp, he said, "That's enough. Tell me a story."

The Vyaasa said, "On the death of Chitrangada, Vichitravirya did not become King right away as he was underage. You became Regent once more. Tell us about Vichitravirya's life in that period."

Devavrata's eyes dropped and he pursed his lips. He said, "That is not a story but a question, asking me to tell you more. Have I not said enough? Will you tell me what happened to Amba?"

"I will, but I do not know much. I would have liked to talk to her first," said the Vyaasa.

"Amba is in custody in this camp," said Yudhishthira.

"She's here?" said Devavrata. "I assumed she had left the camp when I did not hear anything about her."

Yudhishthira said, "We detained her because she was not in her right mind. We intend to send her back to Panchala under guard. But other events have taken precedence, and she is still here."

Shukla said, "It gives me a chance to talk to her. My friend, can you wait a little longer? Distract yourself with our questions. You are the only one here who knew Vichitravirya as a brother. Tell us about him."

Devavrata considered this new postponement of his request. Would Amba talk to Shukla? She knew him from a long time ago, from a time that was less warlike, even if not less tense. *She would certainly not speak to me*, he thought. That decided him.

Devavrata said, "Vichitravirya? There is nothing much to say about him. He was twelve when Chitrangada died, too young to be King. The Co-Regency of Devavrata and Satyavati was revived for another three years. Vichitravirya lived, loved, and died before he could do any damage as King."

Shukla said, "He had children. That should have been good enough, particularly as you remained faithful to your vow."

"Yes, the one thing Vichitravirya did right was to get his wives pregnant before he died. If he had not, I would have become the King I never wanted to be. But it was not enough. My old friend, I needed your advice then, but you were not there. You are right about one thing though – my vow allowed me to be the ruler I wanted to be and let Satyavati's spawn be the Kings she wanted them to be. I had no desire for children."

"You could have sent for me if you had needed my advice. When I arrived you had become Bhishma, the unreachable."

"You do not understand."

"I understand only too well," said the Vyaasa. "I am only sorry I did not tell you Amba's secret sooner."

Amba's secret? The Vyaasa had mentioned it before. What difference could it make?

"Archivist," Devavrata said, "come closer; I will tell you the rest of what I know."

"Vichitravirya was twelve when his world was changed by Chitrangada's death. He had been raised to believe he would never be King, and responsibilities slid off his shoulders like water off a turtle's back. He met Ambika and Ambalika at a young age, when he was not interested in them. They were in shock after the Shaka attack and in awe of the city. Amba protected them as best she could, and as the months passed, they adjusted to their new situation. Amba was much older and had always been like a mother to them, so her role continued naturally. They were aware of their sister's liaison with me, but as Nagas, they were not surprised. They were surprised that we wanted to keep it secret, but accepted the argument that we needed to be careful. City people, after all, were different.

Amba was considered beautiful – I am biased and perhaps my memory has faded, but she was very beautiful – her sisters were even more so. Satyavati, a Naga herself, thought it would be a bond between them. She was unhappy that Amba had refused her hospitality. Satyavati pampered the twins as though they were the daughters she had never had. Amba could do nothing to stop this. Then Amba disappeared, and against their wishes, I attempted to send the younger sisters back to their Naga band. The attempt failed and they lost trust in me."

Shukla said, "Tell me about Amba's disappearance. I know what happened later, but the period leading up to her disappearance has been obscure. How and when did it happen?"

Devavrata said, “I have always wondered if keeping our relationship secret was the cause of her troubles. What if I had simply acted as though there were no vow? I still do not know why she left. Do you?”

Shukla said, “I will surely tell you what I know, but later, after I have spoken to Amba.”

38
Amba Disappears

Devavrata said, "Great happiness is followed by great sorrow – that may be inevitable, and it has been so for me. Hastinapura returned to normal. That was the winter of my happiness. I did not know that come spring, Amba would disappear. Every year during the spring thaw, the snow-fed rivers rose and flooding occurred. I had built dams on the Ganga, so Hastinapura was safe. But we could do nothing about the Yamuna. It was a crazy river in the spring, especially the new stream going east of the Aravalli range. My job every spring was to find a way to keep the flooding rivers from destroying the new settlements along their banks and along the canals.

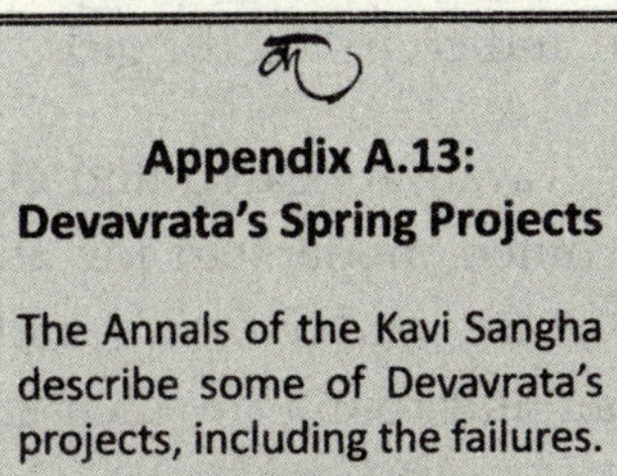

Appendix A.13:
Devavrata's Spring Projects

The Annals of the Kavi Sangha describe some of Devavrata's projects, including the failures.

I was away for two months, almost all of that time just north of the wasteland we call Khandavaprastha. I left six days before the full moon, that being the best time to travel (the moon makes the nights safe for resting), and returned two days before the second full moon after that. When I did, Amba was not in Hastinapura, and nobody seemed to know where she had gone. No one had looked for her. Amba's house, the one I had prepared for her, was empty. It had been cleaned out after she disappeared. I could not ask Satyavati directly for that would have revealed my interest and the relationship I had been keeping secret. In any case, Satyavati never told me the truth when we worked together. So my search for Amba was low-key; the questions I asked indirect, the answers I received evasive.

Her sisters Ambika and Ambalika were of no help in this search. They had been moved in with Satyavati. At their age they were too young to live by themselves. They did not volunteer any information. I was sure they knew something, and as I listened – *lying to my face* – my hands shook. The girls began crying and their sobs attracted the attention of the servants. Most of them were my agents, assigned to Amba, but I had had to include a few provided by Satyavati. Amba was well spied on between these two groups. The attendants came in and consoled the girls.

Satyavati appeared and chided me. The appearance of these women moderated my anger. I knew then I was capable of torture, and I was grateful for that knowledge. I stormed out and found my men standing around in two groups. Both groups had drawn their swords and were prepared to act on my command. They turned when they saw me come out by myself. That was a day when my training with the Kavi Sangha, brief as it was, helped me. I sensed the tension in my men's disposition, calmed myself, and projected calmness to them. Seeing me calmed the men. Their Captains came to me but did not say anything. I was Bhishma, my actions unpredictable. Some of my men considered me capable of torturing the girls. I do not know if I would have done so to discover what they knew of Amba's disappearance if the women and my men had not been there.

So I sent the girls back to their home with the northern Nagas, protected by a small armed party. This was against their will, but I made it clear to all that I had made a promise to their aunts and I could not break it. Satyavati understood, I think, and did not object. The girls themselves were terrified of me.

The entourage returned with the girls and disquieting news. The Matriarch had died. She had been older than the other women but not old enough to die, hence her death had precipitated a crisis. Her sons had died in the Shaka attack. There was no one to inherit the role of Chief. Her daughter had not partnered a man who wished to stay with this band, or else he could have been a viable candidate for the role. Now, the daughter was unable to find a man to take on the role of Defense Chief. A rumour had spread among the other Naga clans that this band was cursed. Without a credible defending force, the band's crops were at risk of being looted by wild Nagas or other hostile, opportunistic Naga bands. Even the Naga soldiers I had left behind had lost hope the band could survive. Ambika and Ambalika had become accustomed to living in Hastinapura and had no interest in re-establishing their band. Their refusal to return to the band, even as Matriarchs, served as a catalyst. With the women unable to agree on a Matriarch, most of the men walked away. There were not enough people left to form a band with a good mix of older and wiser seniors and younger and more flexible youngsters. It would be a long time before such a band could provide a protective home for the girls.

My men, whom I had left behind, had formed a band that offered to help Naga bands in trouble. This was how they ended up as a specialized band of Naga mercenaries. The band sisters asked about Amba. She had not returned to them. I wanted to question Ambika and Ambalika again, for I could not believe Amba had gone away without them.

When the girls returned to Hastinapura, Satyavati took them completely under her control, and I did not have Amba to provide a counterweight. I had to ask Satyavati's permission to interview them and she agreed, with conditions. Her guards would be within sight and I had to stay at least ten hastas away from them. My new name was beginning to influence people and make them fear me."

39
The Interview

Devavrata continued: "Satyavati may not have cooperated, but she did not want to oppose me either at that point. She sent Ambika and Ambalika, escorted by women from her entourage. I asked to talk to them in private, and the women assented with ill grace. Satyavati later chastised me, as though my request had been improper. As usual, she overlooked my rights as guardian of the girls. But I had frightened them when I sent them back to their band and they felt they could not trust me anymore. When Amba was in Hastinapura, we had used my guardianship of the twins as a cover for my visits to Amba. Now I wanted to ask them about Amba's disappearance.

The girls and I went to my chambers, accompanied by one of Satyavati's women and another woman who was married to one of my men. Informal seats had been arranged for us. There were three large stuffed cushions arranged around a low table. In the middle was a large plate with dried fruits, rice cakes made with puffed rice and honey, and a bowl of honey with a number of dipping sticks. I indicated the cushions for them and waited for them to choose. Ambika chose the cushion furthest from the fruits. Ambalika moved towards the fruit and would have sat down next to them, but looked to Ambika, who glared at her. She moved to the other cushion, leaving me closest to the fruits. Ambika looked straight ahead, avoiding my eyes.

'It has been a long time since I have seen you. Are you satisfied with my mother's hospitality? Have you made friends? Do the attendants treat you with respect?'

Ambika replied, 'Yes, Sir. We are well. You too, have been well, we trust?' Ambalika looked at her sister and nodded.

This was not good. *Why was she being formal?*

'I am well, my child. You know that I am concerned about the welfare of you and your sister. I promised your clan's Matriarch that I would be responsible for your health and safety.'

'Yes, Sir. We thank you for your concern,' Ambika said, as Ambalika nodded again.

'With your sister missing, I have not been able to take care of you as I promised.'

'Do not be concerned, Sir. We are well taken care of by your Matriarch, the Lady Satyavati.'

Matriarch Satyavati? What had my stepmother been telling them? In retrospect, it is obvious what Satyavati did, but at the time I was befuddled.

'I have sent my people to many Naga bands in search of your sister, but they have not found her anywhere. Your aunt, the new Matriarch, was not pleased to hear of her disappearance. She has expressly asked after you and I must reply. Would you like to return there?'

Ambika looked away. 'Tell our Matriarch that we are in good health; we are safe in the protection of the Hastinapura Matriarch. We do not wish to return.'

'Ambika, Ambalika,' I said, 'please tell me – do you know what has happened to Amba?'

'You do not know?' Ambalika asked, and her sister frowned.

'No, I do not know.'

Ambika's eyes narrowed as she looked at me directly. I stared straight back. She looked away. I knew then that she was not going to tell me.

Ambalika came surprisingly to my aid. 'Why don't you know? You asked her to meet you. She left in a hurry with a few of your…' Her sister stopped her by squeezing her upper arm.

'My men?'

'Yes, your men. We saw them; they were dressed in off-white half-*panchagachams* and brown *angavastrams,* padded with cotton – your uniform.'

"I don't need to state the obvious to you, Lomaharshana. I had not summoned Amba, nor had I sent an escort to bring her to me. But somebody had done so. *An enemy?* I could not think of anyone in Hastinapura who was my declared enemy. Would Satyavati have the gall to do such a thing? To what end? To kill Amba? I was sure that if she was still alive, she would have contacted me. The men were dressed as my troops. Why make me the culprit? What was the message that convinced Amba to go with the men? *Was she dead?* What had she told the girls before she left, or what had Satyavati told them about Amba?

Amba's disappearance was my fault. I had not protected her. Was she still alive? I could not believe Satyavati would have her killed. The fact that the sisters trusted Satyavati meant that they must have received some reassurance from Satyavati, something that convinced them that she was helping Amba. It was some devious plot by Satyavati. I did not know what she had arranged or why the girls no longer trusted me.

'When was this?' I asked the girls.

'The very day you left, when you sent your men for Amba. We have not seen her since.'

'So, when I returned without Amba, why did you not ask me where she was?'

They were silent.

'Did she send you a message?'

It seemed like Ambalika would speak, but then she held her peace. Instead, Ambika said, 'Sir, we do not wish to discuss Amba with you. Is there anything else you wish to ask us? Please do not ask about Amba, we cannot speak of it.'

I was the Regent, the most powerful man in the city. They were mere slips of girls. Yet, with the backing of Satyavati, they felt they could refuse me.

So the story I heard was that men, dressed in my troop's uniform, had taken Amba away and later the girls had been told, or received a message – *from Satyavati?* – that led them to suspect me and seek Satyavati's protection. I stood up and gazed through the open door at the garden Amba had planted. Before Amba came, it had been choked with weeds and grass. It was on the way to the outhouse, and no one saw a need to decorate the path. Amba said the garden reminded her of her Naga clear-cut fields. *Give me authority over this piece of land,* she had said. *I will set fire to it to clear the ground and prepare it for planting.* She had laughed to see the shock on the face of the old gardener. He appealed to me, terrified that Amba would set fire to all of Hastinapura. I reassured him. Amba had not yet understood the obligations a master or mistress had to their employees, and she treated them as the almost equal members of a Naga band.

I did not know how to reassure the girls that I had nothing to do with Amba's disappearance. Finally, I said, 'I had nothing to do with Amba leaving. Those you saw were not my men. I know nothing of this. Can you believe that?'

They remained silent. I watched them to see if there was any inclination to talk, but they looked away.

'I must find Amba. She is my life. I would never harm her.'

There was a little flutter when I said that Amba was my life, but it died in an exchange of glances. Nothing I said after that had any effect. My heart began to race. I felt I was losing control over my breathing and needed to calm down. I signed for them to leave. They bowed, and I blessed them."

Devavrata paused, closing his eyes. Devavrata's voice, already low, had become rough, his breathing ragged, his recital slow. The Archivist did not mind; the slower Devavrata spoke, the easier it was to rehearse and memorize.

It was an autumn evening and the trees were shedding their leaves, some already bare. Each year, when the Archivist saw a tree bare of leaves, he would worry that it would die, and every spring, when it came to life again, he worried it would be less full or less green than it had been before. It was so much easier to memorize and recall, compose and enact, he thought, than to be a farmer and worry about rain, floods and droughts, planting and harvesting. His life was so much simpler than Devavrata's, devoid of unreachable goals of peace, without subterfuge, without plots. If Devavrata had simply given it all up, he could have gone away with Amba.

Lomaharshana sighed and looked at the Regent, who had fallen asleep. How strange that he could sleep like this even with an arrowhead piercing his lung. *It is time to join the Vyaasa and the other Kavi Sangha members for the evening rituals.* That would be followed by five ghatis, in the dark, rehearsing the material he had just heard, then sleep, which would inevitably bear the stamp of what he had just heard. Refreshed, he would then return tomorrow, with his teacher.

40
THE MARRIAGE PROPOSAL

Devavrata said, "Vichitravirya was twelve when his brother died; he could be crowned King at sixteen at the earliest. He had not expected to become the ruler. The country had been at peace, and his brother had inherited all the martial ambitions of his ancestors. As a result, Vichitravirya's princely training had been largely ignored, his education neglected. Now, he was to be the King. He had to be trained in military matters, to command. His education was my responsibility. He had to be educated in a hurry, so being soft would not do. But I was limited in what I could do, for if I came down hard on the boy, Satyavati complained about my brutish behavior. With Chitrangada, I had had the time and opportunity to develop a rapport; I did not have this luxury with Vichitravirya. Did this have anything to do with what happened? Perhaps. In hindsight, I see a connection.

I rarely saw Ambika and Ambalika. To all appearances, the girls had forgotten their clan and the events in their village. They never brought up the subject of Amba. Was Amba in touch with them? I did not know, nor did I did try to find out. Satyavati took the girls under her wing. They were always in the house when Vichitravirya visited his mother. As the years passed, he began to notice them. They were beautiful girls, close to his own age, and they fascinated him. Satyavati must have been happy to see this, for she had been worried that he would find brides who might not look up to their mother-in-law. Worse, he might acquire a wife who aspired to power. Satyavati was confident that Ambika and Ambalika, as her protégées, would align with her and never turn on her.

The day came when Satyavati raised the matter in open court. 'Elders of Hastinapura,' she said, 'it has been three years since my son, King Chitrangada, passed away. The time comes to appoint my son Vichitravirya as the heir apparent. A city without a ruler cannot prosper; without a Governor it will disintegrate; without a Judge it will not survive. He will be all these – a farsighted Ruler, a stern Governor, a wise Judge. He will be a great King.'

Considering that Satyavati had been an ambitious Naga girl who knew nothing of Hastinapura when she married my father, she had mastered the language of the Kaurava Council.

'Mother,' I said (she frowned at my form of address), 'he is certainly of age. Let him take on the role destiny has bestowed upon him. Let an appropriate and auspicious day be set.'

Satyavati smiled. The court erupted in applause and shouts of jubilation. My supporters could never match the ebullience of Satyavati's courtiers. Her courtiers' actions always mirrored her moods – deathly silence when she was angry, an excess of bonhomie when she smiled. Satyavati's smile was smug; she had a surprise for me.

'We have already suffered through the childless death of one Kaurava King,' she said. This was her revenge for my calling her 'mother'. I was the senior Kaurava Prince; had it not been for my oath to my father, I would have been the Kaurava King.

She continued, 'My son Vichitravirya is of marriageable age. For the sake of the Kuru clan, he must marry soon.'

A chorus of agreement came from the Council. I had not anticipated this and my supporters in the chamber remained quiet, waiting for a signal from me. On the one hand, a crowned Vichitravirya might be an interfering monarch, like his brother, who had wanted to display his authority and ability. In this matter I had no say. He would be crowned when his mother considered him ready, and that was now. On the other hand, a married Vichitravirya would have interests other than public displays of authority and ability. That would allow me to return to executing my plans."

Yudhishthira said, "What plans had you formulated? What role did you expect the King to play in these?"

Lomaharshana said, "Gurudeva, should I include details of these plans in the narrative?"

Shukla said, "Lomaharshana, you are correct to be concerned. The plans are already part of the archives. You can narrate those early plans to the King later this evening. Devavrata, my friend, for now, tell us what you did about Satyavati's plans?"

Devavrata said, "The Kavi Sangha supported my efforts. When Shukla returned from Takshashila, he too, supported me and counselled his sister not to interfere with my plans. Now he is the Vyaasa and very powerful; that is boring. But she does not listen to him anymore, so he comes to squeeze stories from me."

Lomaharshana glanced at the Vyaasa, who was smiling.

Shukla said, “My friend, it is good to see your spirit restored. If I had known that telling stories would cure you of your melancholy, I would have done so from the first day you came back with Amba. I would have been squeezing these stories out of you for a decade at least, instead of in a hurry today.”

Devavrata said, “I like it this way, Shukla. It gives me something to do while I wait for an accident to kill me.”

“True. We both wait to die, you in your way and I in mine. I prefer to squeeze stories out of you in the waiting.”

Devavrata nodded. “I must disagree – the stories of my Regency would dampen any listener’s spirits.”

The Vyaasa and the Regent looked at each other and smiled. It seemed to Lomaharshana that their talk surpassed language, that they were engaged in a conversation he could hear but not comprehend. It was one of the more dubious pleasures of being a memorizer. Occasionally a contract would be incomprehensible, containing encoded or cryptic references, where the word ‘fish’ might refer to a diamond, and ‘pig’ to a coat of armor. Lomaharshana took the opportunity to yawn. Then he rotated his upper body to stretch his abdominal muscles. The movements broke the tension.

Appendix A.14: Devavrata’s Early Plans for Empire

Yudhishthira said, “Grandsire, you have mentioned plans for creating an empire as early as Chitrangada’s reign. What were these plans?”

Devavrata’s reply in the Annals of the Kavi Sangha are in his own words.

Devavrata continued where he had left off. "When Chitrangada was alive, he was suspicious of my motives and insisted that the cadre of armed farmers that I was training vow loyalty to him. Though the Kauravas had begun to use the terms 'King', 'Queen', 'Prince', and 'Princess' for the ruling family, they had not yet begun professing personal loyalty. That was Suyodhana's innovation. He is rigid and unswerving in his demand that all his people vow personal loyalty to him. Though I do not like to acknowledge it, it will make the difference and ensure Suyodhana's victory over Yudhishthira.

But in those times, the old Kuru residents viewed us as senior chiefs and me as the leading representative of the ruling clan. There was much confusion over my oath to my father. Even my ideas about uniting for defense felt like a claim on people's loyalty and they resisted it. Chitrangada's demand for an explicit pledge of loyalty did not sit well with the people. With Chitrangada dead, there was no demand for a vow of loyalty, and as long as Satyavati and Vichitravirya did not ask for it, I could go back to creating a buffer region populated by armed allies who had not vowed loyalty, but worked with Hastinapura out of mutual interest.

By creating an empire I would fulfil my promise to my father that I would protect the Kuru family and his descendants from Satyavati. This goal had yet to be achieved, and I could not accomplish it if Vichitravirya or Satyavati interfered. All in all, the idea of Vichitravirya marrying appealed to me. Both he and his mother would be distracted and disinclined to interfere with me as long as I did not interfere with them. He should marry anyone other than an ambitious Princess, who would question the sincerity with which I had accepted the loss of my birthright.

I was surprised when Satyavati announced in open court that she had found the perfect match but that she was not ready to announce it. The assembled courtiers cajoled and pleaded with her, and then she added a second surprise. She said I was the reason for keeping it secret, that I had not yet given my permission.

I could not banish the surprise on my face, but whatever she was doing, I would go along. Such surprises were the way Satyavati exercised her power in those days, when she was young and certain of herself. She is too old for that kind of melodrama now. In any case, Suyodhana does not permit her to leave her chambers. She has no say in his court. He would certainly not have put up with any drama that did not come with his blessing.

Seeing my surprise led her supporters to exchange knowing glances. More cajoling followed, along with an erudite discussion on the merits and demerits of marrying a local girl as opposed to one from another city. *Of course, they hoped the great Regent Devavrata would bless the event.*

Then Satyavati said, 'They are not local girls.' I knew that instant who she referred and understood her reasons for this rigmarole. Not local girls indeed! I had not seen Ambika and Ambalika for weeks after they had entered Satyavati's clique. My attempts to arrange a second meeting or have them visit, had been rebuffed. That was certainly Satyavati's doing.

Satyavati continued, 'Ambika and Ambalika, the Naga Princesses, have displayed grace and elegance since they came here. My son knows them, and they know him. They are well-matched.' Then she turned to me and stated the obvious. 'Ah, Devavrata, you look surprised. Sometimes the guardian is the last to learn of what his wards are up to.' The court dutifully followed her in laughing at my apparent humiliation.

'You are right,' I said. 'I am surprised. As their guardian, I should know more about what they are thinking. Please arrange to send them to my house.'

There was silence in the court. A hint of a frown showed on Satyavati's perfect visage, but she said, 'Of course, my son. They have been willful not to visit you more often.'

The court hummed and twittered at the overt condescension. I thanked her and left, to await the arrival of the girls."

41
The Second Interview

Devavrata said, "This interview played out in much the same way as the previous one. My staff arranged the chamber so it looked beautiful and smelled of sandalwood and jasmine. They hoped it would please the girls and perhaps they would answer my questions.

I asked Ambika and Ambalika about the proposal to marry Vichitravirya. They behaved as if marriage was a game – in this their attitude was that of the Nagas. Marriage among Nagas was not taken as seriously as among Hastinapuris. The girls spoke quite willingly about marriage and pairing customs among the Nagas, about how the Nagas only celebrated the Matriarch's marriage, which occurred on the same day every year, at the full moon before the spring equinox, one month before the spring sowing season. Other couples might decide to pair up that day as a couple and take part in the celebrations. The Hastinapura Nagas did not follow that practice, for they had moved away from many Naga traditions. Panchala followed the old customs.

Ambika and Ambalika would be disappointed to find that Satyavati was not to take another spouse the same day, and I did nothing to explain. They chattered but avoided the subjects I had an interest in. They were polite but communicated little of value. My occasional attempts to ask about Amba failed to draw a response. I sent them back to Satyavati's care. There was no reason to block the wedding; the sooner Vichitravirya fathered children the sooner I would be relieved of the worry that I would be made King! The announcement was made, and the city prepared to celebrate a coronation and a wedding.

Devavrata paused in the telling of the story. "Shukla, my friend," he said to the Vyaasa, "I have told you all that happened from the day Amba disappeared, to the day my brother was crowned and wedded. Come, tell me about Amba. Yes, yes, I know what you think, that I am dying, but still I grasp at straws. Laugh at me, but tell me what I want to know."

The Vyaasa smiled. "I am not laughing at you, my friend. I smile to see that you still remember the parable of the man suspended by a straw over a snake pit. Indulge me a little longer, for if you relate your memories leading to the birth of Dhritarashtra and Mahendra Pandu, the Archivist will have enough to work on, and then we can exchange places as storytellers."

"There is little to add," said Devavrata. "Vichitravirya was not cut out to be a ruler, but he represented all of Satyavati's hopes and ambitions."

42
Death of Vichitravirya

Devavrata continued, "Vichitravirya was sixteen when he was crowned King. He had to be educated in a hurry, so a soft approach was not an option for the teacher. Despite all the efforts made to prepare him, he was not ready to be King.

I rarely saw Ambika and Ambalika. To all appearances the girls had forgotten their clan and the events in their village and they never brought up the subject of Amba. Was Amba in touch with them? I did not know nor did I try to find out.

The tedium of governance weighed heavily on Vichitravirya. He was expected to lead the Council in decision-making, but the meetings bored him. All that education compressed into a tight schedule had soured any desire to rule and left only the wish to be indulged. He enjoyed the time he spent with his wives and their women, and complained about the time official meetings took. Slowly, more and more of the administration reverted to me, and the Councilors turned to me for guidance and direction while the King spent time with his two wives, at picnics and parties. He enjoyed displaying his martial arts skill before his wives. Satyavati was not pleased.

Seven years passed. The promise Satyavati had extracted from Shantanu – that she would mother a dynasty of rulers – could only be fulfilled if she had grandchildren and great-grandchildren. She looked forward to that day, when she could stop worrying. There was reason to worry. She finally voiced it to me: *Why were there no children? Was there something wrong with Vichitravirya, or with Ambika and Ambalika?* Some of her women tried to assuage her concern: *He was still young. Seven years without a pregnancy between the two girls was unexpected, but such cases did happen.* But I do not think Satyavati ever stopped worrying.

I was out of the city inspecting a dam we had built prematurely on the Yamuna. Premature because, after keeping to one path for many years, an onrush of water down the river had broken a new path upstream, and now the old channel was dry and the dam useless. We had spent much effort on planning and constructing the dam, so the settlers I had sent there were working to send the river back into its old channel. The Yamuna had not yet found a permanent path to the sea. Maintenance of this type was almost a routine task. However, I wanted to see the damage and talk to the engineers about the design so that we did not repeat old mistakes. So that was where I was when I received word that Vichitravirya was dead.

I needed a day to reassign the power and responsibilities I had retained, then I left for Hastinapura, reaching it as the thirteenth day ceremonies were ending. I envied the Shakas' horse-riding ability, to quickly get from one place to another. If I had had a horse, I could have reached Hastinapura in four or five days, following the treeless bank of the Ganga.

At the dam site, the messenger had little to say – he had been sent to fetch me as soon as the King died, so he had not heard any gossip. The news of the King's death changed everything. *The King was dead, long live the… who?* As I prepared to go to Hastinapura, the foremost thought in my mind was the succession. I was reconciled to not being King, but it felt like Shani, the Lord of Destiny and the Arbiter of Fate, demanded that I be King; telling me in so many ways, *You shall be King,* and working matters so I would have to assume the crown I had surrendered so many years before. I did not want the crown, but the rulership passing out of Kuru hands was not acceptable."

The Vyaasa said, "At that point you thought Vichitravirya had died without children. When did you learn that both Ambalika and Ambika were with child?"

"For seven years I had kept my expectations to myself. On hearing of the death, I feared the worst. As I have mentioned before, you cannot make an onager go faster than it wants to go. It took me a week. By the time I reached Hastinapura, almost two weeks had passed since the death. The city was, of course, still in mourning – white and saffron flags were raised at every corner and the colorful gates of the city were draped in white. Preparations for the ceremony of bidding farewell to the departing soul and a warm welcome to the home of its ancestors were in progress, the final ceremony itself having been postponed. I wondered at that – these rituals should not have been held at all since my brother had died childless. But I assumed nobody had dared to correct whatever command had come from the palace. It was a minor matter, and if it helped my stepmother feel better, I was for it.

I could only imagine what Satyavati's state of mind must have been. She had no more sons to raise to the throne, and her sons had given her no grandsons. I think she would have liked to establish a matriarchy, but she had no daughters either. When I reached Hastinapura, the city was in turmoil. The guards, some of them my agents, reported that Satyavati had been issuing commands and threats of revenge if poison was discovered. The funerary rituals usually required the body to be cremated on the third day, but at Satyavati's insistence, the body had not been cremated; it was believed that he had been poisoned and the poison would prevent it from decaying. But the body decomposed and stank. There was no evidence of poison. The poison tester had tasted all the food in the kitchen and any fruits, nuts and even leaves growing near the house; he was still alive. It did not satisfy Satyavati, who was not prepared to believe Vichitravirya had died of a disease or natural causes. She wanted results – the killer who had poisoned her son had to be found, or else... Her guards demanded access to the homes of those she thought were in the plot. No evidence had been found, but that was taken as proof that the conspiracy pervaded the entire city. They were against her because she was a Naga.

I quickly found my worry was unwarranted. I went straight to the palace to express my condolences to Satyavati and to the Queens Ambika and Ambalika. The Queens were nowhere to be found. Their attendants told me they had gone into seclusion almost immediately after Vichitravirya's death. Satyavati was in the Council chamber. As I expected, everyone was busy with administrative trivia – there is no better task to take one's mind off distressing news.

I left my cart with my men and went directly to the Council chamber. Satyavati was sitting on her throne while the Councilors stood before her. She did not see me at first for I did not announce myself as I usually did. The caretaker of the Treasury, an old man who had fulfilled this thankless role for the city for many years, stood before her, trembling. Satyavati was scolding him. 'What do you mean, you cannot account for twenty-five copper seals? They could have been used to pay an assassin.' The man was trembling and his voice had a slight quaver as he said, 'Madam, this discrepancy has existed in the treasury since before your husband died.'

He was right. Satyavati was constantly finding errors and omissions, many of which represented transactions that had not been completed. Once, Shantanu had arranged to 'steal' twenty-five copper seals to see if the loss was reported. The Minister had reported it with such an abject look of fear that Shantanu could not bear to tell him it had been a test. Nor could he return the amount without the man suspecting something. Instead, Shantanu 'forgave' the Minister for having committed such an error. But the Minister kept the loss on the memorized accounts as a reminder. Satyavati had not known about the test. Subsequently, in the complete audit of the treasury, conducted every seven years, when the Treasurer completed the inventory of gold, silver, copper, and tin, he would discover the discrepancy and assume that the caretaker was trying to hide it. The error would be announced, and Satyavati would berate the Minister for his incompetence. At the end of it, he would be ordered to maintain the discrepancy in the archives. Satyavati was berating the Minister once again, but this time the threat of punishment was real, and everyone trembled.

I could not bear to see this continue. I moved so Satyavati would see me. 'Devavrata!' she said. 'You come just in time. I was beginning to fear for my life. Nobody here is competent to protect the Queens as they must be protected.' Then, to the Minister she said, 'You! Go back!'

Satyavati had never before welcomed me in this fashion. I was not comfortable, for as a rule we stayed apart. She burst into tears. *What a miserable being I am – I have suffered the loss of my husband and my children.* It was an old lament of hers, her misfortunes and bad choices. For a moment I felt a knot of sympathy in my gut, but only for a moment, for this lament was usually followed by a demand for some extra consideration. I tensed, waiting for the description of a problem only I could fix.

I walked up to her seat and sat to her right, the seat of the Chief Councilor. I intended it as a signal that I preferred not to rule. She stood up and, as I sat down, said in a quiet voice, 'I have some fortunate news to announce.' She turned to the others in the room and asked them to leave, for she had family matters to discuss with me. They left. Her maids stayed. She asked me to sit closer. Practices of over twenty years were being abandoned in summary fashion. She whispered even though only her maids, and my spies, were in the room. This was all very unusual. I felt certain that some bizarre demand was to follow.

Satyavati said, 'My poor son. Fate is cruel indeed.' She stopped, waiting for me to respond. I nodded. She then continued, 'For seven years he waited anxiously for a child. The day he died, Ambalika missed her monthly flux for the second time.'

She stopped again. I nodded in acknowledgement, even if I did not understand why I was being told this. I had never known when any of the women were bleeding. *Why was she telling me this?* Satyavati's words added to my confusion. Daksha, Lord of the Moon, we are told, fills every woman once a cycle, and afflicts them with pain or tension, not being satisfied with the twenty-seven star-brides he dallies with in that cycle. This fantastic explanation is typical of *bisajs*, seeking the cause of illness in things invisible and unknowable.

Satyavati said, 'The *bisaj* could only come that afternoon. He held Ambalika's hand and listened to her chest. He tasted her spit and smelled her urine, and afterwards told me Ambalika was pregnant. I did not tell Ambalika or Vichitravirya, waiting for them to come in for the evening meal.'

Satyavati said, 'Instead of my delivering the good news to the girls, they reported bad news to me. They were in the garden as the sun was setting. The rains were almost over, signaling the beginning of the harvest season. My son had come into their garden and they showed him the colors lining the clouds. They said he was happy, enjoying himself. He must have been at his poetic best, for I heard giggles and laughter. Then Vichitravirya said, *I have a headache,* and sat down. Ambalika said the shine vanished from his eyes. She put a hand to his temple. He turned pale even as they watched, shook his head and put a finger in his ear, as though trying to dislodge something, and fell back. They rushed to pick him up, but he was already unconscious. They called the attendants, who lifted him and brought him in.

They called the *bisaj* back, and he examined the comatose Vichitravirya. He detected a faint heartbeat and said he was not dead. At the same time, he held out no hope. The young King had no fever or any external symptoms. The *bisaj* could not ask him whether he was in pain or where the discomfort was located. I came in then. I was concerned that my son's spirit was suffering from the uncertainty that he had no progeny and would thereafter suffer in the hell reserved for sons who do not fulfil their duty to their ancestors. Even if he was comatose I felt he might be able to understand – so I informed Vichitravirya and his wives that they were going to have a child. I hope the news gave him some relief. Later that night, he was delirious and called on his brother to help with unseen opponents. The *bisaj* thought that was a hopeful sign, but those were the last words he spoke.

But that was not the end. The next day we discovered Ambika too, had missed a second monthly flux, and the *bisaj* declared her pregnant as well. I immediately informed my son, comatose as he was. I saw no difference in his condition, but in my heart I know he felt me mourning for him. By coincidence, one of the Queens' attendants, a concubine of the King, had discovered that she was pregnant two weeks earlier. A surfeit of babies after seven barren years heralded the King's death.'

Satyavati waited for me to nod, and I did. We were getting into deep waters I knew little of. I had no idea why Satyavati was so concerned about menstruation, perhaps it was a holdover from when the Matriarch ran the family. The women were in charge of every detail and the men superfluous visitors. A woman's partner was not allowed to approach her for a few days every month; they did this so the woman could rest – a luxury young lovers considered superfluous. Why women laid a claim to these rest periods even after their partners had grown old and less driven by *kama*, I do not know.

Satyavati said, 'My only remaining son died that afternoon. He neither spoke nor opened his eyes, but he did become delirious moments after the *bisaj's* assessment that he would not live long. Along with his wives, I held down his hands and legs for he thrashed about even as we told him the news. Then, he suddenly went limp. He was dead.

Ambika and Ambalika were stunned. I took them to our chambers and had my women console them. A messenger was sent to ask you to return post-haste. Others took care of the body, and plans were made for cremation as soon as possible. That is when it struck me that my son could have been poisoned. If we had chosen a date and time and cremated him then, it would have been impossible to discover the cause. I decided to postpone the cremation, overriding the objections of traditionalists. I pointed out to them that Panchnad had the ancient practice of burying people in earthen jars, a practice that had died out in favor of cremation. I offered to return to that practice, so they remained silent.'

In this manner, Shukla, I learned of the conception of my nephews. Satyavati decided that a King with an heir merited an elaborate funeral ceremony, equal to that of a Matriarch of Panchnad. For seventy days I was required to perform an extravagant and solemn ritual Hastinapura had long put aside. At the ceremony I overheard one of Satyavati's maids comment that the Queen Mother had suffered much and life was sad and unfair. I was surprised to hear Satyavati say, 'My son may have passed on, but I am blessed that both Queens, and even a maidservant, have become pregnant at almost the same time. We will have a wet nurse we can trust. A triple pregnancy is uncommon; it is an omen. My line will not die. That is why I have been able to accept the deaths of both my sons.'

After Satyavati's explanation, I realized that the prospect of grandchildren had reconciled her to her son's death. Of course, it was not that simple. She still wanted revenge against a poisoner, if there was one. She felt she would only be respected if she pursued justice and achieved it, so she maintained her pressure on the city's investigators.

Satyavati seemed to become calm after relaying all this to me. She had no choices left. After the deaths she could only rely on my oath; she had to rely on me. The patient hearing I gave her must have reassured her.

It is now common knowledge that Surya, the Sun, and Chandra, the Moon, govern the birth of a baby. A healthy child lies in its mother's womb for at least eight moons and up to one moon beyond that. I thought we had about thirty-two weeks to prepare for the babies' births. It was fortunate the maidservant had become pregnant at the same time. Among the forest Nagas, the freedom of the spring ritual led to many women conceiving at the same time and giving birth at about the same time the following winter. Thus they could help one another in taking care of and feeding the babies. A baby born at any other time was rare.

The Kauravas did not follow that ritual, and the city Nagas had given it up as well. Children were born at all times of the year, and consequently the mother ran the risk of not being able to find a wet nurse. The Kurus of Hastinapura, like the non-matriarchal ruling families of the far West, provided the wife with a trusted maid who would become a mother at the same time. It was controversial. How did they find the maid, how did she become pregnant, what would happen to her child – these were questions I did not ask. The practice stopped because of my father's law, limiting the number of children. Satyavati herself had given birth to Chitrangada and Vichitravirya, and I remember the tense days after each birth, waiting for her milk to flow. I wondered if Satyavati had revived the practice of providing a wet-nurse, then decided this was not an issue worth raising at the time.

Nothing with Satyavati was simple. After poisoning had been ruled out – small pieces of the King's flesh were fed to rats and cats and observed for signs of illness. There were none. But Satyavati was not done.

43
They Shall Be Kauravas

Devavrata said, "The funeral rituals completed, I was called for a meeting with the Queen-Mother. She had an urgent question: *How will these children become Kauravas*? I remained silent until, a few vighatis later, Satyavati said, 'Devavrata, answer my question. If my grandsons are raised without a Kaurava father, they will never be Kauravas.'

My step-mother's question was completely unexpected. Her desperation showed in how she addressed me – 'Devavrata', not 'my son'. She had never done this before. But why was she desperate? *And what did she mean?* As it turned out, she was concerned about conception and childbirth. I knew little of such matters and thus remained silent.

Satyavati continued, 'I have questioned the *bisaj*, and he said there must be almost daily contact between a woman and her husband while she is pregnant. Then the child will inherit the features, strength and wisdom of her husband's family. Otherwise, some stray man passing through at this vulnerable time will imprint the child. We must have a man – a Kuru descendant and a close relative of Shantanu, to stay here for the entire period of the Queens' pregnancies. He does not have to do anything, just be there.'

I was Shantanu's closest relative. His eldest brother had died; the second had renounced his inheritance and vanished into the forest and had not been heard of since. For other relatives we would have to go into the abandoned Panchnad cities or further up the ancestral hierarchy. The difficulty of finding such a person made me the easy choice. But agreement to such a proposal was out of the question for me, and my dissent must have showed in my face.

Satyavati said, 'I told the *bisaj* what he was proposing was impossible and asked for alternatives. He consulted his archives and came up with a compromise. The Kaurava father-substitute was not required to remain for all sixty ghatis, but visit this house daily and spend the whole day with or near the Queens.'

The Kaurava father-substitute under consideration was, of course, me. Spending even thirty ghatis every day in this manner was out of the question. But Satyavati seemed intent on this, and I could not dissuade her.

I asked, 'Wouldn't it be equally possible for the child to be influenced by a woman of Shantanu's family?' Even as I said this, I realized my father had no sisters we knew of. I could not shrug off the responsibility.

Satyavati replied, 'It must be you. You see why it has to be done. If we do not, the children will not be true descendants of your father. It is Shantanu who will suffer.'

'Does it have to be in the same room and all day?' I asked, grasping at straws, anything that would preserve my separation from Satyavati.

'I do not know. I will call the *bisaj*.' She gestured to a maid and asked her to fetch the *bisaj*.

We waited silently. To my relief, the *bisaj* was pragmatic. He was also expert at reading my mind through my face and eyes. The next room would be fine, he said. The night was fine, too, perhaps even better than the day, as the aspect cast by the man would be purer. The complete investment, for it was not guaranteed, would take at least two to four months. In fact, two months would do, but that was the absolute minimum.

I said, 'Send the Queens and their attendants over to my house before dusk. They can sleep in a room adjacent to my chamber. In the morning they can return here.'

It was an uncomfortable four months as I had become used to a solitary life. Initially, I thought it might become possible to ask the Queens about Amba, or even eavesdrop on their conversation. But I did not stoop to these depths; it would have been a scandal if I had been observed.

I had to find other ways to conduct after-dark meetings with spies and other confidential messengers who came to me. We were at peace then, and I learned a lesson in moderation. The girls found it tedious, for I limited them to one attendant each. Shortly after the third month, they decided they had had enough. It took a little longer before Satyavati was satisfied. In the sixth month, she declared that she was satisfied with their exposure to my Kuru aura, and they were clearly showing signs of a routine pregnancy. The nightly walk to my house was getting difficult, and it made sense to stop this ritual.

In the seventh month of their pregnancy, Satyavati announced that, in her opinion, Vichitravirya had been poisoned after all, by a slow-acting undetectable poison. Given when the babies had been conceived, the unborn children could also have received the poison. The Queens were ordered to rest so the children would be healthy. Ambalika and Ambika were kept indoors and out of sight. They did not complain. I was satisfied because it made it much easier to keep them safe. Nor did I have to sleep near the Queens. I could leave Hastinapura and return to overseeing the progress in building water tanks and irrigation canals. I had expected Satyavati to relax as the months went by and the girls stayed healthy, and nothing bad happened, but I was wrong. Satyavati was at her most contrarian self that year.

As the weeks passed, Satyavati became increasingly tense. Lines of worry marked her face. She constantly demanded different kinds of food for the mothers-to-be. At one point, I found that she had arranged to obtain live carrot plants from Takshashila, where they are considered a medicine for blindness. Its leaves, smell and dirty white flowers were impossible to admire. The root, a crooked purple stalk of wood with a pungent taste that the onagers love, is eaten, so cart drivers carry them as treats for the animals. How did I learn of Satyavati's purchase? A month before the Queens were to deliver, a caravan from the west arrived, carrying a hundred plants on the verge of flowering. They had been purchased by Satyavati from Takshashila four months earlier so that when they arrived they were just flowering. The price was staggering – bronze and copper tools for five kitchens, or the equivalent in gold. Satyavati had told me she wanted to order some plants. In those days I was struggling to fit in the day's workload into the time when the sun was up so the girls would not be disturbed at night, and I told the accountant to obey the Queen-Mother. But even someone as cautious as Satyavati can lose their sense of purpose under stress, as she did. Later, I asked her in private why she had spent so much gold. *The carrots are good for pregnant mothers,* she said.

If they were so good, and were so expensive when imported, why hadn't she told me? I would have arranged to buy seed and grow them in my own garden. Satyavati was not troubled by the cost – she was protecting her future descendants. But the worry lines did not fade from Satyavati's brow even after this rare shipment was received.

As the seventh month ended, Ambika and Ambalika grew slowly; by the seventh moon they were still on the small side according to Satyavati, who worried every day. Finally they began to show their pregnancy. I learned a lot from observing them. I received reports on their fluctuating moods, the vomiting over the first one hundred and eight days, their tiredness, Satyavati's worries, and so on. There was nothing I could do but observe.

The seventh full moon passed with no sign of trouble but Satyavati decided it was time to withdraw the two of them from public view. Then halfway into the eighth moon, she announced the news – Ambika and Ambalika had given birth to sons. Ambika was first by a day. But the babies emerged unready and unhealthy, small and sickly. Satyavati walked around moaning and cursing as though she herself had given birth to them.

The Vyaasa was to play a part in our lives once more. If it had not been for him, the children would have died."

"Vyaasa Shukla?"

"No, no, not Shukla here but his predecessor, Jaimini. Shukla, my friend, I have wished to say this to you for a long time. I am astonished by the influence the Vyaasa Parashara has had on this family. Along with the Vyaasa Jaimini, Satyavati had daily visits from Shukla, and Krishna Dvaipaayana Paaraasharya, to whom she was much attached, having cared for him as a baby. Only later did I realize that he was her son.

It is not surprising that Vyaasa Jaimini was concerned. But it was astonishing that the birth of my nephews was also a major concern to our current Vyaasa, Shukla, and to Krishna Dvaipaayana, a potential Vyaasa. It all began with my father's respect for Parashara. As Head of the Kavi Sangha, he influenced my father. He was Shukla's teacher and Krishna Dvaipaayana's father. All three of them were Parashara's children, physically or intellectually. You could almost call Parashara the root of the tree of cause and effect that has led to this war."

"My friend," Shukla said, "I wish it were so. But our influence has not prevented this war, despite the best efforts of the Kavi Sangha. Of Dvaipaayana, the less said, the better. For many years I despaired that he would remain in the Kavi Sangha, for he was a wayward young man. Vichitravirya's death shocked him and made him change his ways."

"Wayward young man? It reminds me that when he was six or so and had just started training with the Kavi Sangha, he would be teased by everybody. They would call him Shukla, to which he would respond with a vigorous *I am not like Uncle Shukla*, as he calls you. Then they called him not-Shukla. He did not like that, and one day he said, *why don't you call my uncle Not-Krishna*? People pointed out that they did, for 'not-Krishna' is what 'Shukla' means. I observed the teasing once and was struck by the role names played in our lives. Take the name Krishna – maybe it is only a coincidence, but life is a mess of such coincidences. Shukla the Vyaasa is a not-Krishna.

There is the Yadava Krishna, whose support for Arjuna and the Pandavas has helped them continue this war and resulted in my capture. There is Krishnaa Agnijyotsna, the Dark Lady, Matriarch of Panchala, whose blistering rage has not allowed this Kuru family to resolve its internal conflicts. Your nephew Krishna Dvaipaayana finds himself in good company.

Pardon me for this digression, but I have one more observation. It is not so strange that Satyavati's family became so central to life in Hastinapura, for she bent all her efforts to ensure her descendants would rule Hastinapura in the future. That makes us no different from Panchala; we too, have our own Dark Lady, whose personal ambitions for her children have precluded compromise.

As for your father's foster-child, Krishna…ah! Krishna Dvaipaayana…what an impressive young man he became after Vichitravirya's death. You were absent, gone to the Kavi Sangha's university in Takshashila, and missed this part of his life. I think of him as a child, even though he is only a decade or so younger than you. He has become a major intellectual force in the Kavi Sangha, something I would not have predicted. As a young man he was well liked, though his behaviour was irresponsible and difficult to condone. He did not like to stay in one place and constantly moved around. He would come along once in a while and wheedle gold and silver out of Satyavati and then disappear. In the beginning, I received reports of his activities that somehow never ended unhappily. An abandoned girl would follow him but, after talking to him, return home with a wistful smile. An insulted bard would come to chide him and leave praising his kindness. The only exception seemed to be Satyavati. Every visit ended with Satyavati getting angry and ordering him to leave. Then she would cry and ask him to promise to return. During your frequent absences, he was her sole link to your father, who had raised them both. I expect he was rebelling against the expectations people had of him as Parashara's son. But, as I mentioned, he changed. He visited me shortly after the birth of Vichitravirya's children. I had not seen him in many years, and I was overwhelmed by his charm. He was polite and asked after my health; made light conversation, and left me babbling about his generosity in favoring me with a visit. I am told he has that effect on everyone.

That was when Krishna Dvaipaayana started building a new life. Satyavati asked him to visit the babies, and he obliged. He even played with them. Satyavati stopped crying after his visits. I stopped getting reports from the places he visited. Then I heard from a proud Satyavati that he had risen quickly in the Kavi Sangha. He was a skilled poet and a rising leader in the Kavi Sangha hierarchy, possibly even a Vyaasa."

Shukla said, "Archivist, that is a long digression. I will help clean it up later. Devavrata, my friend, please continue with the birth of Vichitravirya's sons."

Devavrata said, "On the Vyaasa's advice, Satyavati placed the babies in a warm room heated by a hypocaust[46] fired all through the day. To ensure the babies came to no harm, her maids were in constant attendance on them. A piece of cotton would be dipped in goat's milk and squeezed into their mouths. For two months they were fed like that. By then they were healthier and ready for their mother's breasts, but Ambika and

[46]A system of underfloor heating, used to heat houses with hot air. The Romans used it and claim to have invented it, but there are structures like that in Mohenjo-daro and other Sarasvati-Sindhu Culture sites.

Ambalika were unable to lactate; it had been too long since the birth. The baby suckling at her breast is necessary for the mother to produce milk, and their babies had not done so. As a coincidence, the pregnant maidservant gave birth to her own baby just two weeks before the baby boys were ready to be switched to mother's milk. Her baby was a healthy boy. She was a sturdy woman and produced enough milk for all three boys.

Whoever said that a pregnancy lasting nine moons results in a healthy baby should take heed. The child of the wet nurse, born late in the eleventh month, was named Dharmateja – yes, the same Dharmateja Vidura, whose moralizing lectures discomfit Suyodhana in Hastinapura. Dharmateja Vidura is probably the most kind, ethical, and most far-sighted of Dhritarashtra's councillors. I would rate him as wise as you. His advice to settle this war peacefully enraged Suyodhana.

Vidura was healthy at birth. Even though he was conceived a couple of weeks before the two Princes, he was born well after them. He was a prodigy, born after eleven months. If only the two Princes could have stayed in the womb for another two months, unnatural as that may be, they may have been healthier. Ambika's son was named Dhritarashtra. When he was finally ready to be shown to the public, it became clear that something was wrong with his eyes. He kept them closed. If we tried to hold his eyes open by parting the lids, he would struggle violently and cry. We determined later that he could not bear to let light into his eyes. As a result, he did not look at people's faces when they looked at or spoke to him. There was nothing wrong with his mind, for he listened intently to sounds. Other than this blindness, the stay in the warm room had not hurt him at all. He grew up to be strong and healthy, but blind.

Ambalika's son was named Mahendra. He had been born white as milk – later he would be nicknamed *Pandu* 'the pale'. Even though he shared the heated room treatment with his brother, Mahendra Pandu remained just as pale as he had been at birth. As the years went by, his skin color changed, but unfortunately not uniformly. He developed large patches of pink and white skin separated by areas that were tinted brown. His eyes were pink. He could not tolerate the glare of the sun, but unlike his brother, he learned to cope with it and could see. Otherwise, like his brother he was healthy and grew up to be physically fit."

Devavrata looked at Vyaasa. "There, I have told you of the birth of Vichitravirya's children. Now tell me Amba's secret."

The Vyaasa smiled but only with his lips; his eyes did not and his nostrils flared a little. "Devavrata, in some ways you remain so naïve. I will tell you Amba's secret, but I did not imagine Satyavati's secret, Ambika's secret, and Ambalika's secret, were also hidden from you."

"What secrets? You smile. Are you mocking me? I do not care for Satyavati's secret, she had many. The two girls, Ambika and Ambalika, were innocents. They had no secrets from the world."

"No, I do not mock you," said the Vyaasa. "I wonder… why do you want to know only Amba's secret when there are so many other secrets you do not know? If you learned a new secret, even one about Amba, what can you do with that knowledge? I fear you will not recover from your wound. You may recall the Kavi Sangha's maxim: 'That which does not lead to Action is not Knowledge'. There is no meaningful action you could take even if you knew all their secrets."

"I do not want to do anything. My father appeared in my dreams last night. I assume everyone has occasional dreams of their parents, so this is not unusual. Dreams are creations of the mind. Who can say with authority that they know how dreams correspond to material things? But in the last few days, a particular dream has become constant. In the first dream, my father appeared and told me I had fifty-six days. I didn't understand. Fifty-six days for what? But he said no more and vanished. In the next dream, he told me I had fifty-three days. When he showed up yesterday, he said I had forty days. That is sixteen less than before. Where did my sixteen days go? I have been in bed since I was wounded. Are these sixteen days in bed the ones I have lost? What will happen when there are no days left? Perhaps I will die. It would certainly be considered a miracle if I survived another forty days. What is the meaning of such a dream? I have heard scholars debate about dreams, but they never came to any conclusion. Perchance, in forty days, reason will have prevailed and this war will end. Maybe I will be released in forty days, completely healed, and stop having these dreams. If my father is appearing to me in my dreams, he must think there is something I can do. My task is to determine what that is."

"In any case, you promised," Devavrata reminded the Vyaasa.

"I will do as I promised."

"There is something only you can do in forty days," said the Vyaasa. "Only you can bring the warring parties to the negotiating table."

"I have attempted to do so."

"Oh, no, you have not. Not in the Council and not in private. In the Council, Karna, Suyodhana, and the rest of that gang shouted you down. But you could have stuck to your points and insisted on an honest negotiation."

"It is over. I do not wish to debate it, even if that be the meaning of my dreams; what my father wishes me to do in forty days. I call on your promise. Tell me Amba's secret; no more digressions."

44
Amba's Flight

"Tell me Amba's secret."

The Vyaasa dropped his eyes and took a deep breath. His shoulders slumped. He did not move. Ten vighatis passed as Lomaharshana and Devavrata watched him. It felt like an aeon to Devavrata. Finally the Vyaasa raised his head.

"Devavrata, why is it that you cannot see the obvious? You accuse Satyavati of all kinds of plots and dealings, but the biggest plot eludes you."

"Satyavati has plots in her blood. She had been plotting from the day I met her."

"Satyavati has been trying to make amends ever since that day. For much of what she did, she consulted me. She did not always do as I suggested, but I always knew what she would do. Once, only once, she plotted without asking me for advice – that resulted in Amba's disappearance. I was in Takshashila. I would have stopped her had I been present, but I was not. Why did you, who mistrusted her in everything else, not think she might have had something to do with Amba's disappearance?"

"I did consider it, but did not see why Satyavati would want to get rid of Amba. Even if she knew we were lovers and I had broken my vow, she faced a risk only if a child was born.

That possibility itself gave her power over me, for she could denounce me as an oath-breaker. Civil war would have been my only recourse, and she knew I was ever averse to that. Why then would she have wanted Amba gone?"

"The obvious one. Consider this: Why did you and my sister plot against each other when it would have been so much easier to cooperate? After all, you agreed to split responsibilities after Shantanu died. She handled the internal affairs of Hastinapura, while you extended it into an empire. What did you imagine would happen when you brought Amba into the arrangement?"

"It was a secret between us, for if Satyavati found out, she could have threatened to disclose it and shame me."

"Because you broke your vow?"

Devavrata nodded.

The Vyaasa touched his fingers to his forehead and took a deep breath. Then he laughed. "My friend," he said, "you are a fool. Vows are broken all the time. The tempest caused by that charge would have lasted half a day. No ally would have left your side. Satyavati knew this and did the next best thing she could – she made it appear that you wished to be rid of Amba, but were incapable of taking the decision. That made you look weak. She had not expected it to be so easy to discredit you. Amba probably believed that you would do whatever you thought needed to be done, that you would not flinch, because she knew how the name Bhishma had been earned."

Devavrata silently absorbed the revelation. Satyavati had kidnapped Amba and made it seem the kidnappers were his soldiers. *If they did not kill her, what did they do? She must have been pregnant with Shikhandin – how had she managed during that difficult time? Who had helped her? How did Shikhandin end up in Panchala?*

The Vyaasa watched him for some time and then said, "Satyavati told me much of this when I returned from Takshashila. Your reaction, though, surprised me."

"What surprised me was that no one else seemed concerned about Amba's disappearance," Devavrata protested.

"That was to be expected. Amba had kept aloof from most people during her stay in Hastinapura. She spent her time with her sisters and Satyavati. And you of course. She left without fanfare, saying she was visiting her home. It was your reaction that baffled me."

"My reaction?"

"You seemed preoccupied and distant. All issues that came up were dealt with efficiently. You did not even talk about Amba's disappearance. You did nothing about it."

"What I did, I did secretly. I did not want it to be publicized. She was a gift of good fortune to me, and then, like all such gifts, it was taken away."

"I assumed you knew about her pregnancy. I was puzzled that you did not seem concerned about her health, that you did not mourn the child she was carrying; your child. I was truly puzzled by you."

Devavrata's tried to turn to face the Vyaasa. He regretted it immediately; the movement pressed the arrow deeper and he stopped. He could only look sideways at the Vyaasa. "But the truth is that I did not know," he said.

The Vyaasa leaned closer, his voice a whisper. "You did not know she was pregnant when she disappeared?"

Devavrata shook his head slightly. "No. I only found out a few days ago, during the ambush. How did you learn of it?"

The Vyaasa's eyes narrowed. "You never knew of the pregnancy? I…I cannot believe that."

Devavrata shook his head more vigorously. "I have told you more than once – I just learned of it a few days ago, when I killed Shikhandin. And it was confirmed when Amba tried to kill me. How did you know?"

"Amba's *bisaj* told me. She had asked him not to tell Satyavati. But after Amba disappeared, the *bisaj* felt he had to tell someone responsible. He came to me. I told him to keep it secret until it became necessary to reveal it. I thought you must know, that Amba would have told you, even if she did not tell anyone else."

Devavrata closed his eyes. "Go away," he said quietly. "You can tell me the rest later."

The Vyaasa got up slowly. He felt his bones creaking and his joints complaining. He groaned. He gathered the folds of his upper garment and moved towards the entrance. As he stepped through the tent opening, he heard a sound from the bed. He turned around quickly, and lost his balance. He would have fallen if the Archivist had not stepped forward to hold him up.

"Did you say something?" the Vyaasa asked.

"Come back and finish telling me what happened to Amba."

"I will," said the Vyaasa, and returned to his seat.

"Should I memorize this, Sir?" said the Archivist, who had been silent all along.

"Yes, yes. You have been listening, have you not?"

"Yes, Sir."

"Devavrata, my friend," said the Vyaasa, "should I begin?"

Devavrata nodded silently.

"I used to spend many months in Takshashila in those days. I knew even then that the Kavi Sangha was going to be my life. I returned to Hastinapura once or twice a year. The trip was tedious and took many days. The organizers of caravans had no interest in the affairs of the lands they traversed. It would be some years before I realized how much they knew that was important. They knew the border guards, the officials to go to for various permissions, who could provide protection and who could not, who was predatory and who wasn't, and they knew what could be exchanged where.

Forgive me, I digress. Let me tell you what I found when I returned to Hastinapura after Amba's disappearance. Satyavati was in good spirits. She had taken over the care of Amba's sisters. Amba's absence did not seem to have affected anyone, including you. Satyavati was short with me when I asked about Amba – she had gone away was all she would say. I could not ask you, for you had made it impossible for anyone to approach you except on official business. My status as Satyavati's brother and someone who took care of her interests, allowed me access to her attendants. I found out that Amba had employed a weaver to help her with clothing appropriate to the city. The weaver became Satyavati's eyes and ears, and she talked willingly enough to me. She had realized Amba was pregnant and reported it to Satyavati.

I questioned Satyavati about Amba. Her answer was that Amba had said that she was going on a trip. When I mentioned that Amba had been pregnant, she feigned shock. I then told her that I knew she had known of the pregnancy. I reminded her that she was my sister, and I would protect her interests. She swore me to secrecy. Amba had been pregnant for maybe two moons. Satyavati had always feared that such a thing would happen. She had to act and she could not wait for my visit to discuss what to do. She had arranged for two men, dressed in the style that you, Devavrata, had established for all your soldiers, to visit Amba with a message from you. In the message you asked her to come to your project site as the work was significantly delayed. To Amba, this would have been good news; it would have made your relationship public. Satyavati's spy, one of Amba's maids, reported that Amba hoped that you were thus prepared to acknowledge her publicly, thus ending months of secrecy. She hoped this would include recognition of her future child's standing in this patriarchal city.

Accordingly she left the next day with the messengers. Satyavati said Amba asked her to take care of her sisters while she was gone. She told her sisters little, just that she was going to meet you. The men accompanying her had been instructed to kill her and ensure her body would not be found. That was the first time my sister truly shocked me; I had not expected such ruthlessness. My shock showed, and she began to cry, explaining that she had been afraid. I berated her; she asked for forgiveness. I told her that such forgiveness was not mine to give. Then she threw me a *vajra,* a lightning bolt – neither the men nor Amba returned. Perhaps she had managed to bribe the men or escape their custody. The men would not have returned if they had failed or abandoned their mission. At any moment Amba might return and denounce Satyavati. To prepare for that eventuality, she was kind and solicitous towards Ambika and Ambalika. But when Amba did not send a message of her safe arrival, her sisters began to worry. Satyavati stoked their worries about your intentions. They knew what you were capable of; they too, had been witness to the Shaka massacre. Satyavati sowed doubts in their minds and your apparent lack of concern convinced them.

When you returned from the dam site and said you had not seen Amba or sent for her, they were sure you were lying. They did not wish to deal with you, and avoided you. They felt powerless to denounce you; they were too young. There was no life for them in their band but you tried to send them back to their old settlement; that convinced them you were trying to hide something. But Satyavati was considerate, kind and charming, not brusque like you. They had not seen or heard of her torturing anyone, as you had. For the first time they were told of your oath of celibacy; a vow they knew you had broken with their sister. That only made you more the villain. It was possible that you had arranged to get rid of Amba – maybe not kill her, but make her disappear. Over time they became reconciled to Amba's absence, to life in the company of Vichitravirya and others their age, and finally to marriage.

Satyavati made no effort to determine what had happened to the men who had taken Amba away. Any action by her would have revealed her role. So she asked me to investigate, in secret. She was my sister, and I was concerned about her state of mind. The impulsive and ruthless plot bothered me. It seemed so unlike her that I investigated the matter personally. I went into the forest with a Naga guide skilled in the trails and pathways. We found signs of three overnight camps, suggesting the first three nights of a journey; then nothing. At the point where a fourth camp should have been, there was no evidence of habitation. We traced our way back.

At one point the guide pointed to a trail that some large animal had cut across the path. We followed it and came across some bones. Hidden behind a dense thorny bush was a human skeleton. It had been scraped clean by animals, and two limbs were missing. There was no flesh, nor clothing or any sign to indicate who it had been, man, woman, soldier, fisherman or hunter… I measured the skeleton carefully – the handspan, the length of the arm from elbow to the tip of the forefinger, the circumference of the wrist, and so on. It was not a woman. How do I know? The Kavi Sangha has collected information on the sizes of bones of men and women, hence we know.

If it was a man's body, it could not be Amba; perhaps one of her guards. I was relieved. We continued to follow the trail and a hundred *hastas* further, we came to the banks of the Ganga. It is a fast-flowing and wide river at this point, about ten *kros*[47] south of Kampilya, the capital of Panchala. The forest vegetation grows almost to the riverbank, where it gives way to water-loving plants. Elephant grass grew in clumps there. The trail from the skeleton ended at the water's edge. The water ran too far below ground level, so it was an unlikely waterhole

[47]*Kros* is a measure of distance, a little over two miles.

for animals. The way the trail jutted into the water suggested a natural or artificial dock for a boat, though long abandoned. To the left, a section of elephant grass had been pulled out of a four hasta-square piece of land, about a hasta above the waterline. From there, footprints made by small feet, went north along the river bank. I stepped barefooted next to one of the footprints and made a larger footprint for comparison. It seemed clear that a smaller person had made the old prints. If this was Amba's route, it appeared that she had passed this way some weeks ago. North of there she would sooner or later have reached a town with a ferry crossing and could have made a quick escape to the Panchala side of the river. The road there would lead her to Kampilya, the capital city of Hastinapura's enemy. There was no point in chasing Amba; she would have been long gone, to Panchala if she was lucky. More likely, she had fallen victim to hunger, her own or that of a tiger or a pack of wild dogs.

Some years later, shortly before I became the Vyaasa, the Kavi Sangha managed to place a few spies in Kampilya, the Panchala capital. They reported to me every six months. In the second year of espionage, we received an applicant to the Kavi Sangha from Kampilya, who was a fount of gossip. You know the best bards are natural memorizers of whatever they hear. This bard-in-training relayed rumors that the Matriarch of Panchala was unhappy with her brother Drupada, for having brought an outside woman into his palace. Unlike other men, Drupada, also called the King[48] of the Naga band, never went

[48]The title for the army chief and the brother of the Matriarch could have been "Senapati" ("Lord of the army"), but that usage mixes the two roles. He may well have been addressed as "Rajan" (meaning "resplendent one"), or "Mahanaga" ("great Naga"), or even "Nagarajan" ("Lord of the Nagas" or "King of the Nagas"). "Nagarajan" could also be interpreted as "King according to Naga practice," i.e., the brother of the matriarch. I have translated all of these possibilities as "King."

out of the band to find partners. As King, he could not move to a partner's band; any permanent relationship required the woman to move in with him, leaving her band. It was generally felt there was something wrong with a woman who would thus leave her band.

However, that was not the Matriarch's reason for opposing this relationship. The woman's dialect marked her as a Naga from the Hastinapura territories. A year earlier, a Naga band allied with Hastinapura was reported to have fought off invaders from across the northern Mountains. The invasion had been stopped. There were hints of atrocities committed during that battle. Instead of enhancing the reputation of the band, the victory had led to its collapse, when it could not recruit new members. The assumption was that the woman Drupada had taken in was one of those scarred by that experience. The Matriarch did not wish for any member of such a band in her town, much less in the royal palace. It was said that this woman was so beautiful that Drupada had refused to obey the Matriarch's demand to verify her antecedents.

I learned a lot about Panchala and its rulers from the young bard trainee. In a traditional Naga band, the Matriarch had the power to enforce her commands, but in Kampilya, the power equation between the Matriarch and the King had been reversed. In a deep sense, Panchala and Hastinapura were similar – both patriarchies to be.

The young bard trainee joined the Kavi Sangha in Hastinapura, but stayed in touch with the events and gossip in Kampilya, and I stayed in touch with him. He brought news of Drupada's woman giving birth to a son, as well as the ebbing of the feud between the Matriarch and the King. The woman lived a quiet and secluded life, not seeming to care that her son was not recognized by the Matriarch. The Matriarch may have been reconciled with the King, but she displayed her anger by not acknowledging the birth of the child. Because the mother was not part of the Matriarch's family, the birth was ignored by everyone. The King did not seem particularly distressed.

As usual, all this was reported and recorded in the Kavi Sangha archives. Even then I suspected the woman was Amba. I could not go to Kampilya to verify this, nor could I send another senior Kavi Sangha member. I had to rely on the Naga students who went home annually. When the boy grew up, he played with the other children in Drupada's palace and in the city. He was sensitive about some things; he could not bear to hear gossip about his mother and would attack the gossiper. Questions about his father made him sad and withdrawn.

The Kavi Sangha members in Panchala, though few in number, helped me collect more details about the mystery woman. There is no doubt she was Amba. I do not know how she did it, but she found her way into the protection of the King of Panchala, Hastinapura's enemy, and raised the boy in Drupada's palace. That was Shikhandin, your son. When the boy grew up, he enlisted in a select group of warriors led by the Panchalan army Chief Dhrishtadyumna, brother of the current Matriarch and nephew of the now-retired Senior Chief Drupada."[49]

"Shikhandin," said Devavrata. "He behaved differently towards me. Many men have feared me, but a few hated me. He was one. Why did he attempt to kill me? I had to kill him in self-defense."

---

[49]Dhristadyumna was the son of Panchala's Matriarch, brother of the Matriarch-to-be, and therefore, the King-to-be in Panchala. As such, he is the formally acknowledged commander of the Pandava forces in the Great War.

The Vyaasa was silent. *What can I possibly say?* he thought. Wishing to protect his sister, he had kept Amba's child a secret from Devavrata. It had seemed a small thing. But the loss of Amba was the reason Devavrata became even more *Bhishma* than he had been after the Shaka massacre – opaque, uncommunicative, and difficult to comprehend. It became impossible to tell him the truth. Bhishma was a hard shell; Devavrata only dealt with business of empire. In the meantime, he, Shukla, had become more involved in the affairs of the Kavi Sangha and embarked on the path to becoming the Vyaasa.

Devavrata was also silent, staring intently at the Vyaasa. He finally broke his silence. "Tell me, why did Shikhandin want his father dead? That is, if I am truly his father."

Shukla said, "I could not meet Amba. I relied on the aspiring Kavi Sangha student for news; his brother was married to one of Amba's maids. According to her, Amba expressed hate and contempt for Hastinapura. She raised Shikhandin to hate Hastinapura and you. He had few friends and revealed little, even to those closest to him. He grew up to hate Hastinapura. You realize, Devavrata, that for many, many years, *you* were Hastinapura."

Both men fell silent. For a long time the Vyaasa sat and Devavrata lay still, his eyes closed.

A ghati passed. The Archivist waited for Shukla to continue. When he did not, he stood up to stretch his limbs. Then he said, "Sir, are we done for the day?"

The Archivist's voice aroused the Vyaasa from his reverie. "Devavrata," Shukla said, "how were you captured?"

Devavrata did not reply, and his eyes remained closed. The Vyaasa laughed. It was indeed an opportune moment to fall asleep, to avoid questions. He rose to leave.

Suddenly Devavrata said, “Shukla, you are not done!”

“So you are awake,” said the Vyaasa. “What do you mean not done? What is left to tell you?”

Devavrata said, “You promised to tell me Satyavati, Ambika and Ambalika’s secret.”

“It has been so many years and not particularly interesting.”

The Archivist said, “Should it not be part of the archive?”

The Vyaasa frowned. Seeing this, the Archivist fell silent.

“Come back and finish this,” said Devavrata. “It will not take long. I may know more than you think I do.”

45
Secret of the Three Queens

The Vyaasa said, "Do you recall what you were doing when Vichitravirya died?"

"I certainly do," said Devavrata. "How can I forget? We have gone over it all and your Archivist has recorded it."

"I want you to think back to when his sons were born. Do you recall anything odd?"

"Odd? I think the entire situation was odd. Satyavati was as she had always been – difficult and focused on her ambitions. The anticipated birth of my nephews allowed me to continue postponing decisions about the succession and rule. If I ever became the sole candidate, I would have been compelled to become King, and my stepmother and I would have had to resolve whatever differences we had. Many years had passed since my father's death and that of Chitrangada as well. I had ruled as co-Regent twice during those years. Vichitravirya left ruling to me and Satyavati. I had my time with Amba and now faced many more years of co-Regency. But even so, I felt a knot form in my chest when I thought about ruling Hastinapura and fathering children to rule after me – a knot that had been tied by Satyavati, the girl, and pulled tight by Satyavati, my stepmother."

The Vyaasa said, "This is all true, my friend, but it seems to me that you do not really want to know what you have demanded I tell you."

Devavrata replied, "I am afraid of what you will tell me. I must know it, but I would willingly put it off to the day I die. That day comes soon, perhaps today, perhaps now. But I find I am still afraid. Most of all I fear that which you will disclose."

"I don't know how to allay your fears. You must decide for yourself. The truth is your brother Vichitravirya is not the father of Dhritarashtra and Mahendra Pandu. When he died, the inheritance rules applicable to a trading post could have made a complete stranger the leader. Satyavati arranged for the Queens to bear children by a suitable man. I first thought she had persuaded you, but then it became clear it was someone else."

The Vyaasa stopped, observing Devavrata's reaction to the startling revelation.

Devavrata was silent for a long time. Then he turned to gaze at his friend. "*Niyoga?* She found a surrogate father? That would have to happen after my brother was dead, would it not?"

"Yes."

"But the Queens were a few weeks pregnant when Vichitravirya died. Are you telling me it was done when Vichitravirya was still alive?"

"No, the children were conceived after he died."

Appendix A.15: Carrots and Fatherhood

Devavrata was mystified by Satyavati's actions and demands when Ambika and Ambalika were pregnant – importing carrot plants, secluding the queens, and demanding that Devavrata spend time with his sisters-in-law seemed to be unreasonable and strange.
The Annals explain what Satyavati was trying to accomplish.

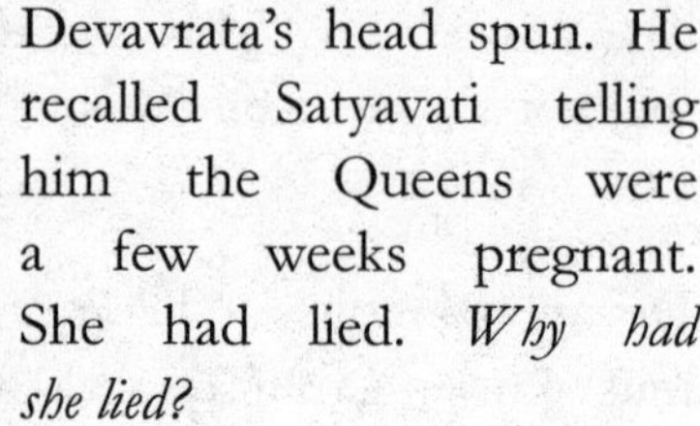

Devavrata's head spun. He recalled Satyavati telling him the Queens were a few weeks pregnant. She had lied. *Why had she lied?*

"Was the father a Kuru; a descendant of Puru? Was he sufficiently honorable to take the place of my brother? Can I still believe that I fulfilled the promise to my father?"

"Hmm…you must be the judge of that. Do you recall us talking about Dvaipaayana visiting Satyavati with her father?"

"Yes, the elusive Krishna Dvaipaayana. What about him?"

"You know he was Guru Parashara's son?"

Devavrata thought back to the time he had first seen the baby with Satyavati. "Yes, and Satyavati took care of him while Guru Parashara fulfilled his vow of silence."

"Do you know he might well be the Vyaasa when I pass on?"

"Yes, I have heard of his brilliant rise in the Kavi Sangha. Why should it matter to me now?"

"Do you know that his mother was Satyavati?"

Devavrata opened his mouth to say something and then stopped. Instead, he started coughing as though his lungs had filled with fluid. The coughing would not stop and the attendant came in and held Devavrata so the arrow would not accidentally move. Shukla waited. The coughing subsided and then stopped.

Devavrata took a deep breath and said, "No, I did not know. Do not tell me that everyone else knew! I cannot believe that."

"Do not fret, even your father did not know. Krishna Dvaipaayana had inherited many of his father's features, but Parashara had not been seen for some years and people forget."

"So what about him? What about Parashara's son?"

"He took the King's place and fathered the children."

Devavrata felt time slow and stop. His thoughts strained to emerge as speech. He managed to say, "What?"

Shukla said, "Krishna Dvaipaayana is the father of Dhritarashtra, Mahendra Pandu and Dharmateja Vidura."

Devavrata said, "You mean…Krishna Dvaipaayana is the grandfather of…" His voice faltered. "…these cousins…the father of their fathers."

The Vyaasa smiled. "You are a perceptive man, my friend, but you refuse to see beyond the tip of your nose. I am not implying anything, I am asserting it. Satyavati asked her son to father children with the Queens Ambika and Ambalika."

"I see." Devavrata's mind whirled. *Krishna Dvaipaayana was not the one responsible; Satyavati was.* Devavrata wanted to rise from his sick bed and confront Satyavati, who, at a single fear-induced stroke, had created this warped world. For an eternity that lasted a few vighatis, everyone was silent.

Then Devavrata said, "Dhritarashtra and Mahendra Pandu are not Kauravas, not descended from Kuru, not my father's grandchildren." The various forms of the statement seemed to rush down a waterfall to a sea of conclusions. *They were not my nephews. Their children are not my grand-nephews.*

"Yes, those are logical inferences. They are not Kauravas."

Shukla's statement evoked more inferences. *They were Shukla's grand-nephews. These children are Shukla's great-grandnephews.* Devavrata felt laughter forming in his throat – mocking laughter that threatened to displace all thought. He needed time. Satyavati's actions were in the past, a long time ago. Shukla's relationship was irrelevant to the war. *What should I do now?*

He made up his mind.

"I repeat my question: Is their lineage worthy of Hastinapura?"

"Dhritarashtra and Mahendra Pandu are the grandchildren of Parashara."

"That is a glorious heritage, descendants of the great Vasishtha. But their mothers are Nagas of unknown descent."

"Does that matter? Must they be Panchnadis? All you asked was whether their bloodline was noble. You had already approved the mothers, thus only the father's heritage can be in question."

The pieces fell in place like the fragments of a broken pot that had been re-assembled.

Shukla continued, "The Queens became pregnant after the King's death. Both sons were born more than six weeks prematurely. Only Dharmateja Vidura, born in the tenth moon after the King's death, was born at the right time. Satyavati had even arranged for the premature delivery with her shipment of carrots – the elixir of its flowers being an abortifacient. It even explained her concern over ensuring that a Kaurava should influence the babies in the womb. She made sure that no questions would be raised, even by me, about the legitimacy of the two children."

Devavrata struggled to focus his mind. *I never bothered to find out why Satyavati was attached to the boy Krishna Dvaipaayana. I just assumed she was attached to him because she had taken care of him almost from birth.*

"Did you know at the time?"

Shukla said, "He is my nephew. I kept quiet when I found out. He was a charming boy, and I was attached to him."

"I have no problem with his fathering future Kings," Devavrata said. "However, I am troubled that I failed to keep the promise I made to my father. Neither Mahendra Pandu nor Dhritarashtra are Kauravas by birth. The empire I have built will pass into non-Kaurava hands."

"That is not true. You fulfilled your promise."

Devavrata shook his head in denial.

The Vyaasa said, "You recall the oath? Of course, you must. Recite it once more."

"I recall it perfectly: 'I hereby renounce all my rights to have children, and give them to my father. To you, O King, I yield my birthright. O Queen, I will not marry, I will not have children, and I will not make love to any woman. O King, my father, my right to a descendant is yours.'"

"There is more to your oath than that."

46
The Unravelling Thread

There was another long silence. Devavrata went over what he had just heard. If Dhritarashtra and Mahendra Pandu were Dvaipaayana's children, they were Satyavati's grandchildren. They were her progeny, even if they were not Shantanu's grandchildren. The prediction that Satyavati's descendants would rule an empire had apparently come true. That long-gone day he had sworn an oath that he would not father children and remain celibate. He had broken the vow of celibacy, but he had been little more than a boy when he had sworn that oath. He knew now that it had been a ridiculous vow. And if Shikhandin was his son, he had also broken the promise not to father children.

There was another oath. Before his marriage to Satyavati, his father had come to him. Devavrata replayed that scene in his mind as he contemplated Shukla's words. Shantanu had said, 'My dear son. To you I owe my great happiness. I asked a lot of you, and you have given me much, much more. I had hoped it would be enough, but I have one more request.'

Devavrata had struggled not to show any emotion. He relaxed his lips, controlled his breathing, and focused his eyes on his father's face – the father who stood before him like a supplicant. He had said, 'You are my father, to whom I owe my life. You are the King, the Lord of life and death in Hastinapura, to whom I owe my allegiance. Ask and it is yours."

Shantanu had said, "I fear what will happen to Satyavati if I die prematurely. What will happen to Hastinapura; the legacy that I inherited? Promise me that you will take care of both.'

Devavrata had closed his eyes in an effort to calm himself. The silence had seemed interminable for his father. Shantanu had construed the silence to mean that his son was angry with his stepmother for the oaths she had extracted from him. A few vighatis later, he had said, 'Son, at least promise that you will take care of Hastinapura and keep it strong and prosperous.'

Devavrata had replied, 'I will swear whatever oaths you wish me to swear. I promise I will take care of your wife, my stepmother Satyavati, if you are unable to do so. I promise that the prophecy she spoke of will come true. As long as I live I will do all I can to keep Hastinapura safe and its rulers powerful and respected."

That was it. His father had left him alone after that. He had made this oath with full consciousness of what it meant and with time for deliberation. The vow of celibacy had been made in the heat of the moment, but this vow was made judiciously, but not, as fate would have it, with full understanding. The first vow was made to a weak man and a fickle woman; the second to his father alone, and to the country he was building; the empire he would create.

Neither Mahendra Pandu nor Dhritarashtra were Kauravas, but they were Satyavati's progeny. By crowning them he had fulfilled his promise to his father, and fulfilled the prophecy that Satyavati would be the mother of many rulers – the only vow he could bring himself to believe in. Or had he? He had taken sides. When the disagreement over policies between Mahendra Pandu and Dhritarashtra became open conflict, he had sided with Dhritarashtra, for Mahendra's proposals threatened his own vision of an imperial city. He had chosen to be neutral between Mahendra's and Dhritarashtra's children, at least in the beginning. He had decided to support Suyodhana's claim when Satyavati insisted the Pandavas, as everybody called them, were not Mahendra's own sons, and not descended from her. The evidence seemed compelling. It was commonly believed that albinism such as Mahendra Pandu's was inherited and none of the Pandavas were albino, though Arjuna, Nakula and Sahadeva were somewhat paler than the two eldest. Yudhishthira's calm demeanor was unlike any Kuru family trait. He reminded Devavrata of Parashara, but Satyavati insisted Yudhishthira had inherited nothing from her or Shantanu. Meanwhile, Bh□ ma's dark skin, broad face, nose and shoulders hinted at a Rakshasa origin. If they were Satyavati's grandchildren through her son Krishna, then any Naga features were natural, but the Rakshasa features required explanation. Was it possible that Satyavati had been justified in requiring Devavrata to provide the Kaurava influence on Ambika and Ambalika when they were pregnant? If he had known that neither branch of the family could claim direct descent from Shantanu, he might not have taken sides in their conflict. He could have refused to support Suyodhana exclusively. Or could he?

It struck him that, anxious to meet Satyavati's conditions, his father had requested the wrong oath. His father was concerned about *his* descendants through Satyavati. For that matter, if Satyavati had been asked, she would have said the same thing. They wanted him to promise to keep the kingdom safe for *Shantanu's* children *by* Satyavati. That is what he had assumed all along. On the other hand, the words of the oath only mentioned the prophecy that Shukla had quoted. In that case, he had actually lived by his oath. He had protected Hastinapura and created an empire to be ruled by Satyavati's descendants. It was not what he had thought he was doing. Was *this* the purpose of his oaths? The meaning he had assigned to his life slipped out of his grasp every time he examined it.

The right oath would have been far more complex, covering all the contingencies he had faced in his life. That right oath could never have been formulated for its every condition would have screamed *treachery*. Where in the oath could he have said, your children will inherit except if none of your children live, in which case my children will inherit? Where in the oath could he have said, only children by birth would inherit and not those by adoption or *niyoga*?

Such a vow had not been demanded of him – it had been his own idea. What if he had refused to make any of these vows and, instead declared his feelings for Satyavati? Would his father have stepped aside and allowed him to marry Satyavati? It was doubtful. Had his father ever guessed what had been sacrificed for him? Unlikely; his father was not one to bridle his desires. *I, Devavrata, have committed a sin against my ancestors by failing in my duties to them. Nor have I performed my duties to my own soul, for I have no descendants. I will suffer for it. I expected to protect my father's children, and that would have protected him and his ancestors. The only one to suffer will be me.*[50]

Another thought occurred to him. If neither the Pandavas nor the Kauravas were descended from Shantanu, then he, Devavrata, was the sole descendant of the King. Inadvertently, he had killed his son Shikhandin, his only offspring. How

[50]In Hindu belief, a person who dies without descendants has committed a sin against his or her ancestors. Some variant of this belief can be seen in many religions, major ones as well as religions of small communities.

ironic that here in this fenced camp-city of the enemies of Hastinapura, the only two legitimate heirs to the Kuru name and fortune lay dead or dying. The descendants of Satyavati and Parashara, Naga and bard, were fighting over an empire that he, a trader and warrior, had conceived and built. He had not ruled as King, but he had constructed an edifice that, if duly maintained, would sustain a great empire. Even Indraprastha had become possible because he had put in place dams and created lakes that controlled the Yamuna upstream. Further downstream, the Yadavas, settling on the banks of the Yamuna, were profiting from his creation. Space was being created for the immigrants from the west, from the lands formerly irrigated by the Sarasvati. They were settling lands all the way from the delta in the south to the northernmost point at Kaalindini, where the Sutudri twisted away from her innumerable children. With the aid of Hastinapura and the Kauravas, these refugees would lay claim to the triangle of land between the Ganga and the Yamuna.

The crisis was not past. Crises, he corrected himself. When you suppress one crisis, another is born elsewhere. The Pandava-Panchala-Yadava alliance would last only as long as the rivers were good fences.

Devavrata frowned; a fog he could not disperse enveloped his thoughts. This obsessive recalling of the events of his life was a foolish old man's indulgence. Dying would be preferable to such unremitting torture. Every time he moved, explosive needles of pain made him shake, his body betraying him. *Even on my deathbed*, he thought, *my ancestors refuse to take me back*.

The Archivist's insistant voice cut through the fog.

Death of Shikhandin

47
An Error of Judgment

The Archivist said, "Sir, you have been silent for a ghati. Are you feeling well?"

Devavrata heard the urgency in the voice. It pulled him away from the emotionally draining morass of morbid thoughts. He could take pride in the empire he had created. What matter who ruled it? Rulers were all the same, whether arrogant like Suyodhana or courteous like Yudhishthira. *A ghati? Had it really been that long?*

Devavrata said, "Where is Shukla?"

The Archivist, the only one present, replied, "He will return, Sir. He had to leave for a short while."

"What do you think, Lomaharshana? You have heard so much from so many different people. What do you think of all that has happened?"

The Archivist said, “Sir, I am merely the memorizer of people’s stories. My opinions do not matter.”

“I will not insist, but I am at the end of my life, indulge me.”

“Sir, it is an honor that you ask my opinion.”

“Be truthful and nothing else.

“Certainly Sir. But I must qualify my opinions, for what I have heard is complex. I have not arrived at a full understanding, the kind of deep familiarity that will allow me to reorganize it as a poem to be recited.”

“I know. At one time I wanted to be a memorizer like you.”

“You flatter me, Sir. May I ask a question?”

“Certainly, you have earned the right. I will answer if I can.”

Lomaharshana the Archivist said, “It is something that has bothered me for some time. Sir, you were asked a question you did not answer; I think you evaded it. It was: How did the seniormost Commander of the Kaurava army get captured in an ambush?”

Devavrata took a deep breath. “Overconfidence and stupidity, my son,” he said. “ Do you wish to make my foolishness part of this history?”

The Archivist nodded.

48
Plan to End the War

Devavrata said, "A man arrived in Hastinapura saying he had come from Panchala and wished to speak with Kaurava army high command. The man was Shi…Shikhandin… *Even saying his name hurts*. I did not know then what I know now, but I trusted him. In some way he must have reminded me of Amba. She was justified in trying to kill me. I wish she had succeeded.

The man Shi…khandin said he was a Krivi, hailing from the smallest clan in the Panchala confederation. He was authorized to make an offer that might end the war, and even if it did not, it would greatly weaken our enemy. The Kaurava Council held a secret meeting, not in the King's court, but in the war room in my house, that had no windows and walls thickened with an extra layer of mud to protect against eavesdroppers. This was where I met our spies and secret agents. Though protected against outsiders, the room had hidden entrances and secret hiding places for my own eavesdroppers. I arranged for a throne to be brought in. The King should look like a King, even to a traitor like this man. Such details are important. All the servants were sent away and only two of my trusted guards remained. Kutaja Drona, Suyodhana, Karna, Dharmateja Vidura and Kripa[51] came in. Blind Dhritarashtra came, accompanied by the bard Sanjaya, and I guided him to the throne.

[51] *Kripa* is Kutaja Drona's brother-in-law and skilled in martial arts. He and his sister, *Kripi*, were abandoned in the forest as babies, found by Shantanu, and raised in the palace.

The man was explicit. His clan did not want to go down the path of war and conquest. Four of the five clans that made up the Panchala confederation did not desire this war. They preferred to trade, not make war. He had been sent by the leaders of his clan to see if peace could be negotiated. 'I can set up a meeting,' he suggested. 'A senior councilor from each of the four clans will attend. Are you interested? Can you send a senior counselor who will negotiate on your behalf?'

Dhritarashtra smiled when he heard this. 'I have nothing but goodwill for my brother's children. Are they in agreement?'

The man looked up at the King, confused. Suyodhana rolled his eyes. 'Father,' he said trenchantly, 'perhaps you should listen rather than speak. My cousins rely on the Somakas, who are Panchala's leading clan. Their common wife, Krishnaa Agnijyotsna, is the Matriarch of Panchala. Her brother Dhrishtadyumna commands the joint Pandava-Panchalan army. This move would take away almost half their army.' Turning to the man he said, 'That is so, isn't it? The Somakas are the fifth clan, and they are the ones who seek war.'

The man said, 'The Somakas are the leading clan, the *first* clan. But my clan, the Krivi, along with the Srinjayas, the Turvashas, and the Keshins, want this war stopped.'

Karna said, 'If that is the case, why not stop it? Surely the four clans are the larger part of Panchala? You do not need to parlay with us to stop the war. Take your troops and go home.'

The man gave a thin smile that did not change his face. 'It is not that simple, Sir,' he said. 'The five clans have been allied for almost twenty generations. Begun as an alliance of equals, it changed ten generations ago to the present status, in which the Somaka are foremost. The Matriarch's family is Somaka. When she dies, the new Matriarch should not be from the same clan, as had been agreed upon. Instead, the Somaka have imposed a new agreement whereby the Matriarch's daughter would succeed. The Somaka control the army; the army controls the cities; the cities oversee the bands. It has been many years since we attempted a rebellion. The last time our senior-most captains were arrested for treason and killed before they could make a single move.'

'So, what is different now?'

'The old King, Drupada, has died. You know the events leading to the assault on the person of the young Matriarch Agnijyotsna, who has taken the Pandavas as husbands. Her brother, the new Somaka King, Dhrishtadyumna, sees an opportunity to avenge his sister and create an empire with Panchala at its centre. He has taken the greater part of his army into the field and is not at present in Kampilya, the capital. Our reserve forces can take the city and hold it for perhaps two weeks, until your forces arrive, but not longer, for our forces are weaker than those the King has at his command. Yet we can hold him off for just long enough. We are not as naïve as we once were. Members of our clans marching with the main army will leave it as soon as news of the takeover is announced.'

'Kampilya will be ours?'

'Yes.'

'We will control both banks of the Ganga?'

'Yes.'

Suyodhana's eyes lit up and his rather hard mouth curved into a smile. He slapped Karna on the back saying, 'The Pandavas and their wife will serve us as slaves yet!'

Dhritarashtra spoke, 'Son, I …'

Suyodhana's eyes glittered dangerously. 'Father, you have a soft spot for these supposed Pandava cousins. The last time, instead of sending them on their way as fraudulent pretenders, you gave them Indraprastha. See what chaos that decision has caused.'

Kutaja Drona said, 'Controlling both banks of the Ganga is a desirable goal. But it can only be achieved at the cost of much blood. Capturing Kampilya by subversion is by far cheaper. This proposal is worth considering.'

Karna, infected by his friend's enthusiasm, said, 'Of course it is worth considering, oh great guru of strategy. We are pleased you have expressed your opinion.'

Dharmateja Vidura spoke. Despite his low birth, I had brought him into the War Council. He usually suggested a peaceful path when addressing a problem. He would have been an excellent trader. As it was, he brought the common man's sensibility to our discussions. I wish we had heeded his advice that day.

'What do you require from us for this alliance?' Vidura asked.

'Yes,' Suyodhana said, addressing the Krivi, 'what exactly do you propose?'

The man's face brightened. 'Four senior leaders, one from each clan, are awaiting an emissary from you. I can take him to the meeting point, three to four days travel from here. It is a crossing on the Ganga.'

'There are a thousand crossings on the Ganga, but none in use since the war began. I know the one where they are waiting and will lead you there.'

Suyodhana said, 'We can avenge the humiliation of Samvarana.'

Samvarana had not exacted revenge for the trouble Panchala had caused him. Avenging Samvarana was an impossible-to-scratch itch on the Kuru psyche, one that afflicted Suyodhana the most. Kampilya had to be captured and its rulers killed, its population enslaved or driven into exile.

Suyodhana said, 'Kampilya will be delivered to us on a platter.'

Kutaja Drona said, 'Whom can we send?'

The messenger said, 'Anyone here would be senior enough to negotiate a peace.'

Suyodhana's smile vanished. 'One from this Council?'

The man replied, 'Sir, any Kaurava war leader would be welcomed. We are serious in what we propose. Whomever you send must be able to create a workable agreement, someone who understands the strategic issues involved in making this alliance work. He should also know your own military capabilities.'

Kutaja Drona said, 'We need to discuss this. Sanjaya, escort this man to the waiting chamber. Return with him in a ghati.'

Sanjaya led the man to the other side of my house. Like the War Room,the waiting room too had been specially constructed to be secure. Back in our meeting, I, Kutaja Drona, Suyodhana, Karna, and even Dharmateja Vidura, who was usually quiet, began talking at the same time and then stopped. In Panchnad councils there was a strict sequence for members to speak.

Karna said, 'I am for it. We can push them back into the jungles they came from. It will cost us nothing.'

Dharmateja Vidura said, 'He makes a good point about trade. This war has slowed commercial activity in all the settlements. We should never have attacked Indraprastha. Instead, we should have proposed an alliance to control all the land from the headwaters of the Ganga and Yamuna to Laghu Nagapura.'

Suyodhana's upper body trembled. Had they been standing he might have attacked Dharmateja Vidura. But we were all seated on our assigned mats; only King Dhritarashtra was seated on his throne – a stool set on a raised platform.

Staring at Dharmateja Vidura he said, 'Will you stop telling me about trade? We are not traders! You are the son of a servant. Your mind is forever stuck in pettifogging details.' Suyodhana's voice rose. 'I will not control the two banks through trade but with the might of my army. The Nagas will witness our power; they will obey us. I will brook no talk of compromise with my so-called cousins. We have defeated them before and we will defeat them again.'

Dharmateja Vidura's face did not change. I admired his ability to give advice calmly and show no emotion, whether the advice was accepted or rejected. He was worthy of the name *Vidura* bestowed on him. Somehow, through his detachment, he had developed wisdom. The rest of us pretended to ignore the break in protocol and looked at Kutaja.

Kutaja Drona said, 'We should consider this development. Any disaffection the enemy people have with their leaders should be exploited. An independent Panchala will always be our enemy; a puppet ruler dependent on us is the best kind of ruler.'

Now it was Suyodhana's turn to speak, but he sat and glowered at us, saying nothing. He had said all he wished to say. He had decided what he wanted to do and it was left for us to decide to go along with him or not.

Dhritarashtra said, 'Can we help my brother's children out in some small way? My brother appeared to me in a dream last night and asked me to end this war.'

Suyodhana rolled his eyes and muttered to himself. I only heard the words 'Stupid old man.' Then he glared at his father.

Dhritarashtra sensed his son's scorn, and he seemed to cringe. He said, 'Of course, we cannot let them hurt or exploit us in any way. Suyodhana, dear boy, you must decide.'

Suyodhana turned away in disgust. The silence spoke louder than any words could have done and Dhritarashtra shoulders stooped wearily.

No one said anything. I was embarrassed. I could guess all too well what the others thought. Then it was my turn, and they all turned to look at me. Vidura nodded towards his nephew, hinting that only I could control Suyodhana now and bring the discussion back to the matter at hand.

That was when I made a mistake. I made the wrong decision. My only excuse for the error was that I did not expect treachery. I can only ascribe it to Shi…Shi…Shi… the man's features reminded me of someone but I could not remember who. In my own defense I can only say that no one expected treachery, Suyodhana included.

So I said, 'This is an opportunity to win the war at little cost. We should follow up.'

Now that the first opinions had been expressed, the discussion began. Kutaja Drona picked up on my proposal. 'Whom can we send? It will have to be somebody who can assess these traitors. Are they serious? Are they strong enough? Will they stay committed? Will they double-cross us, either by plan or in the heat of battle?'

Dharmateja Vidura asked the important question: 'What do we want from this meeting? Do we want to end this war?'

Suyodhana did not disguise his attitude. 'It doesn't matter what we agree to. Once we have Kampilya, the Nagas will pay for their intransigence and the insult to Samvarana.'

Dharmateja Vidura said, 'One should not negotiate in bad faith.'

'I do not care for your moralizing, old man!'

Kutaja Drona continued pressing the issue he thought was pre-eminent. 'You still need to send someone. Who?'

Karna spoke up. 'Let us send our wisest. Send Dharmateja Vidura. He is expendable. And he can prove he is indeed the wisest by bringing us victory.'

Finally Suyodhana smiled, nodding. 'Dharmateja Vidura it is!'

I objected. Dharmateja Vidura was the son of a maidservant. He was not a warrior. He was on the Council because I had put him there many years ago. Suyodhana did not wish to confront me so he had not taken his uncle off the Council. Everyone knew that Dharmateja Vidura, however wise, would not be a credible negotiator in military matters.

But Suyodhana refused to consider anyone else. He turned to me and said, 'I would like you to take this proposal to the man. Tell him that Dharmateja Vidura is your nominee. Let them suggest another name should they disagree.'

Dhritarashtra seconded his son saying, 'That is an excellent idea. Uncle Devavrata, please do as Suyodhana says.'

I could oppose Suyodhana, but not his father, the uncrowned King. Even when he was being browbeaten by his arrogant son, I still owed him that measure of respect.

So I went to the chamber where the man waited, and presented the proposal. He shook his head slowly when I mentioned Dharmateja Vidura. 'Sir,' he said, 'Lord Dharmateja Vidura may be the King's half-brother, but his mother was a concubine. He has never been a warrior. How can you make such a suggestion? It tells me that you are not considering our offer seriously. Are we to be treated as children playing with a ball?'

'The King's Council has asked you to propose a name if our nominee is not acceptable to you..'

'It is not my place to advise the Kaurava High Command, but the martial arts guru, Kutaja Drona, or someone else with his credibility, would be acceptable.'

In the time I was gone, Suyodhana and Karna revised their offer. The successful siege of Indraprastha had emboldened Suyodhana and his brothers. Now Karna and he thirsted for more battle and greater successes. Instead of a heroic victory over their enemies, in particular Panchala, this proposal would corrupt their victory.

I returned to the Council and said, 'Dharmateja Vidura is not acceptable. My recommendation is to take their offer seriously. The clan leaders want trade, not war. The man has been sent to negotiate peace, and they offer a path to it.'

The rest of the Council did not share Suyodhana's belief in the inevitability of victory. The result was an impasse, with Dhritarashtra wavering between giving in to his son and accepting the advice of the Council. Finally, he said, 'Uncle, you have the greatest experience of war and strategy. At the same time, my son has shown his mettle and knowledge of tactics by winning a great victory. What is the right balance between strategy and tactics? What should we do that maintains the greatest freedom of action?'

Suyodhana groaned and then said, 'Father, you have never taken part in a war. Without any experience of either tactics or strategy, it is but theory. There is no need to think about strategy. After our victory we will raze Kampilya to the ground and erase all trace of Panchala. *That* is our strategy. As far as tactics are concerned, we do not need this man's help.'

Dhritarashtra seemed to shrink. I felt sorry for him and said, 'Whatever your strategy might be, you cannot ignore a tactical advantage, however small. I have met the man in private and my opinion has not changed. There is benefit in his proposal.

There is risk as well. Kutaja Drona is our arms-master and war strategist. I rate him more valuable than myself. We cannot send him as an emissary. We need him here. Suggest another name.'

Suyodhana and Karna went into a huddle, ignoring the rest of the Council and me. When they looked up, they were smiling broadly. Karna said, 'The King's father has a companion: Sanjaya. He has the ear of the King's father. Who has greater authority to command the King than his father? And Sanjaya has claimed for many years that he can see activities from a distance. He will be safe from any kind of trap for he will not fall into it.'

With each reference by Karna to Suyodhana as King, Suyodhana's smile grew wider. Dhritarashtra's face darkened, and his eyes remained downcast. Suyodhana had taken over the King's role in public, but until this day Karna and Suyodhana's brothers had maintained the fiction that Dhritarashtra was the King. That bastion had now fallen.

Sanjaya, who accompanied Dhritarashtra everywhere, was sitting behind him. He looked alarmed and said, 'Sir, I do not claim to see at a distance – I am not a god. I have created a *yantra*, a tool that allows me to watch from a distance. If you wish I can show it to you and explain it.'

On hearing Sanjaya's words, Suyodhana and Karna sniggered. They were being impolite and insulting to their proposed envoy, and a close friend and companion of Suyodhana's father. Sanjaya had once been a member of the Kavi Sangha, but left when he failed to rise in its ranks. He was not good at memorizing, his diction was weak, and he was a poor wordsmith. He could not, or refused to, create the archival and historical poetry that was the Kavi Sangha's core reason for existence. The Kavi Sangha never expelled anyone who had been through its school; underachieving students left of their own accord, and that is what Sanjaya had done. He had become friends with Dhritarashtra and had stayed loyal friend even as the King aged and allowed his son to arrogate royal powers to himself. As Dhritarashtra became more and more a figurehead, his erstwhile friends abandoned him and finally only Sanjaya remained. Sanjaya had nothing to gain and nothing to lose from the war. He was not a warrior; nor was he a trader. He cared neither for power nor wealth. He had no family; he was expendable. No one listened to him.

Suggesting Sanjaya as envoy was not a proposal but an insult. Nevertheless the Council agreed. Dhritarashtra said not a word. I was directed to negotiate with the messenger again. But when I took the proposal back to him, he rejected it. Despite being discouraged, the man did not give up. He tried once more, asking for Karna. I was in favour, as were Kutaja Drona and Dharmateja Vidura. But this time Suyodhana rejected it.

'Karna is my right arm,' he said. 'It is a ridiculous idea that we send a warrior from the War Council. Tell him I refuse. Ask him to choose someone else, lower down the hierarchy; one of my brothers perhaps.'

I stood up and said, 'I see no path to agreement. I will send him back.' As I turned to leave, I could hear Suyodhana and Karna still sniggering.

As I reached the door, Suyodhana said, 'Uncle! Listen to me.' I turned to face him. He was smiling; a crooked slant to his lips. There was a sparkle in his eyes. He gave Karna a sidelong glancebefore saying, 'Since you think it is such a good proposition, why don't *you* go?'

Disheartened, I carried the refusal back to the messenger. In his turn he was disappointed and depressed. His sadness tugged at my heart. I now know why I was so accepting of this man – he reminded me of Amba without my even knowing it; so I was willing to trust him. I recalled past occasions when Karna, Suyodhana's closest friend, had expressed his opinion of me in Council: 'At his age, he will be useless in battle.' Kutaja Drona had defended me saying, 'At his age, he is priceless in war.'

The distinction was lost on Suyodhana. My counsel was not wanted. I felt I would be most effective if I could end this war. At my age, it was the most I could hope to do. I made my decision.

49
The Ambush

Devavrata remembered the fateful moment.

"I told the man, 'I will come'. I had credibility with the Council, even when they voted against me. I could converse with the elders of the family. My strategic competence was not in question. If I returned with an agreement, it would be one beneficial to Hastinapura, and Suyodhana would not be able to reject it.

The man considered my proposal. I do not know what I would have done had he rejected it. Finally he said, 'Sir, you are certainly the senior most member of the Council. However, it is generally known that you and Suyodhana frequently clash in Council. Would an agreement made by you be acceptable to Suyodhana and his brothers?'

Even though the man doubted that I would be an effective envoy, his demeanor changed from a gloomy slump to an erect stance. His eyes lit up with hope.

I said, 'I am Hastinapura's senior most Commander. I have credibility. No one will doubt my word.'

"'The man nodded, looking at me as though I were a bird brought down by an arrow, ready to be cooked for a meal. 'I will take you to the meeting place.'

He then laid down some rules. 'We will go alone. The meeting place is on the right bank, the Hastinapura side of the Ganga. The four senior leaders from the Panchala clans will meet us. It will take a few days to get there.'

I said, 'I am no longer young. I cannot walk at a military pace or carry my own supplies. If we are going into the forest for more than a day, we will need a cart or carriers. Unless you can carry all we need.'

The man frowned at me. He had expected a simpler expedition, not having considered the logistics of this conclave.

'It will take about three days. We will be on the King's Path for much of the way and you can rest in one of the many peddlers' huts along the way.'

'I set up those huts, but no one has maintained them during the war. They will be rundown, if not destroyed.'

'That is all for the best for we will not then encounter anyone in them.'

'Can you carry supplies for three days? We will need to share sentry duty at night, for there are wolves and tigers in the forest.'

The lines around his mouth deepened. It reminded me of something, but I could not then make the connection. Now I know – Amba had the same lines on her face when she disapproved of something.

'I cannot take a wedding party to the meeting site!'

'How are your negotiators coming?'

'All they have to do is cross the river at a point across from the meeting spot. Not more than one ghati to cross and another to return. They will be exposed to any watchers only briefly.'

That did not tell me anything about the location. Between Hastinapura and Kampilya there are thousands of river crossings. Only some were ever in use, mostly for trading, but even that traffic had stopped. At the time all the crossings had been abandoned.

'We will take a cart, an onager, and two helpers. We will use the peddler's huts; if they are rundown, no one else will be using them,' he said. 'On the last night we will camp half a kros from the meeting point where we will leave our helpers and head out by ourselves. We will plan to arrive a little before noon. I expect the ferry to cross at noon exactly. If all goes well, the meeting will last only one or two ghatis. We will then return and spend the night at the same campsite.'

That is what we did. For three days we walked through the forest, along a path the man seemed to know. The cart carried the supplies. At the end of the third day, the man, who had been tense all along, seemed to relax. He had been concerned that we would be late, but seemingly we were not. We were but a short distance from the river and that morning we all took the opportunity to bathe in its cool waters. The guards replenished our water supply and then fed and scrubbed the onager. I waited.When the sun was high in the sky, the man said to me, 'It is time to go. We are close to the meeting place.'

My guards looked at me for orders. We had prepared for the eventuality that I would be separated from them, so they knew what to do. I said to them, 'You will wait here. I do not expect to be back until evening. Set up the tents so that we can spend the night here.'

The man with me said, 'There is no need for that. If all goes well, we will be back by early afternoon.'

I put on my armor and tied a scabbard for my short sword at my right hip. On the left hip I tied a small quiver with a few arrows. Armor and swords do not make for easy travel through the forest.

The man laughed. 'There is no reason for these precautions. See, I am unarmed. So will everyone else be,' he said.

I look back and think that, under normal circumstances, these statements from the man should have aroused my suspicions. But the circumstances were not normal and I continued to be blinded by the unconsciously seen glimpses of Amba in the stranger.

The guards set to what they had been instructed to do while the man and I left for the meeting. We walked cautiously for about six ghatis. The sun had not yet reached its zenith when he raised his hand and we stopped. We were at the edge of a clearing. From the absence of tall trees and a uniform growth of small trees, I guessed that it had lain fallow for a year or two at the most. A Naga band must have lived there, for a large thatched hut still stood there. These huts deteriorate slowly, but this one appeared to be in good condition, with an intact roof and fresh mud daubed on the walls. It had been maintained even when the band had left. We headed for it.

The ground was very dry and twigs cracked underfoot as we walked on a path through the new growth. I felt uneasy. Yet there was no reason to suspect anything. I took the precaution of loosening my scabbard so the sword would pull out easily. The man did not notice my action. I thought I heard a twig crack somewhere a little further away, not under our feet. I had arranged with my guards for one of them to follow, unseen. They were experienced trackers and would not have made a noise. But the possibility that it was my own guard led me to ignore the sound. There was no way to unsling my bow from my back without alerting the man with me, so I had to rely on my short sword.

The man, who had been cautious about making any sound till then, now walked boldly forward, as though the need for caution was at an end. I remained cautious. The man glanced at me and smiled. He said, 'We are at the meeting point. We appear to be early; they will come at noon. You should sit down.'

I said, 'Perhaps, but will you remain careful and alert, even if you think it safe?'

He shrugged and said, still smiling, 'As you wish.'

We had been together for three days and I had seen him smile before, but not the smile that now appeared on his face. He was still smiling as he slowed down, and it was a fortunate thing. Just as we entered the hut, a branch shook slightly to the right. When I turned, I saw nothing. The hut was empty and I backed into it, watching the clearing. As a result I saw what I would not have seen otherwise. Right in front of me, across the clearing, an armed man moved from the cover of one tree to another. To the right and left of the hut I heard what sounded like an animal moving through the brush. We were early and Shikhandin had said his negotiators would be here at noon, not for another ghati or more. It struck me then – this was a trap! There were no talks to be held on an impossible future peace. I had to deal with the man right away, not when the trap had closed.

I turned around to face him, drawing my sword from its scabbard. Shikhandin – I can say it now – had entered the hut a few steps ahead of me, expecting me to follow. He began to turn to the right to face me when he heard my sword being drawn. He was too slow; I did not give him any time. I lunged at his back and drove the sword through his chest. It was a fatal blow for it went in the right side of his body and pierced his lung. But it did not reach the heart. He would die a slow death. He fell towards me. Had I been younger I would have sidestepped the dying body, but at the time I was not fast enough and only managed to catch him as he fell.

I intended to use him as a shield if anybody entered through the door of the hut. He lay gasping in my arms, his one good lung struggling to keep him alive. I wanted to know who was leading the ambush. I noticed a gold chain around his neck, constricting his throat. I loosened the chain and found a pendant attached to it. Glancing at the pendant, I pulled the chain free.

The tent seemed to glow with a bright light. I felt that I was in a field after the first monsoon rain, when the earth sings with joy at the sight of the sun. Amba. Amba? Amba! Amba had chosen to re-enter my life at that inopportune moment.

'Where did you get this?' I asked.

Shikhandin was dying, but he answered my question, gasping for breath. 'From my mother.'

'Where did she get it?'

'From my father.'

Impossible! That was impossible. I had to know who his father was.

'Who is your father? Where is he?'

Shikhandin took another deep breath, but it was not enough. He would be losing consciousness soon. *He had to answer my questions.* I had so many unanswered questions. *Was Amba dead? Had she been killed in the forest and her jewelry scattered among thieves? Or was she alive?* There could not be another pendant like the one I had given her. We had designed the motif together – a lotus with two snakes wrapped around its stem. I put a hand over the wound to prevent air from escaping his shattered lung. Perhaps it helped, for with his next breath he said, 'I do not know.'

I groaned. What did that mean? That he did not know his father? Not know where he was? What did he mean?

Then, in the thread of a whisper, Shikhandin murmured, 'Hastinapura.'

That was when I noticed what I had missed all these days when he had worked to build my trust in him. His eyes were the shape of Amba's; his lips and nose were like my father's; his hands, large, with shaped nails, were also like my father's; his stance had the tilt of the head when Amba expressed puzzlement. *Was it these familiar features that had made me trust a renegade from Panchala?*

'Who is your mother?' I asked, though I knew the answer.

Did he say *Amba,* or did I imagine it? If he said *Amma*, it would have sounded like *Amba.* That was his last word before he closed his eyes and lost consciousness.

It is possible that if I had not wasted time with my questions, waiting with pounding heart for his answers, I would have been prepared for the ambushers. But I did ask…and I did wait. It was a critical delay. I had planned to use him as a shield, but I had not moved his body around when I saw movement at the periphery of my vision. There was a sword by my left hand, and I reached for it. I recognized Arjuna, the Pandava, and Krishna, the Yadava, as they entered the hut. Arjuna's bow was drawn and ready. It seemed to me that time slowed and stood still.

I reach out with my left hand for the sword, but even before I could touch it, an arrow, moving oh so slowly, cut through the seam joining my front and back armor pads, under my left armpit. I picked up the sword, but the pain was intense. I gasped. I commanded my mind to ignore the pain, but there was no strength in my arm as breath left my body. I stood up with the sword dragging in front of me; the first time a sword had felt like a burden. I let it drop.

Arjuna and Krishna held their bows ready but kept their distance. A part of me could not understand. *You can come closer*, I tried to say. Pain radiated from the wound and breathing intensified the pain. I reached across the front of my body with my right hand, barely reaching the shaft of the arrow. I wanted to pull it out, but my grasp was too weak. Any movement worsened the pain. I lost consciousness. The next thing I knew I was tied to the cot here, with my son Shikhandin's body at my side for me to contemplate. My first thought on regaining consciousness was, *I have found Amba!*

Devavrata and the Archivist contemplated each other. *If I had become a memorizer, I would have been like him,* Devavrata thought.

The Archivist turned his head for he did not wish Devavrata to see the tears in his eyes. *A long life with so much power and he pines for a lost love.*

The tent flap was pulled aside and the Vyaasa entered. Taking in at a glance the emotional exhaustion of the two men, he said, "Let us break for the day. Tomorrow we will hear about the next generation."

*****

Appendices

A. Annals of the Kavi Sangha

Background: The Floods Of hastinapura

Thirty-six years after the Great War was over and all of its primary participants had passed on, the King Parikshit, son of Abhimanyu, grandson of Arjuna, Emperor of Hastinapura, proclaimed the beginning of a new Yuga. This was to be the Fourth Age of humanity on earth. Despite all the predictions that the Fourth Age would be an age of strife marked by war, Parikshit proclaimed that the peace achieved by Hastinapura was eternal and whatever happened in the rest of the world, Jambudvipa and Bhaaratavarsha would be a center of peace. Parikshit's era has come to be called the "Kali Yuga", the era of Kali, and the Kali Yuga has been all it was predicted to be. Throughout this period, the Kavi Sangha has maintained its oral archives. Hastinapura fell and was replaced as the imperial capital by Mathura of the Yadavas. Then Mathura was superseded by Pataliputra of the Rakshasas, who called their land Magadha. Still, the archives remained housed in Hastinapura, maintained by the bards of the Kavi Sangha.

One thousand and two hundred years had passed when Hastinapura suffered another crisis. A flood destroyed the city, killing most of the kavis. The oral archives were in danger of being lost. Vyaasa Vaishampaayana, Head of the Kavi Sangha at the time, initiated a project to write down the oral archives. In addition to stories with heroes and heroines and gods and goddesses, these archives contain information of interest to historians. The answers to Yudhishthira's questions given in this novel fall in this category. These questions and answers are rarely recited in public, but they are an important piece of the archives.

Below are excerpts from the Annals of the Kavi Sangha that were responses to King Yudhishthira's questions. The Sangha was committed to recording events and conversations after the Great Flood of 1201 Kali Era, under the direction of Vyaasa Vaishampaayana, with the help of Bhargava, the Kambhoja trader and his son, Chandrasekhara.

A.1. A Trader's Education

A trader is a glorified peddler selling goods to faraway cultures on behalf of manufacturers and merchants. A peddler within a culture travels in a cycle of six to nine months – a trader plans a cycle that might last two or more years. A peddler brings back goods to sell at home – the trader also takes orders from buyers for items and quantities and promises delivery. The trader may be trusted to negotiate exchange offers from foreign sellers. A peddler travels alone and must be constantly on the alert – he listens well, speaks little, remembers everything – well, not as much as bards, but still almost everything. The careful peddler makes friends who travel with him or who host him – that is how a peddler becomes a merchant. He makes friends along his route, who will receive him and help him on the next step. He may marry a local woman and establish a household that supports him when he visits. A merchant welcome in every destination along a well-worn path becomes the leader of a caravan for a trading family. The families that support him are also trading families. These families build up links with each other and often consider themselves a single family even if they speak a different language, follow different customs, eat different foods, bow to different gods, and perform different rituals.

Some members of a trading family choose to stay and distribute the imports as peddlers in local markets. Others, usually loners, become explorers, who travel to strange lands looking for new products. Over time, some of the traders become leaders of caravans – their extended families will help them put together syndicates of manufacturers and sellers and buyers at every stop.

Considering all this, the training for a trader, at least in the first year, is not that different from the training for bards. For instance, both traders and bards learn to memorize long lists. A trader trainee or apprentice might be asked to recall a manifest of objects for trade such as a lapis lazuli necklace, a choker of pearls, ear-rings of copper and tin, gold ornaments for the nose, a pendant for the forehead, a jar of unguent for the lips, a whitening cream for teeth, rings for the fingers and toes. A second list might be the directions for a trip of two months with choices to be made every day and distances to be travelled. A third list would be a list of people's names that is then expanded to include how they relate to each other. The difference is that bards are trained with a much wider variety of memorization tasks while traders focus on the marketplace. For instance, a good trader will learn many languages and customs, while bards develop their skills in the customs, and language or dialect of one city.

A.2. The Four Ages of the World

Yudhishthira said, "What did people believe about the state of the world, in particular, the belief that we are on the brink of a Fourth Age of extreme evil, that the transition from one age to the next would be calamitous and traumatic, and that all humanity would be destroyed at the end of the Fourth Age. The scholars of Panchnad had created this explanation for the troubles that followed the earthquakes that had destroyed the cities of Panchnad."

Devavrata's answer: Human history on earth could be divided into three past "Ages" during which Panchnad had progressively deteriorated. This was proposed as a Law of History: The future would be a Fourth Age and, therefore, the Fourth Age would be lesser than the Third Age, just as the Third Age had been lesser than the Second, and the Second in turn had been lesser than a glorious imagined First Age.

The Kavi Sangha records show that the belief in these four Ages of civilization was widespread in Panchnad in its last days. The Third Age was ending and the Fourth Age was beginning; they just did not know exactly when. A thousand years later, we know that the current Age is indeed the Fourth Age, the Kali Yuga. It has been called the Dark Age; the Iron Age, for iron is black; the Age of Strife, for war is its way of life; and, sometimes, the fourth and last Age. At the end of Kali Yuga, the world will be consumed by fire and water, and all human beings shall die, except for the seven immortals whose duty it will be to repopulate the world. The name for the Age comes from the game of dice. In a dice game, a throw of one is called 'kali' for it is always a losing throw, and the Kali Yuga is the era of complete loss.

This story of the Great War is the story of how the Third Age, the Dvapara Yuga, ended. Devavrata lived during that Age. It has been called the Red Age and the Yellow Age, for those are its colors; the Copper Age, for copper is red; the Age of Bronze, the hard yellow metal that emerges from the mixing of soft ores; the Age of Settlement, for the matriarchs ended the wanderings of their clans and put down roots; and, sometimes, the Third Age in the cycle of four ages that make up a kalpa. At the end of the Dvapara Yuga, mountains move, rivers overflow their banks, and people are compelled to abandon their homes and seek new lands to settle in, for human settlement tires the land and drains its soil of life. The land must rest lest it become desert. In a dice game, a throw of two is called 'dvapara' – it loses to all throws except 'kali.' As such, the Dvapara Yuga is the age of little victories and big losses.

This is the common belief, that many scholars see fit to agree with. The Kavi Sangha takes no position on the matter. We use the Kali Yuga calendar that begins in the year of the Yadava civil war that would make Hastinapura the sole center of power in all of Jambudvipa. As to how the belief in the Four Yugas came about, even the archives of the Kavi Sangha have little to say.

A.3. The Rarity of War in Panchnad

Yudhishthira said, "All my life, the prospect of war has never been far. How did Panchnad settle conflicts without war? All the foreign cultures that I have heard about, from travelers and traders, engage in war. How did Panchnad become a war-free culture?"

Devavrata's answer: The Panchnad civilization was a trading civilization. Ships sailed from the ports on the Western Sea to Dilmun and other lands inhabited by Mlecchas. Caravans crossed the mountain passes into the lands of the Asuras, the Medes, and the Parsakas. They left the land of peace and entered a world in which war was endemic. There, gangs of thieves might attack an unprotected caravan. The caravan might blunder into the middle of an armed conflict between cities in foreign lands. The caravans and ships needed protection and a warrior guild existed, that raised competent fighters.

These warriors were a cost when trade was slow. During slow times, they were employed as paid guards who protected settlements from foreign gangs. In Panchnad, land and water was plentiful. No settlement aspired to dominate the others. Why did Panchnad need mercenaries at all if there were no causes for conflict?

As Panchnad grew and expanded, conflicts occurred. You could say it is natural to fight over resources, such as land and water, even if there appears to be enough and even if the residents of a settlement were cousins. The conflicts did not lead to the kind of war we have now, the kind of war that is ubiquitous in the rest of the world. Two settlements in conflict would be encouraged by their neighbors to negotiate. Panchnad had been settled by the steady splitting up of bands with a daughter band settling the frontier with help from its new neighbors as well as its parent band. Neighboring settlements were tied to each other by familial as well as economic and cultural bonds. Conflicts affected everybody, and everybody had an interest in resolving them. The result was that negotiations rarely failed.

Negotiations rarely failed, which is to say that sometimes, often enough, negotiations did fail. Then, neighboring cities would try to help resolve conflicts peacefully. Those too could fail. When reasonable means failed, the practice was to try unreasonable means. For instance, the unreconciled parties would be encouraged to decide by a competition. The winner of a race or a competitive game or the winner in a game of dice would get a favorable decision. These unreasonable means sometimes worked when everybody agreed that there was no fair resolution possible.

War was the most unreasonable of means and as such, the last resort. When the opposing parties were adamant in their positions and would not accept the result of random chance that games or a throw of dice represented, the parties would be allowed to go to a managed war.

Nobody wanted war, even a managed war. More than anything else, the matriarchs who governed each band and clan understood that dependence on uncontrolled war to settle conflicts would change the culture by creating the need for an army. On average, a man was stronger than a woman, and a very strong man was stronger than a strong woman. The difference was slight, but it would be enough to create a preference for an army of men, led by men. Such a force soon became an army for men that would treat women as lesser, weaker beings. This would pose a danger to the power of a matriarch. Neighbors collaborated to prevent or eliminate such developments.

A managed war was a war that felt like another game, like a game of dice. The difference was that warriors could still die. That was the price, and settlements embarked on war with that foreknowledge. A few deaths were preferable to uncontrolled war that might kill the entire culture. A managed war was ritualized to heighten the enormity of death. This is how the practice of ritual war came into being.

Fighting a war is a skill, like any other skill. The guild of guards expanded to become a guild of mercenaries who could be used to conduct war games. The guild of mercenaries provided the warriors, the advisors to the opposing settlements, and the arbitrators who decided who lost and who won.

If negotiation failed to settle a conflict between settlements, the settlements would go to war with mercenaries hired from the guild of mercenaries. This was ritual battle. The settlements stated their demands before the battle and the side that won the battle would dictate terms restricted to those demands. Since a wealthier settlement could always hire better and more mercenaries, a poorer settlement would rarely choose this path, preferring to negotiate instead, or to create a coalition that might oppose the wealthier settlement. As a result, even managed war, when it happened, was between approximately equal coalitions of settlements.

The modern reader would not recognize a Panchnad war as war. One side would issue a challenge by announcing a goal of capturing something of value from the other side, for example, its commander-in-chief. The judges would assign a value to this challenge, specify the time within which the task was to be accomplished (ghatis, days, or other time period), and determine if the challenge had been successfully overcome. The defenders would announce their strategy, perhaps an armed formation to protect its commander for the time specified by the judges. If capture was successful, the challenger won and the challenger's client might declare victory. If enough judges did not accept the claim of victory, the challenge would be reversed. (The required number of judges would be agreed on before the war.) The defending side would issue a challenge in its turn. It did not have to do so; possessing the disputed resource and keeping it secure during the original challenge might be enough to claim victory. The judges might uphold such a claim. There was no limit to the number of challenges a losing side could bring. The cost of such challenges could become unsupportable even for the wealthiest city.

The members of the guild of mercenaries, even those on opposing sides of a battle, were often related to each other. They preferred to capture an opposing warrior rather than kill or even maim them. At every engagement, the goal would be to capture, not kill, one or more senior commanders of the other side. The mercenaries did not overtly change their own behavior. Their clients would get nervous by the loss of the trusted commanders. The arbitrators might make a snap judgement if one side lost enough senior commanders (by capture or, occasionally, death). The result of a Panchnad war was peace.

The trading families taught some fighting skills to their members so that they could protect a caravan under attack from bandits. That is not to say that they were trained as warriors. A trader would never become as expert a fighter as the traditional mercenary of Panchnad.

A Panchnad war was also the training ground for the guards of a caravan. When raiders attacked a caravan, its guards would create a defensible encampment and ward off challenges and try to wound the attackers until they left. Only rarely would a Panchnad troop chase and destroy raiders. They preferred to wait out the raiders or negotiate safe passage, paying tax if it seemed feasible.

Between the Panchnad preference for negotiated agreements, aversion to a standing army, and the guild of mercenaries' preference for bloodless battles, war was rare in Panchnad.

A.4. END OF THE THIRD AGE

Yudhishthira said to Devavrata, "I want to know more about Panchnad and the world in the Third Age. Tell me what you know of the Third Age: the world at large and Panchnad in particular."

Devavrata's answer: This is what the world looked like in the Third Age. At the very center of the world, that unmatched mountain, Meru,[52] rose into the heavens where the gods keep their secrets. That sacred mountain peak is home to Amaravati,[53] the city of the gods. To the extreme north of Meru lies Uttara-Kuru,[54] the original northern home of the legendary Pururavas, ancestor of Puru, who left that home in a time lost to memory. Just south of that is the frozen northern wasteland where the Danavas,[55] asuras by nature, hide from the wrath of Indra in the summer. Through this ice-bound land flow the unnamed mighty rivers that empty into the northern sea. When the sun goes south, these asuras emerge to freeze the rivers and inflict pain on the unfortunate denizens of that land. Still further south, closer to Mount Meru, we find the homes of the brutal, horsemeat-eating Shakas,[56] who range from the eastern desert to the western lakes, from the foothills of Mount Meru to the northern wasteland. To the east of the great peak lies the

[52]Mount *Meru* is a legendary mountain believed to exist north of South Asia, approximately in the centre of the Pamirs in Tajikistan.
[53]*Amaravati* was the city of the gods, located at the top of Mt Meru.
[54]*Uttarakuru* is the mythical "Arctic home of the Pauravas" covered by ice all through the year. The Pauravas claimed to have come from a land far to the north of Mt Meru. Some optimists have located this in the North Pole.
[55]*Danavas*, pronounced Tha(r)-nu(t)-wo(rm)(-s), are demons, children of Danu, one of the wives of the mythical sage Kashyapa who fathered all beings (except the highest gods).
[56]In historic times, the *Shakas* are identified with the tribes that the Greeks called Scythians.

plateau of the Bo[57] and the Ronga and then the plains of Su-wa-Xia.[58] Through this plateau flow great rivers: the mighty river Lauhitya,[59] also called the Bo Ganga; the Xia Ganga that flows to the land of the Xia; and other great rivers called the Ganga because they purified whatever they touched. Immediately to the west of the mighty peak lie the lands of the Mlecchas and the Parsakas; further west are the lands of the brown, the red, and lastly the black people of Egypt. The rivers that flow here are deep and fast, hence called Sindhu (swift) – the Arvand,[60] beloved of Indra; the River of Egypt, sometimes called the Krishna[61] for the color it imparts to the land, sacred to the blue-necked Eashwara; and the Supurna[62] that fulfils all desires. Finally, to the south of Mount Meru lies Jambudvipa,[63] the most fortunate of continents, watered by the rivers Sarasvati, the giver of wisdom, the Sindhu, the swift river, and the Ganga, the purifier of the soul. Many more rivers, of various merits, water this land and empty into the southern ocean, the Brihatsagar,[64] either through the Western or the Eastern Seas.[65] To the east of Jambudvipa beyond the Lauhitya are the rivers

[57]The Tibetan plateau inhabited by the *Botias* and the *Ronga*.

[58]*Xia* refers to the plains of China, through which flow the Yang-tze (Xia Ganga) and the Huang Ho (the Ho Ganga).

[59]*Lauhitya*, meaning the child of Lōhita (iron), is one of the names of the river Brahmaputra; other names include Bo Ganga and Tsang-po.

[60]The *Arvand* is the Tigris (the Swift River, also Sindhu).

[61]The *Krishna* (the Blue/Black River) is the River Nile (also called "the Black River") that flows through lands sacred to Osiris (translates to *Eashwara*, the Lord in Sanskrit). These were the Black Lands, also called the Land of the Temples of Ancestral Spirits. (The Egyptian word translates to *Pitr-vihara-naadu*.)

[62]The *Supurna* ("fulfilling" or "completed well" in Sanskrit) is the Euphrates (meaning "well-fertilized" in Greek).

[63]*Jambudvipa* (The Island of the Jambul) is the ancient name for South Asia (from the Hindukush to Assam and from Ladakh to Kanyakumari).

[64]*Brihatsagar* is the Great Ocean surrounding Jambudvipa (referring to the Indian Ocean).

[65]The Western Sea is the Arabian Sea; the Eastern Sea is the Bay of Bengal.

Iravathi,[66] mother of the Mahanaga Airavatha, and the Hme-Ganga,[67] the great river that vanishes into the unknown world of the east. To the north, the Himalayas, the snow-covered White Mountains, are an endless source of water and a barrier impassable by enemies.

Panchnad, the center of Jambudvipa in the Third Age, is, settled by the most honest, the most honorable, the most peaceful, and therefore the richest and most prosperous people in the known world. Panchnad can be divided into regions, each settled by an ancestral clan. In ancient times, the Bhaarata-Pauravas resided to the west and north of the juncture where the Drishadvati and the Sutudri joined the Yamuna to form the Sarasvati, a wide, swiftly flowing river of legend that has disappeared. Further south, the Vanara,[68] the Raishyava,[69] and the Mayura[70] clans have settlements along the banks of the numerous lakes that slow down the Sarasvati. Having slowed down, the river widened across the flat plain it flowed through. Finally, the southernmost settlements were those of the Yadavas, all the way to the place where the river enters the sea. Over two thousand such settlements lived in peace. The citizens considered themselves fortunate to be born to such prosperity.

Each settlement was independent of others. Each settlement governed itself in the traditional manner, with a matriarch advised by a council of the wisest and most experienced

[66]The Irrawady, which originates in the Himalayas and flows through Burma to the Bay of Bengal.

[67]The Mekong, named for the Hme/Hmu/Hmong people, that flows through Thailand, Cambodia, Laos, and Vietnam and empties into the Indonesian sea, a region not known to the people of Panchnad.

[68]*Vanara* means "ape", probably the langur.

[69]*Raishyava* means "unicorn". The myth of the unicorn is believed to have originated from this source.

[70]*Mayura* means "peacock".

dwellers. The citizens were consulted through assemblies called when requested. The council advised the citizens who were informed and engaged. The seven independent guilds were disciplined, and guild members obeyed the rules and norms established by their guild and the government in performing their tasks. The guild of bards witnessed the acts of the current assembly and reported truthfully on the important events during the time of the last seven matriarchs. Six other guilds – weavers, potters, smiths, builders, farmers, and *bisajs* – reported on their activities, successes and failures, and knowledge of distant events that might affect the settlement. The guild of mercenaries, traditionally not considered a part of any settlement and whose members disavowed allegiance to any settlement, sent observers who would participate if guild-relevant matters were discussed. All the major families participated in trade under the leadership of the founding family. Trade was the usual source of wealth and power and entry into the guild of traders, which was controlled by the leading family. The guild of traders did not need a separate representation in the councils of the state.

A settlement might contain more than one family headed by a matriarch. The matriarch of the first family, the family that had established the settlement, considered herself the chief and headed a council of matriarchs. The families were usually related to each other, and conflicts among the families of a settlement were rare.

There was one aspect of settlement life that was not dictated by matriarchs. The eldest son of a matriarch could expect to be the next male head of the family supporting his oldest sister as matriarch. Consequently, the eldest son was trained to be a chief. Sometimes, one of his brothers might also be similarly trained in case the candidate for chief died prematurely. The other sons of the matriarch did not have that opportunity.

It was the duty of the father of a boy to manage his son's education. The simplest way to do this was to enroll the son in the father's guild as an apprentice. Similarly, the younger daughters of a matriarch, the ones not destined to be matriarch, would be guided by an aunt into an appropriate guild. That aunt would often be performing the same guiding role for her own daughters as well. As a result, entrance into a guild was largely passed on from father to son or from mother to daughter.

The survival and well-being of the settlements depended on all these guilds, but prosperity depended on trade. The settlements traded with each other, of course, and with the far-off lands to the west and northwest. They shipped their fine clay pots, rice, wheat, barley, rice wine, pepper, sesame seed oil, and other goods west to Dilmun[71] and sometimes directly north of Dilmun, to Susa,[72] the capital of Elam, and all the way into Ur.[73] The smiths manufactured faience beads, the most colorful in the world, and fashioned jewelry that was greatly in demand in Dilmun. They exported textiles of cotton that were in great demand. In turn, they imported gold from everywhere, for the people were fond of glittering decoration. They imported tin from secret mines in the far north and exported it to the western world through Dilmun, paying a fortune and making

[71]Dilmun was either Bahrain or Oman. The Sumerians considered it an incredibly prosperous trading centre that allowed them to trade with the mythical land of Meluhha to the east. Meluhha could have been a Sumerian pronunciation of "Malaya", i.e., mountain land or plateau, and referred to the region north of modern-day Gwador on the Makran coast (possibly pronounced "Maghan" by the Sumerians). The name "Himalaya" is a conjunction of "Him", snow and "Malaya", i.e., "Snowy Mountains"; the traditional Sanskrit etymology is Him/Snow and Alaya/Home, i.e. Abode of Snow.
[72]Susa still exists as the city Shush in modern Iran.
[73]The first city of ancient Sumer.

a fortune. They imported decorative objects made of alabaster from Egypt, the land of the Black River, and imported dates from Elam and woolen textiles from the cities of Sumer on the Arvand. The land was at peace and had been at peace for many generations. During the Third Age, in a period long before the events leading up to this war, the Sindhu and the Sarasvati held pride of place among the people of Panchnad. The Master trader Ilina wished to expand the trading for which his clan was famous. Ilina was directly descended from the beautiful Pururavas through the prideful Nahusha,[74] the self-indulgent Yayati,[75] and the self-restrained Puru.[76] The land available in Panchnad on the banks of the Sarasvati was limited, hemmed in by other settlements, and not usable as a trading hub. If he left the banks of the Sarasvati and headed east, he would reach a great river, the Ganga. If he settled there, he would be leaving Panchnad. The Ganga flowed east into uncharted territory and did not connect with any Panchnad settlement at all. Ilina vacillated between staying in Panchnad and increasing trade with the West, or going to the Ganga and developing new markets in the east. Ultimately, Ilina hedged his bets and established Kaalindini,[77] named after his mother, on the upper Sutudri, almost at the foothills of the Himalayas. Kaalindini was close to the other Panchnad settlements. Though the Sutudri was not navigable, the residents of Kaalindini would still share its waters with Panchnad. Kaalindini was closer to the Ganga

---

[74]*Nahusha* was a legendary ancestor of the Pauravas. Nahusha's pride led to his downfall.
[75]*Yayati* was a legendary ancestor of the Pauravas. At the end of his life of over a thousand years, he is not satisfied and asks his sons to give him their youth in exchange for his age.
[76]*Puru* was Yayati's youngest son. He grants his lustful father's desire for one more youthful year. As a reward, he is designated his father's heir.
[77]*Kaalindini* was probably close to the current town of Ropar, just before the point at which the Sutudri changed direction and flowed west to the Indus. It was positioned to be an important trading centre for Panchnad.

and within the reach of the forest-dwelling Nagas. It was positioned to monitor and manage any trade with the east. Ilina was certain that such trade would come about, and he wanted his family to be prepared to benefit from it. Kaalindini was not as hospitable as other Panchnad towns, and the decision to stay was a strategic bet on the future of trade. Ilina's ambivalence about this decision could be considered a family trait. Every generation after him considered the question of moving east (and abandoning Kaalindini), or declaring failure and returning to some Panchnad town, or staying put, doing nothing. The residents felt that migrating to the banks of the Ganga would break their links to Panchnad. They also feared that this separation from Panchnad would make it difficult to attract immigrants who would be needed to grow the frontier town.

Ilina's grandson Bharata was successful in trading with the West and ignored Kaalindini. Interest in the east declined and was not revived until Bharata's great-grandson Hastin determined to try his fortunes in the east.

Hastin stayed on the Panchnad side of the watershed at first, intending to reassure the Nagas that the traders did not want to displace the forest-dwellers but wanted to trade with them peacefully. Previous attempts to settle on the Ganga had threatened the Nagas. The Nagas avoided conflict and did not try to evict the settlers, but they had refused to trade or cooperate with them. With the establishment of Kaalindini, the threat seemed diminished and relationships with Naga bands immediately to the east improved. The bulk of the Nagas still lived a long distance (and past dense forests) from Kaalindini, and trade was not as central to the Naga way of life as it was for Panchnad. Despite that, more Naga-produced goods came to market to barter for Panchnad's products. Nagas would bring unusual produce – fruits, vegetables, or animal meats and pelts; and minerals – rock salt or other minerals used by smiths, but occasionally copper and very rarely, small quantities of tin. They wanted tools, ceramics, and utensils of bronze. Bronze was scarce in Panchnad and not easily found in the market, but an exchange for a larger weight of copper could be profitable. By persistence and some sacrifice, the traders of Kaalindini maintained a monopoly on the Naga trade as it became profitable.

The Panchnadis were familiar with monopolies. They approved of monopolies as a valuable strategic tool for a trader dealing with foreign cultures. Any Panchnad trader could ask to share in the monopoly. The Kaalindini monopoly was different. The Naga trade was risky and intermittent, hard to share, and the profits came from importing into Panchnad, not exporting. The Nagas consumed little, and almost the only product they asked for was bronze. They gave too much in exchange for bronze. This roused both jealousy and anger among traders in other Panchnad cities. By comparison, the Yadavas, who settled around the delta of the Sarasvati, established the great port city of Tripura and controlled the trade with destinations reachable by sea, such as Dilmun, Elam, and Egypt. The Yadava monopoly, though vastly more lucrative than the Kaalindini monopoly, was seen as a service benefitting all of Panchnad. Small things can have magnified effect in society. The Kaalindini traders were considered miserly and grasping, while the Yadava traders were considered generous benefactors, even though the two groups behaved identically.

The traders of Kaalindini were concerned that the other Panchnadi cities were jealous of their success. Hastin, a

Bhaarata,[78] addressed this by deflecting that resentment away from Kaalindini. He set up a caravanserai on the banks of the Ganga, southeast of Kaalindini. Usually, a caravanserai was where caravans stopped on their way to a market or city. This caravanserai was a destination in itself, for there were no known markets or cities to be reached from there. The caravanserai was not a settlement but a service center for trade. It provided a marketplace for Nagas to barter with peddlers and traders from Panchnad. Little changed as far as Kaalindini was concerned, for the profits flowed there. However, the caravanserai provided a service in a potentially hostile environment, and its fees were not resented.

Hastin collaborated with the local Naga clans in establishing the settlement and called it Nagapura in their honor. This further insulated Kaalindini from the disapproval of other Panchnad towns. Nagapura was intended as a trade center that all Panchnad traders could use and nothing else. It was organized like a caravan rather than like a settlement, the leader of the caravan being a male trader who exercised absolute powers. Nagapura did not even try to become self-sufficient as an urban settlement would. Instead, it bartered for food from the surrounding Naga bands. The Nagas became partners in the success of Nagapura, and it succeeded where previous, more conventional, attempts to settle on the Ganga had failed.

A.5. Naga Reaction: Panchala and Nagapura

Yudhishthira said, "You said that the Nagas of Panchala and the other Naga bands as well did not welcome Hastin and his

[78] *Bhaarata* means a descendant of the legendary emperor Bharat, who was said to be the first ruler of a unified Jambudvipa–Bhaaratavarsha.

traders. How was Hastin's settlement of Nagapura established, why did it flourish, and why did you make it the center of an empire?"

Devavrata's answer: The historian will find it curious that an otherwise unremarkable trading post became a city so different from the rest of Panchnad. The changes are extraordinary. It was governed by a Master, not a matriarch. The Kauravas were traders, not warriors. The settlement first collaborated with the Nagas, then became the ruler of some of the Nagas, and, finally became their oppressor, all the while asserting the sincere desire for extensive trade with them. The historian would note that this transition to a militarized state occurred after the Nagas of Panchala tried to destroy Hastinapura.

Hastin, the great-grandson of Bharata, founded the frontier outpost of Nagapura on the west bank of the Ganga. Naga bands were sparse, but the location was near a convenient ford that the Nagas used to cross the river. It was an ideal trading location, and Nagas came to Nagapura often. By the time of our forebear Samvarana, Naga settlements had appeared around Nagapura, for their population had increased. Conflicts were rare as the Panchnadi settlers of Nagapura avoided agriculture and relied on the Nagas for food. The Nagas were used to growing just what they needed and had to be encouraged to grow more so that there would be a surplus to support Nagapura. The exotic cotton textiles, the bright jewelry made from silver, faience beads and lapis lazuli, and the superior metal tools of Panchnad were bartered for food and other products. The Naga population had expanded towards the north on the east bank of the Ganga, despite the thick forest near the river.

Over ten yojanas to the west was the Yamuna, but as it went south, it turned west at the northern ridge of the Aravalli[79] range to join the hundred little streams of the river we call the Sutudri. The unfortunate land to the south and west of Nagapura was protected from rain by the Aravalli range. Deprived of water from the rain as well as from the snow melt, the land was bone-dry. This wild and arid land, unsuitable for cultivation in the Naga manner or for Panchnad settlements, we called Khandavaprastha. This cursed desert land stretched south up to the Charmanavati[80] River, which is also monsoon-fed but drains a vast plateau in the Vindhya mountains.

Nagapura was prosperous because of trade and only because of trade. The Bhaarata Hastin had recognized a valuable opportunity in settling it. Occasionally, the Nagas would come into Panchnad with small quantities of almost pure copper and some tin. The Westerners consider tin to be the most precious metal. It was scarce in Panchnad and in the rest of the world. The Panchnadis had discovered a source far to the north past the north-western plateau and across the valley of the Vakshu. It had been a secret, but eventually that secret was revealed and Panchnad lost its monopoly. Hastin thought he might be able to establish a more lucrative trade in tin and other ores. That was how Nagapura succeeded. It became the destination for tin and copper ore brought by the Nagas from the east in small boats. Nagapura prospered with increasing trade.

In the beginning, Nagapura was managed like a caravan, not like a Panchnad settlement. The head trader was a man who

---

[79]The *Aravallis* are a mountain range in Western India stretching from Ahmedabad to Central Delhi.

[80]*Charmanavati* is the river Chambal.

managed all aspects of caravan life and negotiated barter deals with his Naga counterpart. Over many generations, the head trader's post became the entitlement in perpetuity of the descendants of Hastin. Nagapura never became a Panchnad-style janapada ruled by a matriarch and her council. The head trader's family wanted to retain control and the position of head trader passed from father to son, a practice imported from the Parsakas across the snow-covered Himalayas west of Panchnad.

The settlement was not completely peaceful. On the east bank of the Ganga was Panchala, a confederation of Naga bands. Panchala had slowly but surely extended its rule over other Naga bands of the east bank. Panchala wanted to rule over the Nagas on the west bank as well. The Ganga was too wide to construct a permanent bridge, so such dominance would not have been easy to maintain. When Nagapura emerged, it became practically impossible to dream of unification of all Naga bands. Nagapura's success led to prosperity for the Nagas who allied with the Panchnadis and traded with them. Panchala refused all interaction with Nagapura. The Naga bands on the west bank did not want to join Panchala. Shortly after our ancestor Samvarana, Hastin's great-grandson, became the head trader of Nagapura, he faced an ultimatum from Panchala: You are on Naga land; pay tax on all your deals. When Samvarana laughed off this demand, the Panchalas did the impossible. Their army went north, found a place to cross the Ganga, and invaded Nagapura. They drove a surprised Samvarana and the Pauravas out and took over Nagapura. Samvarana sought refuge in Kaalindini. He did not find support from the other Panchnad cities, for external war was not their forte. Nor did he get support from the guild of mercenaries, for the war to recover Nagapura was unlike anything they had executed in a long time.

The cities of Panchnad dotted the banks of the Sarasvati from its beginnings at the merge of the Sutudri, the Drishadvati, and the Yamuna, all the way south to the western sea. Cities like Moolasthan and Takshashila similarly flourished on the banks of the Sindhu and its tributaries many yojanas to the west. The population was still growing in all these settlements. The great teacher and strategist Vasishtha had established the Kavi Sangha to address the expected problems of growth. Vasishtha believed that expansion to new regions to the south and to the east was essential, but neither he nor the Kavi Sangha managed to persuade anybody.

Samvarana's exile proved to be an opportunity for Vasishtha to establish the credibility of the Kavi Sangha. Vasishtha offered his advice to Samvarana. He and the Kavi Sangha helped Samvarana train an army of warriors, the first such army in Panchnad. It did not consist of mercenaries. Mercenaries fought for an employer. This army was an organization managed, maintained, and pledged to fight for Nagapura and owing allegiance to Samvarana. The Kavi Sangha borrowed one innovation from the other cultures that the Panchnadis knew about: It was an all-male army that did not include any mercenaries or other guild members. This allowed them to build the army without requiring approval from the matriarchs of Panchnad.

In the meantime, the Panchalas had troubles of their own. They did not understand how to run a market or a trade entrepôt. Nagapura's prosperity faded, and the surrounding Naga bands suffered. The takeover of Nagapura was a disaster for Panchala, and as the years passed, they maintained a smaller and smaller force to keep control of Nagapura. When Samvarana returned with his army, he found a disaffected population that welcomed him. The small Panchala force was routed, and Nagapura returned to Samvarana's rule. Vasishtha and the Kavi Sangha gained in stature, and this victory marked the acceptance of the Kavi Sangha as a formidable strategic, political, and intellectual force in Panchnad. Under Vasishtha, the guild of bards merged with the Kavi Sangha. Vyaasa, the title of the head of the guild of bards, became the title of the Panchnad-wide head of the Kavi Sangha as well.

The Panchalas, by evicting Samvarana and then, in turn, being evicted by him, sowed the seed of an empire. Nagapura with its new standing army became the hegemon in its immediate surroundings. Samvarana's army did not consist of mercenaries but of career soldiers who stayed together. The troops remained in the army when the fighting was over and were supported by taxing the surrounding Naga communities in exchange for 'protection' from Panchala.

Samvarana's son Kuru used the army to send expeditions to the east to find the source of the tin and copper. Many yojanas to the east, the Ganga encountered a great plateau to the south and then turned north.[81] A monsoon river, which we call the Hiranyaganga,[82] emerged from the plateau to join the Ganga. At that juncture, Kuru established a small trading

[81]Modern Varanasi/Kashi is located a little east of this turn to the north. Kaushambi is also close by (about 75 kilometres from Allahabad). After flowing past Varanasi, the Ganga turns east again and joins the Sone at Patna (old Pataliputra, the capital of Magadha).

[82]*Hiranyaganga* means the "Golden Ganga", possibly because gold was brought down this river from the plateau. Later the name would change to "Son-ganga", further shortened to Sone.

post called Laghu[83] Nagapura. The plateau was peopled by a different forest-dwelling culture. The Nagas called them Defenders, which Kuru's men translated as Rakshasa. The Rakshasas of the plateau followed two different ways of life. Some lived in permanent settlements that depended on the surrounding forest for game and food. Others lived as miners, whose settlements were located next to a lode of ore – copper, silver, gold, and other tradable minerals. They had developed techniques for extracting almost pure copper from the rich lodes they treated as owned by their settlement. The plateau Rakshasas had access to tin, though they would not, or could not, explain where it came from. Laghu Nagapura became the market in which the plateau Rakshasas exchanged almost pure copper and tin ore for products from Panchnad, such as cotton, textiles, bronze tools and utensils, and fine clay pots.

Laghu Nagapura was not considered a suitable site for smelting arsenical bronze. The Rakshasas did not know how the shiny golden metal was made, there were no local sources of arsenic, and Kuru did not want to create an incentive for raiding. Instead, bronze foundries were established around Nagapura, to smelt arsenical bronze and further work it into tools and jewelry. Nagapura produced copper and bronze items such as cooking utensils, carpenter's tools, expensive armor, and hunting weapons. Smiths and artisans from the rest of Panchnad came to Nagapura. Nagapura prospered as a Third Age manufacturing site, and its surroundings were dotted with foundries in the middle of growing swathes of clear-cut forest. Nagapura began to look more urban, like a traditional Panchnad settlement, and less of a nomadic caravan stop. To

[83] *Laghu* means "Little."

recognize this evolution, Kuru renamed Nagapura. The new name was Hastinapura in honor of the founder Hastin.

Later, Kuru's son Viduratha and grandson Arugvata, the latter also called Anashwa, found a source of arsenic ore in the plateau of Laghu Nagapura and moved the manufacture of bronze ingots there, while the artisans remained in Hastinapura. Arugvat gave the Rakshasas a stake in the production and protection of the bronze by handing over the furnaces to them. A Rakshasa band that raided the site to steal the stockpiled bronze would only hurt another Rakshasa band and the response would be immediate and devastating.

The Rakshasas responded to the new technology and new production methods by increasing native copper production in order to produce more value-added bronze. They also increased cooperation with the Hastinapuris and exchanged information of mutual interest. Arugvat discovered that the tin came through traders who hiked from the headwaters of the Hiranyaganga to the head of a river the Rakshasas called the Great River, which the Hastinapuris translated as Mahanadi.[84] The Great River flowed east out of the plateau and emptied itself via a delta into the Eastern Sea.[85] The traders were met at the delta by ships that claimed to come from the other side of the Eastern Sea. The ships carried tin ore as well as linen, salt-water fish, unusual fruits, and coconut oil and other palm by-products. They took back copper ore and gems – lapis lazuli, beryl, and shell – as well as animal pelts. Live animals – tamed elephants and domesticated dogs – were favorites.

[84]*Mahanadi* means "Great River."

[85]The upper reaches of the Mahanadi are a few days' trek from the upper reaches of the Sone.

The demand for arsenical bronze, tin, and tin-based bronzes in Panchnad led to the establishment of a great trading route from the unnamed land[86] across the Eastern Sea to the mouth of the Great River, across the plateau, to Laghu Nagapura, then up the Ganga to Hastinapura and thence to the plains of the Sarasvati and the Sindhu. Hastinapura, as the entrepôt, controlled the trade and prospered – more than prospered, for Kaalindini and Hastinapura came to be respected in the councils of the Panchnad cities.

Kuru's explorations increased Hastinapura power and profile in Panchnad. Hastinapura had been a caravan. It was going to be a city while retaining its unique features. One difference would prove to be important. Hastinapura was not a matriarchy. The legacy of its long existence as a caravan outpost, headed by a male trader, continued. To conform to Panchnad customs, the chief's sister, or sometimes the chief's wife, was called the Matriarch, but the lineage and power passed through the male chief to his sons and not through the Matriarch to her daughter and son. Kuru, in turn, was recognized as the patriarchal dynast. Hastinapura was no longer the trading outpost of a glorified caravan, but a successful city, controlled entirely by his descendants called Kauravas.

This change in inheritance seemed a minor change. It was expected that when the crisis was past, the traditional Panchnad model would be followed. The Kavi Sangha did not expect the change to last more than a generation or two. However, not only did the new model of patriarchy continue past the next few generations, it has been the standard. Your own claim to the throne rests on your father inheriting from Vichitravirya.

---

[86]Probably Malaysia or Siam.

Many Hastinapuris resented the lack of support from the Bhaaratas of Panchnad during Samvarana's exile. Kuru's success in establishing Laghu Nagapura gave him the wherewithal to declare independence from Panchnad and make Hastinapura a state, called Kururashtra. With its standing army of trained warriors, this state could assert its rights in hostile surroundings.

A.6. An Archive Saved

The Vyaasa explained in the Annals of the Kavi Sangha how the archives contained thc story of the war as seen from the Pandava side.

The Kavi Sangha was accused of trying to please both sides in the conflict. That was not true. The Kavi Sangha was centered in Hastinapura and maintained the archives of the city. The Vyaasa Shukla, also the brother of the Queen Mother Satyavati, King Shantanu's second wife and Devavrata's stepmother, had wanted the Pandavas to return to Hastinapura. He thought they would be easier to manage if they stayed close by, in Hastinapura. His attempts at forging a compromise collapsed with Suyodhana's intransigence on the one hand and, on the other hand, the alliance the Pandavas made with Hastinapura's ancient enemy Panchala. Once the war started, it looked like a foregone conclusion that the Pandavas would lose. When the Pandavas eliminated Devavrata Bhishma, they created a slim possibility that they might win the war, but it was still very unlikely.

The presence of kavis in the Pandava camp was unplanned, if fortunate. (Nobody expected the Pandavas to win.) There were rumblings that the kavis were spies, could not be trusted, and should be expelled, especially as they took directions from Hastinapura.

When the Kavi Sangha, and for all practical purposes that means the Vyaasa, decides to archive history-in-the-making, it appoints an Archivist. The Archivist is expected to interview key persons at the beginning of the major events and debrief them regularly thereafter. The people involved rarely decline the interview request for they know that it is a rare honor for their thoughts to be considered for the archives. In the case of a war with an enemy of Hastinapura, it would have been unusual for the Kavi Sangha to have an Archivist in the enemy camp. An enemy of Hastinapura would not be expected to welcome an Archivist. Even if they did, they would place restrictions on the Archivists to prevent spying.

The Vyaasa Shukla thought that there was no point archiving events on the Pandava side. The Pandavas were on the run, unlikely to win. The rebellion was historic, but the Pandavas were expected to lose, and the events to be documented would happen in the city.

The Vyaasa appointed an Archivist in Hastinapura to memorize and organize the history of the Kuru family. No Archivist was appointed for Indraprastha, nor was one sent to the Pandavas. It was a miracle that they had one in Lomaharshana.

This is how the miracle came about. Many years earlier, when the Pandavas had been allowed to re-establish the settlement of Indraprastha, the Kavi Sangha and its then newly-elected Vyaasa Shukla had offered archival support to the Pandavas. (Hastinapura and Indraprastha were not enemies yet.) When war broke out, the bards and archivists of the Kavi Sangha serving in Indraprastha came under suspicion of spying for Hastinapura and were not allowed to leave Indraprastha if they knew of Pandava war plans. The Pandavas' advisors, many from Panchala, had recommended imprisoning the kavis. Some proposed killing them; feelings against the Kavi Sangha ran high in Indraprastha. The Kavi Sangha had been Devavrata's ally in developing policies for the empire he was building, which were anti-Naga in effect. The Panchala viewed the Kavi Sangha as the instrument of Panchala's defeat so many generations earlier.

Yudhishthira rejected the advice and allowed members of the Kavi Sangha to leave Indraprastha, if they so wished, or to stay if they were willing to archive the events in the Pandava camp. Two of the senior-most members left, leaving behind only four kavis, headed by the young Lomaharshana. The younger ones, being with the losing side, found it difficult to communicate with their leaders and get approval from the Vyaasa. But they stayed on. They would do their job, with or without the Vyaasa's approval at every step. It was some time before the Vyaasa was able to convey his approval and commendation: "Do your job – memorize. You will never be asked to become spies. If asked, pledge loyalty to the Pandavas." In later years this policy of loyalty to the host of the archivists would become part of the ethos of the Kavi Sangha.

This small team initiated the Pandava archives as an extension of the Hastinapura archives. The expulsion of the Pandavas from Indraprastha was followed by a quiet period during which Hastinapura forces hunted for the Pandavas in the forest. Meanwhile, the Pandavas stitched together their coalition and re-built their army, recruiting unhappy Nagas and older residents who felt displaced by immigrants. During this quiet period, Suyodhana declared that any contact with the Pandavas was treason, and even the Vyaasa Shukla felt constrained not to visit the Pandava camp openly.

Since Shantanu's time, the Kavi Sangha had admitted many Nagas as members. This practice began during Parashara's term as Vyaasa and continued under the next Vyaasa, who recruited Shukla. When Shukla became the Vyaasa, he continued the policy. Shukla recruited Lomaharshana, the Archivist who memorized and organized the Pandavas side of this history. Even though very young, Lomaharshana had already built up a reputation as an Archivist. Suyodhana had demanded that this recruitment of Nagas stop, further alienating the Nagas from his rule. The Kavi Sangha deployed its Naga kavis outside Hastinapura. Lomaharshana had been sent to Indraprastha to be Archivist for the Pandavas. He was more than an expert memorizer. He was a skilled elicitor of facts – of the events, conversations, actions that a person had experienced. He was a poet and a storyteller with a keen sense for what had to be archived.

The unresolved debate question is: Is the story of the Kavi Sangha a part of the story of the War? The Kavi Sangha maintains its archives separately from the archives of the city; the history of the War will not tell the story of the Kavi Sangha. The Kavi Sangha is invisible; it is always present.

A.7. The Disaster

Yudhishthira said, "Gurudeva! The Regent will not speak on this matter and threatens to become silent forever. Tell me what you know of the history of the Disaster and how it led to Devavrata's vow of celibacy."

The Vyaasa Shukla's answer: The Disaster took place in multiple acts. The first act was the shaking of the earth. Prithvi, the Earth, shook. It was in the time of Pratipa, great-grandson of

Arugvat, the grandson of Kuru. Some said that such shaking showed Prithvi's anger with humanity. The truth of this accusation was incontestable, for there was always something that could have angered Prithvi. She is a capricious mother who hugs her children and in the next instant turns against them. That must be what happened here. The earth shook, and it changed the world.

The star-gazers have their own language. The quakes, they said, marked the end of the Age of the Bull and the beginning of the Age of the Ram. They pointed to a starry outline in the sky and said it was a bull. Next to it, they pointed out the outline of a ram. If a wise man is one who can see through obscurity, the star-watchers certainly qualify as wise. I frequently wonder, why these two animals and not any other? Do not all animals have a body with four legs, a head, and a mouth? If you can see one animal in the sky, why would someone else not see a different animal? No matter, it is their mystery. They will tell you that the change of Age denoted by the stars is a subtle observation first made by a Samavedin and verified by other Samavedins. Samavedins are bards who specialize in maintenance of clocks – managers of time, if you will. All bards study the Samavedins' art, but only the most skilled who have the greatest fortitude, patience, and focus go deep into that art. A sad consequence of their training is that many Samavedins go mad as they age. Occupied in incessant measurement, they become even more obsessed. They become counters who see numbers in everything. The Samavedins say, and there is no cause to disbelieve them, that this cosmic observation has taken centuries to make and it could only be made because Samavedins, too, maintain archives of their observations. When asked about the significance of the transit from the Age of the Bull to that of the Ram, they defer to the astrologers who see future history in the stars. The Samavedin measures time, not history. In any case, the heavens moved from one Age to the next and shook the world; the world changed.

It is the case though that neither the priests nor the philosophers, neither the star-gazers nor the star-readers predicted any particulars of the Disaster. The shaking of the earth surprised everybody.

Prithvi shook. The river Yamuna, the great tributary of the Sarasvati withdrew her blessings from the people of Panchnad and turned at the northern ridge of the Aravalli range to flow eastward. The river Sutudri, which had flowed in a hundred streams to join the Sarasvati, now abandoned those channels. It no longer went south after it emerged from the Himalayas. It turned sharply to the west to join one of the tributaries of the Sindhu many yojanas away. Kaalindini, less than a yojana away, lost its water supply and, in time, would be abandoned. The River Drishadvati, rain-fed along the western slopes of the Aravalli range and flowing south of the old Yamuna, continued to flow as it did and arrived at the meeting place with the Sarasvati, only to find itself alone. It could only pour into the Sarasvati a fraction of the water that that great river had once received. Other tributaries flowing down with the monsoon rains that fell in the Aravalli range continued to feed the Sarasvati. But it was not enough. The die had been cast and showed kali, the losing throw.

The consequences in the east were tremendous. That year, the east was flooded. The southwestern corner of Kuru territory, once called Khandavaprastha, which had been arid scrubland in the rain shadow of the Aravalli range, became a wooded swamp. The Yamuna's water flowed along the eastern foothills of the Aravalli range as far as where the Sahyadri range was visible and the land sloped up to the south. The Yamuna then turned to the east (many yojanas south of the Ganga at this point) and entered forested regions populated by new Naga settlers along the banks of previously monsoon-fed rivers now overflowing with the snow-fortified Yamuna. The floodwaters then continued parallel to the Ganga until they reached the Charmanavati River emerging from the Vindhya mountain range. The Yamuna-augmented Charmanavati followed its old bed until it merged with the Ganga at the place we call Prayag. Nowadays this stretch is called the Yamuna. For many years there was no fixed riverbed in the upper reaches of the river; it was a floodplain and the course of the river was very unstable. Over the years, as the river made its way through the Naga-occupied forests, a stable bed was formed. The occasional depression collected water to become a pond. Some of these ponds grew to form lakes. For many generations, though, the Yamuna remained an unstable rogue river.

The Kauravas continued to call the river by its old name, the Yamuna. The first region that was traversed by the new Yamuna had few inhabitants, mostly a small number of Naga bands. The Nagas dealt with the new situation as they had always done when displaced by floods or other natural threats to their settlements – they moved to a new location, burned a new clearing for their plantings, and started afresh. Their biggest problem was that they might not have food stores to carry them through a new crop cycle. In this case, the availability of water in an otherwise arid region would increase arable land, but only after the river settled down. A few years later, dormant seeds sprouted, grass and reeds appeared, followed by tadpoles, insects, small fish, and then, finally large fish.

When the fish became plentiful, the river dolphin, a gift of the mother-goddess, would appear and it would be time for the Nagas to return. Many Naga bands on the banks would switch to fishing, like the Meena-Nagas in the northeast of Jambudvipa who lived by rivers.

Downstream from where the Yamuna merged with the Ganga, a few yojanas from Prayag, the increased flow almost doubled the width of the Ganga. Much of this widening was towards the flat northern bank as the southern bank sloped up to the Vindhya range. This was the territory bordering Rakshasa country that saw conflict when Naga bands expanded into this area and met Rakshasa bands also seeking to settle there. Both sides traditionally avoided such conflicts by turning away, so a sparsely occupied no-man's land extended from this juncture to Laghu Nagapura where a river emerging from the plateau, called the Hiranyaganga, joined the Ganga. From that point on, Rakshasas were found on both sides of the river, but the increased water flow of the Yamuna split Rakshasa society into two – one on the north side and the other on the south side of the Ganga. The two communities found it harder to get together and interacted much less. The settlement at Laghu Nagapura flooded and was moved to higher land.

Back in the west, the Sarasvati dried up slowly, its waters disappearing into the sand at its southernmost point just before the point at which it used to split to form a delta to the sea. A slight ridge about five yojanas from the sea had created the last of the Sarasvati lakes. The water would flow over the ridge and find multiple paths to the sea. When the water level in the lake fell permanently below the ridge, the saltwater of the sea moved into the delta but was still a long way from the lake. The land in between was dry and salty, and would become a saltwater marsh in the rainy season. The lake itself dried up slowly as the Sarasvati brought in less and less water.

The other lakes that had dotted the river's path to the sea also received less and less water and slowly dried up. The southernmost lakes dried up first and then the other upstream lakes dried up as the stored water evaporated and was fitfully replenished by monsoon water. The southernmost settlements were abandoned first. Some émigrés went north towards other Panchnad towns, where they were initially helped, but as the magnitude of the disaster became clear, they were asked to move on. Some went to the northwest to the towns on the Sindhu, in particular the great city of Moolasthan, but here too they only received temporary help as these north-western towns struggled to cope with their own floods and shifting rivers. Those émigrés kept going northwest through the passes that lead to the Kubha River, where they stayed and settled. Some émigrés went south to Saurashtra and then proceeded down the shores of the Western Sea.

The émigrés who went north past the other Panchnad towns reached the place where the Yamuna and Drishadvati once joined. Now there was only the trickle of the rain-fed Drishadvati. The Sutudri used to flow through innumerable channels. Its swift flow prevented it from depositing silt; it left shallow beds covered with rocks and gravel rather than soil. The Drishadvati, though slower, did not bring down much silt. Agriculture was not feasible in the areas watered by these rivers. The emigres then went east towards Hastinapura, expecting help but worsening the situation in the host communities. Having come that far, they stopped. The prognosis was poor for going further. The land on either side of the Ganga was clayey, difficult to till. Anyone going further would have to become pioneers opening up uninhabited lands, which they considered a lowering of their status. Some of the area was occupied by Nagas, who would object to losing their land. The Panchnad refugees did not want war nor did the Nagas; they were not eager to start a war whose outcome they could not guess.

From Saurashtra, a large faction went north along the eastern side of the Aravalli range. In the beginning, there was a belief – a hope, rather – that the Yamuna would return to its original course and the Sarasvati cities would regain their wealth and power. That hope faded as the years passed. Moolasthan and the cities on the Sindhu were not in a position to help the Sarasvati refugees. The Sutudri's flow into the Sindhu had increased significantly, and all along the Sindhu, embankments had overflowed and the river had moved to a different channel. The disruption was small in comparison to the lot of the Sarasvati settlements, but the Sindhu towns could not be of much help to the refugees.

Notwithstanding all the differences between the older Panchnad towns and Hastinapura (militarized with a standing army, patriarchal, ruled by warriors not traders, and so on), there had always been a substantial faction in Hastinapura that thought of the city as an outpost of Panchnad. Many citizens still considered themselves the children of Bharata or the children of Puru, who settled by the Sarasvati, and not only the children of Kuru who had secured power in Hastinapura on the Ganga. The Kauravas, who ruled Hastinapura, and their leader Pratipa, recognized that the cities of Panchnad were collapsing and were concerned that they would take Hastinapura down with them. At this point, the Kavi Sangha concluded that the changes in the Sarasvati were permanent and the Sarasvati settlements doomed. Hastinapura was already their stellar success; they made a critical decision to abandon Panchnad and move to Hastinapura and begin the process of creating an urban civilization.

First, a key action was considered necessary. Pratipa[87] was persuaded to justify his name and formally declare the independence of Hastinapura from its Kaalindini parent and from the Puru homeland; independence too from the Sarasvati, to be replaced by a permanent commitment to the Ganga. The significance of that declaration was that he was formally reneging on the implicit promise to support the parent settlement in times of need and to follow their ways of conflict resolution. He would be free of commitments to submit to a matriarchy. This made it possible for Hastinapura to treat the refugees differently from its own population and the Nagas. Though supported by the Kavi Sangha, Pratipa's declaration was not welcomed and caused much debate in Hastinapura. Ultimately he compromised by postponing complete emancipation, leaving it to his son to complete the break-up.

Of Pratipa's three sons, the oldest, Bahlika, objected to the Kavi Sangha-inspired decision and decided not to accept the leadership. He led a batch of refugees to the Northwest, crossed the Sindhu and entered Gandhara via the Kuberakuta[88] road. They intended to return to the old tradition of rule by traders rather than warriors. His group of emigrants crossed the Kubha River into a plateau north of Gandhara. There they discovered that collapse of civilizations was not limited to Panchnad. All over the West, drought and famine had devastated ancient trading networks and wars had become ubiquitous.

---

[87]*Pratipa* means "rebel" or "adversary" (among other meanings).

[88]*Kuberakuta*, meaning "Kubera's Fort," is the Khyber Pass.

The people they were expecting to settle with were themselves impoverished by the changing climate and the collapse of trade. Further migration west would have to be postponed by a few generations. They went as far west as they could and named their settlements and themselves Bahlika. They sent back word of this discouraging development. It made Kururashtra look like the only alternative for all of Panchnad.

Pratipa's second son Devapi was declared Yuvaraja, heir apparent.

A.8. The Panchnad Migration

The Annals of the Kavi Sangha describe how the population of Panchnad abandoned the towns on the Sarasvati and migrated to other parts of Jambudvipa.

In less than a century after Samvarana's return to Hastinapura and the creation of Hastinapura's standing army, patriarchal government and patrilineal inheritance of power were entrenched in Hastinapura. Pratipa's declaration of partial emancipation from Panchnad, followed by the use of the army to control the behavior of immigrants, extended Hastinapura's rule. It became universally recognized as the hegemon of the stretch of land from the western bank of the Ganga to the fluctuating eastern bank of the Yamuna and from the northern foothills of the Himalayas to an undefined boundary with Naga allies to the south. This region came to be called Kururashtra. Trade had been disrupted during the early years of the crisis but was expected to rebound when the crisis was over and normalcy was restored with Kururashtra in full control of trade between the east and the west.

The Panchnad towns were emptying, and a million people were migrating in all directions. To the north and west were other cities that shared their culture, but the earthquakes and the great changes in the flow of the Sindhu had hit them hard. The émigrés who went south established themselves in Saurashtra where the rivers Narmada and Tapti made the land productive. Further south, along the coast of the Western Sea, they established ports and cities that could attempt to continue the commerce that had once been the lifeblood of Panchnad communities.

For all its promise, Saurashtra was suffering from many years of drought. The water in the monsoon-fed Narmada River varied greatly, but it had a large watershed and potentially could enrich the land. For the time being, it could not support a large population. Many migrants, led by the Yadavas[89] of Panchnad, went northeast along the eastern slopes of the Aravalli range in the direction of Hastinapura. The land here was hilly and unpromising. Where it was flat, there was not much water. The Yadavas continued north and east between the Aravalli range to the left and the Sahyadri range to the right into the valley of the Charmanavati. They then followed the Charmanavati River into the Gangetic plain to meet the new River Yamuna. This land, receiving both rainwater and snowmelt, looked like promising territory.

As the Yamuna was unstable, the Yadavas tried to go upstream as well as downstream in search of a place appropriate for settlement. Upstream, the river was still not stable and the situation looked bad. When they tried to go downstream, they met and came into conflict with the Nagas near the river and

[89] *Yadava* means "a descendant of Yadu."

with Rakshasas in the forest. They compromised as well as they could. They wanted to establish a city, to be called Mathura, the "City of Honey".

The Yadavas made many attempts to establish Mathura. The river's constant shifting was a problem, just as Nagas and Rakshasas opposition never ended.

The last group to emigrate from Panchnad was from the upstream cities. The most numerous, the most ancient, and the poorest clan called themselves the Pauravas; then there were the powerful Bhaaratas, who ran most city councils; and a small sprinkling of Kauravas, who were largely up-and-coming traders. These refugees could go north along the old bed of the Yamuna past the point where the river's course had changed and cross it closer to the Himalayan foothills. There was an ancient bridge, but it had been damaged during the earthquake. The local Naga fisher-folk, called Meena (or Meena-Nagas), ferried the refugees over in exchange for textiles, weapons, ornaments, and jewelry. Then, going east, the Panchnad emigrants would first come to the Ganga. Continuing southeast along the right bank, they would reach Hastinapura, where they would request refuge, as family. The familial relationship meant that the request could not be refused. The declaration of emancipation was intended to enable Hastinapura to decline such requests.

A.9. The Refugees in Hastinapura

Yudhishthira said, "Why was it so difficult to manage the refugees who came to Hastinapura seeking help? What did they expect, and what did they get?"

Devavrata's answer: Hastinapura did not have the resources to support all the refugees, so a bad situation was becoming worse. The Kavi Sangha suggested a tough stance. Pratipa's oldest son Devapi[90] had been crowned King but did not have the stomach to deny shelter to the refugees. Reclusive to begin with, Devapi became more isolated when he rejected Kavi Sangha help. Increasingly, he attempted to solve all problems by himself and failed. he common opinion was that Shani had infected him with depression at an early age. This could have been true for he was often melancholic and pessimistic.

One day, Devapi's clothes were found abandoned at the edge of Khandavaprastha. He had disappeared, leaving a message with a retainer: The King had abdicated. He did not want to do it publicly as he knew the counselors would try to dissuade him. He wished his brother well.

The third son of Pratipa, Shantanu, became the leader of Hastinapura. Shantanu realized the magnitude of the refugee problem and requested more help from the Kavi Sangha.

The refugees were from an urban society and lacked the skills needed in building new settlements on uninhabited land. The Vyaasa at that time was Bharadvaja, who preceded Shukla, the Vyaasa who recorded these annals. Bharadvaja was a pragmatic realist. He responded to the disinclination of the refugees to settle new land by proposing positive and negative inducements. In the process, Bharadvaja invented new policies, including harsh ones that were disliked.

It is necessary to note that there were many reasons why the refugees did not want to be pioneers. Their view of themselves

[90]*Devapi* means "friend of the gods" or "beloved of the gods."

as a sophisticated and urban people and not forest-dwellers like the Nagas; their unfamiliarity with the land and the limitations on its use; their knowledge and the skills that they would need to start afresh as pioneers.

First, their view of themselves. They did not want to live like the existing population. That existing population, the Nagas, consisted of nomadic, loosely allied bands that did not build permanent settlements and occupied central and eastern Jambudvipa, that is, the plain of the Ganga from the foothills of the Himalayas and points south. There was fear that the Nagas would not allow any settlement on their land.

Second, their familiarity with the land. Even if the Nagas were amenable to sharing their traditional lands, the methods of farming known in Panchnad could not be used in the new land. The land of the Ganga was heavily forested and the Ganga was the year-round source of water, but irrigation systems would have to be constructed to sustain agriculture far from the rivers. In Panchnad, with the many lakes on the Sarasvati, it was easy to irrigate farms.

The third category of reasons for the refugees not wanting to be pioneers was knowledge, especially of appropriate technology. There had been past attempts by individual Panchnad adventurers to settle along the banks of the Ganga. These failed because the work was hard and the returns meagre. Those settlers in the past had to spend years learning the slash-and-burn agriculture practiced by the Nagas. They discovered that slash-and-burn agriculture was not productive enough to support the Panchnad manner of living in solid houses of brick in a permanent settlement. It wasn't just individuals had to change – systems would have to change. The refugees believed that sooner or later they would be able to return to Panchnad and resisted learning what they needd to learn.

A.10. Panchnad Fails to Come Together

The crisis caused by the drying up of the Sarasvati, and the problem of the refugees, broke the historic unity the people of Panchnad had been proud of. The settlements became unable to cooperate to address the problems.

Well before Devavrata's renunciation, Panchnad was a troubled land. The saving grace was that despite the troubles, there was no war as peace was a way of life. The Sarasvati had begun drying up in the time of Pratipa, Devavrata's grandfather. Pratipa wanted the Pauravas and Bhaaratas in the oldest parent settlements to work together and restore the Yamuna's flow to the west. He offered all the help that he could – this was limited as the Yamuna's sudden appearance in the east was radically transforming the Gangetic plain as well. Hastinapura itself was not in the path of the flood as it skirted along the boundaries of Kururashtra. Naga (and Rakshasas further downstream) bands had suffered the brunt of the flooding in the beginning, but now they were responding to the opportunities created by the new river. Naga bands in the heartland were moving up the Yamuna with new settlements. Rakshasa bands further to the east were preparing to move into the no-man's land that separated them from the old Naga boundaries to exploit the new source of water. The only opponent Pratipa faced who might choose war were the Panchalas who had not been touched by the change. Pratipa had his hands full keeping Panchala from crossing the Ganga again in a reprise of their ancient confrontation.

The upper and middle classes of Panchnad, the Pauravas and the Bhaaratas, were traders first, and builders second. They could not see the need to undertake, at current cost, a huge project with no immediate return. There was no profit to be made in diverting the course of the Yamuna. It was possible that the monsoons might make up the deficit in water. The river might return to its previous course on its own. The communities dithered, and while the impasse continued, migrants from further south overwhelmed the central Panchnad towns. Faced with a population crisis, the towns of central Panchnad were unable to finance such a project. The Bhaaratas repeated their earlier mistake; they considered action only when the southern and central cities failed to handle the refugees. But it was too late, and the Bhaarata cities succumbed to the exploding population of migrants. Pratipa could see the juggernaut building up and wanted to stop it before it arrived in Kururashtra. But he did not control the Yamuna upstream where the problem might have been resolvable. Pratipa felt helpless and failed to take decisive action. In the first years of Shantanu's reign, more refugees arrived at the Kuru borders seeking help. The people of Panchnad were abandoning their settlements as the drought spread north.

Shantanu sought the counsel of the Kavi Sangha and its Vyaasa (Bharadvaja, before Parashara) on developing a long-run strategy to deal with the refugee situation. Something had to be done immediately that would choke the flow. The refugees imagined an unpopulated land with a bounteous river like the Sarasvati on whose banks settlements could be raised. The reality dismayed them. But by then, they were already in Hasapura and had nowhere else to go. Hastinapura itself had to become unattractive.

The broad outlines of the strategy Shantanu and the Kavi Sangha developed were thus: Recreate the Sarasvati-centric way of life of Panchnad on the banks of the Ganga and the Yamuna. Change the pattern of use of arable land from slash and burn to permanent settlement, even if it meant that the Nagas would have to change or would have to leave. Encourage the refugees to be the pioneers in settling the new land. Police the roads from the west along which the refugees came and control their entry. Oppose the work breakdown that the guilds enforced in the old Sarasvati settlements. Slow down the growth of the population to match the rate at which new settlements were established.

The democratic organization of the old settlements would have to be abandoned and a unitary state like the empires of the West that traders described (such as Parsaka, Sumer, and the land of the Black River) would have to be established.

To implement this long-term strategy, it was necessary in the short-term for Shantanu to maintain and expand the army, to deal with any societal unrest, and for the population of Hastinapura and the camled. The immediate and contentious result was the one child-person-one child policy. It provoked unrest that had to be put down by the ever-expanding army. The reported suicide of Shantanu's wife intensified the unrest.

A.11. Satyavati's Ambition

There are no good answers to the questions about Satyavati's ambitions. What did she want, and how did she try to get it? Despite her brother Shukla's rise to the role of Vyaasa, it is generally believed that he was too close to her to be objective.

How are we, looking back at a distant past, to judge the actions of Devavrata and Satyavati. Devavrata's mind must have been in a whirl when his father married the woman he loved. Was avoiding Satyavati's eyes enough? What if they encountered each other on the street? When he visited his father, how could he avoid seeing his stepmother?

Similar questions arise when we think of Satyavati. Shukla reports that she announced to him and their father: *I might as well be dead*. But then she goes ahead with the marriage. How did she find the will to lie with Shantanu? How was it that Shantanu failed to detect her lack of love for him?

Shukla's explanation as recorded in our archives of the time was: Satyavati was born to be a matriarch, a leader of an independent clan. Matriarchs did not follow the norms of ordinary women in our culture. Men were not the all-powerful beings that we have portrayed, nor were women the fragile weaklings of later stories.

Future Vyaasas' reaction was to avoid looking for explanations. They would say, "This was the story that has come down to us. It is history, not melodrama. Even if accidental meetings occurred they were not consequential. Otherwise, the Kavi Sangha would have recorded them as well. So we must accept Shukla's assessment."

Shukla's explanation continued: Why did Satyavati go ahead with the marriage? She was ambitious, and she thought she was going to be the matriarch in Hastinapura. She knew that Hastinapura society differed from the Nagas in the primacy of men in governance. But she may not have been prepared for the extent of male domination. There were no women in superior roles in the state, something unthinkable in Naga bands. All she could be in her new role was the founder of a dynasty. When Devavrata met her and impressed her, she was just beginning her transition from a young girl and early motherhood to an adult. She may have wanted to die at the prospect of losing Devavrata, but she was a pragmatic woman. She may have realized the silliness of her announcement and did not act on it. Devavrata's impulsive vow was similarly silly. It would have impressed her as extremely foolhardy, if not foolish, and she would have been amazed when nobody attempted to dissuade him and the seriousness with which he followed it. She had compromised and found other reasons to live. He should have found other reasons to back away from his vow. She had not asked for celibacy, she had not asked that he never make love to another woman, just that he not have children who aspired to be Crown Prince. Even then, as Queen, she would have managed the expectations of his children if he had had any.

It is interesting to observe the reactions of the audience when this story is narrated. They do not question Devavrata's impulsive and daunting vow. Nor do they question his father's behavior. Would a father leave on a trading caravan while the son he left behind exhibited dangerous tendencies? But Satyavati is judged.

A.12. Shantanu Modifies Kavi Sangha Policies

The older Annals of the Kavi Sangha are incomplete when discussing the changes of policy under Shantanu. The Kavi Sangha went through some difficult leadership transitions and failed to record the archives completely.

This is a summary of what the Annals of that time say: After Shantanu married Satyavati, the Kavi Sangha retreated on some of its policy directives. Part of this retreat was forced; the one child policy had to be abandoned, and that decision was controversial. Meanwhile, Devavrata saw himself as the only person who could bring balance to the absence of empathy in the Kavi Sangha's approach to managing the crisis.

Parashara's policy of bringing Nagas into the Kavi Sangha was intended to make it more acceptable to the Nagas and not appear as an imperialistic extension of Panchnad. But the process of the Nagas participating in the discussions inevitably led to compromise, sacrificing the immediate reward for a future promise.

For instance, the Kavi Sangha approach to creating new settlements effectively took land away from the Nagas. It is reasonable to wonder why the Nagas in the Kavi Sangha did not object, especially given the high ranks they reached. Shukla was the first Naga to become the Vyaasa, and after him, there would be many.

The Nagas who joined the Kavi Sangha often felt that the policies proposed were in the best long-term interest of the Nagas. Like all such policies, much would depend on honest and sincere implementation, even though we know that the implementers are human, error-prone, and corruptible. The war broke out because the sons of Mahendra Pandu decided that the Nagas had been treated unfairly, extremely unfairly. Meanwhile, their opponents, the sons of Dhritarashtra, refused to see unfairness in practice but theorized about principles. As this benefited them, they objected to any change.

Everything would be sacrificed on the altar of fairness – the selfish who stole from the poor; the refugees, now called immigrants, who wanted to restore their old way of life; and the Nagas who were short-sighted, focused on the present, and refused any compromise. The Pandavas would sacrifice everything on this altar of fairness.

When Shantanu married Satyavati, he abandoned one element of the Kavi Sangha strategy. He backed away from the short-term plan to stop population growth by limiting family size. Such impulsive individual decisions, usually by male decision-makers, have often created problems for the plan.

The alliance that the Pandavas cobbled together to oppose Hastinapura included Panchala, even though there was still enmity between the Naga city and Hastinapura. Panchala had been opposed to Hastinapura from its founding as a trading outpost. The Yadavas were in the alliance too. Their leader Krishna kept his own counsel but wove a path to a Yadava empire that would rival a Kuru empire centered on Hastinapura. In principle, the Kavi Sangha was not opposed to the Yadava plan. The rise of the Yadavas under Krishna had not been anticipated. Though the Yadavas, descendants of Yadu, were cousins to the descendants of Puru, Yadu's brother, their imperial plans would not mesh with Devavrata's goals. Those plans were also inimical to Yudhishthira's goals, but the Yadavas allied with him to oppose Hastinapura and Devavrata. Added to this incongruous mix were the southern Nagas represented by their army chief Virata, who styled himself King of the Matsyas, that is, the Meena-Nagas. The Meenas may be Nagas, but their interests diverged from those of Panchala. They had fared well under Hastinapura's policies, so why did they oppose Hastinapura? All they saw, like many others, was the unfairness of Kavi Sangha policies.

A.13. Devavrata's Spring Projects

Devavrata planned a number of Spring projects, incuding a proposal to build channels that would divert the Yamuna back into its old channel to the west. Then the Sarasvati could become a great river again, instead of the monsoon-fed, drought-prone stream that it had become. These channels were difficult to cut for the mountain-fed rivers never dry completely. During the winter, the cold, white snow freezes in the mountains, creating glacial ice dams at unexpected locations. Melted water from higher grounds accumulates behind these natural dams. When the dam bursts, a torrent of water is released. We cannot predict when such a dam might break upstream. The breakage of a dam deeper in the mountains might release enough water to break the next ice dam downstream, setting off a chain of dam collapses. When that happened, the floods overwhelmed our best efforts. The best times for constructing water-works are late fall, after the first ice dam forms in the mountains and holds back some water, and early spring before the ice-dams break releasing gushers.

Unfortunately, spring was also the best time for the refugees to leave their homes or temporary shelters and migrate. The weather was not too hot or too cold or too wet, though fearsome animals ranged in the forests. A spring migration could end in settling down on fallow land and creating a permanent settlement. A fall migration followed a summer spent accumulating supplies to last through the winter before continuing east. Many of the water projects were right on the migration route to Hastinapura, and Devavrata planned to use the refugees as laborers. But he miscalculated. The urban refugees were in no sense ready to labor on a canal project. A settled urban life changes people; they become unable to perform physical tasks or work with soil. These refugees were repelled by physical labor as a child shrinks from the fire that burnt it once.

A.14. Devavrata's Early Plans for Empire

Yudhishthira said, "Pitamaha, you've mentioned plans for creating an empire as early as Chitrangada's reign. What were these plans?"

Devavrata said: After Chitrangada's death at the hands of the Shaka, I concluded that the only way we would repel future invasions was by presenting the Shakas with a united defensive line across the foothills of the northern mountains. I needed support from the Panchnad republics on the Vipasa and Jahnavi rivers. Even if the far western republics of Moolasthan and Takshashila would not join me – they had their own refugees – I would at least prevent the Shakas from establishing a foothold on the gateway between the west and the east. To create such a defensive line, I needed to have a unified entity, an empire, if you wish. This empire would have to command the loyalty of the Nagas, the original Kuru settlers of Hastinapura, and the new Panchnad refugees.

These days the idea of an Emperor is bandied about easily – Emperor Yudhishthira and Emperor Suyodhana, as they call themselves. In those days, there was no 'Kuru Empire', even in fantasy. The refugees from the west brought along their ideas of running cities by guilds organized around critical functions, but this did not sit well with the Nagas who wanted to live in bands. It was not even acceptable to the immigrants settled in border areas, who could not wait for service from a guild member with the authority and training to perform a specialized task. The Nagas had no concept of empire, though Panchala, the hostile Naga confederation across the river, was developing into a military state with imperial ambitions. To this day, we point to the Shakas and what they did to a peaceful Naga band to define and justify the empire I have created.

The best argument for a Kuru empire came from the work I had done. As I built dams and lakes along the Ganga and tried to control the Yamuna, I realized that the local residents, whether new immigrants or older residents, had to be organized to maintain the waterworks. How were we to convince these local people – urbanites, farmers, Nagas, and even traders – of the value of long-range planning and long-term maintenance? I could see it and acted to foster it through my waterworks projects. These hydraulic systems would survive forever if they were kept in good repair. The taxes collected on the produce of the farmers and the goods shipped by traders would more than pay for the maintenance. The problem, as always, was finding qualified people to do the work.

My focus on the long-term issues created an alliance between Hastinapura and the new immigrant-turned-farmers, who saw their interests tied to the interests of Hastinapura. If they could be trained as fighters, we could rely on them for defense. When defense was not needed they would rely on the empire to support them and their economy as needed.

A.15. Carrots and Fatherhood

There is an explanation for Satyavati's demands that puzzled Devavrata. The source of this information is not named, but it must have been a bard who knew both agriculture and the medicine used by women.

This is what the older Annals say: Devavrata had been confused when Satyavati imported carrot plants as medicine for Ambika and Ambalika. The Queens had been secluded and then Satyavati had asked Devavrata to spend time with them so that their sons would inherit Kaurava features.

The carrot, a small purple root that comes from the northern hills, can be used to produce an abortifacient that causes a fetus to be expelled prematurely from the womb.[91]

Satyavati did not want Devavrata or anybody else to suspect that the children were not the sons of Vichitravirya. She used the wild carrot plants to produce a concentrated liquid that was administered to Ambika and Ambalika in the seventh month. Thus the two babies were born prematurely in the seventh month. Satyavati let it be known that the babies were full-term but because they had received some of the poison that killed Vichitravirya, they were weak and needed special care. She prepared the warm room and other facilities knowing that the two boys would need special care. After two months in the warm room under special care, the two sons of Shantanu Vichitravirya were ready for a regular diet based on their mothers' milk.

---

[91]The carrot's cousin called 'Queen Anne's lace' can be used to produce an abortifacient which causes a foetus to be expelled prematurely from the womb. The modern carrot has evolved greatly from the original – a small purple root that originated in South Asia.

The maid-servant who also had intercourse with Krishna Dvaipaayana bore Dharmateja Vidura as a full-term baby two months later (in the ninth month). Vidura was born healthy. Vidura's mother started producing milk just in time for the premature royal babies to drink.

The use of the wild carrot as an abortifacient was not known to Panchnad, but may have been a Naga secret. The beliefs about how the father's characteristics are inherited were common Panchnad knowledge. Heating rooms with hypocausts was ancient knowledge in the Sindhu-Sarasvati culture and the plateau of Gandhara. Unfortunately, Devavrata had no knowledge of what was going on. His goal was to keep the peace. He wanted Vichitravirya's sons to be born so that he would not be forced to reign as King.

B. NOTES

B.1. Standardization

A recurring theme in Panchnad culture was *standardization.* This can be seen in the archaeological sites of Mohenjo-Daro, Harappa, Chanhu-Daro, Lothal, and others, where uniformity reigns to a far greater extent than other contemporary urban cultures such as Sumer. Bricks were manufactured in sizes in a standard ratio of 1:2:4. Weights are found in the sequence 1, 2, 4, 8, 10, 16, and 32. (It is surely a coincidence that the #2 weight is within 10 per cent of the British ounce.) Towns are constructed on a precise north-south axis. Every town's architecture is very similar. There are other such standard features.

I have assumed that this approach to standardization applied to other areas of endeavor, such as the calendar, seasons, time, distance, arts, and even the conduct of war.

B.1.1. Annual Calendar of Panchnad and Hastinapura

Melas (fairs) are held on the occasions of the two equinoxes and the two solstices. The winter solstice marks the Sun beginning its journey north, but it also marks the beginning of the winter harvest period (January to March or April, depending on latitude). The spring equinox heralds the arrival of spring and is considered the start of the year. The summer solstice is the beginning of the monsoon planting season. The autumn equinox marks the end of the monsoon harvest and the beginning of the winter planting season, ending with the winter harvest. In the parts of South Asia where three crops are possible, the summer planting and harvest season extends from March to June (spring equinox to summer solstice). Traders leave home after the winter harvest to reach their destination(s) before the monsoons begin (a leading separation motif in Sanskrit love poetry) and start on the return journey after the monsoons end to arrive home in time for the winter harvest.

B.1.2. Seasons of the Year

Sanskrit Season	English Season	Gregorian Months
Vasanta	Spring	Mid-April–Mid-June
Grishma	Summer	Mid-June–Mid-August
Varsha	Monsoon	Mid-August–Mid–October
Sharada	Autumn	Mid-October–Mid-December
Hemanta	Winter	Mid-December–Mid-February
Sishira	Preveral	Mid-February–Mid-April

B.1.3. Measures of Time: Ghati and Vighati

G^haṭi and *Vig^haṭi,* pronounced "Gut-e" and "We-gut-e", and spelled "Ghati" and 'Vighati', are the measures of time that have been used in India from ancient times (with regional variations, such as *nāzhi* and *vināzhi* in Tamil). I have appropriated them for this period though we do not know what terms were used then.

The day is defined as the time from sunrise of one day to the sunrise of the next day. A day was defined as approximately 60 ghatis. The measure is approximate because the "day" defined in terms of the sunrise varies during the year. Each *ghati* in turn was divided into 60 *vighatis.* For comparison, one *vighati* is 24 seconds and one *ghati* is 24 minutes.

B.1.4. Measures of Distance: Yojana

The earth rotates once every 3600 vighatis (through 360 degrees, the modern measure of angles of a circle). In one vighati, the earth will have rotated one-tenth of a degree. In that one vighati, a vertical rod that casts a small shadow pointing north at high noon (say local time in New Delhi, India) will cast a slightly bigger shadow angled slightly east by one-tenth degree with respect to north. At the same time, some distance to the west, it will be high noon (local time) and a vertical rod placed there will cast its smallest shadow pointing due north. The distance between these two rods was considered one *Yōjənə* (pronounced "Yo(re)-ju(t)-nu(t)" and spelled "Yojana") in Panchnad.

The above definition of yojana as a measure of distance is dependent on latitude. Such a dependent definition, while useful in a culture spreading in an east-west direction (such as Europe, West Asia, the Russian steppes), is not useful for a culture oriented from north to south (such as South Asia or Egypt). A definition created by a north-south oriented culture would be a constant, but establishing it would depend on the exact determination of longitude (or, the circumference of the earth), which requires the use of synchronized clocking. Such a capability did not exist until late in the history of Panchnad, when the Samavedins perfected their techniques for keeping time.

A standard definition of yojana can then be obtained by selecting a well-known spot, for instance, Takshashila. Takshashila was the famous center of learning and thought in historical ancient India, and in this book is depicted as the Panchnad center of learning, culture, and philosophy, where Kavi Sangha members went for their advanced education. The standard yojana is measured on the ground at that latitude and composed of smaller standardized units, such as the hasta (or cubit). The latitude can be determined easily by measuring the declination of the sun at noon on the spring or autumnal equinoxes, and other spots at the same latitude can be identified if necessary.

If measured at the equator, one-tenth of a degree would be about seven miles (11.13 km). At the latitude of Takshashila, it would be the "standard yojana" of about six miles (9.24 km), or 21,120 hastas or cubits (see below). All of Panchnad used this definition of yojana.

An average "casual" walking pace is about fifty steps per vighati or three thousand steps per ghati. The average stride of the average South Asian is about two feet. So the average walking speed is approximately one mile per ghati. In six ghatis (one-tenth of a day of sixty ghatis), an average person could walk about one yojana.[92]

Allowing for meals and other breaks, and by walking only in the daytime, a traveler could hike between three and four yojanas, i.e., about twenty miles in a day. Walking at that pace, it would take about three months to go from Kamarupa in the east of South Asia (in Bangladesh) to Takshashila in the west of South Asia (in Pakistan), a distance of about sixteen hundred miles.

Another measure integrating time and distance is the cartwheel. A fully loaded cart with large wheels (about four feet in diameter) pulled by a single bullock or onager makes between one to five turns of the wheel every vighati. The smaller wheels

92Note that this definition of the "standard yojana" is speculative and based on average speed of walking. At the latitude of Takshashila, the sun will "move" in one vighati, a distance that a person walking east (or west) can go in six ghatis.

of two feet in diameter make about four to eight turns in the same time. A peddler's cart pulled by either animal moves four to eight miles/hour, not an unreasonable speed. But a single bullock will work less than four hours a day at that pace. A caravan of such carts will go slower, perhaps half the speed, at eight to sixteen miles/day. The trader can make the outbound trip starting in early to mid-October (after the monsoons end) and arriving in mid-April (just before the summer heat makes it difficult to travel).

B.1.5. Measures of Distance: Classical Sanskrit

These definitions are from Kauṭilyā's *Aṛtaśāstra* (approximate equivalents in inches are also provided):

1 angula = a finger-width, 3/4 of an inch

4 angula = 1 dhanurgraha [bow grip], 3 inches

8 angula = 1 dhanurmushti [fist with thumb raised], 6 inches

12 angula = 1 vitasta [a handspan], 9 inches

4 vitasta = 1 aratni= 2 hasta [cubit], 18 inches

4 aratni = 1 danda or dhanus [bow], 6 feet

10 danda = 1 raja, 60 feet

2 rajas = 1 paridesha, 120 feet

2000 danda or dhanus = 1 krosa or gorutta = 4000 yards or 2 1/4 miles, nearly 3.66 km

4 krosa = 1 yojana = 9 miles, nearly 15 km

Note that, by the time of Kauṭilyā, believed to be around 300 BCE, a yojana is no longer defined using the motion of the sun but is composed of smaller measures built on human dimensions.

B.1.6. Fine Arts

Centuries later, the *Natyashastra* of Bharata-muni would codify the theatrical arts and techniques, establishing *standardization* in theatre. This began, I assume, in the cultural ideal of standardization inherited from Panchnad before 2000 BCE. The techniques and methods of instruction used by the guild of bards became the pattern of all theatrical instruction. Speech sounds had been classified into *swara* (vowels) and *vyanjana* (consonants) and systematized. This made it possible to teach memorization in a uniform manner. Every bard was capable of reciting an epic poem in exactly the same way, and development of the skill of learning and reciting was attributed to the mode of instruction.

This mode of instruction was applied to all the elements of the theatre. Hand movements were named *mudras* and became the basis for a semi-secret alphabet of signs and signals. Exercise routines that actors practiced were named *adavus* and standardized for formal instruction. Emotional states were named *rasas* and there were eight, arguably nine, of these. The art of expressing the rasas on stage was named *abhinaya.*

B.1.7. *Vyuhadyuta*: War by Mercenaries

A *vyuha* described the deployment of an armed force intending to attack or to defend against an attack. The Panchnad mercenaries' guild had developed a theory and classification of vyuhas that suited their mode of battle in which troops hired by two cities would set up challenges or duels to determine victory as efficiently as possible. Actual battles between armies only occurred if one side developed an overwhelming superiority in numbers or position, but this was rare. Thus, the

Sarasvati-Sindhu Culture had standardized war, with the result that full-scale all-out war never happened. Until the Great War.

B.2. Panchala Versus Panchnad

The names are, unfortunately, very similar.

Panchnad is the land defined by five rivers. These are the Sarasvati, the Sindhu, the Sutudri, the Yamuna, and the Drishadvati. This region extends from approximately today's Ropar (Kaalindini) in the north to the Arabian Sea in the south, the Aravalli range in the east to Multan (Moolasthan) in the west. Note that Panchnad is not the same as "Punjab." That province, divided between India and Pakistan, overlaps with Panchnad. Punjab also means the land of five rivers. But as it turns out, only the Sutudri (today's Sutlej) and the Sindhu (renamed Indus) are common to the two regions. Punjab also extends further northwest into the Himalayan range, but stops well short of the sea in the south, whereas Panchnad goes all the way south to the sea.

Panchala is the name of a confederation of five Naga clans. The clan is a unit much larger than a band or a family. Panchala became the name of the region controlled by these five clans. The region lies on the northern side of the Ganga from Ahichhatra in the north to (possibly) as far as modern-day Kashi to the south.

B.3. Cultural Elements

B.3.1 Dress

Both men and women dressed in two primary pieces of cloth, usually made from woven cotton. A longer piece was wrapped around the waist to form a skirt. (It would be called the *panchagacham.*) Another piece of cloth was wrapped about the upper body, which would be called the *angavastram.* The guild of weavers produced these to order and decorated them as required by the wearer.

A bard at a recital of a historic poem would wear a new white (undecorated) panchagacham and angavastram.

Men and women tied the panchagacham and angavastram differently. The male style of panchagacham used a longer cloth whose first section was used to gird the loins, while the woman's style was more like a skirt hanging off a girdle. The men used the angavastram as a kind of shawl, while the women used the central section as a crosspiece to support the breasts.

An angavastram padded with cotton and wrapped securely around the chest and shoulders functioned as rudimentary armor. Cotton armor was the main protection of the "Indian"[93] infantry of the Persian Empire under Cyrus the Great as described by Herodotus. I believe that one of the earliest uses of felted cotton may have been as armor.

B.3.2. Renaming the Characters

The reader familiar with the Mahabharata might be puzzled by some names. I believe that during the composition of a *jaya* (a lay celebrating a victory), the names of the participants were modified to highlight some attribute of or action by the character. In addition, as the jaya is composed by the winners, the names of the warriors of the losing side might be changed

[93]The soldiers in this infantry division were from the provinces ("satrapies") of Arachosia and Gandhara, which lie to the west of the river Indus. The men were most likely mercenaries.

to denigrate them. Occasionally, these became the name by which they were later remembered.

For instance, the martial arts teacher *Drona* may have been renamed from Kutaja, meaning "highest mountain peak." An alternative meaning of *kutaja* is "born in a jar." The word *drona* also means "jar". More specifically, the drona was a wooden jar that held soma during a fire sacrifice. As soma was an intoxicating drink, the jar and the people who handled it were supposed to be drunk from its fumes. So "Drona" may have been a mocking name for the teacher of the vanquished Kauravas. Similarly, Duryodhana ("bad warrior") may have been renamed from Suyodhana ("good warrior").

The reason for such transformation by a poet is that a person can be identified by names as well as attributes. Using a descriptive name that tells of some action by the character keeps the audience interested and signals what to expect. It allows the poet to avoid repeating a name multiple times in a single verse. In addition, names can be used to signal to the audience what they should think of a new character that appears on stage.

B.3.3. Naga Culture as Imagined in This Book

The Hastinapuris gave the name "Naga" to the forest-dwelling, matriarchal bands living along the Ganga. These bands occupied the forests along both banks of the Ganga, ranging from south of Hastinapura to a little east of Kashi. They translated the matriarch's title as "Nagini" ("Mother or Female Serpent"), and the title of the male chief, usually the brother of the Nagini, to "Great Serpent", i.e. "Mahanaga". This was the origin of the name "Naga" as applied to the culture. It is likely that the bands had a different name for themselves.

The Nagas practiced slash-and-burn agriculture. Each band would burn a grove in the forest near a source of water for growing food plants and raising chickens and barley. They would settle nearby, usually at the edge of the grove, for a few years, from five to twenty, depending on the fertility of the grove's layer of ash. Then they would move to a new location not adjacent to the exhausted grove. The old grove was left fallow for at least two more cycles, generally over twenty years.

The women made most decisions in the band, which was a haven for the women and the children. The matriarch's brother was the traditional head of the men's fraternity. Except for the matriarch's brother, the rest of the men joined the band on invitation. The popular men often moved from band to band, while the others acted to keep the matriarch and the women satisfied. Boys were expected to leave their bands after puberty and find other bands to join, but matriarchs and other powerful women could keep their sons in a band indefinitely. The men who were not invited by any band were considered "rogue." They lived by their wits without social support and usually died soon after leaving their mother's band. Rogue men who survived for a long time could be dangerous, as they were often anti-social or otherwise had difficulty in social settings. If a group of rogue men formed a gang, they could be a big threat to bands. But most rogues could not cooperate with each other and found it difficult to form a large band of rogues.

There were a number of rituals that the Nagini and the Mahanaga were expected to perform. Four of these had to do with the equinoxes and solstices; the rest divided the quarters evenly. At the spring equinox, the Nagini and the Mahanaga emerged from a sacred fire and led a bacchanalian nine days. Most children were born about nine months later (around the winter solstice), and the number of children born was an indicator of the matriarch's inner strength.

B.3.4. Redistributive Festivals Among the Nagas

Naga bands often celebrated parties with other Naga bands, both close and far. A group of nearby bands (typically five) would get together once a month. A larger group of twenty-five bands might meet twice a year. Festivals involving even larger groups might be held every few years. These events were organized by the men of the hosting band, sometimes in collaboration with the men of other bands. It provided an opportunity for the men to display their ability to organize, collaborate, make friends across bands, and create alliances that crossed family boundaries.

The word "potlatch" is derived from a redistributive feast held by the Trobriand Islanders of New Guinea. Similar festivals occur in other cultures as well, usually as part of a transition to settled agriculture. In the beginning, all the clans or bands would bring food and gifts for exchange. Later, a clan might host the entire event by itself, and the attending clans would acknowledge the host's "big man" superiority. A feature of the Trobriand Island culture was that the men of one tribe led by a "big man" would challenge other tribes through potlatch events. Occasionally, conflicts broke out, and even though their conflicts rarely led to actual battles, the more successful "big men" or those with bigger teams would usually win by intimidation. "Big Men" whose teams won often grew in prestige and with time became "Big Chiefs", leaders of larger groups of men. From time to time, a prototypical "Big Chief" would host a potlatch to show off his superior organizational capabilities as well as breadth of popularity. Over time, Big Chiefs became kings and did not have to sacrifice themselves to host a potlatch; taxes would pay for redistributive feasts.

The confederation of Panchala came into existence by a military merger of five Naga clans. The men of these five clans got together to handle the menace of "rogue males," who had been organized into a gang by a charismatic leader. Such cooperation between bands is an example of how the ritual of potlatch maintained a critical skill and makes possible coordinated responses to unusual events.

B.3.5 Language Questions

We do not know what language was spoken in 2000 BCE or, for that matter, in 850 BCE. We know that after 850 BCE, many texts were written, though few samples from that early era exist. Those we know of are in Sanskrit, and after 300 BCE, in PailPali. I have used Gondi in a few places for personal and intimate forms of address (such as "Avva" for mother, and "Bābā" for father) used by Shantanu's children. Satyavati's brother, a Meena-Naga, uses the Dramila (or Tamil, as Tamil spea kers are called in many ancient texts) word "akka" for his sister. For the more formal words (e.g. ghati, yojanas) spoken by the upper classes in 850 BCE, I have used terms from Sanskrit, translated when it seemed necessary. I've used "Namaskar" and "Guru" as well as "-deva" and "-ji" as honorifics. This too may be an anachronism. In addition, Sanskrit does not use "-ji", so it assumes a vernacular language that was not Sanskrit. Keep in mind that over four thousand years, a language will drift along with its speakers. Some of the changes are well known. For instance, 'k' drifts to "w". There are many such changes possible, and not all that is possible happens.

On the whole, I don't believe that this experiment in trying to convey an imagined language has been wholly successful. Whatever language is used in this book as the base, including English, some results struck me as ill-fitted. So I only use a non-English word when a candidate word or concept is first used, and a footnote provides the meaning. Subsequently, I use the English form.

B.4. Myths and History of the Kauravas

B.4.1 Myth: Pururavas the Handsome

Pururavas loved Urvashi, the semi-divine *apsara*, who agreed to live with him on the condition that he would never show himself to her naked. Indra, the king of the gods, was unhappy that Urvashi no longer graced his assemblies but lived with a human. He used his *Vajra* (the thunderbolt) one night when Pururavas and Urvashi were lying together, and she saw Pururavas naked and immediately left him.

B.4.2 Myth: Nahusha the Proud

Indra, the King of the gods, had committed the sin of killing a brahmin when he killed Tvastr and Vritra. As a result, he could no longer appear in the courts of heaven and hid himself in shame. After many years, the gods chose Nahusha as their King. Initially a good king, he became proud and lusted after Indra's wife Sachi. Sachi prayed to the great god Shiva and was told to ask Nahusha to come to her on a palanquin hoisted by the seven Sages. The Sages were old and slow, and Nahusha was in a hurry. He kicked Agastya, the shortest Sage, and shouted *"Sarpa! Sarpa!"* (which means "Faster! Faster!"). Agastya lost his patience and cursed Nahusha to become a *sarpa* (another meaning: 'snake'). Immediately, Nahusha fell to earth as a giant python.

Later, Agastya modified his curse and allowed Nahusha to be freed by his descendant Yudhishthira. Centuries later, the python Nahusha attacked Bhima and they fought. When Yudhishthira appeared and tried to save Bhima, Nahusha was freed of the curse. This is clearly a myth as the young Yudhishthira then counsels the aged Nahusha and helps him attain liberation.

B.4.3. Myth: Yayati, the Needy

Yayati figures in two myths, the first being about his marriage to Devayani, the daughter of Shukra, the preceptor of the demons, and the second about cheating on his wife by making love to Sarmishta, the daughter of the king of the demons, punished to be Devayani's maidservant. Yayati had two sons with Devayani (Yadu and Turvasu) and three sons with Sarmishta (Druhyu, Anu, and Puru).

The second myth is the founding myth of the people of South Asia and the rest of the world. It begins when Yayati was granted a thousand years of youth by the gods. When he reached the end of that period and began to suffer from the debilities of old age, he found that he was still unsatisfied. He wanted a few more years of youth to satisfy his desires. He had an additional gift from the gods, he could extend his youth if he could find somebody to exchange their youth for his old age. Yayati asked, but nobody would give up their youth. Finally, he asked his own sons. Yadu, Druhyu, Turvasu, and Anu refused, with particularly harsh words from Anu.

Puru freely gave up his youth. After a few more years of extended youth, Yayati felt sorry for the son whom he had deprived of youth in this manner and gave Puru back his gift.

He then made Puru his heir and sent Puru's brothers to other parts of the world. The oldest, Yadu, remained behind to go to the south of Jambudvipa and became the ancestor of the Yadavas. Druhyu's descendants are the *Bhojas*, the clan that Kunti comes from (though the Bhojas also claimed descent from Yadu, and were one of the Yadava clans forced to migrate from the banks of the Sarasvati).The other brothers gave rise to other people, generally classified as Mlecchas, Yavanas, and so on.

B.4.4 Myth: Puru the Obedient

Puru gave up his youth to his father, Yayati, and in exchange became the dynast. His descendants, the Pauravas, settled on the banks of the Sarasvati and established the first cities of Panchnad.

B.4.5 Pauravas: From Puru to Bharata

This book reimagines the history of the Pauravas from Ilina, a descendant of Puru to Bharata. They developed the trade routes from Panchnad in all directions and made Panchnad a well-known trading culture.

Puru's descendant Ilina founded the city of Kaalindini (named after his mother Kaalindi, the matriarch) among the foothills of the Himalayas on the banks of the Sutudri (Sutlej). Kaalindini was on the trade route to the north into Kashyapura and points further north. Ilina developed long-distance trade to the north and to the south across the Western sea. Ilina's grandson, Bharata, began the first tentative moves towards the east, but he encountered dense forest populated by Nagas not used to long-distance trade. He pulled back and continued Ilina's work of creating a single integrated trade route from northern Gandhara and northern Vakshu (the land around the river Oxus) to the port of Tripura in the south and across to Dilmun. Tin, lapis lazuli, and cotton textiles became staple exports from the Sarasvati-Sindhu culture to the western world.

B.4.6 Bhaaratas: From Bharata to Kuru

This book reimagines the history of the efforts by Panchnad to trade with the Nagas to their east in the Gangetic plains.

Bharata and his descendants continued their attempts to trade with the Nagas. It was not until Hastin's reign that a trading center was established on the banks of the Ganga at a point where the river expanded and slowed down. They sold cotton textiles and felted cotton pieces in exchange for exotic animals and fruits. Occasionally, almost pure copper ore would turn up, and there was great excitement once when a small sample of almost twenty-five per cent pure tin ore was brought in. There was little explanation of how or where this was obtained nor of how much was available.

This trading center, managed by a head trader, was called Nagapura. It would grow to become the capital of a great empire, but it began as the outpost of a trading caravan.

The Naga polity had been changing during these years. "Rogue males" had always existed among the Nagas, but their inability to cooperate with each other meant that they lived lonely lives and died young. However, many generations before Hastin, a band of rogue males led by Takshaka had begun to threaten normal Naga life. To counteract Takshaka's band, a confederacy of the Nagas called Panchala had been formed. After much difficulty, Takshaka was defeated, his band dispersed, and he was killed. In the process, a settlement called Kampilya was established on the northern bank of the Ganga about 150 miles[94] south of Hastinapura. Kampilya functioned as a cantonment for a permanent standing army. Like the other Naga bands, Kampilya was ruled by a matriarchy, but it had a special status among the Nagas and continued as a training center for a permanent army. The confederacy also grew by absorbing more and more Naga bands within its protective umbrella.

Trade expanded slowly, and Nagapura grew in prosperity. By the time of Hastin's descendant, Samvarana, it had become the single biggest settlement on the Ganga. The Nagas around Nagapura had refused to join the confederacy. That made Panchala feel threatened. Panchala attacked Nagapura, and Samvarana was driven out. Samvarana did not retire to a Panchnad city. Instead, he started working on regaining control of Nagapura.

Meanwhile in Panchnad, a teacher named Vasishtha had been developing new ideas of governance. This was in response to the observation that the world outside Panchnad was different. Traders returned with stories of great wars, of fortified cities under siege, of drought and famine and mass migrations. It was all a bit too much for the ordinary Panchnadis to believe.

---

[94]One hundred and fifty miles is a critical span for many Bronze Age empires. A messenger walking twenty-five to thirty miles a day would take about a week to go from one end to the other of such an empire. (A riverboat could cut that time by two or three times at most when rowing with the current and a favorable wind.) This creates a two-week round-trip time for administrative actions in response to events, probably a limiting factor in managing such empires. Only after the arrival of the horse did larger empires become feasible, Mesopotamia being a good example.
For what it is worth, the distance from Kaalindini to Hastinapura was approximately 150 miles and so are the distances from Hastinapura to Kampilya, Hastinapura to Agra, Agra to Kanpur or Jhansi, Kanpur to Allahabad, and so on, all of these being ancient sites of settlement after the disappearance of the Sarasvati.

Samvarana proved to be an excellent pupil. Having suffered a loss to war, he could believe in Vasishtha. An army was organized with the help of Vasishtha's Kavi Sangha, with the help of the ex-mercenary Vishvamitra. The soldiers were all men, trained to fight and committed to the aims of the Kavi Sangha and to recovering Nagapura. After ten years in exile, Samvarana returned and found a demoralized Naga force defending Nagapura. Trade had dropped to nothing, the settlement was decrepit, and the surrounding Nagas no longer looked to Nagapura for luxuries obtained through trade. The Panchala army melted away, and Samvarana was back in power. The Kavi Sangha's and Vasishtha's reputation for wisdom soared.

After Samvarana returned to power, a steady, if small, stream of ores, mostly copper, but occasionally tin, would come by boat from the east. Tin, in particular, was extremely valuable, but there seemed to be no way to increase its supply. Samvarana's son Kuru took up the challenge to extend Nagapura's trading network to the east. Far to the east, he discovered a plateau south of the Ganga from which the river Hiranyaganga flowed. The ores came from the plateau. A small settlement called Laghu Nagapura was established. Laghu Nagapura was positioned to satisfy an increased demand for ores.

The Panchnadis encountered a new forest-dwelling culture of hunter-gatherers – the Rakshasas – whom they had only heard about until then. The Rakshasas were hostile to trade, and this hostility took many years, almost two generations, to overcome. In the meantime, Laghu Nagapura could only be used for shipping the ores out to Nagapura for smelting into bronze.

Kuru renamed Nagapura as Hastinapura after his ancestor who founded the settlement.

B.4.7. Kauravas: From Kuru to Pratipa

This book is the reimagined history of the Hastinapura trading settlement as it gained power over the local Naga inhabitants and the city's role changed from being only a trading center to being a hegemon.

The first few generations after Kuru were peaceful ones. Hastinapura grew in prosperity, but maintained its army because Panchala continued to be a threat. The presence of a standing army made Hastinapura the most powerful proto-state entity in its neighborhood, the effective hegemon over the surrounding Naga bands. The surrounding Nagas had also become integrated into the trading network. The biggest problem in moving away from the slash-and-burn agricultural way of life was the difficulty of agriculture on the heavy clayey soil of the Gangetic plain.

Many local Nagas found it simpler to switch to fishing as a source of livelihood, becoming Meena-Nagas. There were many differences as well as similarities to the old way of life. Settlements tended to be permanent. Building on stilts was expensive, and so old settlements were not abandoned. In addition, the river's ability to provide fish did not degrade as fishing continued, so frequent moving was not necessary. It was harder to spin off a new band. A new site had to be found, and it had to be located along the riverbank. There were fewer places available for sites.

The new way of life was a riskier way of life. It would be put to the test by the crisis.

B.4.8 Kauravas: From Pratipa to the War

This is the period of the crisis caused by the tectonic events and the resulting changes in the flow of major rivers.

The crisis broke out very early in Pratipa's time. His son Shantanu took the lead in trying to solve the problem. However, personal issues and weaknesses dominated the family. Shantanu's first wife died, leaving a son Devavrata. The story of Devavrata from an early age is the subject of Book 1 of this series.

Spoiler Alert: What follows is a summary of this book and a commentary on some aspects related to the crisis.

Wishing to marry again, Shantanu disinherited Devavrata to fulfil a promise to his second wife Satyavati. Shantanu had two sons with Satyavati. While Shantanu abandoned his duties in the pursuit of pleasure, Devavrata administered the state in consultation with the Kavi Sangha. Steps were taken to help the thousands of migrants, but the crisis grew in magnitude every year. Waterworks were constructed along the Ganga to provide water for agriculture. Land was set aside for new settlements. Disputes with the Nagas over land rights increased, and the Hastinapura military had to be deployed. The Nagas were not a combative culture. If two Naga bands came into conflict over land, it was usually easier for one or both to move. Therefore, the Nagas moved, and moved again. Lands they would have left fallow did not remain fallow but were occupied by migrants. Though Devavrata tried to be even-handed between Panchnad immigrants and Naga inhabitants, the Nagas were slowly pushed away by a growing circle of immigrant settlements centered on Hastinapura.

When Shantanu died, his son Chitrangada was crowned king but died childless. Chitrangada's brother Vichitravirya also died, leaving two sons, Dhritarashtra and Mahendra. The older son, Dhritarashtra, being blind, could not be crowned, so Mahendra became King. Mahendra was nicknamed *Pandu* (meaning "the Pale") and this name stuck. Dhritarashtra had many ("a hundred") sons. They were called the Kauravas to distinguish them from the sons of Mahendra Pandu, the five Pandavas. Suyodhana was the oldest Kaurava, and Yudhishthira was the oldest Pandava. Yudhishthira should have been crowned King, but in a compromise, the Pandavas left Hastinapura to rule half the kingdom from Indraprastha, a settlement originally founded by Mahendra Pandu. Suyodhana, the oldest Kaurava, was declared heir to his father Dhritarashtra, but he could not be crowned while his father lived. Nevertheless, he titled himself King while Devavrata continued as Regent.

In summary, after Shantanu's death, Devavrata was Regent for about four years. After Chitrangada's death, Devavrata was Regent for about six years. After Vichitravirya's death, Devavrata was Regent for sixteen years, the regency ending when Mahendra Pandu was crowned. After Mahendra Pandu went into exile, Devavrata acted in his stead, acting as Regent for over fifteen, possibly as long as twenty, years. This regency should have ended when the Pandavas returned and Yudhishthira crowned. The compromise that sent the Pandavas to Indraprastha averted conflict but did not resolve the succession dilemma. It allowed Devavrata to continue as Regent de facto until the end of the Great War.

B.4.9. The Great War: Pandavas and Kauravas

This story is dealt with in this series of Books.

B.4.10. Pandavas: From Arjuna to Janamejaya

This is also dealt with in this series of Books.

B.4.11. The Family Tree

The Kuru family tree is shown in the end of the book. It shows the chain of ancestors from the mythical era – Pururavas to Puru. Some of Puru's descendants, the Pauravas, are identified in the yellow box. The list only identifies the rulers whose actions are mentioned in this book and skips over many intervening rulers.

To the left is the "Vyaasa Chain" that names the sequence of Vyaasas, the head of the Kavi Sangha. The extent of a Vyaasa's role is approximately parallel to the Hastinapura ruler they were associated with. Vasishtha, for instance, is associated with Samvarana. Samvarana's ancestor Hastin founded the town of Nagapura, and Samvarana's son Kuru renames the town Hastinapura.

Kuru, a Paurava, i.e., a descendant of Puru, is considered the dynast for the Kauravas, his descendants. The label "Kaurava" denotes all the descendants of Kuru, referring to the sons of Mahendra Pandu as well as the sons of Dhritarashtra. However, in the most common usage, "Kaurava" denotes only the hundred sons of Dhritarashtra and "Pandava" denotes the five sons of Mahendra Pandu.

The crisis described in this book began towards the end of Arugvat's reign – a trickle of Panchnad refugees that slowly grew into a population problem in Shantanu's time. Shantanu's two wives (Ganga and Satyavati) are shown along with their children, including Satyavati's child with Parashara (who also appears in the Vyaasa list).

Kunti, the Bhoja Matriarch, who comes to live in Mahendra's settlement of Indraprastha, is shown with a dotted line back to her ancestor Druhyu, skipping many generations. Kunti does not have daughters. Her three sons grow up in Indraprastha with the twin sons of Madri. These five are, of course, the Pandavas, named after Pandu, the male head of the settlement.

Colored boxes surround the warring cousins, the Pandavas and the Kauravas. The five Pandavas are joint husbands of the Panchala Matriarch Krishnaa Agnijyotsna. She and her children are not shown. Arjuna is also husband to Subhadra, the daughter of Devaki, the Matriarch of the Vrishni clan, by Vasudeva, army chief for the Bhojas and brother of Kunti. That is, Arjuna and Subhadra were first cousins. Subhadra's ancestry from Yadu is also indicated by dotted lines.

Arjuna's son by Subhadra is Abhimanyu. He died young during the war. His son Parikshit is the only descendant of the Pandavas who survives the Great War. Following the patrilineal model of Hastinapura, Parikshit becomes the ruler of Hastinapura.

B.5. A Brief History of the Kavi Sangha

The Kavi Sangha is a completely invented organization. The names of its leaders (the Vyaasas) have been chosen to correspond with sages in Hindu mythology, but everything else is invented.

B.5.1 Vasishtha

The first Vyaasa was Vasishtha. Vasishtha was a bard. Bards had always been a key part of Panchnad society for they provided the memorization and archiving service that was used to manage the marketplace in the oral culture of those days. The demand for bards was growing and the guild of bards was not able to expand fast enough. Vasishtha established a school to teach these skills to any student, and the best graduates of the school were organized into the Kavi Sangha. When Panchala drove Samvarana out of Nagapura, he came to Panchnad looking for help. Vasishtha took him under his wing and trained him to be a warrior. He then helped the newly minted general to put together an army of men prepared to fight a real war, unlike the mercenaries of Panchnad. The martial arts teacher Vishvamitra was an ex-mercenary, but one with experience in the Western world, and knew about fighting such wars. Vishvamitra's unusual intellect had got the attention of Vasishtha, who made him a protégé.

The Kavi Sangha's role in restoring Samvarana to Nagapura greatly enhanced its prestige and Vasishtha's reputation for wisdom. After the restoration, the Kavi Sangha and its members, especially the Vyaasa, became much sought after and every Panchnad town invited them to participate in civic affairs at the highest level. Vasishtha was the head of both the guild of bards and the school, which he managed as a single operation. He received support to train more bards and in response, he increased the range and extent of the archives maintained by the guild, now merged into the Kavi Sangha.

Many Kavi Sangha members aspired to succeed Vasishtha in the role of Vyaasa. As Vasishtha grew older, the virus of patriarchy had begun to infect him and he wanted to make his son Shakti the next Vyaasa. Shakti had been born very late in Vasishtha's life and was still a child when his father died, and another Vyaasa, Vishvamitra, was selected.

B.5.2. Vishvamitra

Vishvamitra was the obvious next candidate, but many bards objected to him as he was not a bard but had been a mercenary. Vishvamitra had to prove his qualifications many times, but finally succeeded in obtaining universal approval. After Vishvamitra, Bhrigu became the Vyaasa.

B.5.3. Bhrigu

Bhrigu was a systemic institution builder. He established practices and precedents that made the Kavi Sangha a permanent institution in the life of Panchnad and Hastinapura. During this period, Hastinapura grew in power and established itself as a major trading center. After his death, Bharadvaja became the Vyaasa.

B.5.4 Bharadvaja

Bharadvaja was the Vyaasa when Pratipa was King and the crisis of refugees began.

The Yamuna and the Sutudri changed their course, the Yamuna going east and the Sutudri further west, and both were lost to the Sarasvati. A worldwide drought that lasted almost four hundred years coincided with the riverine changes. As a result, the Sarasvati also lost the other source of water and started drying up. Refugees streamed into Hastinapura. Hastinapura was overwhelmed, and Pratipa asked the Vyaasa Bharadvaja for help.

Bharadvaja was a pragmatist and realist who looked for rational solutions to all problems. The flood of refugees had caused hardship. There was not enough food to go around, and the Naga mode of production precluded ramping up food production rapidly. The Nagas could not be displaced easily, but their practice of leaving groves fallow for two generations made it possible to house the refugees there, even if the land was not productive. However, that was not enough, and the population had to be controlled. Already, babies were dying of starvation. Bharadvaja suggested the "one child per person" policy, that child preferably a son. A girl would contribute much more to population growth a generation hence than a boy could.

This law would apply to refugees in Hastinapura, creating a disincentive to settle in the city. Bharadvaja wanted to encourage the Panchnad refugees to go as far east as possible, well beyond Laghu Nagapura into Rakshasa land or beyond, or to go as far west as possible, to Bahlika or even Parsaka and lands beyond. He floated a proposal to work on diverting the Yamuna back into its old channel. This would be backbreaking and dangerous work, but it would restore the Sarasvati and allow the refugees to return to Panchnad. In order to encourage the refugees to participate in the diversion project, workers on this project would be exempted from the one-child-per-person policy. This concession aroused anger in the older residents of Hastinapura as it was seen to favor the immigrants.

The diversion project was given up and the one-child-per-person policy applied without exemption. Thus began the policy disputes that led to the Great War. Shantanu applied the policy to the whole population of Hastinapura in the spirit of equity, but the policy was only enforceable because Hastinapura had become a permanently militarized state.

Bharadvaja began to use the army to construct waterworks in areas deemed fit for settlement by immigrants. Conflicts with local Nagas were addressed quickly. As the land being expropriated was lying fallow, the Nagas frequently let the land go without a fight. Among Nagas, conflicts only occurred when two groups wanted to move to the same place at the same time. Such a coincidence was rare, and most often, the conflict was settled by one Naga band going somewhere else. The Nagas took the same approach towards Hastinapura. But the Hastinapura-supported settlements were permanent, and the Nagas were being slowly pushed out of the region. When conflict did become worse, the army dealt with the uncooperative Nagas harshly.

Bharadvaja died a few years after Shantanu's wife Ganga died. He was succeeded by Parashara.

B.5.5. Parashara

The Vyaasa title returned to Vasishtha's family when Parashara, son of Vasishtha's son Shakti, became the Vyaasa. Parashara was known as the "walking Vyaasa" for he walked everywhere. He had been asked by Bharadvaja to assess if the Nagas would tolerate being thrown off their land to make room for the immigrants. Parashara concluded that the Nagas would not tolerate it. In the course of his travels, he also encouraged many Nagas to join the Kavi Sangha, with the long-term goal of extending the Kavi Sangha to the Nagas. Parashara had hidden his involvement with Satyavati from the senior members of the Kavi Sangha. The affair was not a problem, but hiding it was, and he was sentenced to a vow of silence for a few years, even though he was the Vyaasa. During this period, Satyavati married Shantanu through Shukla's machinations.

Parashara died before the term of his punishment ended. He was followed by Jaimini.

B.5.6. Jaimini

Jaimini became Vyaasa a year or so before Chitrangada was born. He was the opposite of Bharadvaja. Where Bharadvaja had been practical and hard-nosed, Jaimini was compassionate and flexible. In particular, Jaimini objected to the use of the army to build the waterworks that helped settle immigrants and dispossess Nagas. But there seemed to be no alternative. An army was needed to keep Panchala at bay. The army had to be fed. The only way to feed it was to use it to increase food production or enforce laws that controlled the population. Some years after the death of Shantanu's first wife, the one-child-per-person policy was annulled. That left the army only one choice, increase food production by replacing Nagas with settlers.

Jaimini continued the recruitment of Nagas into the Kavi Sangha. As Devavrata expected, this made the process of settling immigrants a little harder, as Naga concerns were taken into account in each project. However, addressing these concerns reduced the conflict in the colonization of Naga lands.

Jaimini died a few years after Vichitravirya's death.

B.5.7. Shukla

Jaimini's successor was Shukla, the brother of Satyavati, and the first Naga to be named Vyaasa. He was the Vyaasa through the period of this novel. When he died, his nephew Krishna Dvaipaayana, son of Parashara by Satyavati, became the Vyaasa.

B.5.8. Krishna Dvaipaayana Paaraasharya

Krishna Dvaipaayana as Vyaasa worked with the Archivist Lomaharshana to create order out of the archives of the war years. He composed the *Jaya*, a poem about the war, and performed it at a Spring Festival at King Janamejaya's request.

The Archivist Lomaharshana (introduced in this book) followed Krishna Dvaipaayana as Vyaasa.

B.5.9. Lomaharshana

Lomaharshana made it his mission to spread the story of the Great War. He made its recital an annual event coinciding with the Spring Festival.

B.6. Neologisms

Terminology invented by the author.

B.6.1 Nishkamakarnarpana

The Kavi Sangha's bards and memorizers learned early in their education to enter a trance state in which they would listen without judgement and without attachment to what was being said. With practice and experience, the memorizer would learn to dispense with the trance state when listening, but the skill was available for use under unusual conditions. I have named this skill *niṣkāməkərṇārpəṇə* (pronounced "nish-calm-u(h)-cur-narp-un-u(h)", and spelled "nishkamakarnarpana"). The word means "paying attention without attachment."

B.6.2 Nishkamasmaranadharanam

The Kavi Sangha's bards and memorizers practiced a collection of mental exercises and practices to erase unneeded memories while retaining the important ones. These exercises and the skills developed were called *niṣkāməsmərəṇədhārəṇəm,* pronounced

Nish-calm-u(h)-smu(t)-runner-th(e)-ah-run-um, and spelled nishkamasmaranadharanam, "holding on to memory without attachment."

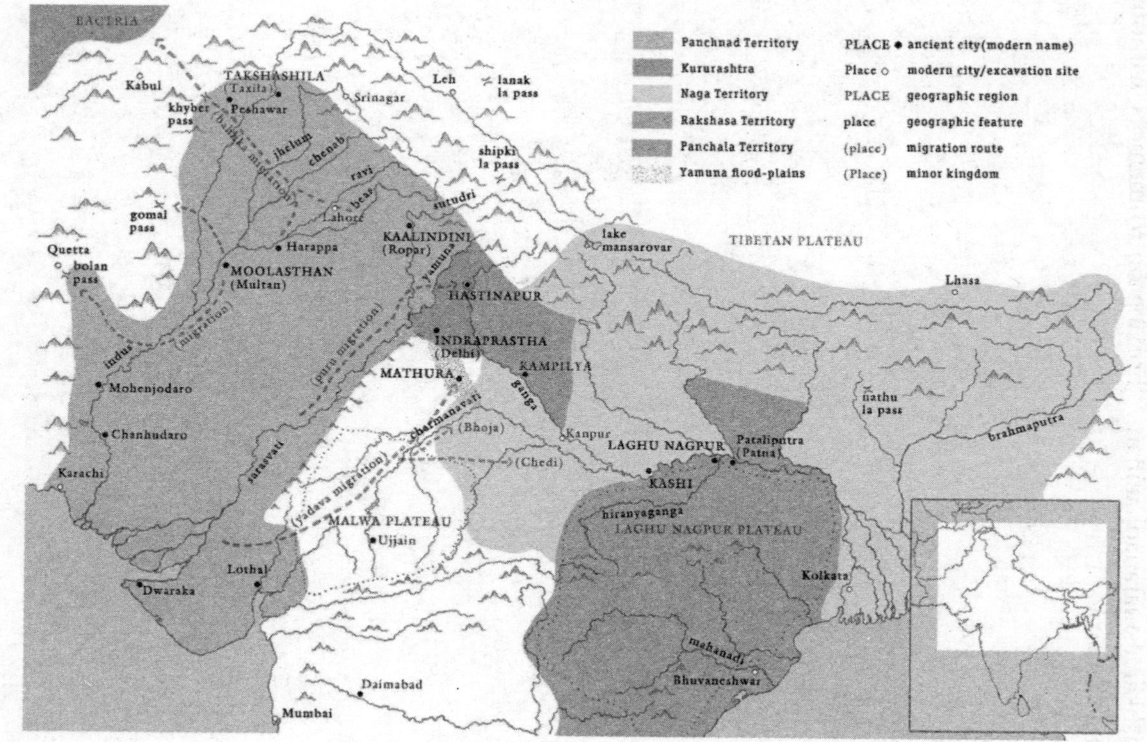

Panchnad Territory
Kururashtra
Naga Territory
Rakshasa Territory
Panchala Territory
Yamuna flood-plains
PLACE ● ancient city(modern name)
Place ○ modern city/excavation site
PLACE geographic region
place geographic feature
(place) migration route
(Place) minor kingdom
BACTRIA
Kabul
TAKSHASHILA (Taxila)
Peshawar
khyber pass
Srinagar
Leh
lanak la pass
shipki la pass
jhelum
chenab
ravi
beas
sutudri
Lahore
gomal pass
Quetta
bolan pass
Harappa
KAALINDINI (Ropar)
MOOLASTHAN (Multan)
yamuna
HASTINAPUR
INDRAPRASTHA (Delhi)
KAMPILYA
MATHURA
ganga
(migration)
(puru migration)
indus
Mohenjodaro
Chanhudaro
Karachi
sarasvati
charmanavati
(Bhoja)
(Chedi)
(yadava migration)
MALWA PLATEAU
Ujjain
Lothal
Dwaraka
Daimabad
Mumbai
lake mansarovar
TIBETAN PLATEAU
Lhasa
nathu la pass
brahmaputra
Kanpur
LAGHU NAGPUR
Pataliputra (Patna)
KASHI
hiranyaganga
LAGHU NAGPUR PLATEAU
Kolkata
mahanadi
Bhuvaneshwar

B.7. Geography, Politics, and History

A map of Panchnad and Northern South Asia is shown in the front of this book. It shows the geopolitical situation in 2000 BCE (the time of the events in this book). The following conventions have been followed:

- Regions occupied by different groups and/or cultures are shown as shaded areas.
- The Laghu Nagapura and Malwa plateaus are demarcated using a dotted line.
- Cities and regions mentioned in this book are labelled in uppercase.
- Some modern cities are marked to help readers orient themselves. These names are in lowercase with initial capital. The label is placed within parentheses if an ancient town, village, or city was close by.
- Rivers' names are in all lowercase and are placed alongside the river.
- A number of cities outside South Asia are also indicated.
- Some of the major passes (Khyber, Gomal, and Bolan passes in the west, the Lanak-La and the Shipki-La passes in the north, and the Nathu-La in the northeast) are shown. They were major routes into South Asia for both trade and human migration.
- Lake Mansarovar in Tibet is shown. It is generally held to be the source of the four great rivers of North India (the Sindhu (Indus), the Ganga, the Yamuna, and the Brahmaputra) and is a place of pilgrimage for both Hindus and Buddhists. A number of other great rivers of China, Myanmar, and Indochina also have their watersheds within a short distance of this lake.
- At bottom left, Mumbai and Daimabad are shown. Daimabad's claim to fame is that it is the southern-most point of the sub-continent where "Bronze Age" Sarasvati Sindhu Culture artefacts have been found.

B.7.1. Nagas and Rakshasas

The map shows a light brown region to the north and east, extending from Lake Mansarovar in the west to the eastern end of the Brahmaputra (Tsang-po) river and incorporating the delta of the Ganga and Brahmaputra. This area was heavily forested and sparsely populated by the Nagas who were slash-and-burn agriculturalists. They had migrated here from the north (Tibet) and east (China and Indochina through Myanmar) many thousands of years earlier and spread over the Gangetic plain.

The region colored reddish-brown contains the Laghu Nagapura (now called Chota Nagpur) plateau and extends south into the South Asian peninsula. This region, too, was heavily forested and sparsely populated by the hunter-gathering culture Rakshasas (the name the Nagas used for them). The Rakshasas were descended from the earliest human migrants out of Africa (~60,000 BCE) who had left bands in settlements along the shores of the Deccan peninsula (probably 40,000 BCE to 20,000 BCE. These bands had slowly expanded into the plateau and up north into Laghu Nagapura where they may have first encountered the Nagas. The Nagas initially responded by retreating. They avoided conflict, and the land seemed unlimited. As a result, the Rakshasas had come down from the Laghu Nagapura plateau, crossed the Ganga, and occupied land all the way to the Himalayas. Meanwhile the Nagas, who had discovered that land was not limitless, began to resist, leading to the situation shown in the map.

The Rakshasas in Laghu Nagapura had developed significant mining and copper smelting skills.

B.7.2 Panchnad

Panchnad is the brown region to the west on the map, extending from the Sarasvati in the east to the Western Himalayan foothills in the west and from the northern Himalayan foothills to the Western Sea (now called the Arabian Sea) to the south.

The city of Kaalindini (near the modern town of Ropar or Rupnagar) in northwest Panchnad is located on the banks of the Sutudri ("'Hundred rivulets'"), as it leaves the Himalayas. Before the crisis brought on by the earthquake, the Sutudri drained to the south. The land being a very flat alluvial plain, the Sutudri split into a multitude of streams (hence the name). The crisis changed the Sutudri into the modern Sutlej, which turns west at Kaalindini/Ropar (and is not shown in this map). The map shows the approximate ancient course of the Sutudri as it heads south.

Before the crisis, the Sutudri merged with the Yamuna to form the Sarasvati. Tectonic events, i.e. earthquakes, changed the course of the Yamuna as described. It turned east at the northern ridge of the Aravalli range. As a result, the Sarasvati lost its two primary sources of water from the Himalayas. It did not dry up immediately as a third monsoon-fed river, the Drishadvati (not shown here), came from the Aravalli range to join the Sarasvati.

B.7.3. Kururashtra

The Yamuna (in its old course) formed the northeast boundary of Panchnad. The river Ganga flows parallel to the Yamuna. The town of Hastinapura (begun as the trading center Nagapura) was founded on the western bank of the Ganga. Hastinapura controlled the land between the Yamuna and the Ganga all the way to the northern foothills. To the south, Hastinapura's control extended just past the Aravalli ridge into a scrub forest that was called Khandavaprastha. The Hastinapura-controlled area called Kururashtra is shown in pink.

B.7.4. Panchala

The eastern bank of the Ganga was under the control of Panchala, a confederation of five Naga clans that considered Hastinapura a dangerous foreign interloper. Panchala, shown in purple, was managed from the military cantonment of Kampilya. It extended along the northern foothills of the Himalayas past Hastinapura to the point where the Ganga emerged from the mountains.

B.7.5. Migrations out of Panchnad

The map shows the routes that the refugees leaving Panchnad followed. To the northwest, they went through the major passes towards the Afghanistan plateau. From the northern settlements on the Sarasvati, the refugees went towards Hastinapura. From the southern end of the Sarasvati, the refugees, who called themselves Yadavas, went east past the southern end of the Aravalli range and into the Malwa plateau (shown in white). From the Malwa plateau, the Yadavas split into four branches: The Andhakas stayed in Malwa. The Chedis went east towards Kashi. The Bhojas went along the Charmanavati River gorge and tried to settle the region between the rivers Charmanavati and the Betwah. The Vrishnis headed north and tried to create settlements on the banks of the re-directed Yamuna.

The Chedis and Bhojas came into conflict with the Nagas on their territory. The Chedis responded by allying with Rakshasas. The Bhojas retreated to Malwa after many failed attempts to establish settlements. The Vrishnis were lucky. The instability of the Yamuna meant that neither they nor the local Nagas had much to fight over right away. But that same instability frustrated the Vrishnis' wish to create their urban center Mathura.

The Vrishnis followed a different model for settlement. Led by their army chief Gopala Krishna (son of the matriarch Devaki by her husband the Bhoja army chief Vasudeva), they tried to create alliances with all the local powers – Hastinapura in the north, Panchala on the other side of the Ganga, and the Meena-Nagas who had migrated up the Yamuna streams. But that caused rifts with their cousins the Bhojas and Chedis.

B.7.6. Prehistory

This map does not show the other ancient migrations that led to the tripartite division of South Asia between the urban civilization of Panchnad, the hunter-gatherer Rakshasas, and the slash-and-burn Nagas. This division had come into being well before the time of the Sarasvati disaster.

B.8. JAMBUDVIPA

The traditional name for all of South Asia is *Jambudvipa,* the Island of the Jambul. Unfortunately, South Asia is not an island, and there is some debate over the identity of the Jambul fruit.

B.8.1 The Jambul

Wikipedia describes two different "Jambul" fruits. One is a purple berry, tart and sweet (*Syzygium cumini*[95]), that grows at higher

[95] See http://en.wikipedia.org/wiki/Syzygium_cumini

elevations all over India. The other is a pear-shaped but smaller fruit (*Syzygium samarangense*[96]) with a melon-y pulp ranging in color from white to red that grows all over South Asia and South East Asia. The Wikipedia reference calls both of them "Jambul", but it also calls the latter the "rose apple". It seems that the rose apple may be called "Jambul" in some parts of South East Asia as well. However, Indians asked to describe the "jambul", will describe the berry. To add to the confusion, the jambul berry is called "naga pazhum" in Tamil, i.e., "snake fruit", or "fruit of the Nagas".

So, is "Jambudvipa" the "Island of the Rose-Apple" or is it the "Island of the Purple Berry" or "Island of the Snake Fruit"? It is unclear to me why most Western authorities in Indian mythology prefer one meaning ("rose-apple") over the other. The Tamil name conjures the possibility that the name Jambudvipa acknowledges the original possession of the land by Nagas.

B.8.2. The Island

A Kashmiri legend says that in the center of Kashmir was a great lake with an island paradise in the middle. When the Earth was kidnapped by the demon Hiranyaksha and hidden in the depths of the Sea of Milk, Vishnu, incarnated as a boar, killed Hiranyaksha and retrieved the earth from the milky depths by carrying it on the tip of his tusk. The tip of the tusk punctured the edge of the great Kashmiri lake at a place called Varahamoola, which drained the lake and created the land of Kashmir. Varahamoola is now identified as Baramulla.

I have 'extended' the Kashmir myth to cover all of South Asia: A hypothetical Panchnad myth identifies South Asia as that central island and the draining of the lake with the emergence

[96]See http://en.wikipedia.org/wiki/Syzygium_samarangense

of the subcontinent of South Asia (then called Jambudvipa) from the drained lake.

There are problems with this unification as an interpretation of the myth (as with other interpretations). Jambudvipa is clearly not an island, so some people believe that it refers to all of Asia or Eurasia. Others believe it refers to Asia, Europe, and Africa as a single landmass. And then (a deep breath is called for here) there are people who believe that this name is a residual race memory of ancient Gondwanaland, from a time when India, Africa, Antarctica, and Australia formed one island, a mere one hundred and eighty million years ago. This is, of course, conclusively proved by its name, which translates as *Land of the Forest-Garden of the Gonds.*

B.9. Geography of the Western World

B.9.1. Egypt

B.9.1.1. Names

From the Wikipedia entry for "Egypt":

> The English name *Egypt* is derived from the ancient Greek *Aígyptos* (*Aἴγυπτος*), via Middle French *Egypte* and Latin *Aegyptus*. It is reflected in early Greek Linear B tablets as *a-ku-pi-ti-yo*. The Greek forms were borrowed from Late Egyptian (Amarna) "*Hikuptah* of Memphis", a corruption of the earlier Egyptian name *Hwt-ka-Ptah*, meaning "home of the KA (soul) of Ptah", the name of a temple to the god Ptah at Memphis.

The god Ptah was considered an ancestor of all Egyptians. One variation of the name of Ptah's temple was "Home of the Temple of the Ancestor." In Sanskrit, this would be *Pitr-vihara* ("temple of the ancestors"). Adding "*naadu*" ("land" from vernacular languages) as a suffix to make *Pitr-vihara-naadu* might be a culturally appropriate way to refer to Egypt.

Other names of Egypt include "The Black Land," "The Red Land," and "The Land of the Black River." The word "black" or "red" refers to the color of the silt that the Nile carries and deposits on the land after floods. This soil is responsible for the extraordinary fertility of the land bordering the Nile, converting a desert into one of the most productive agricultural lands in the world. The ancient Egyptians also referred to themselves as the "black" or "red" people.

The "Black River" is the Nile and it would be translated to "Krishna" in Sanskrit.

B.9.1.2. Egypt: Places, Gods, and People

Osiris (the Greek pronunciation of "Au-ser") is the great god of the ancient Egyptian religion. Indian interpreters of Egyptian religion have made much of the similarity between "Au-ser" and "Eashwar" (as the great god Shiva is known in Hinduism). There are many similarities. Au-sera could mean "the great prince or lord" and Eashwar means "lord". Au-ser could mean "the receiver of ritual offerings," while "-eashwar" as a suffix could mean the one who has the right to a sacrifice (or ritual offerings). There is no known link between the two names, but they are ancient names in two civilizations that traded with each other.

Egyptian history mentions a people called "Punit" or "Punt" from before 1500 BCE who traded with Egypt, but came from an unknown homeland to the "east". Around 1500 BCE, the

Queen-Pharaoh Hatsepshut sent an expedition to Punt with a guide. They came back with stories that could have been from eastern Somalia, but could also describe the land around Kerala in India. Later Egyptian chronicles mention the attack of the "Sea People," who are said to be related to the people of Punt. The Sea People, also called Panit by the Egyptians, came to dominate trade on the Mediterranean Sea and were called Phoenicians by the Greeks. I've called them the "Western Panias", the "Pani-s" or "Bani-s" being the traders of ancient India, forerunners of the Banias in later times.

B.9.1.3. Egypt: From Matriarchy to Patriarchy

Egypt's transition from matriarchy to patriarchy took place in many ways. One example of a transitional structure is the inheritance model of the Pharaohs of Egypt, which was followed for almost four thousand years. The successor to a Pharaoh would be his son who was a *stepson* of the Great Queen (the senior-most wife of the Pharaoh). The son had to marry the Great Queen's *daughter* (not stepdaughter) to establish his legitimacy, and she would become the next Great Queen. (This is the source of the claim that Pharaohs of Egypt married their own sisters; they married a stepsister to establish their right to the throne. In practice, the system was frequently abused as some Pharaohs, once established in power, would marry other women, declare one of them the Great Queen, and usurp the half-sister's title.

One collateral effect of this mode of inheriting power was that any other sisters of a Great Queen would be barred from marrying *anybody*. In the few cases they were married, it was to men incapable of being a Pharaoh. In many cases, these sisters died of unknown causes, possibly murdered by their brother to forestall a husband from challenging the Pharaoh's fitness to rule (as *any* daughter of a Great Queen could lay claim to be her successor as the Great Queen).

B.9.2 Rivers

The land of the Shakas (said to be descendants of Druhyu, a son of Yayati) was called Scythia by the Greeks. North of Scythia, the Danavas (the children of Danu, one of the wives of the Sage Kashyapa) were said to occupy Siberia and Eastern Europe, through which some of the greatest rivers of the world flow, though they are frozen for several months of the year. Many of these rivers were not known in India, though by coincidence a number of great rivers have names beginning with "D-n". Some river names from Iran to Mesopotamia are easily translated into the Sanskrit names used in this book. The Euphrates ("Well fertilized" in Greek) becomes the Su-purna ("Fulfilling well" or "Completing well"); the Tigris ("Swift" in Greek) becomes the Sindhu-of-the-west.

All the rivers to the east of India that came out of Tibet are given names that are a variant of "Ganga." The Bo Ganga is Tsang-po or Brahmaputra or Lauhitya (Lohita's child). The Shia (Xia) Ganga is the Yang-tze. The Ho Ganga is the Huang-Ho. The Hme Ganga is the Mekong. The Naga Ganga is the Irrawady (also mother of the Great Naga Airavatha). The rivers that flow west are fast rivers and are called Sindhu. The rivers to the northwest were known but do not appear in this book. The Syr Darya was called *Yaksh-arta*, which means the *Pure Pearl* in Persian, which is close to *Laksha-Rta* in Sanskrit, the Greek name being *Jaxartes*. The Amu Darya, was *Vakshu*, possibly meaning "good or beneficent river", the Greek name being Oxus.

B.9.3. Names of Countries

Afghanistan is part of the South Asian cultural landscape, but is difficult to reach, so its cultural connections with mainland India were intermittent and driven by trade. Gandhara (Kandahar in modern Afghanistan) had the closest relationships. Further north, Shantanu's brother Bahlika is said to have settled in Bactria (the Greek form of Bahlika). The similarity of the names "Bahlika" and "Baluchistan" could be mere coincidence, but note that Brahui, spoken only in Baluchistan, is one of the oldest Dravidian languages known. Bactria forms part of the Vakshu (Sanskrit name for the Oxus) civilization, also called the Bactrian-Margiana Archaeological Complex (BMAC). BMAC was an extended civilization of fortified towns contemporary to Harappa and Mohenjodaro. The design of the settlements of BMAC could arguably be a response to the hostile conditions under which Bahlika left Panchnad.

B.9.4. The Khyber Pass

The name Khyber is supposed to be derived from the Semitic/ Hebrew word for "fort". There is no other name used by the West. Unfortunately, I have not been able to find a Sanskrit word for the pass. A plausible derivation is that the word "Khyber" is a translation of the name used by the residents. This would be "kuta" meaning fort (among other meanings). Kubera is the god of wealth in the Hindu pantheon. The Khyber was a pathway to wealth for traders going west and for raiders coming south. Hence the name "Kuberakuta", i.e., Kubera's Fort. The translation in a Semitic language to "Kubera's Khyber" is a bit strange because it sounds like "Fort's Fort", and it was simplified to "Fort", i.e. Khyber, by the Westerners.

B.10. FATHERHOOD

The reader of this book may consider incredible my assertion that the ancient culture of South Asia did not understand the connection between sexual intercourse and fatherhood and did not understand how the baby developed, how it inherited the characteristics of the father, and so on.

This claim is not limited to South Asia, but is generally true for many, if not all, Bronze-Age cultures. The evidence for my claim can be found in various stories and rules found in religious myths, scriptural documents, and other ancient writings. An example of such a story is Jacob tricking his father-in-laworah. An Torah. An example of such a rule is Manu's rule, "Any child born in the 'field' owned by a man is his."

When I discuss this, I have found many listeners unwilling to listen carefully and jumping to conclusions about what I am saying or not saying. Their view is that we know the following:

1. A single act of intercourse, about nine months earlier, makes the woman pregnant
2. That a child has exactly one father and cannot have zero or multiple fathers
3. One and only one of the sole father's sperm cells fertilized a single egg/ovum of the mother
4. That the child inherits characteristics from the mother through the egg
5. The child inherits characteristics of the sole father from the single sperm cell.

Multiple births are a bit more complex and raise other possibilities than single births – we still do not know all the different possibilities that can occur. So the following observation is limited to single births.

To many people it is incomprehensible that three propositions listed above are not known to humans "naturally", i.e., without any kind of experimental or other verification. People want to believe, apparently, that we are all born with this knowledge and that fathers know who their children are by some non-conscious and non-deliberate chemical or alchemical process.

There is no question about motherhood as the mother's role in creating the child is very obvious.

My claim is that observation #1 above is not innate to humans but had to be discovered by some empirical observations. The observations became possible when humans domesticated animals, specifically the dog, which has a short gestation period. This still does not establish the knowledge of #2, #3, #4, and #5. If the mother had sexual relations with more than one man in the critical period (just before the first missed menstrual period) then maybe the child has multiple fathers. The seminal fluid is the visible product of the man that enters the woman and is the "obvious" source of the foetus. The knowledge of spermatozoa requires the invention of microscopes. It is "obvious" that the mother's characteristics are inherited because the foetus grows in the woman's womb. This leaves us with the conundrum of #5 – how does the baby inherit the characteristics of the father? It has to be more than just the seminal fluid because then a woman who had multiple sexual relationships would give birth to children with the characteristics of many fathers – not a usual occurrence.

The environment is an "obvious" choice, as exemplified by the story of Jacob in the Torah. In that case, the father can also influence the child by being part of the environment.

One feature of #1 – it is based on empirical data collected by women! The knowledge that a period has been missed following a sexual act would not automatically be conveyed to a male observer. I propose that this requires a settled or partially settled community, not a frequently moving nomadic band. In such a band a minimum number of men are needed for hunting and for protection from other predators. An excess of men creates instability and cannot be tolerated as men are expensive toys!

C. Glossary

Name of Person or Place/ Pronunciation GuideWW	Definition of Word and Description of Person or Place
Amba / (H)um-ba(h)	Member of Naga band; goes to Hastinapura; escapes
Angavastram/(H)ung-gov-us-trum(p)	Upper cloth or covering; covers the torso and shoulders
Arjuna/Urge-june-u(h)	Son of Kunti and Mahendra Pandu; third Pandava
Bahlika/Bah-lick-u(h)	Shantanu's brother who abdicates and migrates to Bactria or Baluchistan
Bakakula/Buck-ark-cool-u(h)	Name ('Family of Baka') of Shantanu's driver
Bharadvaja/Burr-oth(er)-va(st)-ju(st)	One of the Vyaasas
Bharata/Burr-rut-u(p)	Ancestor of Samvarana; in legend the first king to unify all of Bhaaratavarsha (eponymous "land of Bharata")
Bhima/Beam-u(p)	Son of Kunti; the second Pandava
Bhishma/Bee-schmu(ck)	'The Terrible', a title attached to Devavrata's name
Charmanavati /Chur(l)-mon(day)-(c)arver-thi(ef)	River; now called the Chambal

Name of Person or Place/ Pronunciation GuideWW	Definition of Word and Description of Person or Place
Chitrangada/Chit-ra-(su)ng-othe(r)	Son of Satyavati and Shantanu; rumored to have been killed in a battle with a Gandharva
Devapi/They've-up-pea	Shantanu's brother who walks off into the forest
Devavrata/They've-of-(b) rothe(r)	Son of Ganga and Shantanu; earns the name "The Terrible" (Bhishma)
Dhritarashtra/Thee-ri-the-ra-sh(h)-tru(ck)	Son of Ambika and Vichitravirya; blind at birth; father of Suyodhana and his brothers, the Kauravas
Drona/Thee-row-nu(t)	Possibly pejorative name for Kutaja, the martial arts instructor of the Kaurava and Pandava cousins and others
Duryodhana/Thee-ree(d)-yo-the-nu(t)	Bad Warrior; pejorative name of Suyodhana
Dvaipaayana/Thee-why-pa-yen-nu(t)	'Born on an island', Krishna Dvaipaayana is the son of Satyavati and Parashara
Dvapara Yuga/Thee-va(st)-purr-u(h) You-gu(t)	The third of the four Ages of mankind
Gana/Gun-nu(t)	The masses; the people at the bottom of the social hierarchy
Ganapathi/Gun-nup(tial)-per-thie(f)	Lord of the Gana(s); also a god in later times; patron god of Hastinapura, who removes obstacles to trade and business

Name of Person or Place/ Pronunciation GuideWW	Definition of Word and Description of Person or Place
Ganesha/Gun-hey-shhh	Another name for Ganapathi; meaning "Lord or God of the masses"
Ganga/Gun-ga(h)	Devavrata's mother; also, the river called the "Ganges" by the ancient Greeks and modern Englishmen
Hastinapura/Hus(h)-tea-na(h)-poo(h)-ru(m)	A trading post established just beyond the frontiers of Panchnad on the banks of the Ganga, in Naga territory; also called Nagapura as it was built with Naga help
Himavat/Him-marve(l)-th(ief)	"White Mountain Range," the Himalayas
Hiranyaganga/Here-un(do)-near-gun-gu(t)	A tributary of the Ganga coming from Chota Nagpur; now called the Sone
Indraprastha/In-the-ra-pr(op)-us-thu(d)	Settlement founded by Mahendra Pandu; capital of the Pandava kingdom before the war
Jambudvipa/Jum(p)-boo-the-vee-pu(n)	The Island of the Jambul Tree
Jaya/Ju(mp)-yea(rn)	"Victory;" also a victory lay; when capitalized, as in "Jaya", it is a lay of the Great War that is the central story of this novel
Kaalindini/Kaa-lindy-nee	Panchnad settlement in the Himalayan foothills closest to the point where the Sutudri emerged from the mountains; possibly, the town of Ropar/Rupnagar (though "kalindi"'s meaning "from the Yamuna" makes this dubious)

Name of Person or Place/ Pronunciation GuideWW	Definition of Word and Description of Person or Place
Kali Yuga/Cull-ea(se) You-gu(t)	Fourth age of humanity, supposed to be in the future for Panchnad
Kampilya / Come-pill-yea(rn)	The capital of Panchala
Karna / Cur-nu(h)	Friend, supporter, and provocateur to Suyodhana
Kaunteya / Coun(t)-The(odore)-yeah	Descendant of Kunti, generally used for Yudhishthira, Bhima, and Arjuna, the three oldest Pandavas
Kaurava / Cow-ru(n)-ver(se)	Descendent of Kuru
Kaushambi / Cow-sharm[||calm]-bee	Site occupied by the citizens of Hastinapura escaping the floods of 850 BCE
Kavi Sangha/Cu(r)-vee Sung-gu(t)	Means 'Society of Poets'; established by Vasishtha to fulfil his plan to prevent Panchnad from possible stagnation
Khandavaprastha/Khan-dove-up-russ-thu(d)	Land to the southwest of Hastinapura, suddenly inundated with the waters of the Yamuna when it changes course; over a century, Khandavaprastha changes from scrubland to green and fertile forest, setting the stage for conflict
Krishna Dvaipaayana/Cree-shhh-nu(t) Thee-why-pa-yen-nu(t)	Krishna Dvaipaayana is the son of Satyavati and Parashara, Krishna meas "“blck”'
Krishna Vaasudeva/Cree-shhh-nu(t) Vas(t)-sue-they've-u(p)	Leader of Yadavas who supports the Pandavas' claim to half of Hastinapura's land

Name of Person or Place/ Pronunciation GuideWW	Definition of Word and Description of Person or Place
Kuru/Coo-roo	Dynast of the family ruling Hastinapura; changes name of Nagapura to Hastinapura; establishes Laghu Nagapura; establishes riverine trade between Laghu Nagapura and Hastinapura
Kutaja/Coo-touch-u(p)	'Mountain peak' or 'jar'; may have been original name for the martial arts teacher of the cousins
Lomaharshana/Low-mu(ss)-her-shun-nu(t)	Storyteller who makes hair bristle or stand on end; Kavi Sangha Archivist in the Pandava camp
Mahanadi/Mu(ss)-ha-knee-thee	'Great River', so named by the Rakshasas; goes east from Chota Nagpur plateau to the Bay of Bengal
Matsya/Mu(tt)-th(ud)-sir-yeah	Panchnad name for Meena Naga clan
Mayura/Mu(tt)-you-ru(t)	Peacock; totem of Yadava clan
Meena/Me-nu(t)	Naga clan
Meru/May-roo	Mythical mountain; the home of the gods; often located in the Pamirs of Tajikistan
Moolasthan/Moo-lus(trate)-sthan	Panchnad–Gandhara settlement near Bolan pass and Gomal pass that enter modern-day Afghanistan; one of the oldest urban settlements known in the Sarasvati Sindhu Cultur.

Name of Person or Place/ Pronunciation GuideWW	Definition of Word and Description of Person or Place
Naga/Na(h)-gu(t)	Forest-dwellers occupying most of the Gangetic plain except towards the east, where Rakshasas lived; organized as matriarchal bands with a male war-chief; slash-and-burn agriculturalists
Nagapura/Na(h)-gu(t)-poo(h)-ru(t)	"The City of the Naga"; later renamed Hastinapura by Kuru after his father
Nagaraja/Na(h)-gu(t)-ra-ju(t)	Chief or ruler of a Naga clan
Nishkamakarnarpana/Niche-calm-u(h)-cur-nu(ptial)-pun-nu(t)	'Focused listening' practices taught by the Kavi Sangha
Nishkamasmaranadharanam/ Niche-calm-u(h)-smur(f)-run-u(h)- thar-run-(dr)um	'Memory management" practices taught by the Kavi Sangha
Panchagacham/Punch-ugh-(m) uch-(dr)um	Lower cloth or covering; covers the body below the waist; predecessor of today's "dhoti" or "veshthi"
Panchala/Punch-ah-lu(ck)	Naga confederation of five clans controlling the land north of the Ganga up to the foothills of the Himalayas
Panchali/Punch-ah-lea(d)	Title of Matriarch of Panchala; the Matriarch Agnijyotsna whose consorts are the five Pandavas
Panchnad/Punch-na(h)-d	Land between Sindhu and Sarasvati rivers; center of modern-day Pakistan; home to more than two thousand settlements from the Bronze Age (3000 BCE to 1500 BCE)

Name of Person or Place/ Pronunciation GuideWW	**Definition of Word and Description of Person or Place**
Pandava/Pa-(u)nder-vu(h)	Descended from Pandu
Pandu/Pa-(u)ndo	Named Mahendra at birth but called Pandu because he was very pale (albino); considered the father *de ju*re of the five Pandavas
Parashara/Per-harsher-u(h)	One of the Vyaasas; father of Krishna Dvaipaayana
Paurava/Pow-ru(t)-vu(h)	Descendant of Puru; describes people of Northern Panchnad and settlers of Hastinapura
Pitr-vihara-naadu/Pit-r-we-har(sh)-un(do)-na(h)-du()	Land of the Temple of Ancestors; Egypt
Pratipa/Pru(ssian)-tea-pa(h)	Father of Shantanu; the name means Rebel or adversary;
Puru/Poo-roo	Ancestor of Kuru; Yayati's youngest son; gives up one year of his youth to his father Yayati; becomes the heir
Raishyava/Wry-she-eve(r)	Unicorn; one of the iconic totems of the Sarasvati-Sindhu Culture, portrayed on many seals
Rakshasa/Ruck-sus(tain)-si(r)	Hunter gatherers; "Defender" in the Naga language; name given by the Nagas to the hunter-gathering tribes who dwelt in the forest to the east of modern-day Patna
Samavedin/Sa(ga)-mu(d)-way-din	A Kavi Sangha bard specially trained to keep time; the "chronometers" of Panchnad
Samvarana/Some-vu(h)-runner	Driven out of Hastinapura by Panchala; returns under Vasishtha's guidance; establishes a standing army

Name of Person or Place/ Pronunciation GuideWW	Definition of Word and Description of Person or Place
Sanjaya / Sun-ju(t)-yu(m)	Guru and advisor to Dhritarashtra
Sarasvati/Sir-russ-vu(h)-tea	Hidden river of Hindu mythology; river bordering Panchnad on the east; dried up when it lost the snow-melt from the Yamuna (before the events in this book)
Sashidhara / Su(m)-she-the-ru(n)	Name of Shantanu's Chief Minister or Advisor
Satyavati/Su(m)-tea-yeah-vu(h)-tea	Naga wife of Shantanu; has two sons Chitrangada and Vichitravirya; co-Regent with Devavrata; politically ambitious and capable
Shani / Shun-ea(se)	The god of destiny; traditionally associated with the planet Saturn in Indian astrology
Shaka / Shucke(r)	Scythian
Shantanu / Sha(rp)-(hu)nter-noo(se)	King of Hastinapura; husband of Ganga; father of Devavrata, Chitrangada and Vichitravirya
Shikhandin / Chic-und(id)-in	Pandava spy who leads Devavrata into an ambush; killed by Devavrata
Shukla / Shook-lu(g)	Brother of Satyavati; the Vyaasa at the time of the Great War
Sindhu / Sin-do	Ancient local name for the river Indus (which is the name given by the Greeks)
Sutudri / So(me)-(s)tood-ree(l)	Ancient name of the River Sutlej; Himalayan river that used to flow south to the Sarasvati; changed direction near the town of Kaalindini (Ropar) to flow west and is a tributary of the Sindhu (Indus)

Name of Person or Place/ Pronunciation GuideWW	Definition of Word and Description of Person or Place
Suyodhana / Sue-yo-the-nu(t)	Also called Duryodhana; mortal enemy of Pandavas; son of Dhritarashtra; leader of the Kauravas
Takshashila / Thuck-shush-ill-a(hh)	One of the oldest settlements in the world; center of learning established by Vasishtha
Vaishampaayana / Why-shum-pa-yen-u(h)	Vyaasa in 850 BCE; charged with writing the archives of Hastinapura
Bisaj	Medical practitioner of ancient Indian medical system
Varahamoola / whirr-aha-moo-lu(st)	From Vishnu's incarnation as a Boar, this refers to the tip of the Boar's tusk that held the Earth at this point; ancient name of the modern town of Baramulla in Kashmir
Varanavata / Whirr-runner-vu(h)-tu(b)	A town west of Hastinapura on the northern bank of the Yamuna river; founded by Devavrata
Vasishtha / (L/W)ush-ish-ta(h)	The first Vyaasa and head of the Kavi Sangha, created by merging the guilds of bards, poets, and archivists
Vichitravirya / We-chit-ru(n)-vee-riya	Son of Shantanu by Satyavati; marries Ambika and Ambalika; uninterested King; dies young
Vidura / We-do-ru(t)	"The Wise;" half-brother of Mahendra Pandu and Dhritarashtra; born of a maidservant, therefore not a citizen but a commoner; named "Dharmateja" at birth; considered both learned and street-smart

Name of Person or Place/ Pronunciation GuideWW	Definition of Word and Description of Person or Place
Vyaasa / We-yeah-sir(ilst)	Title of the Head of the Kavi Sangha; also arranger, organizer, or editor, capturing the many roles of the Head of the Kavi Sangha
Vyuhadyuta / Viewer-d'you-ta(h)	A duel between two armies that consists of setting up opposing battle formations but not actually fighting
Yadava /Yeah-the-vu(h)	Descendant of Yadu
Yamuna / Yum-moo-nu(h)	A river; changed direction and created a crisis of flooding in Khandavaprastha and of drought in Panchnad
Yayati / Yea(rn)-yeah-tea	Ancestor of Kuru; enjoyed a thousand years of youth but wanted more
Yudhishthira / You-dish-tea-ru(t)	The oldest Pandava; the King of Hastinapura after the Great War

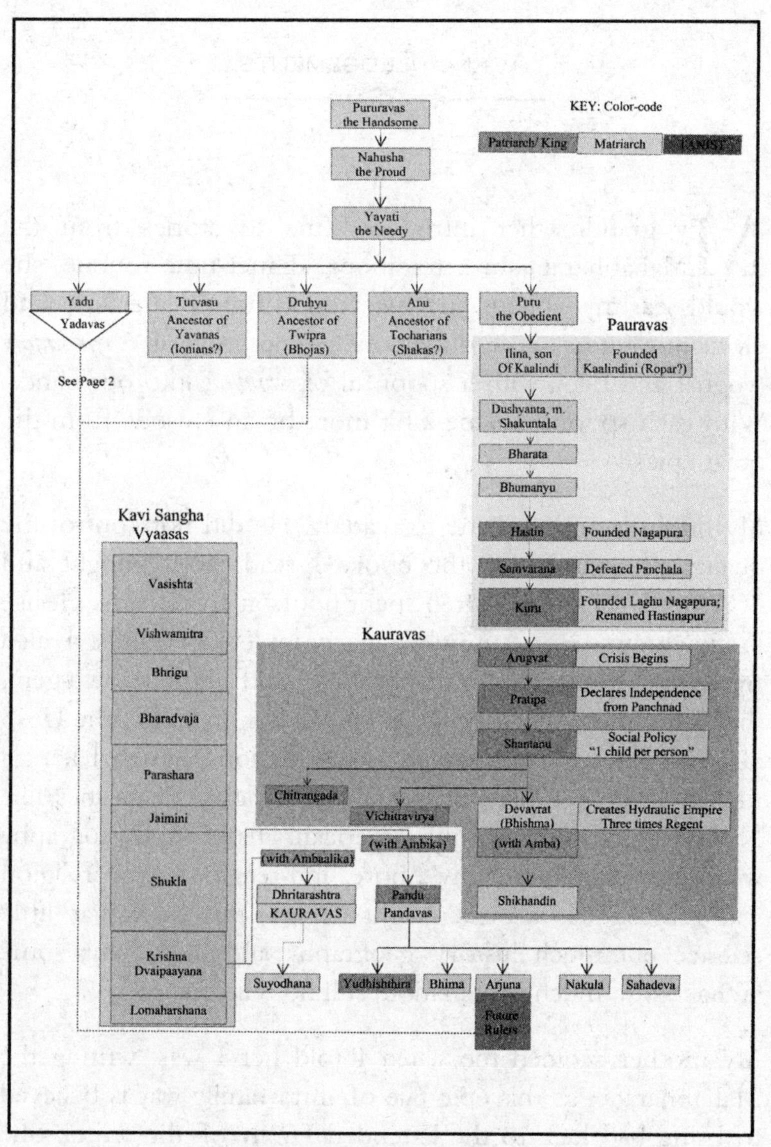

The Kuru Family Tree

Acknowledgements

My grandmother introduced me to stories from the Mahabharata. In a traditional dinner-time routine, she would seat my siblings and me around her on the floor and efficiently get us to eat, doling out a tablespoon of *thayir-sadam* (yogurt and rice), with a spoonful of *sambar*, into our hands. With each spoonful came a bit more of an episode from the great epics.

My father introduced me to reading. He did not control the quality or quantity of the books I read, both bought and borrowed. As a boy I often spent hours at India Book House in downtown Bombay, while he completed errands. I also frequented the British Council Library and a little-known gem, the Vaho Mano Theosophy Library. Later, in Delhi, the USIS libraries. I read at random – usually fiction, though I kept a firm hold on my nerd credentials by reading magazines like New Scientist and Scientific American. History and geography were anathema, biography a bore, and religion…well, religion was religion. As a cynic might expect, this book has little science but much history, geography and biography; some archaeology, much imagination; still no religion.

My mother scolded me when I told her I was 'writing the Mahabharata', as this epic tale of intra-family war is believed to bring bad luck to the extended family of the writer. She surprised me by asking for a copy of my work-in-progress and read the whole manuscript of Book 1 in one long sitting. She then told me that we need not worry – what I had written was not the Mahabharata after all – the curse would not apply. She was the first reader of this curse-free version. She even said she enjoyed the story, an accolade never bestowed easily. After that ringing affirmation, I had no choice but to get on with it and publish the book.

My wife and daughters have tolerated my obsession with the Mahabharata for a long time and were overjoyed that I was finally done with the book. I appreciate their patience; their love and support created a world in which I could write.

Living as I do in the United States, I have found it difficult to find readers who could help me with my writing. Indian readers were distracted by the changes in the plot and preferred to debate them rather than critique the actual manuscript *pace* Amartya Sen's The Argumentative Indian; non-Indian readers, all American, struggled with foreign names, and being unfamiliar with the original plot, suggested ideas that did not fit my version.

Many writers and texts have influenced me. The great scholar and poet A. K. Ramanujan's collection of folktales acted as an inspiration; likewise, Iravathi Karve's analysis of the main characters of the epic *Yuganta*. J.A.B. van Buitenen's translation of the critical edition compiled by the Bhandarkar Oriental Research Institute- was a key reference. Information about ancient India came from the *Brihatkatha*, the *Jataka* tales, and the *Panchatantra*. The controversial anthropologist, Marvin Harris (*Cultural Materialism),* provided a theoretical foundation for the response to the crisis proposed in this series. Insights into ancient cultures came from Robert Graves (*The Greek*

Myths and other works). The amazing novelist Gore Vidal (*Creation* and *Julian),* provided a model for the writing.

Harshad Marathe admirably translated my comments into a visual and illustrated the annotated map of South Asia, showing my hypothetical distribution of the ethnic groups – the Panchnadis, Nagas, and Rakshasas.

Notes

Notes

Notes

Notes

Notes

Wish To Publish With Us?

We are always keen to look at interesting content across genres. Please email your submission to: **submissions@leadstartcorp.com**

The submission should include the following:

1. Synopsis

A summary of the book in 500 – 1000 words. Please mention the word count of the manuscript.

2. Sample chapters

Two chapters, not necessarily in order; just send the two best.

3. A Note About The Author

An interesting note about yourself (about 200 words).

4. Additional Information

- Target audience,
- Unique selling points
- List of illustrative content (if any)
- Other comparative titles
- Your thoughts on marketing the book.